She closed her eyes

and drifted into oblivion. She raised an arm toward the slip stream. Before she was caught up in its electrical surge, steel fingers wrapped around her arm and yanked her around. She looked into Garrett's hard gaze.

"You've done enough damage. I won't let you cause anymore."

"And how are you going to stop me? I've evaded you before." She was getting weary of his pestering. Didn't he understand she was trying to fix her mistakes?

"Like this." He moved closer. The heat of his breath trailed her skin, tickling the back of her neck. He kissed her, sending shockwaves of need charging to her most private places. The smell of cinnamon and cloves drove her to a frenzy. Fire coursed through her veins. The charge sizzled on her lips. She fell into him, kissed him back. Her traitorous arms circled his neck. His hands locked against her spine, sending warm shivers through her.

She dragged her lips from his, gasping for air. Her heart ached, but she willed herself to stay put. This was all a game to him. A desperate ploy. "I know what you're trying to do. It won't work." Her mind reeled.

He smirked. "If you knew what I was trying to do, we wouldn't be in your head. You'd be in my bed."

"I told you this would not happen again." She balled her fists, refusing to give credence to the pleasure of his words. Oh, to fade into oblivion, here, with him. So easy to give in. But the bastard was only trying to distract her like she had him. Did he think her that stupid?

Shadow Dancer

by

Krysta Scott

Shadow Dancer

Cover Art by *Debbie Taylor*

The Wild Rose Press, Inc.
PO Box 708
Adams Basin, NY 14410-0708
Visit us at www.thewildrosepress.com

Publishing History
First Fantasy Rose Edition, 2017
Print ISBN 978-1-5092-1350-4
Digital ISBN 978-1-5092-1351-1

Published in the United States of America

Dedication

For Mom—Thank you for believing I could write.
Dad—for giving me the science fiction bug.
Phyllis—for always supporting me and believing in me,
and of course my wonderful husband, Scott, and my
lovely daughters, Taylor and Isabelle—Thank you for
your unwavering encouragement and support.

Acknowledgments

A very big thank you to all those who read my
manuscript in part or in full: Alicia Dean, Kathy
Wheeler, Betty Sanders, Sheila Fields, Kelly Cox,
Donnell Epperson, Jordan Dane, and Cindy Sorenson.
Publishing my manuscript would not have been
possible without you. Also, a special thanks to Ally
Robertson, my awesome editor who liked my book
enough to take it on.

Chapter One

"You can't do this, Mrs. Hanover. Think about your daughter." Nikki Angelus stood stiff-armed, her fingers curled against her thighs. She was unable to stop the increasing volume in her voice, but it was unlikely any of the people milling around the halls of the Hazelwood County Courthouse were listening. Who cared about one lone attorney locking horns with an unreasonable parent? They were more concerned with their own cases rather than the mess she'd stepped in. But it wouldn't do for Nikki's eight-year-old client to hear her panic. The child was in the Judge's chambers—only a few feet away—awaiting her fate, and the courthouse walls were thin.

"I am thinking about her." Amy Hanover's chin quivered, her mass of blonde curls pooled at her shoulders. A tear dripped over the large bruise on her cheek—a mark so fresh it hadn't yet discolored to yellow. She wiped the tear away and shook her head, her empty blue eyes never landing on Nikki. Unbelievable. Amy Hanover's concern for her child was as weak as a potato chip

Nikki leveled her gaze on Amy's attorney, Alec Brigg, who was doing nothing to help. He just stood there, lips pressed together, letting Nikki do all the talking. Nikki ground her teeth. There had to be a way to get through to the woman. "How? By sending her back into a household filled with trauma?"

Amy tilted her head toward Alec. Her doe eyes pleaded for assistance.

"I understand your concern, Ms. Angelus." Alec held up a protective arm between Nikki and Amy. "I had this same conversation with my client last night. I haven't filed the dismissal, hoping she'd change her mind. But it's no use. She insists on dismissing her divorce action."

Nikki lowered her voice, though it vibrated with fury. "She's putting her child in danger."

Alec nodded. "It's not too late to reconsider, Amy. Keeping the divorce case in place is the best course of action."

Amy gazed across the hall at her husband leaning against the wall. Her face flushed as her lips curved into a shy smile. Parker Hanover, a muscular man with brown hair cropped with precision, laid his hand over his heart and patted his chest three times. Amy giggled. "I'm not going to change my mind."

"I'm sorry, Ms. Angelus. My hands are tied." Alec's shiny head glinted under the fluorescent bulbs. He looked like a macabre cue ball on a collision course with the eight ball. "Mrs. Hanover has made her decision. There's nothing more to discuss."

"Yes, there is. The district attorney's office has more than enough evidence to convict her husband of assault and battery. All she has to do is cooperate with the DA. As long as that case is pending, the emergency custody order will remain in place. He won't be able to go near her or the child." That fact alone should persuade Alec to step up and convince Amy to see reason. But Amy didn't have enough money for that kind of motivation. She had no one to stand up for her, and soon, Amy would return to the man who'd put the bruises on her face and arms. Alec's silence did nothing to dissuade her of the opinion.

"Lori needs her father. She deserves a family." Amy crossed her arms, exposing finger marks from wrist to elbow. Her gaze remained glued on the floor. She looked so lost—the picture of the perpetual victim. A pang of sympathy stirred inside Nikki, but she squelched it. This woman was ready to shove her child back into turmoil, all for the sake of an imagined ideal of a happy family.

"Going back to him won't give you a family. All you have to look forward to is more bruises."

Amy's eyes widened as if she was truly surprised by Nikki's statement. "No, he's going to get help. He promised."

"Amy's been through enough, Ms. Angelus. I'm not going to let you upset her any more. Let's take this before the judge." Alec took his client's arm and led her into the courtroom.

A sharp snort caught Nikki's attention. Parker Hanover peeled away from the opposite wall, his eyes downcast. As he passed, he whispered, "It will be good to be back home with my wife."

Nikki dug her teeth into her lower lip. The man wanted to appear so submissive, he didn't even hire an attorney. He swung the courtroom door wide and moseyed inside. Underneath that timid veneer lurked an unbridled temper with a hair trigger. Surely, Judge Weatherly would see that.

She counted to ten before she followed. The chill in the courtroom matched the ice water coursing

3

through her veins. She sucked in a lungful of air. It wasn't unusual for a battered woman to return to her spouse. She let the breath out through her nose. But how could a mother betray her child like this? It was mindboggling. Her head spun, searching for every possible argument she could use to protect Lori.

Nikki sat in an empty chair with the other attorneys waiting for their cases to be called while two attorneys battled for dominance before Judge Weatherly. Their voices droned on about some piece of property that probably cost less than the fee they charged their clients to argue the matter. Nothing was as important as a child's welfare. She rubbed the back of her neck. The tension in the air was so thick it was hard to breathe. Parker Hanover sat in the gallery, bent in a repentant pose. Nikki clenched her jaw. She couldn't let the bastard win.

"Prepare a court minute before you leave." Judge Weatherly's voice resonated through the room. As the litigants departed, Alec rose. Nikki sucked in a breath. It was time. She leaned forward, poised and ready.

"Your Honor, may we approach on the Hanover matter? We have a short announcement." The weariness in Alec Brigg's voice did nothing to alleviate the damage his request would cause.

Judge Weatherly motioned them forward. It was sickening how quickly Amy and Parker Hanover rushed to the bench. With a sigh, Nikki took her place before the judge.

"My client," Alec began, "is dismissing her case. Mr. Hanover is in agreement with this action."

"I see." Judge Weatherly flipped through his papers. "I seem to remember there was a victim's protection order entered in this case?"

Alec opened his mouth, but Nikki beat him to the response. "Yes, Your Honor. Mrs. Hanover was beaten by her husband in front of the minor child. The DA is considering filing charges. I object to Mrs. Hanover dismissing this divorce action."

Alec bristled like a rooster shaking out his feathers. Any indication he felt bad about Amy's decision dissolved at the first sign of battle. "Now look here, Your Honor. Ms. Angelus doesn't have standing to object. If Mrs. Hanover wants to dismiss her action, she can. We don't need anyone's permission."

"And yet—" Judge Weatherly raised an eyebrow. "You are here in front of me. It's my understanding this case was scheduled for a review of Mr. Hanover's suspended visitation."

"Yes." Alec rubbed a hand over his bald head. "But Mrs. Hanover is dropping the matter."

"Your Honor," Nikki said. "Dismissing the case will not solve the Hanovers' problems. If Mr. Hanover doesn't seek help, he will continue to injure his family. He won't get help if this matter is dismissed. I believe Mrs. Hanover has been bullied into dismissing by her husband."

"Mrs. Hanover," Judge Weatherly said. "Is this true?"

Amy's head snapped up. Her chin trembled, but at least this time she made eye contact. "No. I made a mistake rushing to divorce."

"I see." Amy shrunk under Judge Weatherly's scrutiny. For a long time, he held her gaze. She shifted from foot to foot. She rubbed her arms and swallowed. "Mrs. Hanover, if you have been beaten, the odds are, it will happen again."

"I wasn't." Amy's head dropped, her long curly hair masking the bruise on her cheek. She clasped her hands behind her, shielding the marks on her arm. Unbelievable! She knew exactly what she was doing. Didn't she care about her daughter at all? "I fell against the window sill. My husband was trying to help me."

"That's a lie." The only sound Nikki heard was the steady pulse of blood whooshing past her ears. She had to make this right, and time was running out. "This is the first time I have ever heard this version of the incident. She has told the police and me that her husband beat her. Just look at her arms. You don't get marks like that from someone trying to help."

Amy looked to her attorney. Her wide eyes held the same plea of every client caught by surprise in a hearing.

Alec didn't disappoint. "Your Honor, it doesn't matter. She can dismiss her case if she wants to. We are wasting time that you can use on cases that actually need a decision from you."

Judge Weatherly nodded. "Well—"

"Your Honor, you can't let them do this." Nikki had to make him see reason. "Think of the child. This result isn't in her best interest."

"Ms. Angelus," Judge Weatherly's tone was gentle. Too kind. He was going to let her down. "I don't have jurisdiction over a dismissed case, and I can't force someone to pursue an action if they don't want to."

Parker Hanover gave a slow, contrite nod. He slipped his arm around Amy, and they walked out of the court room.

Nikki's insides turned cold. The monster had

actually won.

By the time she exited the court room, the Hanovers had already retrieved Lori. Of course, they wouldn't want Nikki to have any say in what Lori was told about today's events. She caught Lori's blonde locks bobbing in the crowd as her parents led her out of the building.

Nikki followed the fractured family to the door. She pressed her hands against the glass, watching the child. One tiny hand gripped her mother's, the other clutched her doll. With blue eyes like her mother's, Lori looked back at Nikki. The only difference was Lori's eyes were clear, sharp, and frightened.

Nikki's fingers curled into the glass pane. She was weak. Powerless. She couldn't even stop a man without a lawyer from getting his way.

"Rough day?" An old man stepped next to her, casting a shadow across her vision. "I'm sorry you were unable to save that little girl, Ms. Angelus."

Nikki glared at the man standing casually next to her, hands in pockets, pity reflected in his gray eyes. He was tall and wiry and dressed in an expensive suit. "Do I know you?"

"Not really." His lips tugged into an affectionate smile, and a wisp of a memory cloaked in fog and smoke tapped at the edge of her brain. Someone had looked at her exactly that way once. Not the man in front of her, certainly. She didn't recognize him. But someone who'd given her milk and cookies to lift her spirits on a bad day.

"Then how do you know my name?"

"Doesn't everyone? You're well known on the domestic floor as an effective Guardian *Ad Litem*."

"Not today." She blew a breath, fogging the pane and absently trailed a finger through the mist.

"A minor setback." He shrugged. "Not everything can be corrected."

The man's glib attitude flipped her switch to defensive mode. "It's my job to correct this situation."

"Really?" The man fixed her with a gaze so intense she dare not look away. "What if I told you you had the power to correct this situation?"

Every nerve stood on end. She should walk away but didn't. "You have information I could use about the Hanovers?"

"Them and…" He nodded in the direction the trio had gone. "You."

"What?"

"I have something for you." He placed a small parcel in her hand. Nikki took it automatically. It didn't weigh much. Based on its size it probably didn't hold much either. It was addressed to her but had no return address. Reason returned in a rush.

"I can't take things from strangers. It gives an appearance of impropriety." Not to mention his actions were just plain weird. She moved to hand it back, but he held up his hands.

"You might as well take it. It belongs to you anyway and will remind you of who you are."

"Which is?"

"A very powerful person."

Her eyes narrowed. "Who are you?"

"That isn't important."

"What is this?"

"A family heirloom." He backed away. "I'll be in touch."

He faded into the crowd. She wanted to run after him, but her legs had turned to lead. With a sigh, she sank onto a marble step. She pondered the mysterious box, barely registering the people leaving the building. With the swipe of a finger, she slit the top and pulled out a black velvet jewelry box. She lifted the hinged lid. A necklace nestled in a cushion of soft material. With trembling fingers, she picked it up by the chain. An amulet swung in the air. Silver flames shot outward from the center where a green gem was set inside a circle.

She peered underneath the lid. A piece of paper was wadded up inside. She pulled it out. A message scrawled with large loops and even spacing read, *To Nikki, now you're one of us and have the power to find the answers you seek. Love, Mom.*

Nikki's hand flew to her mouth, and her throat went dry. She turned the note over, looking for some clue where the necklace had come from. One thing was certain, her mom did not send this.

People didn't send packages from the grave.

****

Garrett Nightshade sustained a confident pose—the complete opposite of his snarling sputtering counterpart. He had pissed off his opposing counsel this morning, an inevitable byproduct of his tactical decision to protect his client from wasting her time on a hearing that might not even occur. The Judge had been ill so often lately, it was hard to predict when matters would be heard. Unfortunately, Judge Calder was here and Arnold Darning was in fine form, spewing his ludicrous bullshit.

"This is an urgent matter for my client. Mr.

Nightshade's client should be here." Arnold pointed an accusing finger in Garrett's direction. "There is no excuse for her absence."

Of course, the man conveniently omitted his client had cleaned out the bank account two months ago. The parasite masquerading as a doting husband had moved to Oklahoma with more than one hundred thousand dollars in cash. Garrett didn't have the necessary documentation to prove his actions, but he would soon. He opened his mouth to respond, but Judge Calder's sharp glare at Arnold's antics sent its own message. Garrett kept quiet and allowed Arnold to make his case for him.

"We're here on your motion to modify support alimony, is that correct?" Judge Calder asked.

"Yes, Your Honor." Arnold clasped his hands behind his back, ready for argument.

The judge turned in Garrett's direction. "Since we have already had a hearing regarding your client's income, is it necessary for her to be present today?"

Arnold's head snapped toward Garrett. Hope flickered in his expression. Garrett cleared his throat, prepared to douse those expectations. "Yes, Your Honor. My client's income has changed considerably since our last hearing. In these hard economic times, Ms. Gardner has been forced to take a pay cut. It's difficult for her to pay the ten thousand a month sum you ordered last time. But she is making those payments every month and on time. Mr. Gardner is requesting twenty thousand per month. She just doesn't have that."

"That's absurd. She owns the company," Arnold said.

"Be that as it may, the business is not as lucrative as it once was. We will need an evidentiary hearing to prove her lowered income. Besides, Mr. Gardner can always mitigate his situation by getting a job."

"My client was laid off."

"More like quit."

"That's not true. In any case, Ms. Gardner should have been here today. It's not like this hearing came out of the blue. She's had two months to prepare her arguments." Arnold pounded his fist on the bench. Judge Calder's eyes narrowed but Arnold was too far gone to notice the icy mood that descended upon the courtroom. "I insist we hear the matter today without Ms. Gardner. Mr. Nightshade is completely capable of protecting the interests of his client."

"Mr. Nightshade." Judge Calder peered at him over thick glasses. "Why isn't Ms. Gardner here?"

"Your Honor." Garrett offered a half-shrug. "Ms. Gardner lives out of state. Times being what they are, she can't afford to make numerous trips for hearings. Because you have been sick so often lately, I wasn't sure your court would be in session today. Rather than have my client make a wasted trip, I advised her not to come."

Arnold smirked. No doubt waiting for Garrett to receive a huge ass chewing. It would be a long wait. Arnold didn't have Garrett's uncanny powers of persuasion.

"I see." Judge Calder rested his chin on his shaking hands. "That actually makes sense."

"What?" Arnold lifted his hands in an 'are you crazy?' gesture. "Ms. Gardner lives in Dallas. That's two and a half hours away. Three if you drive slowly.

There's no good reason for her not to be here."

"Mr. Nightshade's correct," Judge Calder said. "I've been ill a good portion of the past year. It would be a large imposition for someone to travel from out of state only to have to turn back without relief from this court."

"That's not an excuse." Arnold's face infused with red, deepening his ruddy complexion. Garrett stifled a grin. Appearing too cocky would undermine his efforts. "This hearing has been on the docket for months. A quick call to your clerk would have been all it took to let him know court would be in session today."

"I did call your clerk. She couldn't confirm you would be here today."

Judge Calder nodded. "I'll continue this matter two weeks. I expect your client to be here on that day, Mr. Nightshade. My health is in very good condition at present. I expect this matter to be resolved at our next hearing."

"Absolutely, Your Honor." Garrett collected his file and turned to leave.

"Your Honor…" Arnold wiped his forehead with a white handkerchief.

"You're excused, Mr. Darning. I've ruled."

Garrett hurried out. The court couldn't do anything without both attorneys. If he stepped back to the bench, he risked a re-hash of the arguments. He pushed the doors open and exited into the hallway. A hand grabbed his arm in a vice grip.

"You arrogant son of a bitch." Arnold's face turned purple.

"Okay." Garrett narrowed his gaze on the hand at his wrist.

Arnold's hand fell away as if burned.

"What do you have on Judge Calder? You couldn't have gotten your continuance any other way."

Garrett looked down his nose at his defeated opponent. "Mr. Darning, if you think I have been unethical, file your lawsuit. Otherwise, I suggest you mind your tongue. Slander is expensive."

With one last sputter, Arnold stomped off. His recently vacated space was replaced by Garrett's boss, David Barnes. Barnes clapped him on the back. "Making friends?"

"Arnold accused me of being unethical."

The two men walked toward the exit. In just a few short steps, they would be out of the courthouse and away from the hate infused floor.

"Interesting. Why is that I wonder?"

"Seems to think I have Judge Calder in my pocket."

Barnes chuckled. "He'd shit bricks if he knew the truth."

Garrett's chuckle froze in his throat as he walked past a woman slouched over a small object in her hand. Her brown hair draped around her face leaving him inexplicably curious about her. There was something so defeated about her posture. He placed a hand on her shoulder. "Are you all right?"

Startled green eyes met his gaze. Then a slight wisp of a smile curved her lips. "I'm fine. It's been a tough morning."

There was nothing weak about her rich husky voice. Even the mundane words held fire and determination.

"Hey, you coming, Garrett?" David held the door

open with an amused glint in his eyes.

"Yes, just a second." He returned to the woman possessing way too much of his attention warranted by the situation. For some reason, he wanted to stay and help her through whatever had sullied her day. But that was foolish. She probably didn't need his help anyway. He offered her a wide grin. "I hope your day gets better."

"Thank you."

With a nod, he was out the door.

****

The evening sun cast long shadows over the ramshackle wooden porch of a house that leaned a little far to the left. If this was a normal business call, Nikki would have been itching to get inside to have a look around. But she already knew what she would find behind the door with white peeling paint. A life in the midst of failure. If she could avoid coming here, she would. But she had to be here, because the man inside was the only person alive who could give her the answers she needed.

Inhaling deeply, she knocked. Rustling like sewer rats accompanied the heavy clomps as the inhabitant stumbled his way to the entrance. Nikki shuddered. It had been a while since she'd been here. From the sound of it, the interior was worse than before. Finally, the door opened. A wrinkled face with an unruly white beard peered through the crack.

"What are you doing here?" The sour smell of alcohol wafted over her with each of his slurred words.

"Hi, Dad, I need to talk to you."

"At this time of night?"

"It's only six. I'm coming from work."

He sneered, clearly not impressed. Evidently, he hadn't forgotten what had transpired the last time they spoke. Neither had she, but she wasn't going to let him know that.

There was a brief stand-off until he finally rolled his eyes and barked, "You better come in. This isn't the neighborhood for people dressed as hoity toity as you." He opened the door a smidge wider, and she stepped inside the musty house. She followed him through a narrow hall lined with stacked magazines and newspapers on either side.

Things had gotten bad for her dad. She doubted that she could get any meaningful information out of him. But she had to try. He stopped in front of a bar with neon beer signs on the wall behind. He stood there while she removed a stack of papers from a stool. She preferred to stand, but that would give away her impatience. She gingerly took a seat at the edge and waited him out.

He pulled out a large bottle of scotch and rummaged through the debris on the bar for two glasses.

"Dad, could you not do that while I'm here?"

"Now, look here, Miss Prissy Britches, this is my home and you won't be telling me how to behave here." He filled both glasses a third of the way and offered one to her. She shook her head. He did his usual half-nod-eye-roll thing then tossed back a swig of scotch.

"You know, it's hard to talk to you when you're like this." There were so many things she would like to say, but it was useless. Simply put, her dad didn't care about her opinion. Never had. She smoothed her skirt and waited for the onslaught of his usual criticism

"Look here, missy." He punctuated the words with his glass, as if giving an exuberant toast, but all he managed was sloshing alcohol over the side onto the bar. He made no move to wipe it up, or even acknowledge the spill. But then, living in a pit like this, what was one more stain on the woodwork? "I'd be a little more grateful if I were you. I've done right by you and how do you repay me? By taking that low-life government job, Guardian whatever."

"Guardian *Ad Litem*." He'd had higher ambitions for her, but how could she work for one of those mover and shaker firms when the whole reason not to was right in front of her? She sighed. There was no reason to tell him again that she represented children in high conflict divorce cases. The importance of their voices being heard. He never listened anyway.

Nikki picked up a framed picture, the only thing standing upright in the bar area. The family—her family—stared back at her. She traced the images lightly with her finger. Her mother, her father, Cassie, and herself. It was from sixteen years ago—the last time they were intact and happy. Tears surfaced and the years melted away. Once more she was a little girl staring into a casket at her dead sister. An ache pierced her heart, and she drew in a deep breath, wiping her eyes before the tears fell…before *he* knew she was crying.

The man who stood across from her in his stained undershirt and ripped jeans bore no resemblance to the well-groomed man from the photo dressed in an expensive navy suit. But she guessed she didn't resemble the dark-haired girl with the gazillion-watt smile, either. They needed Cassie and her mom to make them complete. Both were gone.

She set the picture back in its place and focused on her dad.

"Why are you here?" he grumbled.

"I received a weird package at work today." She fumbled in her purse for the small velvet box. She wrapped her fingers tightly around it. The soft fabric was cool, but its contents burned with the promise of illumination. "The message said it came from Mom."

He stiffened but didn't ask any questions, yet she had the impression he was waiting for the sick punch line at the end of her statement. As if he knew what was coming next. She rested the box on the counter and opened it without ceremony. The green gemstone reflected the dull light coming from the fixture above them. "Did Mom own this?"

He turned his head as if to look away, but his narrowed eyes never left the pendant. His face seemed to pale, but surely it was a trick of the neon lighting behind him. He didn't say anything for several seconds. He just stared at it like it would jump out at him and slit his throat. He knew what it was, but was he going to tell her?

"Where did you get that?"

"A strange old man gave it to me after court. It came with this note." She pulled the note from her suit pocket and handed it to him.

He scanned the message then tossed it into the sink as if it had thorns. He slammed his glass onto the hard surface and placed both hands on the edge. Hanging his head, he took several deep breaths before he kicked the bar, shaking all the contents. "She never owned anything like that, and if you know what's good for you, you'll stay away from those people."

"Who?"

"The Guild," he spat, showering the air around him with moisture. "They'll pretend like they're going to help you and then bend you over backwards and fuck ya. They'll strip you of everything you care about. They don't even protect their own. Don't trust them. Don't trust any of them."

Nikki swallowed. "What are you talking about?" She didn't know what else to say. This was the longest, most emphatic speech he had made since he lost his job at the firm. She had never seen him argue a case when he practiced law, but word on the street was that he was something to see before his fall from grace.

"The Guild, that's what." He drained his glass, then grabbed hers.

"You aren't making any sense."

"Just stay away from them, Nikki. You don't need any part of them. Now leave me alone."

****

Nikki was drained, emotionally and physically, when she crawled into bed that night. She closed her eyes and tried to shut out the disturbing confrontation with her father. But her mind refused to obey, and sleep was a long time coming. She took in deep, slow breaths and willed her pent up muscles to relax.

The body didn't belong to Nikki, but somehow she was layered within the essence of the woman, crawling for her life along the damp ground. Nikki sucked in the same breath, reached out the same arm, and strained to move inch by precious inch along the thick overgrown lawn. The woman's every move was somehow hers.

She tried to separate her experience from the

woman's, but they remained one. She dug her fingers into the soil, splintering her nails, sending sharp pulsing pain up her arms. With one voice, she whimpered, "Why are you doing this?"

There's no time for that. Move! *Nikki urged the woman onward. In turn, the woman redoubled her efforts. Straining with all her force, she yanked them incrementally further along the cold, hard ground.*

"Where are you going?" a cruel voice said just behind them. The loud crack of a gunshot echoed, then a bullet tore into their calf muscle. Hot searing pain coursed through their flesh. She screamed, grabbing the injured leg, twisting to look up at their tormentor. The darkness of nightfall hid all but the moonlight reflecting off the muzzle of the rifle. Warm, thick blood leaked between her fingers.

"Parker, stop," she pleaded. "Don't do this."

"Why not?" Parker laughed. "You deserve this, you bitch. You dare to take my daughter away from me? You deserve this and worse."

"I didn't do that. The judge—"

"Don't give me that shit. He wouldn't have known anything if you hadn't told him. You started it, and I'm gonna end it." Parker pointed the gun at them.

She raised her hands to block her view. Nikki squeezed her internal eyes shut. This can't be happening.

"No! For God's sake. No!" Nikki braced herself for the end, but Parker didn't fire.

She opened her eyes, and he was lowering the gun. "I'm not going to shoot you."

She dropped her hands. Hope surged through them.

"Shooting you would be too quick." He flipped the gun around and slammed the butt down on her head.

Get out! Get out! *A new masculine voice roared within Nikki's mind.* Get out! Now!

The ground beneath her quaked, hurtling Nikki forward. Finally free of the other woman, she was falling, and there was nothing beneath her. She grabbed for something to stop her descent. Her fingers found nothing but the air that whooshed inside her ears. She was going to hit bottom.

She jerked upright up in bed, clinging to sweat-soaked sheets, her heart hammering against her chest.

"What the hell kind of nightmare was that?" she gasped.

****

Garret sat up in bed, jerked the covers off, and swung his legs over the side. His toes stretched against the cold, hardwood floor, grounding themselves and him back into reality.

The phone on his nightstand rang for what had to be the eighth time. He cursed himself for not removing the phone from his bedroom, and for not setting up his voicemail. All that did was prompt the caller to redial every time Garrett failed to answer. He dropped his head into his palms as the incessant ringing continued. Although he was required to be available at all hours, he would never get used to the early morning interruptions.

He snatched up the phone. "What?'

"Mr. Nightshade?" an unfamiliar masculine voice asked.

"Yes." Who else would it be at 1:00 in the morning? Garrett stilled his annoyance and waited for the caller's next move.

"My name is Lars Hanover. Adelaide gave me your name and number. There's been some trouble."

Garrett rubbed his forehead with his palm. It was never a good situation when his mother was involved. He needed to clear his mind—to wake up. "What kind of trouble?"

"My son lost his temper tonight and beat his wife badly enough to land her in the hospital. He's been arrested."

Garrett took a pen and a small pad from the drawer of his nightstand. Dread burned through his stomach lining. He didn't have a problem using his talents to influence a judge for a client with a righteous cause. But there was no way he would use them to benefit some jerk who put his wife in the hospital. "What's his name?"

"Parker Hanover. He's being held at county jail."

"Look, I'll visit him in the morning and look into the matter. After I meet with him, I'll know whether or not I can represent him."

"Fair enough." A pause on the other end of the line alerted Garret there was another reason for the call. "There is one more matter I need you to attend to."

"What is it?"

"You are the protector of our rights, correct?"

"I try to protect the rights of all my clients, once they actually become my client, that is."

"Cut the bullshit, Mr. Nightshade. I know you're one of us. You're part of the Guild and the scuttlebutt is that you enforce for us."

There it was. Mr. Hanover was a member of the Guild of the Celestial Night. One of Garrett's kind, but more importantly… "Mr. Hanover, the fact that I don't know who you are means that you are one of the dissidents. You're the type that I, shall we say, take care of."

"No, that's not true." Although Mr. Hanover was clearly attempting to keep his voice calm, panic crept around the edges. "Your mother sent me to you. We aren't nonconformists. We follow the edicts of the Guild."

"Then how is it your existence has escaped my notice?"

"We left the Guild shortly after our son was five. He's always been temperamental and he didn't respond well to the direction of the casters. We felt it best to raise him outside of our culture and leave him untrained. He is an isolate now."

"I see." An isolate. That could be a problem.

"No, I don't think you do. But you will."

Why had his mother left this family off the radar? He leaned back against the headboard, not liking the direction this conversation was taking. He'd always considered himself well versed on the secret workings within the Guild. One phone call from this stranger had dispelled that notion, leaving him as anxious as an untrained novice. He ground his teeth. There was no way he'd be able to take his seat at the council table with spotty information. "What does the Guild have to do with your son's trouble?"

"There is a child. My grandchild. She is—talented. We tried to get custody initially, but they gave her to her mother. Now, the Department of Human Services has her. She hasn't been traditionally trained. If she stays there—"

Now Garrett understood. The Hanovers had compounded one mistake with an even bigger problem. One that his mother wanted him to solve. An inexpertly trained child of the Guild.

Garrett sighed wearily. "Be at my office by seven-thirty."

Chapter Two

Nikki rushed through the steel door of the juvenile shelter. As soon as she entered the waiting area, Officer Gunderson met her with a cup of coffee.

"Black, right?" His attempt at a smile faltered as his eyes met hers. She took the coffee from him, sipped the hot bitter liquid, and grimaced.

"It's one in the morning." She was still shaking off the fog of sleep. Her voice held a sharp edge, and she had a creeping sensation that she had been yanked from the rim of a deep abyss. It was that creepy dream. Her subconscious screaming at her for not being able to protect Lori Hanover. She would do better next time.

"Sorry about that, but your boss says you're the assigned Guardian *Ad Litem* for Lori Hanover."

"What?" Nikki blinked. "Are you sure you have the name right?" Lori couldn't be here. It was too soon. Nikki pulled her free hand through her hair. She swallowed as the dream rushed back. Every thump. Every crash. The desperate scream as the butt of the gun came crashing down. She cringed. All of a sudden she was certain. Parker Hanover was a powder keg ready to explode. Nikki couldn't fathom what had set him off so soon. Whatever it was sent Lori here. This morning she'd failed this small child. She sure as hell would not fail again. "What happened?"

Officer Gunderson opened the file. "The Hanover

child was brought into the shelter an hour ago. The investigating officer discovered her in the backyard hiding in her playhouse. It appears the father severely beat the mother. He's locked up, and the mom's in the ICU at county hospital."

"Wow, this is a tough one." An image of a body slamming against a wall flashed into her consciousness. Nikki drew in a deep breath and grabbed the file from Gunderson. She flipped through the pages scanning the details of an incident that sounded all too familiar. Like that dark dream was real. Even though the idea was nonsense, a pall of impending danger clung to her like a shroud of darkness that wouldn't let go. But no semblance of reason could shake the strange sense of déjà vu. It felt very, very real. "Mr. Hanover reconciled with his wife this morning. What could have possibly set him off?"

Officer Gunderson glanced at the floor. "No one knows. The mother is unconscious and the child won't make a statement."

"Poor Lori." Nikki took another sip of coffee, as if the liquid had the power to grant her strength. "Where is she?"

"Right this way." The officer motioned, and she followed him down the dimly lit hallway. Fluorescent lights flickered above her head like she was in a scene from a bad horror movie, but instead, she was en route to interview a traumatized child. And that was worse. Much worse.

Gunderson stopped in front of the third door.

"Well, I'll leave you to your business." He let out a long sigh. "Gotta hand it to ya, I wouldn't be able to do what you do."

Nikki gave him a half smile. Sometimes it took all the fortitude she could summon to do what she did.

Taking a deep breath, she forced her face into a pleasant expression before opening the door. She stepped into a tiny room that held only two chairs and a table. Nikki quietly closed the door behind her.

Lori occupied one of the chairs. Her golden curls hung limply down her thin shoulders hiding her face. In her arms she clasped a stained rag doll with a shock of red hair. The doll's stuffing protruded at the seams of both arms and one leg. Memories assailed Nikki, the emotions so strong, she was nearly paralyzed by them. The child reminded her so much of Cassie, she wanted to reach out and take the little girl into her arms.

"Hi, Lori, do you remember me?"

Lori didn't look up, or otherwise acknowledge Nikki, even when Nikki sat in the chair across from her. Nikki couldn't really blame her. It'd been her duty to protect Lori from her abusive father. After what the child had been through tonight, there was no reason for Lori to trust Nikki. Searching for a way to get Lori to open up, Nikki's eyes lit on the doll.

"Who's this?" Nikki indicated the doll. Lori looked up, her blue eyes suspicious behind her veil of hair. She remained silent, so Nikki continued. "My sister used to have a doll like this when I was a kid. My mom told me that the spots and rips mean she is well loved."

Lori sat up a little straighter. "My mom says that, too. Does your sister still have it?"

She couldn't tell her the truth about Cassie— couldn't speak as she recalled placing the doll in the coffin with her dead sister—so she just nodded. It wasn't really a lie.

26

"What's going to happen to Rags?" The girl's face crumpled, and she burst into tears as she held the doll tighter.

Nikki guessed the question was more about what was going to happen to Lori than her doll. She chose her next words carefully to encompass both interpretations. "I'm here to help with that. Remember, I'm what's called a Guardian *Ad Litem*. I'm going to help figure out what's best for you and Rags."

Lori's eyes widened with hope and another emotion that rested between suspicion and relief. She cocked her head to the side and stared through Nikki, as if she were attempting to confirm her identity. "Mommy said my guardian would help me fix this. But you didn't do so good last time."

Uneasiness gnawed at Nikki's insides. It wasn't the accusation that unnerved her, but the weird sense that there was a deeper implication she was unable to translate. Lori watched her expectantly. With every second that ticked by, disappointment and distrust re-entered her blue eyes.

"No," Nikki said. "I didn't. I'm so sorry you had to go back. This time I will work harder at getting what's best for you and," she added at the last minute, "Rags."

Lori squinted and pursed her lips. "Mommy told me about court and that she would send me a guardian."

"It's important for you to understand that I don't work for your mommy or your daddy. I work for the court."

"Oh."

"What does it mean for your mommy to send you a guardian?"

"I just thought…" Lori shrugged. "Nothing."

Lori's gaze traveled to the table. Just like that, a door of emotional acceptance had opened and slammed shut. Nikki didn't know why, but the sensation that she'd missed an opportunity quivered through her. Ignoring the feeling, she opened the file.

On the surface, the Hanover case was the typical scenario of a fractured family. Mrs. Hanover filed for divorce two months ago. In the pleadings, she accused the father of committing domestic violence in front of her daughter. The photos of a black eye and bruises up the arms in the shape of fingerprints still made her shudder. No new photos of what happened this evening were available, but it still looked bad. The judge was right to suspend his visitation the first time. Then Amy Hanover went and dismissed her case and Nikki was powerless to stop it. Acid gnawed at her insides. This time she would make sure Lori was protected.

"Where's Mommy?" Lori clutched Rags, as if her doll were the only thing that grounded her to earth. She was so alone and lost.

Dark depths of pity consumed Nikki as she searched for a way to answer the potent question. But there was never a good way to share this kind of news. "She's in the hospital. The doctors are taking good care of her." A lame response, but it was the truth. "I'm trying to figure out who will take care of you until your mother gets better. Is there a person you want to live with?"

Lori's expression closed off. Her message was clear. She wasn't going to discuss this topic. Out of everything that had happened to this small child, where she would stay should have been the easiest subject to approach first.

"Is there someone you would like to stay with until your mother gets better?"

Silence.

"I know this is hard, but I need to know what you want."

"I'm not supposed to say."

"It can be hard to talk to a stranger about private things, but I'm here to help you."

"You wouldn't get it."

"Well, I haven't been through what you have, but if you talk to me, I'm certain I can help you."

"No, not the bad stuff. I told the other lady all about that. I mean you aren't like us."

Nikki couldn't erase the impression there was something a little off with this child. Like there was a hidden message beneath every word she spoke. Lori's responses weren't unusual, but her reactions were out of sync.

"Someone has already spoken to you before you came here?"

"The other lady that came to my school."

More than likely, she was referring to the DHS caseworker on the abuse action. Nikki took a deep breath.

"Did you talk to her about where you wanted to live?"

Lori nodded soberly. "I picked my mommy and now she's…"

Realization shook Nikki. Lori felt guilty. She had chosen her mother, and now her mother was in the hospital. Maybe Lori wasn't so unusual. "What happened to your mother wasn't your fault."

Lori's only response was to curl up in her chair,

hold her doll closer, and stare vacantly at the institutional wall.

"Lori, I want to help you."

Still no response.

"Would it be okay for me to tell the judge to place you with your grandparents?"

Lori sat up straight, dropped her doll on the table, and shook her head. "I want to stay here, but Rags doesn't."

Nikki frowned. "Where does Rags want to stay?"

"She wants to go with you."

****

For the second time that night, Garrett was ripped from a peaceful slumber by the insistent shrilling of his phone. "Hello." He rubbed his free hand over his face to push away the last vestige of sleep.

"She is awake." The familiar, raspy voice eroded any hope of a restful night.

"Mother." Garret pulled his clock to face him. "It's five in the morning."

"I know what time it is," she barked. "This is important. She is *awake*."

"What the hell are you talking about?" Garret pushed himself to a sitting position.

"The Shadow Dancer is awake."

Garret's mind instantly cleared. "The Shadow Dancer is just a myth."

"I raised you better than that. Stop thinking like a fool, boy."

His mother's stern reprimand propelled him back to his childhood, when he was forced to listen to endless lectures about his family duty. Garrett squirmed as if trying to release himself from her grasp. But he wasn't her protégée anymore. "This can wait. I need sleep."

"Don't you hang up on me. The Shadow Dancer is real. And now one is awake. I shouldn't have to remind you how dangerous that can be. No one should be able to dream cast and alter events beyond the forty-eight hour window. That won't only affect our kind. It will be catastrophic for everyone."

"What makes you think the Shadow Dancer exists?" He hated himself for asking, but sometimes the best course of action was to let his mother's tirades run their course, even if it was in the middle of the night. *Especially* in the middle of the night.

"Ever since the Hanovers contacted me, I have experienced a flux of energy. This pattern is strong and willful."

"Really?" He stiffened.

"Yes. I think the granddaughter is the key."

A steel cable seized his insides and wound itself tight around his gut. He'd taken care of dissidents before, but could he do that to a child? There had to be limits to how far his responsibilities went. "Are you sure it's not Parker?"

"It couldn't be Parker. He was removed from training and allowed to atrophy. I sense an expertly trained caster."

"You think a child could be that well-trained?"

"Who else could it be? But perhaps you're right. Look into the matter and report back to me."

Garrett hung up the phone and headed to the kitchen to brew some coffee. It was unlikely he'd get back to sleep anyway, and now he had work to do.

****

Nikki drew her hand through the full length of her hair as she headed into the office building. The strange dream she'd had last night haunted her. She couldn't shake the feeling an important connection had been severed, and she couldn't articulate what had been lost. Whatever it was strained the edge of her nerves. She normally didn't dream about the parents of a child she represented. She hadn't been on the Hanover case long enough to have an intimate knowledge of the events, and nothing in the case file was as graphic as the dream.

She entered the elevator and pushed the button for the seventh floor. A man stepped in before the doors closed. He glanced at the panel, then to her. Leaning one shoulder against the wall, he shoved his hands into the pockets of his navy blue slacks, making his paisley gold tie tilt to one side against the open suit jacket. His short brown hair was moussed into wind-tossed perfection and was the same shade as his rich chocolate eyes. His penetrating stare was neither subtle nor innocent.

"Is there something I can help you with?" she said, conscious of the snippy tone and too tired to rein it in.

"You look familiar. Have we met before?" he drawled with an unrepentant air.

She crossed her arms in front of her chest and shifted against the side wall, taking in the full support of its steel structure. He looked vaguely familiar but she couldn't place where or if she had ever seen him before. "I don't think so."

"I'm sorry, I don't mean to be rude," he stated smoothly, but the grin never left his face. Everything except his suit and the well-placed hairs on his head oozed nonchalance, as if nothing in his world was urgent. He maintained his casual pose and continued monitoring her with an amused expression. "But I need to speak with you, Ms. Angelus."

Nikki's pulse sped up. How did he know her name? Suddenly, she needed out. This stranger was crossing professional boundaries, his attention making her feel as if he were a hunter and she his prey. She watched the lights as the floors ticked by. Why did everything move in slow motion when she was in a hurry? Finally, the elevator stopped on her floor. The doors slid open, and she dashed off.

The man followed. She spun around to face him.

"Should I know you?"

"No, Ms. Angelus. I only know who you are thanks to the kind lady at the information desk. She pointed you out for me." He held out his hand. She reluctantly shook it, ignoring the warmth in his grasp. She took a minute to assess his grip. Strong. Solid but not overbearing. Probably not a threat. Maybe if he hadn't come on so strong. Appeared so in charge, she wouldn't have overreacted. That dream coupled with the connection to the Hanovers filled her with the jitters. Really, she needed to pull herself together. "I'm Garrett Nightshade, and I've been retained to represent Lars and Carrie Hanover, the paternal grandparents of the Hanover child. It's my understanding you're the Guardian *Ad Litem* in the custody case."

"Yes, I am." The sense of foreboding shot up a notch. She regarded him with a stiff dose of skepticism. Having an attorney as a buffer between the Guardian *Ad Litem* and the litigant was usually a good thing. In this case, Nikki wasn't so sure. She drew herself up to her full five feet nine inches. But his tall well-built figure still dwarfed hers. "What can I do for you?" Garrett stood calmly, hands stuffed in his pants pocket unruffled by her lame attempt to claim the dominant position. She refused to appear disconcerted and met his wide set eyes head on. Their depths reflected a keen intelligence that would not easily be outwitted. Under different circumstances, his inconsistencies would fascinate her. Right now, it was the wrong place, wrong time, and wrong situation.

"My clients would like custody of the Hanover child. I need to know if you oppose their request."

"I'm not sure. There is a maternal aunt also seeking custody." She waited, shifting back and forth from foot to foot, increasingly agitated at his scrutiny. Fighting the urge to look away, she forced herself to meet his gaze.

"You do know she's a stripper?" He raised an eyebrow to punctuate the question. She hadn't been aware of the maternal aunt's profession. The thought of him knowing something she didn't irked her more than she cared to admit. Not to mention that little nugget didn't fare well for the other side. A profession as unstable and chaotic as exotic dancing usually didn't sit well with her either. But something about his confidence in his position weighed on her last nerve. She wasn't ready to back down. Not yet, anyway.

"There are worse things a person could be."

"Like what?" His expression remained civil, but coldness crept into his voice. He crossed his arms, and a small green gemstone on his finger winked at her. Her focus shifted to his ring. She knew the pattern instantly. It matched the amulet in her purse. A cold shiver passed through her. *He's one of them.* She looked him straight in the eye, hoping to gain some insight as to why his people were all of a sudden knocking on her back doorstep.

"Like the parents of a son who has a propensity for beating his wife senseless and abusing his daughter, that's what."

For an instant, his eyes turned into small, icy slits. Then he recovered, and his face went blank. "Have it your way. You need to be aware that I know Judge Abernathy."

"So do a lot of people. So, unless you're suggesting I file a motion to disqualify you from this case, I would chuck the bravado."

"Bravado, huh?" His lips curved in an inviting smile. "I'm not suggesting anything."

"I didn't think so," she said through clenched teeth. There was no way she would be taken in by his glib charm. "Now, if you'll excuse me, I'm needed in court." She whirled and strode over to the receptionist without giving him a chance to respond. The receptionist buzzed her in, and she breezed through the door, leaving Garrett Nightshade on the other side.

A modicum of guilty pleasure swept through her when the door promptly closed on his shocked face.

She pulled the amulet from her purse. The disquiet she'd felt earlier returned as she studied the necklace.

What the hell was going on?

Chapter Three

Garrett cracked his knuckles and stepped off the elevator onto the family court floor. It had been a mistake to sneak up on Nikki Angelus, but he'd been so sure she would succumb to his charm. She should have been an easy mark. After all, a Guardian *Ad Litem* was nothing more than a social worker in attorney's clothing. Nikki had thrown him with her intelligence and sure-footedness. Not to mention her out-and-out sex appeal. He wouldn't let that happen again. For now, he needed to do a little extra reconnaissance.

With steady purpose, he approached Judge Abernathy's chambers and pulled open the door. The bailiff looked up from her desk, a large smile spreading across her face. She was semi-attractive, with blue eyes accented by silver-framed glasses. Fluorescent lights from above highlighted the shine in her blonde hair.

"Good morning, Mr. Nightshade. What can I do for you?"

He pulled his suit jacket straight, attempting to take solace that at least the bailiff was receptive to his charms. But it did nothing to ease his bruised ego. Her pleasant expression held none of the fire Nikki Angelus had. Strange after that one short meeting he reeled with self-doubt he'd never before experienced. He considered her words. The Hanovers did raise an abuser. But it didn't necessarily follow they weren't good parents. Bad seeds cropped up out of nowhere. He groaned. Nikki Angelus be damned. He knew the best course of action. It was only a matter of time before he swayed Nikki's opinion to be more in sync with his. Until then, there were more practical ways to get what he wanted.

Garrett sat on the edge of the bailiff's desk and leaned in, making her blush. "Hi, Judy, is the judge available?"

Judy's smile never wavered, but a hint of sadness shadowed her face. "I'm sorry, Mr. Nightshade, but the judge won't be in today. He had to take the day off for personal reasons."

"Really?" Garrett frowned. Although he was aware Judge Abernathy had recently separated from his wife, he was under the impression the judge had his personal issues under control. Apparently, he'd been mistaken on that count, just as he'd been with Nikki Angelus. An odd sort of apprehension filled him. He'd never been so off his game before. "I'm sorry to hear that."

If his response sounded insincere to him, he was certain Judy would think so too, but the silly schoolgirl grin never left her face. It was as if she only had one setting.

"Did you have a case set with him today?" she asked.

"Yes. The Hanover matter."

"I see." Judy referred to a docket sheet on her desk, her finger tracing each case until she reached the one whose name matched. "Ah yes, actually this case has been consolidated with the lower case number. Judge Weatherly is handling this case. A transfer order has already been executed."

"Thank you, darling." Garrett was out the door before Judy could respond.

The morning kept getting more complicated. Judge Weatherly had only recently been appointed to the bench, and Garrett wasn't familiar with him.

He maneuvered his way around people in the hallway, some meeting with their lawyers in the middle of the corridor, others leaning against the marble walls or reading the names on top of the doors, no doubt looking for the right judge's chambers.

When Garrett stepped into the courtroom, Judge Weatherly was already on the bench. Garrett made his way to a vacant seat where he eased onto the cool wooden surface and waited his turn.

He searched the sea of faces, but Nikki Angelus was not among them. His clients, looking every inch the sweet old grandparents, right down to the wiry gray hair and horn-rimmed glasses, were in the back corner of the room.

As the judge called case after case, each attorney stood and announced their presence. Finally, Judge Weatherly said, "Hanover vs. Hanover."

"Garrett Nightshade, present for the grandparents, Your Honor."

"Sam Carr, present for the maternal aunt," a thin voice said.

Garrett looked in the direction of the speaker. The man was elderly, with gray hair, watery blue eyes, and a body so frail it was a wonder his torso was strong enough to support him. He had the air of an attorney who had practiced law far beyond a reasonable number of years.

"I see Ms. Angelus has been appointed as Guardian

Ad Litem," the judge said. "Has anyone heard from her?"

"I met with her early this morning, Your Honor," Garrett said. "She should be on her way."

"We'll give her fifteen more minutes."

Garrett allowed himself a slow smile as Mr. Carr fidgeted with his tie. Garrett hadn't lost this case yet. Like him, Mr. Carr had probably been hired the night before, possibly even this morning since, despite his discomfort, he gave the impression he hadn't lost a minute of sleep. Given the fact that Carr's client was a stripper, it shouldn't be too hard to craft an argument in the Hanover's favor.

He turned to view the people sitting in the galley, searching for Mr. Carr's client. His eyes slid over all the occupants until he saw the most likely candidate—a woman with long blond hair and a tight fitting pink tank top. She twirled a strand of hair around her finger as she gazed off into nowhere. She couldn't be more than twenty, but already, lines had formed at the corners of her eyes and around her mouth. She wasn't emaciated enough to argue a meth addiction, but maybe she was tacky and spacey enough to discourage Nikki from recommending her as an appropriate custodian. Even if that were not the case, the matter hinged on whether Judge Weatherly respected Nikki's opinion. Was his estimation of her high enough for him to blindly follow her recommendation?

He was summoned from his brooding when Nikki Angelus swept through the door. She never once looked in his direction. Instead, she nodded and smiled at someone over the top of his head. Garrett swiveled around to see Judge Weatherly returning her smile.

That answered one question. A surge of competitiveness engulfed him. Let the games begin.

****

Nikki entered the courtroom feeling more confident than she should, considering she was only armed with current information from an eight-year-old child. But, it was a relief to know that Judge Weatherly would be hearing the case instead of Abernathy. She wouldn't have to fight Abernathy's good ole boy mindset and penchant for skirt chasing. She was free to concentrate on the facts and not tussle with side issues.

"Welcome, Ms. Angelus, glad you could join us." Judge Weatherly's bottom lip twitched, signaling his sarcastic sense of humor.

Nikki grinned. "It's my pleasure, Your Honor. Sorry I'm late. I reported to Judge Abernathy first and was informed about the transfer order."

"Are you ready to proceed?"

"I haven't met with both attorneys yet." She set her file on one of the tables next to an empty seat.

"Very well. Let me know when you're ready."

Judge Weatherly continued to call his docket. A flutter from Nikki's periphery drew her attention to a tall, thin, gray-haired man. Sam Carr waved in her direction. Some of Nikki's optimism sank at the sight of his strained expression. Mr. Carr meant well, but was seldom up to date on new developments in the law. If he was the maternal aunt's lawyer, it would take more than being in the court's good graces to keep her ward from ending up with the paternal grandparents.

As she headed in his direction, a hand wrapped around her wrist sending warm shivers up her arm. She stared down at the man whose long fingers held her captive. His thumb traced small circles on the tender area of her wrist. How could the man who aggravated her earlier do something that was just so…pleasant?

"Ms. Angelus." Garrett's smooth voiced crawled inside her. "Weren't you going to greet me, too?"

He sat casually at the counsel table, totally at ease. If she didn't know better, she'd swear he was draped over a bar stool, ordering a drink. But his gaze was far from relaxed. He was focused in on her like a hawk tracking a fish.

She removed his hand from her wrist. Not only was he being too familiar, she didn't like the warmth his touch evoked. A flicker of something not entirely unpleasant—attraction—desire? No, no way. She wouldn't allow it. With all the disdain she could muster, she said, "As I recall, we've had our meeting, Mr. Nightshade."

"I didn't think that went so well the first time. I was hoping for a do over."

"I'm not into do overs." Nikki moved past him, keenly aware that he watched her progress and not entirely sure she disliked the attention. Good grief, Garrett was going to be a pain in the ass. She couldn't wait for this case to be finished so she wouldn't have to contemplate the many ways he stoked her heat barometer. She sat next to Sam Carr and smiled as if nothing bothered her.

"Hi, Sam, you on the Hanover case?" Nikki kept her voice low, as much to prevent Garrett from hearing their conversation as to keep from interfering with the cases in progress.

"Yeah. I represent the maternal aunt. She was going to try to do this herself but I warned her she shouldn't proceed without an attorney."

Nikki agreed, but didn't add that sometimes having an attorney wasn't much better than having none. At least Sam always tried to do the appropriate thing, and that was a step in the right direction.

"What do you know about Mr. Nightshade?"

Sam wasn't the best person to ask, but some information was better than no information.

"His main focus is estate management and criminal law. He only recently started taking family cases. A sign of the economic times, I guess." Sam leaned back, pondering his opposing counsel.

Nikki resisted the urge to turn around and look at the subject of their discussion. She sat stiff in the wooden chair, feeling Garrett's eyes bore holes into her back. His attention shouldn't have bothered her, but it did. It wasn't the first time she'd been annoyed by opposing counsel, but Garrett's scrutiny unnerved her. Her skin tingled as if he could see through her façade and reach into the depths of her psyche to pull out every buried insecurity. She bent in closer to Sam, hoping Garrett didn't perceive the shudder that passed through her.

"This case doesn't strike me as a big money maker."

"I believe he knows the family."

"Hmmm." No longer able to stop herself, Nikki glanced in Garrett's direction. Just as she suspected, his eyes were on her. He cocked his head and smiled. That same odd sensation traveled through her, and she forcefully pushed it away.

Hoping to tamp down the unsettling feelings his intense gaze elicited, she took stock of him—

purposefully clinical—detached. His style of dress didn't indicate a man merely scraping by. The parents had no money, so it had to be the grandparents paying his bill. But, if they had the funds, why hadn't they gone the route of hiring a high profile family attorney? Garret's presence fit right into her weakness for solving puzzles. She would crack his code soon and be done with him.

"He doesn't intimidate you, does he?" Sam's paternalistically worried expression almost made her laugh.

"No, but I think he's going to be trouble. What's your client's story?"

"She's the mother's younger half-sister."

"Is she a stripper?" Nikki held her breath, hoping the answer was no.

"She says she tends bar in a strip club. She doesn't make a lot of money, but she has her own apartment and a place for the child to stay."

"A bartender's probably a step above a stripper from the Court's perspective. But that could mean she works nights."

Sam exhaled, his slight frame diminishing even further. "I don't have a strong case, do I?"

She patted his gnarled hand. "You're not defeated yet, Sam."

****

Nikki and Sam leaned in close, their heads bowed, like long lost friends planning a surprise. Garrett strained to hear, but only indistinguishable whispers reached his ears. He peered at them over his steepled fingers. Their discussion was taking far too long for his liking. How much could they have to go over? He suspected Nikki was the type of woman who didn't give in too easily. In another circumstance, he would find that quality fascinating. But in this instance, it just plain pissed him off.

Garrett glanced at his watch. Damn. Ten-thirty. Much later than he expected to still be dealing with this case. If other attorneys weren't at the bench arguing another matter, he would have demanded they proceed. The other case droned on with no sign of stopping.

He rose and approached Nikki and Sam's table. Nikki glanced in his direction, the flash in her eyes signaling she wasn't too pleased with the intrusion. At least now he wasn't the only pissed off person here. "Anything I need to be involved in?"

"No." There was no apology in Nikki's tone.

Garrett pulled out the chair next to her and sat down. A trace of lavender filled the air, urging him to lean closer. "You might want to rethink that train of thought. I suggest we agree that the paternal grandparents be granted custody while the mother is in the hospital."

"Sorry. I'm afraid I can't agree to that." Nikki held his gaze but added no explanation.

"You can't seriously be considering the stripper."

Sam sputtered. "She's a bartender not a stripper."

"Are you honestly attempting to hand me that line? She works at the Blue Moon Saloon and while people do tend bar there, I happen to know none of them are women."

"From personal experience, I presume." Nikki's lips curved as she cocked her head to the side, exuding innocence that Garrett didn't buy for a second.

"Counsel?" The judge's voice interfered with any

response Garrett might have made. "Are you ready?"

Nikki stood. "Yes, Your Honor."

"Please approach." The judge motioned with his hands.

Garrett narrowed his eyes and pursed his lips. He wondered if Nikki's cool veneer would crumble when he turned up the heat. She couldn't possibly win this fight, and he was going to make her pay for every agonizing second he had to wait to argue the case. Both Sam and Garret motioned for their clients to approach the bench. The woman in the pink tank top stepped forward, giving Garrett's clients a wide birth as they walked toward him with measured steps.

Judge Weatherly thumbed through the documents before him. "This case looks a lot different from the last hearing. Apparently, we have all new players. Ms. Angelus, can you bring me up to speed?"

"Your Honor, at the last hearing, the mother dismissed her case against the father. At that time, there were concerns over domestic violence and physical abuse perpetrated by the father. Apparently the reconciliation didn't go too well. Last night, the father beat—"

"Objection, Your Honor," Garrett interrupted. "Irrelevant."

****

Nikki inwardly groaned, cursing herself for rising to his bait. She inhaled deeply, resolving not to allow Garrett to rile her. "Oh, I think it's highly relevant since he was found at the scene with a gun in his hand."

"I disagree, Your Honor." Garrett waved a dismissive hand. "The GAL's statements assume facts not in evidence and are highly prejudicial to my clients."

Judge Weatherly peered over his glasses at Garrett. Nikki swallowed the impulse to grin. She knew what was coming next.

"Well." Judge Weatherly shuffled his papers and tapped them on the surface of his bench before laying them back down in perfect order. "Is the father here?"

"No." Garrett's shoulders squared. A mottled red tinge crept up his neck when just moments before he sauntered arrogantly up to the bench. *Not so comfy now, are you?*

"Where is he?"

"May I say something?" the paternal grandfather interrupted.

Judge Weatherly silenced him with a quelling look. "No, your attorney will speak for you."

Garrett's hand flew to the knot in his necktie, but he didn't loosen it. Instead, his arm drew slowly back to his side, as if he was forcing it to obey his commands. The corners of Judge Weatherly's mouth raised in the familiar twitch that signaled he was going in for the kill.

Garrett's Adams apple bobbed up and down as he choked out, "He's in jail."

Judge Weatherly raised a quizzical brow. "And why is that?"

"Your Honor," Garrett started. "Neither the mother nor the father are able to take care of their daughter. Although the reasons may be relevant at a later time, the simple fact is that neither parent is present today, ready or able to attend to the child's needs. The paternal grandparents are here to care for the child during this time—"

"As is the maternal aunt, Your Honor," Sam interjected more gracefully than Nikki would have thought possible, although his client didn't augment his position. She stood staring vacantly ahead at nothing in particular with no reaction to the proceedings.

"The point is"—Garrett slammed a fist into his palm, punctuating each word—"that the qualifications of the applicants here today are what's material to your decision."

Judge Weatherly leaned forward, holding Garrett's attention. "That's all well and good, counsel, but you still haven't answered my question."

"What I am trying to say, Your—"

"I know exactly what you're trying to say, counsel. But I am not persuaded that the circumstances of the parents aren't material to my decision today. So tell me, why is your client in jail?" Judge Weatherly tapped his index finger on his papers as seconds ticked by. "It would not be advisable to have me ask a third time, counsel."

Garrett met the judge's gaze but didn't answer. Nikki had never seen anyone this stubborn or this bold. What was he thinking?

"Very well." Judge Weatherly turned to Sam. "Mr. Carr, where is the mother?"

"She's—"

"Objection." Garrett slammed his hand down on his file. "This is irrelevant."

"Overruled, Mr. Nightshade. You may continue, Mr. Carr."

"She's in the hospital."

Judge Weatherly turned back to Garrett. "Mr. Nightshade, are you aware of the reasons the mother is in the hospital?"

"Yes."

"And would those reasons tie into why your client is in jail?"

Garrett's face turned red, and his eyes glinted under the dim lights. "Yes," he ground out.

"Ms. Angelus, I think I understand the situation. Do you have any input into placement of the child?"

"Yes, Your Honor."

"I object to any recommendation she might have." Garrett pointed a finger in Nikki's direction. "She has only spoken to the child once and hasn't had the opportunity to speak with the paternal grandparents."

"Your point?" Again, the twitch of Judge Weatherly's lips.

"She hasn't gathered enough information to form an opinion."

"Ms. Angelus? Would you like to weigh in on this?"

Nikki breathed deeply to silence the urge to wrap her fingers around Garrett's neck. She clasped her hands behind her back as she considered her next words. "Your Honor, it is true that I only visited with the child last night after she was removed from the home due to the…incident. In fact, I have received contradictory information regarding the status of both the grandparents and the maternal aunt. The child is safe for the moment, and I would suggest that a thorough home study be conducted to insure optimum placement for this child."

"Now wait a second—"

Judge Weatherly silenced Garrett with a wave of his hand. "Mr. Carr, do you have any input?"

"I agree with the Guardian *Ad Litem*. A home study is the best course."

The paternal grandmother whispered into her husband's ear. The grandfather pulled at Garrett's arm and spoke in a low tone, glancing nervously at Judge Weatherly. Garrett shook his head.

"Your Honor, a home study requires we hire a social worker to assess the appropriateness of each home. My clients can't afford something like that."

"That's not a problem." Nikki had to admit the look of pained confusion on Garrett's face proved much more satisfying than squeezing the life out of him. Way better. "The child was taken into protective custody last night. The Department of Human Services will conduct a home study to determine placement."

"Counsel," Judge Weatherly began, pausing at length, meeting Garrett's gaze, then Nikki's as he met both attorneys at eye level. "Has DHS not been notified of this hearing?"

"I didn't notify them." Sam gave Garrett a lost look. "Did you?"

Garrett didn't answer right away, nor look in Sam's direction. His focus remained on Judge Weatherly. Nikki had to admire his stamina while facing defeat square in the face. In a record fifteen minutes, he'd boxed himself into a tight space he couldn't wriggle out of. "No."

"Would you agree that DHS is a necessary party to this action, given the child is in protective custody, counsel?" Weatherly's eyes narrowed to impenetrable obsidian. His light tone masked the serious nature of his question.

Both attorneys answered in unison, "Yes."

"Good, then I have no alternative but to continue this matter until DHS can be properly notified of these proceedings. See my clerk about selecting a new date. Allow enough time for DHS to complete a home study."

Nikki offered a smile in Garrett's direction. His expression remained stony. Good, her message had been delivered and received. Loud and clear. Score one for Nikki.

****

Garrett ushered his clients out of court and into a nearby conference room. After he closed the door, Lars Hanover attacked. "What the hell just happened in there?" Lars pointed his bony finger in the direction they had just come.

"Apparently the judge isn't willing to make a decision until he sees a home study." Garrett didn't want to admit it, but he had just been sideswiped by Nikki Angelus, something that wouldn't have happened if he'd had time to prepare the playing field. He squelched a twinge of uninvited admiration. She wouldn't get the best of him next time. He'd make sure of it, but first, he had to console his clients.

"How are we supposed to protect her?" Carolyn Hanover spat from her seat at the table. "She's in there all alone with no support. There's no telling what can or will happen if—"

"Surely, you can monitor her activity from the outside and prevent her misusing her powers on the other children and the gatekeepers"

Lars' face crumpled into a veneer of sheer hatred and venom. "No. Our daughter-in-law would never allow us to keep a single item of Lori's. She never trusted us to oversee our granddaughter's progress. She kept Lori's training to herself and taught her never to ask for our help. Even last night, she remained silent."

"But every child of the Guild cries out when trapped."

"Not this one."

Garrett met Lars' gaze with a measured look. "Are you suggesting that an eight-year-old has enough control of her impulses not to reach out when she's frightened? I've never heard of such a thing." Lars didn't turn away, but his cheek twitched slightly under Garrett's scrutiny. "Is there something else you haven't told me, Lars?"

"No." Lars' eyes widened as he placed his hands out in a placating gesture. "I've told you everything, I swear."

Garrett put a steady hand on Lars' shoulder and squeezed. "You better be telling me everything."

Lars winced and nodded as his gaze traveled to Carolyn, who sat frozen in place. Her thin lips pressed together in silent fury.

"Fine." Garrett shook Lars to get his attention. "I will see what I can do about reaching Lori."

"And how're you going to do that?"

"If we can't go through the front door, we'll just have to go through the back."

****

"Ms. Angelus." Garrett's voice whipped up from behind her. She'd only met Garrett this morning, but already she recognized the man's husky tone. Too bad hearing it meant more confrontation. "Can I talk to you for a minute?"

Her fingers curled into a fist. She didn't want to

deal with him, but couldn't think of a good enough reason to avoid this conversation. "Sure."

"You can't really believe that it's best for this child to remain in the juvenile shelter?"

As she scrutinized his pious face, her blood boiled. What did this estate lawyer know about children, let alone what was best for them? "What's more crucial to this puzzle is why Lori would request to stay there rather than go with her grandparents. Until that home study is finished—" She pointed her finger at him wishing it was a sharp object so she could really drive her point home. "I'm not recommending she be removed."

"Good Lord, the child is eight years old. She can't possibly know what she needs."

"In my experience, children are much more attuned to their needs than most of the parents I work with."

"Don't be naïve—"

Nikki raised her brow.

Garrett ceased speaking but didn't appear to be ashamed. He probably came from the ancient 'children should be seen and not heard' ideology. She clamped her jaw tight and turned to leave. There was no reason to engage in this type of dialogue. He gripped her arm and swung her around. His soft brown eyes shifted from anger to amusement.

"Come on." His voice dropped to a sultry octave. "Don't be like that."

She pulled away from him, ignoring the intense tingly sensation traveling up her arm. "Like what?" She blew the words out through clenched teeth.

"Suppose we call a truce, okay?" While his expression remained impassive, Nikki sensed something more insistent about this approach than the one he'd initially taken. "Do you have a card?"

Surprised by the mundane request, she jerked a card from her docket book and thrust it at him.

"Thank you." He smiled a little too broadly, as if he'd gotten away with stealing her virginity rather than a mere business card.

****

Garrett held Nikki's gaze. Establishing dominance as quickly as possible suddenly seemed vital. She had succeeded in slipping past his influence, but now that he had her card, it was a done deal. Such a small ordinary personal item but it would do the trick. Still, he couldn't resist the urge to push a little further. "I know you have concerns regarding this child. Perhaps if I talked to her, I could convince my client to let it be for the moment."

Her blue eyes filled with venom. "You know you are prohibited from speaking to that child by the order that appoints me." She pointed her thumb at herself. "I won't agree to anyone speaking to the child."

He allowed his lips to curve, noting her annoyance. "We'll see."

She rolled her eyes and waved him off. He watched her retreating back, grateful he had another way to break her spirit. He went in search of Sam to retrieve another business card. He couldn't resist a little chuckle. "Looks like I'm back in business."

****

Parker Hanover tightened his hold on the steel bars and wedged his face between them. He tried to let the cold metal distract him, but it was no use. There was no way to get fresh air. The cinder block walls closed in around him, constricting his ability to breathe. He took big gulps. How long would they imprison him with no real light and no room? The two other occupants confined in the small space rustled around in the cell, disturbing his focus.

"You're gonna hurt yourself, buddy." One of the men spoke from behind, not even trying to suppress his amusement.

Yeah, they thought he was a chump. But they were fool-hardy jerks who had no idea who he was or how powerful his family was. But these idiots would learn as soon as his attorney got here.

"Shut up." Parker let the words drop menacingly, although they sounded petty and childish to his ears. That's what Amy would say anyway. *Petty and childish, that's what you are. You need to grow a pair. You disgust me.* He grinned. Bet she wasn't thinking that now. She should have been more cautious with her suggestions. He would bet his meager pay check that last night hadn't gone as she planned.

"Hey," a second voice, deeper than the first, sounded. "Don't punish the messenger. Carl here was just trying to help out."

Parker pulled his face from the bars for a better view of the two buffoons. What did they know about the terrible twist fate sent his way? Or anything else for that matter. They were the desperate, muted twits who couldn't see people the same as his kind did. His people used skills to get inside a person's mind and twist it to their liking. How ironic that years ago his parents isolated his mind forcing him to live among these bottom dwellers. His hold tightened around the steel rods. The only thing that mattered was his precious daughter. Rage crackled inside him like a magma flow, threatening to erupt through his head. Who would protect his daughter now?

Fuck this! Where the hell was his prick of an attorney? He deserved so much better than this. He should be revered, not mocked by pond scum.

"I don't need his help or yours." A guttural growl accompanied his words, and for the first time, both men appeared off balance. "That's right, keep away from me." He circled around them. "Go to the corner and keep quiet."

The men looked at each other as if in silent communication. Parker didn't think they could really do that, but both seemed to receive the message. The smirks returned, and the men once again appeared at ease, eager for a confrontation.

"Come on." This from Carl as he swiped his hand in the air. "No need to be so crabby. You, me, and Ben here might be stuck in this tank for a while."

Parker scoffed. They weren't really looking for peace. More likely they were itching to fight, and Parker wouldn't stop them if it went that far. He sneered. "I won't be here long. My attorney's going to bond me out."

"Right." Ben chuckled. "You've been here twelve hours and he ain't seen you yet. Looks like he's right on it, dude."

Parker's grip tightened around the bars. Ben's words stung. Not only because he was laughing at him, but because he spoke the truth. His attorney should have been here first thing this morning. His stomach clenched. Had his parents lied to him when they assured him they would get him an attorney? Worse yet, what if nobody took the case and he was truly alone? He shoved his face back through the bars. "He'll be here."

"What are you in for, anyway?" Carl asked.

His mind went back to last night and excitement hummed through his bloodstream. He could still hear the thud of Amy's body as it banged against the wall, hear the glass shattering as the picture had fallen to the floor. His heart beat faster and blood rushed to his head. *He'd* been the one to cause all that destruction. And it had felt fan-fucking-tastic.

"Ah," he sighed, closing his eyes at the bloody images and smells. A tiny prick at the edge of his conscience warned him that he should feel remorse. But he couldn't help himself. It felt good. Never had he felt so in control. Never had he been so powerful. The heady feeling of making his family bend to his will surged through him, just like it had when he'd slammed the butt of the gun into Amy's head. Yeah, last night was good. Very good.

"I was told I put my wife into the hospital." He thought it was best to leave out the rest of the details. Let them wonder what he had done. Let them imagine the worst.

"You hurt your wife?" This came from Ben who sounded incredulous.

For the second time, Parker pulled away from his vigil to face Ben.

"That's what they say." He stared them down, grinning. Proud.

"You hardly seem the type." Ben changed his position and now rested on a metal cot, hands locked behind his head. Carl stood with an arm draped around the pole of what passed as bunk beds, and wore a similar expression.

"Oh, yeah, what do you think my type is?"

Both men's eyes glazed over as they appeared to be taking his question seriously. Then a vicious smile lit Carl's face. "You look like a kiddy diddler."

Parker lunged at him, blinded by fury and indignation. He hammered Carl's head against the pole. Stunned, Carl reeled backward, his hands grappling for a steadying grip on loose sheets, to no avail. He fell to the ground.

A malevolent glint entered Carl's eyes. "Oh, you want to play, do you?" He rose and raced toward him. Carl's knuckles landed squarely on his jaw, dropping Parker to his knees. Pain exploded from his cheek bone into the backs of his eyeballs. He grimaced and reached to claw Carl's face. His fingers slid into the tender spot of Carl's eye, and he pressed hard. Carl screamed and drew back. Ben grabbed Carl from behind and dragged him off Parker.

"You don't want to do this," Ben said as he pulled his buddy to the opposite side of the cell. It wasn't far, but enough to keep him out of reach. Parker struggled to his feet, poised to take another run at him.

"Let go of me!" Carl yelled, struggling with Ben. "I'm going to fuck that piece of shit up so his own momma won't recognize him."

"We want out of here, remember. Not more time," Ben hissed. Parker made a move in their direction. Ben glared at him, halting him in his tracks.

Anger still boiled and burned inside him, demanding satisfaction.

"You heard what he called me." As if that was enough for Ben to step aside and allow Parker to finish

Carl off. But Ben held Parker's gaze and shook his head slowly.

"Asshole, don't you remember where you are? Jail! Do you want to get into more trouble?"

Parker couldn't comprehend being in more trouble than he already was. *You're a kiddy diddler.* The words uttered by the dregs of the cell block resonated in his mind.

"You're thinking it too! You're just like him." It was worse than being called a wife beater. As usual, the authorities had misunderstood the situation. He just couldn't take her incessant nagging. They didn't understand. All they were interested in was making him the butt of a joke. Well, he couldn't take that and be a man at the same time. Rage made his vision go red and he propelled himself forward, toward the men, wanting to hurt someone. Ben shoved Carl to the side and doubled his fist, slamming it into the center of Parker's face. The cracking sound came just before the pain.

"Augh!" Parker clutched his fractured nose, the pain searing his mind. His eyes watered. The metallic taste of blood trickled into his mouth. "Bastard! I'll kill you! I'll kill you both!"

"You need to calm down, fella. It don't matter what he called you. You struck first and that's exactly what I'll tell the guards when they show up. Now sit the fuck down."

"Asshole." Parker spit a mouthful of blood at them and sank back down onto his cot. Ignoring the blood still dripping from his shattered nose, he leaned his head back against the wall. He was tired of following orders, but he wasn't feeling so empowered now. His fatigue was made worse by his bewilderment. No one had come for him as promised. Where was his fucking attorney, anyway? Why wasn't there someone to defend him?

The only one who cared about him was Lori, and she'd been taken away by that crazy bitch. Amy was always playing the victim, just like now. Being all pitiful and weak. Everyone feeling sorry for her. No one cared how any of this affected him. Now Lori was further away than ever. It would be different if he could touch her mind the way his kind could but his suffocating parents prevented him from that long ago. They said it was for the best, but the truth was, they were scared of him. As a child, he'd been powerful. More powerful than the adults of the Guild. They had all feared him, and now look at him. But he would show them all. He smiled grimly. It was only a matter of time.

Then he could be with his Lori as it should have been all along. A father should know his daughter in the true sense. Not even the father-daughter bond they shared could satisfy him. It should be more. So much more. What if she thought he had abandoned her? He couldn't do that to his sweet child. He wouldn't do that. He held out his arm and scratched a wide groove into his flesh. Blood trailed the line, mixed with the blood dripping from his nose. He ignored the pain. It was the good kind. Pain with a purpose. Like his mom said when she described giving birth. His cell mates didn't come near him as he completed his work. *Yeah, now you get it.* He made another slash in his flesh, then another, until Lori's name was carved into his arm. He hoped it would leave a good scar, so Lori would know he hadn't left her.

Chapter Four

Nikki pushed through the entrance of the juvenile shelter and walked over to the front desk. Marilyn, the receptionist, smiled as Nikki approached. Her frizzy red hair fell in haphazard curls barely contained by her headband. "Good afternoon, Nikki. Which child are you seeing today?"

"Lori Hanover." Nikki leaned into the counter, taking a few short breaths to slow her respiration. "I phoned ahead. She should be waiting."

Marilyn held up a finger and punched some numbers. "Hi, Nancy, Nikki is here to see the Hanover child. Umhmm. Right." She hung up and smiled at Nikki. "She's waiting in room ten."

"Thanks." Nikki waited to be buzzed in, and then headed in the direction of the room. Just before she arrived at her destination, a high-pitched voice stopped her.

"Hey, Nikki, could I have a word with you?"

Nikki turned to face the elementary dorm supervisor. "Yes, Valerie?"

"I know you're visiting with the Hanover child today." She lowered her voice and ducked her head conspiratorially. "Some strange things have happened since Lori was placed here."

"Really?" Nikki inhaled deeply. Valerie was prone to exaggeration. To her, a small tiff over not getting a turn on a swing would be perceived as a violent brawl. What could Lori have done in the twenty-four hours she had been here to merit this kind of concern?

"Yes, I mean, it's really weird." Valerie couldn't quite meet her gaze. Did she feel guilty or was she trying to hide something?

"Ok…"

"The girls in her dorm were all complaining that some of their stuff was missing. It was little things, like a headband, barrette, and plastic bracelet. You know, things like that. Every single child, other than Lori, was missing something. When the dormitory was searched, the items were found underneath Lori's pillow."

"I see."

"But that's not the strangest part" Valerie placed her hand on Nikki's arm. "Lori said they were hers. Because it was late, the night supervisor said they needed to go to bed and we would resolve the matter in the morning. She made explicit notes so that we could deal with the situation during the day shift. But when the girls were questioned, they all said it was a mistake. Claimed they had given Lori the items. What makes matters even more bizarre, the girls are very well behaved and cooperative with each other. There hasn't been an outburst all day."

Nikki wasn't sure how to digest this news. One minute, Lori was stealing from her dorm mates and the next instant, they were bestowing gifts upon her. Certainly strange behavior. But what really struck her as odd is that Valerie felt it important to divulge this information. It might be unusual for children here to get along well, but maybe they were just having a good day. "Are you sure the night supervisor got the story right?"

"We checked with her. She is adamant the girls were upset. I thought you should know, since you're seeing her today."

"I'll talk to her about it."

"Thank you."

Nikki proceeded down the hall and opened the door to room ten. At least this time they'd put Lori in the more kid friendly room. As much as it could be with a wallpaper apple tree fraying at the edges and blue butterflies with missing wings dotting the wall. Long purple and orange crayon lines scribbled across the surface marring what was supposed to be a picturesque picnic scene.

Lori looked up and smiled. Dressed in tan shorts and a t-shirt speckled with pink and red hearts, she could have been waiting for the school bus instead of court personnel. So much childhood had been robbed from her and yet she beamed as if she were actually having a picnic. "Nikki, they tell me I get to stay here for a while."

Nikki took the chair across from her. "That's true. The Judge thought that it might be a good idea for someone to check out the homes of your grandparents and aunt."

Lori pulled the ends of a lock of hair over her mouth but said nothing. Her eyes were brighter than last night. Her hair was combed and pulled back by a headband. She didn't tense at the news, but also didn't seem interested in talking about what happened in court.

"Could you tell me," Nikki said. "Why you want to stay here?"

Lori tilted her head and looked her straight in the eyes. "Because I'm safe here," she said, then began blowing at her hair.

"Why don't you feel safe with your grandparents?"

Lori stopped messing with her hair. She folded her legs in front of her and wrapped her arms around them. Resting her head on her knees, she peered keenly at Nikki. "They're bad people."

"What makes them bad?"

"I don't know. I just can't trust them."

"Why?"

Lori rolled her eyes and sighed. "Look, they just can't know me okay?"

"They don't get to see you?"

She slammed her hand down on the table. "Noooo. They get to see me, they just can't know me."

"I don't understand."

"You would if you were my mom." Her voice caught, and she swiped at a tear. Her feet abruptly touched the floor. Her head dropped into her hands, and she peeked through them. "They just can't know me, okay?"

"It's okay." Nikki nodded at the perplexing child. She didn't want this ordeal to be any harder on Lori than it had to be. But, she wasn't sure how to read between the lines. The play on words was significant to this child. To Nikki, it was as meaningless as gibberish. She decided to take another tack. "What about your aunt?"

At the mention of her aunt, Lori's mouth drooped. "She can't keep me safe. She's my mom's step-sister. She's not blood." Lori's blue eyes were serious.

"She doesn't have to be a blood relative for you to

go live with her."

Lori took on a 'you really don't get it' expression. "Oh, yes she does. Or else she can't protect me."

"From what?"

"I can't tell you. It's a secret, but it's bad. Really bad." Her whisper sent a skittered chill up Nikki's spine.

****

That night, Garrett sank into bed with a shroud of guilt hanging over him. He knew he should have gone to see Parker Hanover today. What stopped him? It wasn't like he hadn't dealt with clients of his ilk before, but a dark inkling niggled at him like an itch he couldn't reach. That itch took the shape of Nikki Angelus. It wasn't just her silky black hair and bottle green eyes that held his attention. Power lurked beneath her passionate exterior. A power so compelling it reached into his soul and exposed him as a fraud. She threw him off his stride, and it bothered him more than he cared to admit, or had time to deal with. It was imperative to return things to their natural order before he lost his edge.

He lay down, holding Sam's and Nikki's business cards. Talismans of sorts. They were his gateway to restoring the balance. But who should he visit first? In truth, he was anxious to get into Nikki's head, but it struck him as rude. An odd enough notion since he entered people's minds on a daily basis. Even so, his instincts urged him to deal with Sam before Nikki. Besides wouldn't Sam's mind be the easiest to manipulate? He'd go there first, then he would be able to turn his full attention to Nikki.

He lifted Sam's card, allowed the first wave of

sleep to catapult him into Sam's mind. The usual stretch expanded his mind outward, creating a sense of nausea as he floated in a formless vacuum. A crack propelled him forward until he was outside his own body. He hovered over his sleeping form. A glowing silver line of energy extended from his spiritual form down to his physical body, connecting the two, so even in separation they were one.

Garrett searched for the slip stream that would lead him into Sam. He squinted, as if his eyes were still in corporeal form and waited for the astral world to take shape. He crouched, ready for the tingle and the white undulating river of light to reveal itself. When it appeared, he dove into it, swimming at first until its force pulled him into the undertow. He pulsed through the metaphysical torrent until he smacked against the barrier of Sam's mind. The impact was softer than most. That was a good sign.

He retrieved the astral image of Sam's card to slice a slit from the top of Sam's psyche to the bottom. The motion was smooth. The membrane offered no resistance. Garrett stepped through and, as he suspected, Sam's mind was pretty straightforward. There was no myriad of doors for him to choose from like he often found in the most guarded minds. Instead, there was one door at the end of a corridor.

Only one option.

One choice.

One path into the center of Sam's psyche. Garrett smiled at how easy his task would be. He pushed open the door and entered Sam's consciousness.

Images of Sam's life flashed past. Riding his tricycle as a boy. Accepting a Boy Scout patch for mastering the art of tying a tourniquet. As an adolescent, shyly approaching a young girl with blonde hair, terrified of her rejection, instead she smiled. Later, standing with his right hand raised, taking the oath of an attorney while his mother wept in a sea of other parents. Garret chuckled. Sam passed the bar by a nose.

Garrett slid past Sam's images of youth, finding more recent memories. In some, Sam got a guilty verdict for his client with a sentence of life without parole. Glancing back at his client's family weeping in the gallery, remorse at not being able to do a better job misting his eyes. His adrenaline rush at successfully winning another client a judgment of alimony when everyone told him he wouldn't get a dime. With reluctant admiration, Garrett acknowledged these experiences mirrored his own.

Jury trials were the worst. So many people to influence, but Sam succeeded without Garrett's special brand of power. Garrett envied Sam's triumph. Could Garrett have won his trials with no ability other than an acute mind and quick tongue? Sam's was not the strongest mind he had encountered, but there was more to him than first impressions indicated.

When Garrett reached Sam's memory of the hearing before Judge Weatherly, he carefully monitored Sam's mood as the events of the day played out. Sam's nervousness as he discussed the case with Nikki. How could he convince the Judge that his client wasn't as bad as his opponent would make her? She wasn't really a stripper, but she did tend bar at a strip joint where methamphetamines were consumed for breakfast, lunch, and dinner. Not the optimal situation to expose a child to, even when it was a parent instead of an aunt who wanted custody. But his client wouldn't necessarily take the child around these people. Then again, everyone knew that the people you work with often times show up at your doorstep unannounced or by invitation.

Sam's nerves spiked as he approached the bench where the judge put a period to his angst by rendering judgment. Garrett took note of the anxiety and filed it away for future reference should he encounter Sam again. But he didn't need to manipulate this emotion to gain the advantage. The moment Garrett needed to see came after the judge ordered the parties to submit to a home study. Sam was surprised by this turn of events, and it took several minutes for him to absorb the shock of the decision, as well as the ramifications. Relief folded around the older man like a blanket, turning his agitation into bliss. He hadn't lost. A surge of pride followed. Then he realized his client had limited funds. The agitation burned nipping at his fingers like a bunch of fire ants. There was no way his client could afford a home study. Then another miracle, the judge ordered DHS to foot the bill. He wasn't sure how his client would fare under the scrutiny, but at least she had a chance.

Garrett seized his opportunity. Pulling at the fabric of this memory, he extracted the necessary parts to twist them around. *Your client will buckle under the pressure of this investigation,* he began. *DHS won't pay for the home study. She will take out a loan but be unable to pay it back quickly enough. She will be forced to work longer hours impacting her ability to care for the child consistently. Constantly worried, she will show up late for work, then begin missing full days with no phone calls. Her boss will fire her. All because she fought against the Hanovers. Fine upstanding people who only want what's best for little Lori. They will end up with custody, and your client will be worse off. Do the right thing. Back out of the case.*

He smiled, shoving the tendril of guilt at crushing the work of a good man. Truth was, Sam had little hope of actually winning this case. Garrett was just speeding up the process. It was the perfect adjustment. Subtle with no hint of interference. Satisfied with his work, Garrett returned to his physical body for the next round. It was time to prepare for Nikki.

****

In the darkness of his bedroom, Sam Carr tossed and turned in his sleep, unable to let go of the events of the day. For one thing, there was no guarantee his client could pass a home study. What if she couldn't handle the financial pressure? She could even begin to overcompensate by working longer hours. That wouldn't end well. She could lose her chance at custody, even lose her job. The more Sam contemplated, the more he was convinced he'd sent his client in the wrong direction. A direction that would eventually ruin the girl's life. Hell, she was only twenty. How could he have done such a thing? Hadn't he sworn to protect his clients? He had to get her out of the ditch he had dug for her. But how?

After wrestling with the issue, the solution finally came to him. He would convince his client to drop the case. Then she wouldn't have to lose everything. Yes, that was what he would do. Decision made, he fell into a deep, peaceful sleep.

****

After a long, hard day, Nikki looked forward to the bliss of sleep. However, she found herself grappling with what to do with Lori's rag doll. The toy had been entrusted to her care and it seemed disrespectful not to have a specific place to put it. The night before, Nikki placed her at the foot of the bed. She'd been too tired to think of anything else but sleep. Tonight, she wondered if she should put it with the rest of her ragdoll collection on the window seat in her bedroom.

Since Cassie's death, Nikki had purchased a rag doll on the anniversary of her sister's birthday each year. She now had one of every type. The Christmas doll, the anniversary doll, the patent doll, the city doll, the country doll, and so on. There were sixteen. It might be all right to put Lori's doll with them. It wasn't as if Lori's doll would get lost among them. Nikki's dolls were in mint condition. Not a hair out of place, no rips, tears, no smudges of affection.

Rags was, well, a child's beloved plaything, unlike the shrine of dolls Nikki collected in Cassie's memory.

It didn't seem right for Rags to join them. She wasn't a tribute to a dead girl. Lori might be in trouble, but she was very much alive. Unlike Cassie long ago, Nikki could help Lori. She could make sure this child was well cared for in a safe home. At least, she hoped she could, and that potential was enough to convince her to place Rags somewhere of her own.

After much deliberation, Rags ended up on the nightstand. Nikki looked at the doll's unwavering smile of trust. *I will protect her,* she promised Rags just before she fell asleep.

****

Garrett lay on his bed with Nikki's business card

clutched between his fingers. He forced himself to relax, and willed his mind and ghostly body to rise into the slip stream and pass through. A shiver of anticipation shuddered down his spine at the thought of his destination, but he shook it off as the excitement of bringing yet another matter to a finish. What else could it be?

Nikki's psyche was thicker and tougher to slice, but he had her card. Even if she knew what he was doing, she didn't possess the ability to deny him access. After a long grueling moment, he was through the unusually solid mental barrier. Twelve doors greeted him. More than he expected. How had one so young amassed so many compartments when people twice her age had less? What sort of trauma had she endured that required that many blockades? He found them compartmentalized in a series of events, and now he had to choose the right one to enter.

But where to begin?

The doors were arranged in a semi-circle. They were not scattered like most minds. Her sub-conscious had lined them up in order of significance. But did that mean youngest to oldest or least important to most important?

There was no indication from the doors themselves. They were universally the same shape and size. All were fashioned of dark mahogany wood. That was interesting in and of itself, as most minds gave themselves away by dressing their doors in an obvious portrayal of their personalities. Juveniles doors were often colors consisting of pinks or blues, some emblazoned with race car decals, daisies, or other childish symbols. As the memories aged, the colors faded, but the character was still represented by some type of symbol such as bumper stickers or posters. Nikki's mind gave none of those indications.

As he neared, he examined them more closely and realized that Nikki did have a tell. More subtle than most, but easy to read once discovered. The door knobs were different. One was shaped like a cat. Another, like a dog. Garrett dismissed these as being from her childhood. The next three doors, offered a peace sign, a maple leaf, and a corvette. Adolescence? His curiosity piqued, he almost opened one of them, but stopped himself.

No. No use getting off track. He would have time to delve into these idle musings later, if he so desired. A twinge of guilt pricked his conscience. He wasn't the intrusive type. This was a job. Nothing more.

He walked past a door with a crystal knob, then brass, gold, silver. These were much harder to decipher, but his gut told him he was not yet at the right door. The third door from the end had an antique ivory knob with an old fashioned key hole. He paused, then reached out and turned. Locked. Whatever lay behind this door, Nikki kept even from her own awareness. Garrett wanted—no *needed*—to know what that was.

He bent down and peered through the key hole. Nothing. No light, no flash of color, no images. The memories there were hidden, buried deep. Again, off track. He wasn't going to be able to solve this puzzle tonight. Reluctantly, he turned to the last two. One had a white knob with a doll painted on it, and the other was a scale.

He smiled, thinking he should have started on this end first. The door he needed was the one with the scales of justice. He turned the knob and walked through. Nikki wasn't hiding this part of her life.

Garrett saw her sitting for the bar exam. Her thrill at being selected to act as Guardian *ad litem* for children. Her first case showed her arguing with a mother. Determined to convince her that it was in her child's best interest to visit his father, and when she wouldn't listen, recommending the child be placed in the custody of his father.

In another case, Nikki admonished a father not to speak to the child regarding her mother's infidelity so that the child could know and love her mother on her own terms. In case after case, Nikki worked to help parents get off drugs, to work through their grief, to let go of their anger, all for the benefit of the children. When she lost a case, she was heartbroken, crying over a grilled cheese with fries kicking herself for not being good enough to help her young charge.

The sight of her hunched over mindlessly eating a fry, eyes misting with tears tugged at Garrett's sympathy. If only he could console her somehow. Let her know she wasn't alone. But he could only watch as these visions passed. They were outside the forty-eight-hour window. Garrett was unable to help. Nikki intrigued Garrett further when she won a case. She wasn't filled with arrogance, she was happy that those children—*her children*—would have strong healthy bonds with their parents. What an amazing woman.

She was elated when she got it right and horrified when she got it wrong. Torturing herself for days over what she should have done to alleviate the child's pain. Her devotion to doing the right things was so strong that he wondered if he should listen to Nikki's reasons before he tweaked her mind. But her choices weren't always correct, and by staying in her mind, he could be saving her from the same disappointment she'd experienced before.

Sorting through her memories, he located the Hanover case. Nikki didn't feel the same anxiety as Sam. Although nervous, she navigated the courtroom with ease. She listened to Sam's tale and took every outcome into consideration before reaching her conclusion.

His lips twitched when he discovered that his presence irritated and distracted her. *Turnabout is fair play*. Nikki had been telling the truth when she stated her reasons for not recommending his clients. Another factor in her favor, she played fair. So Garrett decided to give her a straight message. *The grandparents are the best choice. Parker is a bad seed. An aberration. Lori is a good child. They will take good care of her.* Then, as an afterthought he added, *allow me to speak to Lori*.

Briefly, he considered placing a thought that she found him irresistible, suggest a casual dinner. Afterward she would be filled with an aching need to rip his clothes off and have her way with him. But just as it occurred to him, he discarded the notion. Not only was that *not* fair play, it would be no fun if he couldn't win her over on his own.

This was business no matter how tempting it was to make her hot for him. Purpose completed, Garrett left her mind.

Chapter Five

Nikki's dreams that night were much more pleasant than they'd been the night before. *Hawaii was bliss, digging her toes into the sand, her long sundress billowed in the wind as she walked the line between beach and ocean. A breeze ruffled through her hair. She breathed crisp clean oxygen into her lungs. The illusive peace she craved enfolded her in a hug. The scene shifted. She lay in bed, staring up at a bamboo ceiling fan. A small smile curved her lips. Garrett's face appeared over her. "Are you happy?" His fingers traced her bare arm. Her smile broadened. "Yes." Although she disliked this man, his touch ignited her desire. She moved in to kiss him.*

He vanished.

She woke, heart racing. Closing her eyes, she willed herself to return to the dream. She threw the pillow over her head in disgust. Why the hell would she want to be in his arms? But she did. She groaned realizing the thought both shocked and excited her.

****

Garrett entered Nikki's office with Sam trailing him. Mountains of paperwork and files were arranged in neat piles. The only vacant space on the surface was the place in front of her chair.

Her walls were equally chaotic with a mish mash of art from local talent and a multicolored array of children's drawings. The drawings had uneven lettering stating 'thank you for helping me' or 'for Nikki, you're awesome!!!!' amongst flowers, stick figures, and two dimensional houses.

There was only one thing that indicated he'd stepped in an attorney's office. The bar license that hung in the center of the wall behind her desk. It wasn't much of an ego wall. Just her license. No other awards, certificates, or professional accomplishments joined the lone indication that she was indeed an attorney.

"To what do I owe the honor of seeing the two of you so early in the day?" Nikki speared him with a narrowed gaze over the stack of files. Without waiting for an invitation that would never come, Garrett took one of the two chairs in front of her desk and indicated to Sam to do the same. The old man perched on the edge of his seat prepared to flee at the first opportunity. He really needed to calm down, but he didn't know this was all a matter of formality. Nothing could change the outcome of this meeting. Garrett eased into his chair, flung his arm over the back, and waited.

"Well…" Sam fingered his tie while his eyes traveled over the décor of her office rather than her. "I've discussed matters with my client and…well…"

Could the man not get it out?

"What's wrong?" Nikki demanded.

"My client can't afford this litigation. With a home study on top of that, there's just no way. I've recommended she dismiss her case."

Finally. Garrett let out a breath, waiting for Nikki's acquiescence. Instead, she clicked her pen. In and out. In and out. In and out. Her face twisted into an expression of confusion.

"The expense of a home study isn't an issue. Don't you remember? DHS is picking up the tab?"

"Oh, come on." Garrett locked stares with Nikki, willing her to remember the subliminal suggestions. Last night, he was sure he made an impression, that his message had sunk in. "You have to agree that dismissing the aunt's action makes sense."

Nikki's gaze did not waver. "In point of fact, I don't."

Nor was he given any indication that her resolve had waned. What had gone wrong? He wasn't a novice dream caster. A shiver of apprehension shot up his spine. He squeezed the arm rest of his chair until his knuckles whitened.

Her mind was his to control. He convinced judges to reduce their sentences from life in prison to twenty-five years. With a simple flick of a mental switch he changed the course of a wandering unfaithful spouse into a dutiful and considerate husband. How the hell could he fail to change the position of one powerless woman? It made no sense. Sharp teeth gnawed at his conscience, provoking a notion that couldn't be true. If it was, all certainties in his life would be sucked into a meaningless vacuum, and where would that leave him? More importantly, what would that make him?

Sam loosened the crooked knot of his tie. "That's not the point. It's the litigation. With discovery and how many days of trial it will take. My client doesn't have the stamina to handle that kind of scrutiny. She feels she can't deal with it."

Nikki rested her mouth on one fist as she turned her attention to Sam. The intensity of her gaze had not lessened, and stubborn determination crept onto her face. "You aren't thinking this through, Sam. A home study might resolve the issue of custody, and there would be no need for a trial. I insist we wait until the home study is complete."

Garrett couldn't believe what he was hearing. Worse, Sam's face had smoothed into a comfortable pose of contemplation. The bastard was actually considering Nikki's words. Garrett refused to let her ruin his plans. "Are you forgetting that the aunt is a stripper?"

"That's not true," Sam sputtered. He didn't utter another word but he sat straighter his expression alert. Now he was strong and confident. A man who wouldn't back down. In one small act of defiance, Nikki stripped away all of Garrett's work from the night before.

"She's a bartender." Nikki smiled a 'don't mess in my territory or else' challenge. Her expression, smooth as silk and too slippery to grab hold of and crush. White hot anger seethed beneath his skin. How dare she meddle so casually in his affairs?

"You don't know that." Garrett's words barely escaped his clenched jaw. "She could be lying."

Her smile broadened. "Even if she were a stripper, I wouldn't rule her out."

Sam's head swiveled from Nikki to Garrett.

"How can you be so naïve? That type of person is not suitable to raise a moral, law abiding citizen."

"Right," she said blandly. "And your clients have really done a great job there. You're letting stereotypes rule your decision making and that's not wise."

Truth be told, Garrett wasn't prepared for a fight. He had been so sure that his work last night was complete. He'd gone through the door and sown the seeds of a different opinion. His work should have taken hold. Instead, Nikki appeared as certain of her opinion as she was when he'd first met her. No one born into solitude should have been able to counteract his will. Yet she had, and that meant only one thing. Someone else had intervened. Someone he didn't know.

"So, you're going to let a meth head have custody of this child?"

Nikki leaned forward. "None of that has been proven. I don't let surface appearances dictate my recommendations. Sometimes the one who *seems* most appropriate ends up being the most detrimental to a child's well-being."

"I've never known that to be the case." Garrett straightened his tie with a swift tug.

"You've practiced family law for...what...twelve seconds? You haven't come near to seeing the atrocities I have. I had a case once where the mother was a stripper. The judge gave custody to the dad. That weekend, the dad took the child camping and while she was swimming, the father got high on marijuana. Because he wasn't paying attention, his daughter drowned."

"That's horrible." Sam looked back at Nikki, slack jawed.

"You can't let one case control your opinion." Garrett tried to remain in charge of the conversation that was quickly slipping from his grasp.

"That isn't the only one. I had a guardianship where the paternal grandmother obtained custody on very slim grounds. Even though there was a court order, she wouldn't let the mother visit her children. However, she had no problem letting her alcoholic son see the kids. Before the situation could be resolved, the grandmother allowed her son to drive the children to school drunk. They died in a car crash."

"Is that true?" Sam eyes grew wide.

"What's your point?" Garrett noted that Sam's resolve to dismiss the case was crumbling with every word Nikki spoke. He shook his head in frustration. It was time to wrap up this conversation.

"My point is that the very people who think they are protecting children, sometimes end up harming them."

"I think we're done here." He wasn't going to get anywhere today. Until he discovered who protected Nikki, he would have to go through with this farce of a custody battle.

She grabbed a stack of papers, tapping on the desk to straighten them. "Fair enough," she said.

Garrett searched her expression for smugness before signaling to Sam, who rose with him. Garrett hung back as Sam slipped out, and leaned over Nikki's desk until they were nose to nose. "Who's protecting you?"

She leaned back, steepling her fingers and locking her eyes with his as if she were in perfect control of the situation. The frustration of their encounter melted off her face, replaced by a self-assured smile. "I have no idea what you're talking about."

Her gaze held his, waiting him out, unhinging every notion he knew was true. It was a fact that she couldn't sidestep his mind-push without help. Unless she was hiding a secret of her own. His eyes traveled down her neckline, searching for the tell-tale bulge of the amulet, but there was no hint of anything beneath the smooth surface of her turtle neck sweater. "Someone has to be protecting you."

"You're used to getting your way all the time, aren't you?"

If she noticed his perusal of her attire, she gave no indication. She sat still, watching him. No huff of indignation. No spark of outrage. No reaction. Irritation burned a trail from within. Where had this cool veneer come from? If he couldn't influence her actions in her dream world, then he had to find another way to get to her. Problem was, the conscious world was not his playground. It belonged to people like her. Except people like her shouldn't be able to thwart his power. And now she had the edge because she had done the impossible.

Fury and the burn of competition fueled him. Things were about to change. She was either protected or one of his kind. He had to know the answer for sure. He rounded the corner of her desk and took great satisfaction when her eyes grew wide.

****

Nikki bolted from her chair, distancing herself from Garrett. But that proved difficult. She found herself wedged between her desk and credenza with nowhere to go. Garrett drew closer. He was so near she could feel the warmth of his breath. He smelled of cinnamon and cloves. Not an unpleasant aroma. She squirmed in discomfort. "What are you doing?"

He didn't reply. An electric tingle passed through her at his nearness, compelling her to lean into him. She gripped the edge of the credenza to hold herself in place, determined to resist. She considered yelling for help. Just what she needed, her colleagues thinking her weak. Her own fury took hold. After all, what could Garrett do to her in such a public place? She took a deep breath, ignoring the pleasure his scent created, and stood her ground. Waiting.

"You're afraid of me aren't you?"

She raised her chin. "You're confusing me with Sam," she said haughtily. His arrogance stirred a resentment she rarely felt. Irritation snaked its way from the depths of a past she had thought long since managed. Through clenched teeth, she continued. "I can't be bullied by you like he can."

"Is that what you think I'm trying to do?"

"Aren't you?"

Garrett shook his head, slowly extinguishing the last remnants of her anger with his gaze. His finger traced her collar bone leaving a blazing trail of heat in its wake. She froze conflicted between the notion to move closer and the desire to flee. The tenderness in his touch made her inhale sharply. His spicy scent soothing her into submission to his will. She parted her lips as her head bent backward. Was she truly succumbing to Garrett simply because he touched her? She ground her teeth together annoyed at her confusion.

"Why do you cover such a pretty neck?" The question swelled with sexual innuendo. She swallowed hard to keep from responding in kind. His finger trailed her neck line. She sucked in a breath. Then abruptly, he pulled his hand away and stepped back. The wave of disappointment that engulfed her surprised and annoyed her. Why was she just standing there letting him get away with such disrespectful behavior? "You need to leave."

Instead of obeying, he folded his arms and favored

her with a measured look. He pursed his lips. Heat rose up her cheeks at his scrutiny. She glanced down at her desk, anything to avoid his gaze. She hated herself for the display of weakness. Her eyes lit upon the golden pen he had handed her to sign the papers. She grabbed it and thrust it outward. "Here's your pen. You can go now."

He raised an eyebrow, a flicker of amusement crossing his face. She knew how she must look to him. Fumbling. Awkward. Not the least bit a worthy adversary.

"Keep it." His low tone undermined her command, agitating her further. Why wouldn't he leave? Infuriating didn't begin to describe this unwanted intruder standing there acting as if there was something wrong with her. She could call for security. Have him escorted out, but all she could think of was the snickers she would hear behind her back. That she didn't have enough control to oust another attorney from her domain.

"Get out now," she hissed. "Or is your abominable behavior a quality of the Guild."

His eyes narrowed. "What do you know about the Guild?"

"I know you wear the ring." His fingers fiddled with the very object of their discussion. "I've been told you are dangerous. Wasn't sure I believed that until now. But you walk in here demanding I kowtow to you. Expecting it as if it is your due. Is this type of thing something I can expect from you in the future?"

"I'm not the enemy."

"You could have fooled me."

The jangle of the phone filtered into her awareness.

She made no move to pick it up, keeping her attention pinned on Garrett. He stopped. Took on the appearance of a statute. A slow easy smile crept across his well-groomed features. "Answer your phone."

Before he exited her office, he added, "Pleasant dreams, Ms. Angelus."

Nikki watched Garrett leave with mixed emotions. On the one hand, she respected his desire to zealously represent his client. She even understood his need to blindly pursue their objectives. She wasn't the least bit shocked he behaved a little too entitled, as if there were no other side to his case but his own theory. He acted in step with the person she met yesterday, the type of attorney who would bully his adversaries into submitting to his objectives. Sam was easy prey to a person like Garrett Nightshade. It wasn't the first time she had to stop an aggressive attorney from taking advantage of a weaker one.

What bothered her most was how easily Garrett thought *she* would bend to his will. That was insulting. She had expected more from him. More to the point, she had wanted him to expect more from her too. Disappointment seared her bruised ego. She sighed. He thought as little of her as he did Sam. She wasn't worthy of his respect or admiration. Once again, she was the flawed sibling who had the audacity to survive when the perfect one had perished. She bit her lip at the realization she had allowed Garrett to get to her. Maybe that was why she hadn't been as firm as she should have been when things got so heated she could barely breathe.

Nothing excused his rude actions. More troubling was why she had let him get away with his intrusiveness. Her hand flew to her neck. Her skin still tingled from his touch. The reaction to him was so unexpected it clogged her ability to process her feelings. What did he want from her? More importantly what did she want from him? She tossed his pen onto the desk unable to deny the attraction. It was that stupid dream.

If she hadn't woken with every nerve ending screaming for his caress, she would've kept him from getting close enough to diminish her ability to reason. If she was honest, she was pleased to see him this morning and his nearness felt natural. Most likely the remnants of her dream. But that didn't explain his question or why he seemed to talk in riddles. He thought someone was protecting her because she wouldn't agree to dismiss the case? That was the strangest statement of all. She was pulled from her musings by another blaring ring of the phone. With trembling hands, she lifted the receiver.

"Hello?"

"What do you think of the package?" a raspy voice said.

"Excuse me?"

A low chuckle. "The amulet I gave you?"

A cold chill swept through her. "Who is this?"

"The one who can give you the answers you seek."

Her nerves were stripped bare. How much ambiguity was she supposed to endure? It seemed the universe had deemed it fit to deliver every bizarre situation to her personally this week. She had had enough. "Look, I don't have time for games. If there is something I need to know, this would be the time to tell me. Let's start with your name."

"My name is William Songe. We need to meet."

Disappointment plummeted to her darkest core as tears rose unbidden. The necklace had come from this stranger. Not her mom. In a brief moment, the last tie to her mother vanished. She wasn't about to take this venture down the rabbit hole, even though the origins of the amulet plagued her and the man on the other end of the line promised to answer her questions. She could simply hang up, but found herself unable to let go that simply. Surely, there was more information to be had.

"Why did you give me the necklace?" The brisk words echoed her need to swing at the man who had sullied her mom's memory.

"Because it is your legacy. I repeat, we need to meet." His voice took on a soft pleading tone. "The corner diner."

"What time?" Was she really considering his offer? "Wait. No way. I don't even know you."

"I am not a stranger to you, Nikki."

"I don't know a William Songe." Like it or not, her well-structured life had morphed into burning questions. No matter how much she thought she knew, she couldn't depend on one fact in her life. Everything had dissolved into gray vapors of uncertainty.

"Six-thirty, and I will explain everything."

"I don't think so."

As she hung up the phone, she wondered if Mr. Songe knew as much as he claimed. She pulled the velvet case from her purse and opened it. Vivid green jewels winked at her, keeping the buried secret of its past from her. Whatever was happening, this tiny emblem played a significant part. She had to find out more about it. Now she had a name to begin her search.

She sat in front of her computer and typed the name William Songe into the data base.

****

Garrett flipped open his phone and dialed.

"Hello."

"We have a problem."

"What kind of problem?" His mother's cranky voice indicated her day had gone about as well as his. And this imposition was not welcome. If he could have avoided this phone call, he would have. The next best thing was to get right to the point and keep the conversation to a minimum.

"I dream casted Nikki Angelus last night, but it didn't take."

"What do you mean didn't take?" His mother drew the words out as if trying to decipher the meaning of each one before she uttered them. From past experience, a sure sign that his mother hadn't anticipated this outcome. None of them had. An outsider resilient to the discreet ministrations of the guild? It was unheard of.

"I mean I altered her decision on the Hanover case. She should have acquiesced to the suggestion that the case be dismissed. Yet her mind remained unchanged, and she challenged the solution." Uttering the words aloud increased his concern.

There was a long pause on the other end as his mother considered the information. "She's protected? But that doesn't make sense."

"There isn't another explanation. I've checked. She's not one of us. So why would a member of the Guild protect her?" Garrett leaned against the wall just outside Nikki's office. Through the glass walls that encased the entrance, he had a view of the receptionist answering the phones. She looked up from her work and scowled at him as if he were an uninvited guest at an invitation-only party. He had to admit that lurking around after his business was finished was a bit creepy, but it eased the growing tension in his gut to stay put until he sorted this puzzle out.

His mother's curt voice cut into his musing. "The Hanover matter has already been addressed by the guild. They unanimously voted to handle the family crisis internally. I know of no Guild member who would openly oppose the wishes of the council." There was an accusing edge to her tone. She blamed him for this mess. "All known dissidents are accounted for, and there has been no unusual activity on that end."

"Which means there is someone out there unaccounted for. Someone who has a stake in the outcome of my case, and you don't know who this person is." Satisfaction consumed Garrett when he heard the hiss at the other end of the line. It wasn't often he was able to shift the axis of his mother's innately ordered world.

"No need to sound so smug," she said with a level of amusement that set his teeth on edge. "Once you head the guild, these problems will fall on you."

"I'm not going to head the Guild. I've told you that before."

"You can't run from fate. You're next in line, and that's final." His mother sounded so sure of herself. Mocking him. Daring him to prove her wrong. But Garrett had long since formed a plan to remain on the outskirts of the Guild. He wasn't going to let guild business consume him like it had his parents. As a child, he'd watched them give every last inch of themselves to the Guild until they had nothing left. For him. For anyone. That would not be him. It would *never* be him.

"Mother, I suggest we stay on task."

"Spoken like a true leader."

"Cut the crap." The sacrifice his parents paid on the altar of the Guild's welfare stopped here. "How do you suggest I handle this problem?"

"Investigate her, find out who she knows."

"On it." He snapped the phone shut.

Chapter Six

Garrett sat across the table from Parker in the small rectangular cubicle provided by the jail for client interviews. The cinderblock walls and stale air always gave him the impression that he was in a shallow grave. He reminded himself to breathe. Soon, he would be out of this room taking in fresh air. Parker wouldn't be so lucky. His parents refused to post bail, ensuring the lowlife would be in county jail until his trial.

"So, you're the highbrow attorney the Guild sent?" Parker said. "'bout time you showed."

"I'm here now. Let's not waste time, shall we?" Any flicker of guilt Garrett had about not seeing Parker sooner paled against Parker's entitled attitude. Time to let the weasel know Garrett was in charge. "So, tell me what happened that night."

"I beat the shit out of my wife, that's what." Parker laughed. The cruel mocking sound echoed off the walls. Now that was different. Most clients didn't admit what they did. Let alone state it so bluntly. Parker's statement bordered on gleeful. Almost proud. He also made no effort to make eye contact with Garrett. Instead he pulled at the skin of his arm as if that was the most important use of his time. Like he was beyond human caring. An insanity defense was more probable than Garrett first surmised.

"So I've heard." Garrett kept his voice low hoping

Parker would follow his lead to take this interview seriously. "Do you want to let me in on what set you off?"

Parker's head snapped up. The maniacal glint in his eyes was alarming. He slammed his hands palm down on either side of Garrett's note pad. "She's a fucking whore. What other reason do I need?"

Parker went back to pulling hairs from his arm, in a bizarre grooming ritual. Was he trying to alleviate his anxiety? More likely he had lost touch with reality. Perhaps he was experiencing a form of shock. Regardless, he wouldn't be much use to Garrett in this condition. Garrett hoped he could get enough information out of his client to create a sufficient defense for his case. Mental instability was at the top of the list.

"How often does your wife frustrate you like this?"

"All the time." Parker's flat effect clashed with his obsession with his arm. He made faces as he pulled at the hairs but not like he was in pain. The depth of focus on his task, squinting, biting his lip, methodically examining each hair was like a scientist handling a highly combustible fluid. It wasn't only the fixation with his appendage that was disturbing, but the lack of concern he appeared to have about his incarceration.

"Were you drinking alcohol or had you taken any drugs?" Garrett hoped the answer was yes. If he had been under the influence then a case could be made for diminished capacity, and that could at least eliminate the intent portion of the aggravated assault and battery charge.

"Nope don't drink or do drugs." After stripping one area completely bare, Parker turned his arm over to the underside. Deep red gashes spelling out his daughter's name were carved in his flesh.

"What happened to your arm?"

Parker lifted his head and regarded Garret in a calculated fashion. Goosebumps prickled over Garrett's scalp to the nape lifting the hair at his neck. The fiend was more aware of his situation than he'd been letting on. An unpleasant glint flashed in his eyes before his expression went blank again. Garrett gripped the edge of the table and wondered what this guy was up to.

"None of your fucking business."

Garrett narrowed his eyes on the bastard. "As long as you're in here, everything about you *is* my fucking business right down to how often your diapers were changed as a child." Garrett crossed his arms. His pose remained casual but every alarm sparked and jumped through his veins. Parker didn't move with the exception of an almost imperceptible quiver of his upper lip. Then his shoulders slumped.

"You wouldn't understand."

"Try me."

"It isn't right, you know. What they did."

Now they were getting somewhere. "What did they do?"

"Do you know what it's like when they strip you of everything you are?"

"No, but I'm not sure what this has to do with you and your wife." It was difficult to generate any sympathy for the man. Sure, he'd had some tough breaks but that didn't excuse the egregious actions toward his spouse. Parker wouldn't be the first criminal who attempted to use childhood events to explain away untenable behavior. From time to time, Garrett used these events to mitigate a client's circumstances. Except, he wouldn't use any Guild business to defend Parker. Matters of the Guild weren't common knowledge. Besides, this guy was a trip. Garrett hadn't been told what Parker's particular problem was as a child. However, his behavior today indicated his parents had made the right decision to isolate his mind.

"It's awful. I can't know people the way you can." He examined the end of his finger nail. "But you're lucky aren't you?"

"This isn't about me."

"No," Parker's lips curved in a sad smile. "I'm just trying to inform you how fucked up Guild business is."

Guild business. Every sense went on alert, but Garrett forced a benign tone. "What does that have to do with why you're in here?"

"I thought you wanted to know about my arm." His expression turned hostile and he sneered with contempt. "I can't reach my daughter. Your precious Guild made sure of that. She's out there all alone with no one to reassure her. All because of the Guild."

"No, Parker, your daughter is all alone because of what *you* did. I am trying to help you with your criminal charge. So far, I have nothing. No defense. What do you want me to do?"

Parker laughed and Garrett expected him to go back to his weird grooming but his hands remained neatly folded in front of him. There was no evil glint in his eyes or any sense that he was verging on a nervous breakdown but his words stopped Garrett short. "I don't need your help. I have a plan of my own."

"What do you mean?"

"It's only a matter of time before I'm out of here."

"The only way you're getting out of here is with the court's permission and you need me for that."

"Have it your way." He shrugged. "But I think I can bank on that guardian whatever."

"Nikki Angelus? What makes you think she can or will help you?" For a second, Garrett thought Parker was reverting back to apathy but that wasn't it. He detected a spark of self-assurance in his expression. The kind that promised certainty in what he had to say. There was no waver. No suggestion that he was promoting a lie.

"Because I know who she is."

A chill of premonition coursed down his spine. "And who is that exactly?"

Parker smirked. "If you don't know, I'm not saying, but I recognized her right away. Are *you* in for a surprise."

****

Garrett inched up the cracked cement steps. A precarious structure that leaned a little to the left just like the rickety house attached to it. Peeling paint flaked off the sides of the humble abode exposing rotting gray wood. At first, Garrett thought his investigator had gotten it wrong. This couldn't be the address of Nikki's father. Anyone involved with the Guild would live in far better circumstances. Then again, maybe Garrett was the one who'd gotten it wrong and Nikki wasn't a Guild member. There was no one protecting her. He'd just let his imagination run away with him. Except she'd evaded the mind push and refused to settle the Hanover matter. He could think of no other reason she had the power to that. And then there was Parker's cryptic remark.

An uncomfortable feeling gnawed at his insides since he'd left Nikki's office this morning. His discomfort spiked to overload after he'd met with Parker. Garrett was certain someone was protecting Nikki. The thought left him feeling weak and filled with the compelling need to find out how far his investigator had gotten regarding his inquiry into Nikki's past.

A quick phone call to his investigator led him here. To a house with a screen door hanging loosely from hinges too far rusted to be of any useful purpose. The mailbox no longer hung in the usual place but leaned carelessly against the wall on the porch. Nothing about this situation was right. He was missing something huge. The only way to fill in the gaps was to ask. Garrett rapped on the door with a renewed sense of purpose. Several minutes passed. He was about to knock again when the door opened a sliver. One glittering brown eye met his gaze.

"Can I help you?" The raspy voice was accompanied by the sour stench of stale whiskey. Garrett grimaced resisting the urge to wave his hand in front of his face.

"Mr. Angelus?"

The man nodded and the door opened wider. He was clad in a T-shirt and pants two large for his slight frame. Garrett crossed his arm exposing his Guild ring. Mr. Angelus' gaze drifted toward the insignia then snapped back up. "I was warned someone like you might show up one day."

"Is that right?" So Mr. Angelus knew the Guild insignia. Garrett was right, the Angelus family was involved in Guild business. It was time to find out just how much. "I have some questions for you."

"Figures." Mr. Angelus glared at him like a man who'd like nothing better than to rip Garrett's throat out. "But I've got nothing to say. You're not welcome here."

Mr. Angelus shoved the door with more strength than Garrett thought possible. But it wasn't good enough, Garrett held up his hand stopping the door before it shut. "You don't want to do that. I'm here on official business."

Mr. Angelus scoffed but allowed the door to ease back open. "What possible use could your kind have for me? You've already taken everything. I've got nothing left."

"I'd like to talk to you about that." Whatever the man had done, it must have been pretty bad to lose the favor of the Guild. He'd never been a member. That kind of scar left a very distinctive mark filled with shame and vile hatred. Although it was clear Mr. Angelus didn't think much of Garrett, he didn't spit that kind of animosity. His anger carried the fear of a trapped animal. Lunging and snarling hoping Garrett would just go away but with no real bite to it.

"Appears like I can't say no." He turned and skulked down a narrow aisle.

Garrett followed the man's defeated back, curiosity about what had happened to the Angelus family urging him through the stacks of periodicals and old newspapers. Angelus stumbled to one side toppling a stack. Magazines and papers slid into the narrow aisle, sending dust particles straight to the back of Garrett's throat. He wrinkled his nose as the burning tickle of an almost sneeze lodged behind his eyes.

Angelus lumbered on, never acknowledging the

periodicals he'd strewn over the only vacant area in his house. Garrett briefly considered stacking the magazines back in their place but if Angelus didn't care about the clutter why should he? Garrett shook his head and stepped over the mess.

Angelus reached behind what might have been a wet bar. The surface was covered with crumpled up napkins, knickknack figurines and more papers. Beer signs cluttered the wall. More things Garrett couldn't even identify filled every corner of the house. Angelus pulled out a crystal decanter, pushed away some of the refuse on the counter, and set it on the recently cleared area. He smiled as if he had performed a complicated magic trick. Garrett almost believed he had. The decanter glinted under the dim light. A relic from a past days of glory Angelus would never recapture. "Wanna drink?"

"It's ten in the morning."

Angelus curled his lips, exposing clean even teeth. An oddity Garrett couldn't reconcile with the state of the man's house. Garrett half expected to see one or two teeth missing. "Judge away, Mr. High and Mighty. It wasn't so long ago I was dressed in a suit as nice as yours."

"I meant no offense."

"Right." Angelus grabbed a glass and filled it three quarters full. He lifted his glass, quirking an eyebrow. "You mind?"

"Not at all."

"Good." He took a big gulp. "I'd offer you a chair, but I don't plan on you staying too long. State your business."

Garrett didn't mention there was no vacant seat

available. It just wasn't good form. Whatever the reasons for his circumstances, Garrett had no desire to rub his nose in it. Like Angelus implied, it was better to get to the point. "I wanted to ask you about Nikki."

"Why?" Angelus's eyes narrowed. "What's she done now?"

"Nothing. But I found a birth announcement for your youngest daughter but not for Nikki. That just seems odd." Except avoiding Garrett's mind push. But he couldn't just blurt that out. Not until he understood exactly what Angelus knew. Maybe he'd been too blunt. He needed to try a different tactic. "It's clear you know about the Guild. Just what is your involvement with them?"

Angelus snorted. "I don't have anything to do with *them*."

"But you did."

Angelus drained his glass and poured another. "Not for a long time."

"What happened?"

Angelus leaned his skinny arms against the counter a wicked gleam in his eyes. "How is it you don't know?"

Garrett swallowed the burn of the put down. He would not be chastised by this fallen man. "Doesn't matter. What is the Guild to you?"

"Nothing. That's what." Tossing his hands in the air taking the glass with them. The acrid smell of whiskey permeated the air as it sloshed over the side of the glass. "You people come in with your promises. Oh, do me this favor and I'll make you rich. But that's a lie. You use people then you destroy them."

"How did the Guild destroy you?" Given the

amount of alcohol Angelus drank, the Guild may have nothing to do with his current situation. It was just as likely his little vice had sunk him into an aimless life of hording and despair. Except the Guild could have helped him. Their own little version of rehab. Instead, they sat back and allowed Angelus to derail his life. It all went back to the same question. What had this man done?

"They didn't keep their promise."

"What did they promise?"

Angelus issued a couple grunts. He slammed his glass on the bar. His free hand massaging his neck. He gasped. "I've said too much. I can't say."

Well wasn't that convenient. Someone from the Guild had blocked Angelus from leaking pertinent information. Garrett hadn't come this far to be denied. Angelus couldn't talk about the promise but that didn't mean everything was out of reach. He just had to find the right back door. "I wanted to talk about Nikki."

"You know it all started with her." His breathing was even. His voice clear. Promising.

"Tell me about that."

"I was an Oil and Gas attorney. Did you know that?"

Garrett shook his head. "Go on."

"I was at the top of my game. My wife and I couldn't wait to have a child." He swallowed. "When Nikki came into our life, my wife was so happy. She just doted on her. After Cassie was born. Things got a little different."

"Nikki didn't like her sister?"

"Oh, she adored her. That wasn't the problem." Angelus walked to the far wall and dug around in the mountain of paper. He pulled out a large box labeled photo albums in curved hand writing. An inch of dust covered the top. This was a box Angelus hadn't opened in a long time.

"Then what was?"

Angelus caressed the top of the box sending a chunk of dust cascading to the floor. "All my sweet wife wanted was to be a mother. For us to be a family. After Nikki, she became forgetful. It started small, you know. Nothing that would alarm anyone at first. She would misplace her keys. Hell, anyone could do that, right?"

Garrett wasn't sure he needed to respond, but he nodded anyway.

"Then it got a little worse. She'd be microwaving tea and just leave the cup in there for hours. Or doing laundry and leaving the clothes in the washer so long they mildewed. But she was taking care of two children, it's possible that things would slip her mind." He gingerly lifted the lid and pulled out a photo album. He hugged it to his chest. Tears glistened down his cheeks. "Then one day, she left the house to go shopping leaving the front stove burner on. We had a gas stove. An oven mit near the flame caught fire. If I hadn't come home for lunch, the whole house would have burned down."

Icy prickles shivered up Garrett's spine. A young woman losing her grip on reality was disturbing enough. Add Guild involvement and the eeriness shot through the roof. He bit back the copper taste rising in his mouth. "What did the doctor's say?"

Angelus glared at him, still clutching the book, his eyes full of pain. "They called it organic brain syndrome. But really that is a catch phrase for 'I don't know what's really wrong'. There was no medicine to give her. And she just kept failing."

"I see."

"No, you don't." He gulped in air. "Then Cassie died. The doctors said it was pneumococcal meningitis. That it was easy to miss your child was sick until it was too late. My poor wife couldn't handle that. She killed herself." Angelus bent over. The tears spilling down his cheeks. Wracking sobs heaving from his chest.

"I'm so sorry."

Angelus straightened. "It was Nikki. She caused this, and I got left with that brat. But still, I did right by her. But the Guild abandoned me. He..." His voice stilled and Angelus grabbed his throat. His mouth working but no sound emerged. His eyes bugged. He held out his hand and fell forward.

Garrett knelt down and placed his hand on his head. "It's all right, Mr. Angelus. Relax now. I won't ask any more. You're in no danger of telling your secret."

After a few grunts, he stilled and drew in a huge gulp of air. "Thank you. I just need a little rest."

Garrett helped him up and assisted him to the couch. After swiping the litter off the surface, he eased Angelus onto it. Within seconds he was snoring. Garrett made his way back to the dropped photo album. He flipped through pictures of family picnics, visits to Santa and trips to Disneyland. He smiled at a young Nikki holding up three fingers with the caption *Nikki at three years* in the same feminine scrawl as on the box. Once they'd been a cohesive family unit until they'd been ripped apart.

But Mr. Angelus was wrong. Nikki didn't cause this, but someone who knew her did. The mysterious *he* had used Nikki's mother as a training ground to hone someone's skill as a dream caster. And he had to find out the man's identity soon. He searched through the album for the earliest picture of Nikki. Funny. There were pictures of Cassie, a cute pudgy infant, at one month, three months and six months. The album didn't contain any infant pictures of Nikki. Curious. He rifled through the box just in case it contained Nikki's baby book. It didn't. Interesting. He snatched a picture and left the house filled with more questions than when he'd arrived.

****

Nikki crumpled another page and tossed it onto the living room floor. It was hard to concentrate on the case files. Maybe it was the warmth of the heavy blanket she lounged under on her couch enveloping her with fatigue. Or maybe she was tired because the Hanover case sucked more time and energy than she had available with so many other cases to attend to. Her cell phone buzzed. She picked it up. Her father. Again. She'd avoided his calls all evening not wanting to deal with whatever rant had caught his fancy. She just had too much to do. In an effort to get caught up she'd lugged several files home. They now lay strewn across the floor and ottoman. She turned her phone off and tossed it aside. Ignoring the twinge of guilt for her much needed silence, she reviewed her current task.

She'd started a letter to the attorneys in the Carter case only to nod off leaving indecipherable scratches on the page made with the very pen Garrett handed her that morning. She rolled it between her fingers mesmerized by sparkles the light caught. There was a rich golden color to the pen. The initials GCN were engraved into the body. A pen made for him in her hands. She wasn't sure why she'd brought it home. It had a nice weight and stroked smoothly across the page. But that wasn't the only thing. She liked the way it glittered in the light, liked the way it felt in her hands, and liked the way it made her feel…special.

She ignored the last thought trickling across her mind and went back to drafting the letter. It wasn't a difficult subject. She was only asking for the attorneys to consider moving the date of their hearing because she had five others set that day. It required less than three sentences plus her signature. Still, she had trouble committing her words to the page. She yawned. Her eyelids drooped and everything went fuzzy. Enveloped in a warm haze, inviting her to doze, it was so tempting to succumb to the gentle prodding. After the last two nights of restless slumber, she relished real rest. Just for a minute, she promised, closing her eyes.

She must be dreaming again because no one can float upon air. Yet here she was soaring through the atmosphere with nothing holding her up but her arms and legs propelling her forward. On impulse, she dipped her head toward the floor and somersaulted three times before righting herself, once more hovering. She pirouetted in a tight spin and laughed at the freedom of movement drifting here and there, going in no particular direction. In a space filled with gauzy mist there didn't appear to be any route or any specific direction to take until she felt an urgent tug.

She was swept up in an undercurrent powerful enough to topple her over and over. It wasn't the soft tumble of the somersault or the exhilarating spin of her pirouette. The force was much more compelling. An apprehension squeezed the breath from her lungs. She froze, attempting to orient herself to this new development. The stream was much too bright and fast for her to identify where she was headed. She closed her eyes against a dizzying wave of nausea. The brilliant light scorched the backs of her lids. A rhythmic pulse pounded her ear drums raw. Then silence before she was hurled into a solid barrier and sent sprawling to the ground.

Her head throbbing, she stood and contemplated her surroundings. It was darker and the air dense. Other than the solid wall in front of her there were no corners or edges that gave the black void any definition.

"Would you like some help navigating from here?"

She stiffened when she heard a deep gravelly voice. It was familiar. She'd heard it before but couldn't place where. Though she knew she should turn around, she fought the urge as if she would find an evil clown behind her. She forced herself to look and was relieved to find an old man standing there. He was tall, thin, and did nothing to hide the amused glint from strange blue eyes. Nothing hostile or unfriendly. He was the man who gave her the amulet.

"Are you?"

"I'm William Songe." The man nodded.

That explained the familiar face and voice. His phone call that morning made a larger impact on her than she realized, for him to materialize inside her dream. This representation of him might have been conjured up in her imagination. She didn't know what was going on. Maybe her mind was trying to make some sense of their conversation, or trying to figure out who he was to her. Whatever the reason, he was here. For now, she decided to play along with the scenario to see how far her mind was willing to take this matter. "Why did you bring me here?"

"I didn't." He grabbed her wrist, jerking the hand that held the pen in front of her face. "This did."

"What are you talking about?"

"You were brought here because you are holding an object that belongs to someone else." He took the pen and studied it. Its golden surface dull in the darkness. "Hmmm, GCN who might that be?"

"An attorney on an opposing case."

His clear blue eyes met hers with an intense gleam. He didn't quite believe her words. She frowned. There was no real reason for him to doubt her but beneath the surface she detected a subtle flicker pass before he tilted his head to one side. "What business do you have inside the mind of your colleague?"

She frowned. "I don't understand." It was hard enough to accept the premise of her dream without having to puzzle through the significance behind his bizarre questions. It became increasingly clear that Songe was having an entirely different conversation with her than she was trying to have with him. Perhaps he was touched in the head.

"You're here." Songe waved his arm indicating the dark vacuum. "There is something you need from him or something you wish him to do. What is it?"

"Mr. Songe, please. I truly do not understand."

The elderly man grimaced. She knew that look. It wasn't anger really; but more the expression of a frustrated parent striving to enlighten a three-year-old to the way of the world. But a piece of information was missing from her comprehension. Something that he believed she already possessed. His irritation stretched to its limits at having to explain again. "This is the first time you've done this on your own. You have a purpose for being here. Just tell me why you're here," he growled.

"I don't know. All I remember was working on a case and falling asleep. And now I'm here. Talking to a madman in my dream," she smirked.

He stared at her with such intensity, Nikki had to forcibly keep from squirming. Finally, he said, "I see. Perhaps we should start from the beginning, shall we?"

"Please." Was this a dream? Everything felt so real. She glanced around her. She stood on a solid surface breathing air and though she failed to understand the content of their conversation, the words were coherent and more precise than in her previous dreams. The surroundings didn't change abruptly. The events took place logically and systematically. Perhaps this was a walking-dream. She'd heard of those. Though she sought for some sort of justification an uneasy feeling fluttered deep in her gut. The kind of feeling she knew spelled life changing news.

"This object"—Songe held the pen out—"is a gateway into the mind of its owner. Sleeping allows access to that owner's conscience, allowing us to influence judgment and actions." He paused, watching her reaction to his words. But somehow she found them incomprehensible. He was a candidate for Bedlam. Nikki took a cautious step back.

"When you fell asleep holding this pen, you were

naturally drawn to this person's mind." His eyes took on a maniacal light. He smiled and lowered his voice. "All you need to do is use it to open the door."

The words began to filtrate. The idea was absurd. "You must be crazy. Are you saying I'm psychic?" Only con artists claimed to have that type of power. She wasn't a con artist. She wanted to slap his amusement into the next universe.

"In a manner of speaking." He grinned. Apparently thrilled she was starting to "get it" and his tone took on a smug countenance. "It isn't that simple, my dear. You are descended from a race of dream casters known as the Guild. You are here because you want something. However, I can't assist you, if I don't know what it is you seek."

"I don't need anything from him." She snatched the pen from Songe's hand and plunged it through the barrier. "Take that Garrett Nightshade."

To her surprise, it ripped apart leaving a gaping hole. She pulled the rift further apart and peered inside. Doors? Was she seeing doors? Curiosity propelled her onward but a firm grip held her back.

"Did you say Nightshade?" Songe demanded harshly.

"Yes. The bastard," she muttered.

"Then I wouldn't do that if I were you."

She twisted her hair into a ponytail in frustration. Was she standing on the precipice of Garrett's mind because of their interaction earlier? Why was this happening? She didn't like this dream anymore. "I want to wake up now."

Songe nodded. "That might be best for now. One last word before you go. The Nightshades have long been the law within the Guild. You would be wise to stay out of his mind for now."

She shuddered. "That isn't going to be a problem."

He studied her, the scrutiny unnerving. For the second time she forced herself to not shift. She didn't know why but she sensed that she needed his permission before leaving. So she waited.

"Good." He let go of her arm. "Don't let anyone tell you you're not a proper child of the Guild. You have great power. Don't misuse it but feel free to test it out." His cackling laughter was the last thing she heard as his image faded.

Nikki woke with a start, sending her case file crashing to the floor. She rubbed her eyes. When had her dreams gotten so surreal? If this trend kept up, she would be a sleep deprived zombie before the end of the week. She scowled at the pen still clutched in her hand. She gripped it so tightly, it left a crease in her palm. Irritation flared at the sight of its metallic gleam. She threw it against the wall.

The amulet was the beginning of all this. Before she had been given the necklace she had never heard of the Guild or of Mr. Songe. Now the Guild had been mentioned twice and Mr. Songe had invaded her dreams. Since her father wouldn't tell her anything, she would have to find out about these strange events from somewhere else. Mr. Songe appeared to have an agenda that increased the queasiness in her already unsettled stomach. Garrett wore the ring but she didn't trust him to tell a straight story. Never-the-less, the amulet had disrupted her well-structured life. She was determined to find out why.

Chapter Seven

Nikki sat at the breakfast bar nibbling on a piece of toast spread with strawberry jam, rehearsing the list of things to accomplish at the office today. Her files no longer littered the floor but were stacked neatly in her briefcase. She sipped her coffee and grimaced at all the tasks left unfinished by her bizarre dreams. No matter how many signs indicated that the experience was real, she couldn't convince herself that it was more than a dream. She hadn't been raised by fools. And she wasn't about to start believing in flights of fancy now.

The phone buzzed. She dug it out of her purse. Damn. She almost shoved the cell back in her purse. What could Garrett want now? The text message was sent last night. After she had turned her phone off. She chewed her lower lip wishing she'd never turned the damn thing back on. With a sigh, she scanned the message. *I know I'm not your favorite person right now but I really need to talk to you. Could we call a truce? I'd make it worth your while. Dinner tonight?*

Now he wanted to play nice? She could almost see the saucy wink at the end of his message. The slow seductive way his lips curved into an inviting smile. His solid confident posture intermingled with the scent of clove and cinnamon that turned her knees to jelly. Even now, the temptation to accept his invitation overwhelmed her ability to reason. Tiny shivers of anticipation trickled down her spine. Nikki dropped the phone on the counter. She really needed to get a grip. Garrett was the enemy not a sexy dinner date.

She glanced at the clock. Crap. Half past eight. Didn't leave her much time. She jumped off the stool, slammed her mug on the counter, grabbed her briefcase, and headed for the door. Before she slipped her cell phone back in her purse, it rang. Double damn. Her persistent dad. But she couldn't continue to ignore him. She flipped it open. "Hello, Dad."

"You would think I would hear a little more joy given you crashed my gate just the other day."

She flinched. "Sorry." Besides his penchant for calling at the wrong time, like on her way to work, the man had a point. She had just dropped by the other day knowing he wasn't keen on surprises. "It's just that I'm late for work."

"Again?" She didn't have to see his face to know he sneered. It was ingrained on her brain *and* in his voice. "Didn't your mother always tell you that you're on time for the things that are important to you? Maybe you could be punctual if you had taken that other job."

"I didn't want to be a tax lawyer, Dad."

"The pay's better than what that shit hole pays you."

"You're in a foul mood." And probably drunk. Lately, she couldn't think of a time when they'd spoken that he wasn't inebriated. But she wasn't about to bring that topic up. She leaned against the wall of the apartment wishing she had the guts to just hang up. But this man was her father and she just couldn't bring herself to treat him that way. "What prompted this little call?"

"Someone paid me a visit yesterday."

"So?"

"He was asking about you." Her father's tone didn't indicate the casual kind of someone informing her of a fact. His voice had a sharp edge to it, like he was accusing her of a sinister deed.

Nikki ran her fingers across the rough stucco wall suddenly feeling ice cold. Not because her father seemed to think she was up to no good, but because someone had been to his house asking about her.

"Who was it?"

"Some asshole claiming to be investigating you."

That didn't make any sense. Why would anyone be asking about her? She hadn't committed a crime or been involved in anything nefarious. Up until a few days ago, her life had been pretty typical. Boring. But something had changed. "What did he want?"

"He asked if you were born somewhere else."

"Why would he care about that?"

"He'd found Cassie's birth announcement and obituary. Wanted to know why you didn't have a birth announcement." A slosh and the sound of a gulp alerted her that her father had in fact been drinking. But that wasn't what concerned her most. A man was skulking around inquiring into her past and she had no idea why. She pulled her hand through her hair wondering how life had gotten so complicated.

"Why should he care about that?"

"I have an idea." Another gulp accompanied by a cough. "I'm willing to bet he knows about that little necklace you have."

She bit her lip. "What would that necklace have to do with my birth announcement?"

"Why else would anyone be interested in you?"

Nikki jerked the phone away from her ear and stared at it. No matter how uneasy their relationship, the ugliness and revulsion emanating through the phone hurt and surprised her. He'd never spit this kind of venom at her.

Breathing deep, she raised the phone back to her ear unsure how to deal with this unexpected mood. She veered away from the subject of the amulet. "I thought birth announcements were automatically placed in the paper."

A grunt from the other end was the only response. Had he lost interest in the conversation or was he stonewalling? Every instinct urged her to end the conversation. She was late enough for work as it was. But she couldn't bring herself to do so. Like it or not, she wanted to know why the man couldn't find her birth announcement and her father had answers. "Is there something you're not telling me?"

He emitted a choked laugh. "Darlin', there's lots I don't tell you. It wasn't that long ago I was a respected attorney with all the devastating secrets that go with it."

She bit back a sharp response. "I mean about me," she said softly.

"Honey, you wouldn't sleep a wink if I told you all the things I know about you. But I'll tell you one thing, you better run because they're after you and if they get you you're fucked."

"Who?"

"That, I'm honor bound not to say." He paused. "But you need to extricate yourself from them. Take my advice. Get rid of that amulet."

"Consider me warned." She should do exactly that

but there was a pull to the necklace she didn't understand. And she wasn't the only one that had a piece of jewelry like that. A chill tore through her freezing her in place. She wasn't the only one. "Dad, did the man who visited you have a name?"

"Garrett Nightshade." A sharp click severed the call, leaving her in a whirlwind of confusion. Garrett had been asking about her, and she had no idea why. She wasn't dismissing the Hanover case like he preferred but that wasn't enough reason to be rifling around in her life. That pesky dinner invitation made a lot more sense. He wanted answers. What business was it of his that she didn't have a birth announcement anyhow? That had nothing to do with the case. There was no doubt that the amulet had her dad spooked. Somehow he connected the visit from Garrett with her gift of the jewelry. What made sense in his mind was muddled in hers. It was time to find out more about the Guild.

****

Nikki spent a long morning catching up on her caseload. Regardless of the hours she put in, the mountain of work would never be completed. It didn't help that the mystery of the amulet and Garrett's persistent interest kept inserting itself into her thought process, making it impossible to remain on task. Finally, lunch. She grabbed her purse and rushed out. Maybe, she could get some answers.

There weren't many antique shops in Hazelwood. Even less, close enough for her to get to in an hour. She stared in dismay before a little antique store called Lost and Found Antiques. The exterior wasn't anything special. Every window was smudged with dirt. The shop's name was written in golden letters peeling around the edges. Several rusty wheels, plant pots, and gates dotted the entryway, giving the place the appearance of a yard full of junk rather than a shop filled with valuables.

Having no better option, Nikki took a deep breath and pulled on the door. A bell jingled when she stepped inside.

The interior didn't dispel her earlier impression. Musty mildew permeated the room. The floor was cluttered with furniture that could be antiques but hadn't been kept well. Wall to wall chairs in disrepair lay under thick layers of dust. A wooden dresser's varnish, scuffed and gouged with course gaps would have shown brilliantly had it been finished to its natural deep cherry wood. A table with chipped corners and deep grooves on the surface, candle sticks too tarnished to recognize whether they were tin or brass. An armoire was painted pink with flowers stenciled on the doors which might have been pretty if crayon markings hadn't covered the bottom and the sides. Surely, this was not the place that held the answers she sought. She turned to leave.

"May I help you?" A strong male voice stopped her. She glanced over her shoulder. A stick of a man leaned against the back wall behind the glass case counter. He held a broach in one hand and a cloth in the other. Deep brown, almost black eyes regarded her seriously under thin, shoulder length hair.

"I, uh, was hoping you could answer a question or two."

He beamed and spread his arms wide, bony fingers still grasping the cloth and jewelry. Bell sleeves ballooned beneath his limbs. With some amusement, Nikki noted the man certainly dressed the part of an idiosyncratic dealer. She wouldn't be surprised if he wore pantaloons and pointed shoes.

"My shop holds answers for many." He smiled. "My name is Arthur, how may I be of service?"

Nikki held back a laugh. All that was needed to make the atmosphere complete was some sawdust and circus animals. She checked her watch. Too late to back out now, she approached the counter. "I have this piece of jewelry and wondered if you could tell me where it originated."

His eyes lit up with interest. "Let me see it and I'll see what I can do."

She fished around in her purse and clasped the velvet case. For what seemed to be the thousandth time, her fingers curled around it. She placed it on the counter and opened the lid. The emerald jewel winked under the dim bulb of a tarnished chandelier. Arthur was instantly mesmerized. His long fingers grazed the silver work around the gem.

"This is very fine work," he murmured. His eyes never left the piece. "Wherever did you get it?"

His voice took on a soft tone almost reverent about an object that had caused nothing but scorn from her father. Her father had been afraid of it, whereas this man seemed to appreciate its beauty and worth.

Telling him the package had mysteriously been given to her seemed unwise. "A friend."

He glanced up his face registering surprise. "That's a nice friend you've got there."

She coughed. "Yes, it is." It was clear he didn't believe her. No doubt he thought she had stolen it. If she had been in a pawn shop, the proprietor might have checked up on the ownership, but not here. Besides, she wasn't there to sell. "All I want is some history on this object. Can you help me or not?"

He raised an eyebrow. "No need to get testy."

"Thank you."

He reached behind the counter and pulled out a box. After a few minutes of rummaging through its contents he extracted an eye piece. He placed it over the amulet examining all sides. "The emerald is genuine. It looks like the casing is made of platinum rather than silver." He held it up to the light. "I'm not seeing any signature or mark that identifies the artist."

Wiping his face with an old handkerchief, he set the eye piece and necklace back down on the glass top. As he did, the necklace made a scraping sound. With both hands planted firmly on the counter, he rocked back on his heels. His eyes fixed on a point over her shoulder. Glancing in the same direction, she couldn't see anything more than clocks and other artwork hanging on the opposite wall. He sucked in a breath. She turned around to face him.

"I think I might know something about this piece. Hold on a moment." Arthur retreated into the back room. Rustling noises and clanks like he was moving papers and boxes continued a few minutes before he emerged holding a large tome. He positioned it just right of the necklace and thumbed through it. The pages were yellow with a fancy script that appeared hand-written rather than type set. The odor of dead leaves wafted through the air at each page turned. She watched, fascinated, his fingers move swiftly over the pages.

He stopped. "Here it is." He flipped the book so she could read it. "I knew I had seen it before. Your little piece of jewelry is renowned. It's the mark of The Guild of the Celestial Night. See?"

"Right, I've heard that before but what does that mean?"

He scowled at her. "How is it that you come in possession of such an item without understanding the significance of it?"

"As I said, a friend—"

"No," he laughed. "Not true. A member of the Guild would never pass this on to a nonmember."

"Except someone did, because I have it." She pointed to the amulet as if the mere fact it was there indicated he was wrong. Then she remembered the man in her dream had called her a child of the Guild. But that wasn't possible because, according to Arthur, she wouldn't need to be here if she was.

"Have it your way." He waved his hand in the air with flourish. "It doesn't matter to me. Would you like to know the legend of the Guild?"

"Please." Queasiness churned in her gullet but she had to know.

"No one is quite sure of the origins of the people who created the Guild. It is a very secret society, and not much is available to the public. All I know comes from my grandfather who had some past dealings with its members. He was able to account for it in this book and his journals."

Nikki chewed her bottom lip. She was being told a fairy tale. In fairness, he was recounting a legend which amounted to the same thing. But she couldn't be sure that anything she would hear could be taken as fact.

Regardless, she would listen. It might give her an idea of where to go from here. As Arthur prattled on she silently cursed herself for not having the foresight to get Songe's phone number.

"It is believed that people with special abilities—possibly Celts—migrated to America and established a community here in Oklahoma. They all settled in the same area and didn't mingle with outsiders."

"Obviously, they did eventually," she muttered.

Arthur paused, giving her a reproachful look. "Did you want me to tell you the legend or not?"

Nikki folded her hands in front of her, and murmured. "Sorry, please continue."

"Now where was I?"

It wasn't that he was taking a long time to tell the tale. After all, she did ask for the history but a jittery sensation lodged in her stomach. She just wanted him to cut to the chase. It seemed she would be denied this wish.

"Oh, yes, they didn't mingle. Then shortly after the dust bowl when they were building all those lakes, they were forced out of their homes."

"You mean the government seized their town by eminent domain."

"Exactly right." He beamed her a smile of approval.

She had the impression Arthur enjoyed having an audience and might drag this moment out as long as possible.

She sighed, resigned. Late to work again, twice in one day even. Her father was right. The important things came first.

"That's when they scattered and the mark of the

Guild became so important. The one who wears this."
He held up the amulet. "Identifies themselves as one of
them. That's why I'm so surprised you have one and
don't know what it is."

She pursed her lips. Where the hell *had* this little
trinket had come from? Her mother? According to her
father, her mother never owned it. Even though he
wouldn't say, she was sure her father knew more than
he let on. Mr. Songe gave it to her but where did he get
it? He must be one of them. But what did that mean
exactly? Oh, it was all so confusing, frustrating.

"Do you know anything about the Guild's
activities?'

"Not much. My grandfather swore by them. He
said they made him a very rich man. But I never
thought they did much to really help him. Grandfather
had an eye for antiques. A much better one than I do.
He had this knack." Arthur closed his hands into fists
then flit them open as if he was a magician in the
middle of a magic trick. "The Guild entrusted him to
their history and relics."

"What did he say they did for him exactly?"

Arthur lifted his eyes to the ceiling as if looking
there for an answer. After a pause, he blew air from
pursed lips, pushing bangs that had fallen into the
middle of his forehead to the side. "That's where he got
a little vague. Near as I could figure, the Guild was into
some metaphysical malarkey. They're a weird bunch.
That's for sure."

"What did he say they do?" She persisted.

He squinted and drummed a forefinger on his chin.
"It wasn't reading minds, exactly. It was more like
mining a person's subconscious to make them stop or

do stuff. Grandfather was very loyal to them. Treated them like royalty. But the Guild always seemed a bit sketchy to me. Like they had an agenda of their own. I never saw it. But there were grumblings they destroyed people who got in their way."

A cold chill passed through her. "How could they do that?" She didn't know what she'd expected to hear but being able to reach people through their dreams was not it. Songe's words came back to her. *Don't let anyone tell you you're not a proper child of the Guild. You have great power. Don't misuse it but feel free to test it out.*

He shrugged. "I have no idea. I don't believe in psychics. I just thought my grandfather was a bit nuts. But it wouldn't be fair to say the Guild didn't have an impact. When they were around things happened. Successful people failed when they shouldn't. Then there were those who'd never done a good thing in their life all of a sudden gained a fortune and respect."

A few days ago, Nikki might have thought the same thing. But that was before her little adventure into *Guildville*. Now she wasn't so sure what she thought, and she'd hung up on Songe, the only person who could tell her. Left with no way to contact him, there was only one other to give her the answers she needed.

Garrett. Damn. The man she was warned to stay away from. But she had to know. She just had to.

Chapter Eight

Garrett scrutinized the photo he'd taken from Mr. Angelus. Nothing in the appearance indicated that it could give him any real answers. It was a typical depiction of family life when Nikki was young. At approximately age three, she rode a hobby horse, smiling as an adoring mother looked on. Her wide-toothed grin—finger in mouth, hamming it up for the camera—gave no indication that she was unhappy or that her childhood was complicated. It was a snapshot of a moment in Nikki's life that was sane and normal. And yet, there were no pictures prior to this age. Something wasn't right. A chunk of Nikki's formative years was missing in the family photo montage. Garrett intended to find out why.

He stretched out on his office couch, the leather creaking as his weight settled into the cushions. He shut his eyes, relaxed his muscles, and allowed the silence to send him into nothingness. He fidgeted a little as he waited for sleep to claim him. Daytime was not his best casting period but with all the Guild shit going down lately, he hadn't slept worth a damn anyway. Minutes later his body surrendered to unconsciousness and entered the slip stream.

Jorge Angelus's mind proved no problem. The man had conveniently passed out and was ripe for the foraging. There were no walls or other obstructions to impede Garrett's progress. He found the access route he needed to ask his question. *Why are there no baby pictures of Nikki before the age of three?*

Images swirled around in a gray fog with brief glimpses of activity. Jorge at the park with his family pushing Nikki on a swing, whoops of laughter filling the air. "Higher, daddy," she screamed. "Higher." Eva answering with her own laughter and Jorge proclaiming, "Look how high you are, Nikki, look how high." A broad grin crossed his features at the sight of Nikki's joy. Satisfied glances passed between the parents at their daughter's happiness. A regular weekend afternoon for a typical family of three.

The image shifted to a hospital room. A small infant lay in the plastic hospital bed for newborns, a pink bow on her dark fuzzy hair. The baby sucked noisily on a tiny fist crammed into her mouth. Nikki sat on the edge of Eva's hospital bed, examining the baby's activity. She pointed. "Baby doll." Eva giggled. "No, this is your little sister Cassandra." Nikki's small face screwed up in confusion until Jorge handed Cassie to Eva for feeding. As the baby was brought to her mother's breast, panic lit Nikki's face. "Mommy!!!" Eva smiled. "Come, sit next to us." She patted the free area beside her in encouragement. Nikki patted her little sister's arm while she breast fed.

The fog cleared and the weather turned colder. A much younger Jorge sat next to his wife patting her back as she wept. Eva rubbed her eyes with a tissue and wailed, "We'll never have children." Jorge pulled his wife closer and kissed her head. "Don't worry. We'll figure this out."

A slight shift showed Jorge in an attorney's office.

To Garrett's shock, he recognized the lawyer speaking. His hair was dark auburn rather than gray and the glasses thick rimmed rather than the wire, but there was no mistaking the man who studied Jorge with a somber expression. The head partner of Garrett's firm, David Barnes.

"My client can give you what you want if you agree to his terms." David peered over his glasses at Jorge.

"I understand." Jorge acquiesced, but his fingers gripped the edge of the armrest, knuckles white under the pressure. "Are you sure no one will find out?"

A wide, self-assured grin spread across Barnes' face. "Of course. There is no one to tell is there? The parents aren't in a position to question any of this and my client will ensure they don't."

Jorge shook his head.

"Please understand, although she is three years old, she will not remember her past existence. Once placed in your home, she will already believe you are her true parents. There will be no adjustment period. It will be as if she was born to you and your wife and you are never ever to inform her she is adopted."

"How can you guarantee that?" Jorge leaned forward, the muscles in his neck taut. "Surely she can remember where she was just before she comes to us."

"Does it really matter?" Barnes moved to sit on the edge of his desk, his leg dangled in the air. He folded his hands at his waist and offered Jorge his most ingratiating look. "I can't go into specifics, of course. But let's just say there is a bit of tweaking. Brain washing—for lack of a better term."

Jorge fixed Barnes with a horrified stare, lips in a

tight thin line. His next words were short bursts. As if it cost him a great deal of strength to utter them. "Will it hurt?"

"Certainly not." A condescending smile. "It is a completely painless process. Don't worry. My client knows what he is doing."

Jorge remained silent, his hands clasped together in a vice grip.

Garrett's first thought was to urge Jorge to walk away from this maniacal deal. But he had no power to influence the past. All he could do was watch the events unfold. Instead, Garrett sent out his next inquiry. *Who?* He stiffened, preparing for a rush of new images that would reveal the man behind the adoption scam but they never came. Garrett remained rooted to this spot in time. Jorge didn't know his strange benefactor which was odd because he seemed aware of the Guild dealings. Barnes continued his recitation of the rules.

"My client will be allowed access to the child's information and progress in order to assure her family the child is thriving. However, no one but you will realize his true relationship to her."

Jorge did know his benefactor. Silky tendrils of anxiety filtered through Garrett. Someone had blocked Jorge's mind from revealing this particular piece of information. This powerful dream caster had to be Barnes' client. Garrett continued to observe the scene, curbing his irritation. There were no shortcuts. Frustrating, but the answers would come in time.

"That won't be a problem," Jorge said.

"Good." Barnes nodded, pleased. "My client requires pictures at least once a year."

Although the request wasn't so unusual, a shadow

of suspicion skittered beneath Garrett's awareness. There was something about this agreement that set him on edge.

Jorge shifted in his seat and made no direct eye contact with the attorney. Garrett had the impression that Jorge wanted to back out of the arrangement. In the end, Jorge just nodded. Somber but eager to wrap things up. "My wife desperately wants a child. I will do as you ask."

Another shift. The atmosphere hummed with excitement in Judge Ratcliff's chambers. Ratcliff's torso bulged with muscles. His biceps would be the envy of any football player. In his prime he had been an amazing running back but had declined a promising NFL career in favor of becoming an attorney. Service to his community was an important factor in his decision. But the bastard lost sight of his goal in favor of lining his pockets. A shady deal here and there, guaranteed fancy cars, summer homes, and women.

"How wonderful to see families willing to give an orphan a home." Judge Ratcliff beamed as he passed the decree of adoption to the Angeluses.

"Sign here and here." Barnes indicated to Eva. She bent over the paperwork, a smooth scratching on the surface before the decree was passed to Jorge, who followed suit.

"Congratulations, you are now the proud parents of a young girl." Judge Ratcliff signed with a flourish and handed off the decree to Barnes.

It was done. Nikki was an Angelus. All ties to her previous life severed by an order of the court. Garrett clenched his jaw. It was wrong. What had happened was all wrong. What was worse, Jorge knew the child wasn't in need of parents. He'd signed the documents knowing the transaction was illegal. All to avoid the hassle and to quickly offer his wife what she wanted most—a child. It was despicable the way the judge justified his actions with a wave of his hand over a file in order to create the ideal family.

But Nikki didn't need a new family. No one paused to reflect that a child had been stolen—lost to her blood relatives. All for the sake of pandering to someone else's need. Therein lay the crux that gnawed at Garratt's insides. Then it occurred to him. This was all an experiment. Someone in Nikki's family needed to sever her ties for their own hidden purposes. Whatever the reason, it was a fucking rotten thing to do to a child, let alone her parents.

Remorse burned a hollow groove inside him for such a dirty deed along with a deep seeded grief in the pit of his stomach. But it didn't matter. Even having witnessed the images of the happy family events that followed the adoption. Nothing failed to erase the cold calculation it took to remove Nikki from her home obliterating her family history. She'd been wronged in a way that could never be recovered. Time was the one thing a person couldn't buy back, even if she discovered the life she led was a lie.

A gentle nudge jostled Garrett awake. A face hovered over him, blurry at first, then his focus sharpened. "Nikki?" he muttered.

Somehow, she'd come to him. Had his dreams summoned her? Was that even possible? None of that mattered. What did matter was that her soft, full lips were only inches from his. He could see the pain buried in her green eyes. He now knew why it was there. His hands rose to rest gently on her upper arms, tugging her to him. She didn't resist.

Her body slanted across his, breasts pressed against his chest. A low moan vibrated from his throat as his lips captured hers. Sweet. God, she tasted so sweet. Heat rushed to his loins. His tongue probed the warm recesses of her mouth. Need replaced reason. Mind-numbing desire overpowered any instinct to comfort.

Some part of his brain registered a change in the softness of her surrender. Her muscles tensed beneath his touch. She dragged her mouth from his, pushing against his chest, and vaulting upright.

A hand dragged jerkily through her hair before twisting it at her nape. "What the hell was that all about?" Green eyes flashed fire, her breaths coming in short gasps.

He was having a hard time breathing steadily too, but where hers were fueled by anger, his were due to the pounding hard on he was unsuccessfully trying to control. He gritted his teeth, coming fully awake. What an ass he'd made of himself.

"I'm sorry." How could he explain that he'd been dreaming of her, that the sorrow she'd endured had touched him, made him want to comfort her? The lust had been a result of having a desirable, complex, yet vulnerable woman in his arms. But he couldn't explain that to her. Nor could he explain what he'd learned. She wouldn't believe him if he did.

Her lip curled with derision. "Don't tell me you're the type of guy that molests women in his sleep."

He jerked to sitting. Her righteous indignation had the effect of a dive in ice water. Reason returned and, with it, irritation. Nothing like being caught in a compromising state. He shoved a hand through his hair. "Look, I said I was sorry and if I don't miss my guess, you kissed back."

She huffed as she straightened her suit jacket. Amusement touched him when she didn't deny the accusation. He crossed his arms over his chest enjoying her scattered attempt to recover her equanimity. He raised an eyebrow questioning her presence not ready to utter the words. Garrett leaned against the thick leather savoring her discomfort. A flicker of movement drew his attention to the doorway.

"I'm sorry." His breathless receptionist, Donna, stood in the threshold balancing precariously on thin high heels. Normally, he enjoyed the way her blouse dipped to reveal her cleavage or the way her hooker pumps elongated her shapely legs. Right now, the interruption was *not* welcome. "I just left my station for a moment to retrieve a brief for Mr. Morrison. She must have slipped in during that time." He bit back a grin at her over-the-top husky tones. Donna glared at Nikki with distaste.

Garrett just wanted Donna to leave. "It's okay, I, uh, needed to see her anyway." He returned his attention to Nikki who had an engaging grimace marring her face

"Really? You needed to see me." Her composure once more intact, she glowered at him. A gradual burn crept up his insides but he refused to squirm. She was the one interrupting his work not the other way around. He fixed her with a stare and smiled.

"Are you sure?" Garrett was startled by Donna's simpering voice.

"I am," he replied not taking his eyes off Nikki.

Nikki chewed her bottom lip swollen by their brief but pleasurable encounter. If Donna hadn't been there, he'd try to finesse another kiss from Nikki. The need to have her near him, feel the heat of her embrace was undeniable. What a fascinating walking contradiction she was. Icy one moment and full of blazing passion the next. He hadn't experienced this much desire in years.

"It was a mistake to come here. You're not the one that can help me anyhow." Nikki pushed past his receptionist disappearing from sight. Donna glanced at him and after Nikki. She remained frozen in place as if unable to decide whether it was better to stay put or chase after his unexpected guest.

Garrett was entertained at the amount of trouble one attractive, hot-headed attorney could stir up. "It's okay, Donna, let her go. I have a question for you."

Her shoulders relaxed. She let out a small sigh. "Yes?"

"Is David Barnes in?"

She considered a moment. "He hasn't checked back in from court yet."

"Notify me when he returns."

****

Nikki stared at the stacks of files cluttering her desk and office floor. Needing something mindless to do, she sorted her cases into two piles. Attend to now and attend to later. She picked up the Baker file and slammed it into the Now pile, spilling its contents into the chair. Annoyed, she shoved the papers back into the folder and jerked up another case. McCracken's case bulged in an already fraying accordion file. She thumped it on top of the other one a little more gently. Resentment blazed a trail of shame that rooted in her consciousness. She couldn't let go of Garrett's heated kiss. It was disgusting how alive she felt in his embrace. How her body had reacted to his touch.

She couldn't fathom why her mind turned to jelly every time he was near. She banged another file into its designated pile. It wasn't as if she hadn't been around a multitude of men like him. Attorneys who wielded their power to suit their needs regardless of who it cost. She'd never been attracted to men like that. Not once. Until now.

No matter how hard she tried to push them away, the memories tumbled back on her. Weighing her down. Torturing her with tantalizing realism. His smooth firm jaw, his mouth firmly pressed against hers, opening, plundering hers, weakening her knees. The heat of his chest pushed against her breasts awakening a need she didn't know existed. There was nothing rough or aggressive about that kiss but it wasn't tentative either.

It was as if he had kissed her dozens of times and knew the exact amount of pressure to apply. Like he'd known her own mind. Her mouth went as dry as the sand under a cactus. After what she'd learned today, that was very possible. Had he visited her? Goose bumps pricked up her arm at the thought of Garrett rummaging through her mind garnering information about her. As disconcerting as that thought was, he hadn't used whatever he found against her. Yes, his action was impertinent but the kiss was soft and tender giving her the impression he meant no harm. She exhaled slowly through her nose, cheeks hot at the real truth. She kissed him back and she'd wanted more. Much more. Groaning, her head fell in her hands. She'd been so flustered she couldn't bring herself to ask about the Guild. Not with him taunting her with his naked sexuality.

How the hell was she supposed to handle the Hanover case when every time she found herself standing beside Garrett electric shock waves coursed through her? Just looking at him muddled her mind.

Nikki sank into her desk chair and stared at the two stacks, frustrated she'd made no real progress. All she'd accomplished was moving the files from one spot to another. Her head dropped onto her desk. She had to get her feelings under control. She was no longer a teenager pumped full of errant hormones. She was a grown woman who should be able to deal with the pitfalls dumped in her lap. She drew herself up. No matter how she felt, none of this was about her. It was about little Lori Hanover's welfare. She had to focus on that.

Riffling through the papers, she located the Hanover file and went over the facts. Had she missed something? Anything? No. Studying the pages failed to unearth a single detail she could use to strengthen her position.

Except for the police report and the divorce pleadings, her sole source of information came from an eight-year-old child. With Lori's mother unconscious, Amy couldn't be interviewed. Nikki pursed her lips. She needed to speak to Parker Hanover. And that required going through Garrett.

She scrunched further into her chair unable to ignore the inevitable. Every time she saw the man, things got screwy. No matter how uncomfortable Garrett made her, she had to deal with him for the sake of the child in her charge. Building up her nerve, she reached for the phone. It rang before she picked up the receiver. She snatched it up.

"Hello?"

"Let's try this again. Nikki, are you ready to see me now?"

Nikki started at the sound of the superior gravelly voice at the other end. Her heart beat with dread, though she needed to speak with him. She sucked in a deep breath and said coolly, "Mr. Songe what took you so long to call back?"

A deep chuckle answered her. "As I recall you hung up on me."

"True," she admitted. "But I didn't understand the Guild the first time you called."

"And you do now?" Amusement tinged his gruffness.

"Not really. But I am willing to listen." In fact, she was more than willing. She was desperate to find out why she was having those strange dreams. It was hard to believe that a few days ago she was a normal member of the human race, only to find out that she belonged to a secret society. So secret, salient details were undiscoverable. But Mr. Songe and Garrett had the inside track into her newly found lineage. It was her turn to learn how the Guild affected her life.

"Good. Meet me at—"

She cut him off. "Forget it. I'm not waiting another minute. I demand to know why I'm hearing from you now."

"So demanding for someone who isn't in a good bargaining position."

She let that go. "I suspect you don't hold all the cards either." His self-assured manner irritated her. He acted as if he did her a favor rather than manipulating her into doing what he wanted. If this was his attempt at playing some nasty game to bend her to his will, he could think again. She hadn't spoken to him enough to know whether her instincts were correct, but her job as Guardian *Ad litem* taught her enough to rely on her own instincts. "Frankly, I don't trust you. And until I learn more, it isn't the safest bet for me to run off and meet you."

"Fair enough sweetheart, but I have nothing to give you so that you'll feel safe. You're going to have to take it on faith that I am here to help."

A tremor rushed through her at the endearment. It was too intimate for someone she'd just met. Yet, there was a quality in how he said the word. It flowed easily from his tongue in a way that signaled the frequency he called someone this nickname. Who was she kidding? It sounded as if he had often used the term to refer to her. But he was a stranger. "Who are you?"

"William Songe."

"That's not what I meant and you know it." She paused allowing the notion to take root. An odd sense of déjà vu seized her with an electric anticipation that refused to let go. "Who are you to me?" she demanded softly.

"I am the one who looks out for you."

She swallowed hard. It wasn't fear unfolding but something else. "What are you talking about?"

"Meet me at the corner café at 5:30." The connection severed.

Nikki stared at the receiver in her hand. She didn't need any further coaxing. If she wanted answers, cooperating with this strange man was necessary. It was as if a strong gust of wind shoved her from behind.

It was essential to know why the amulet had come to her, and there was more she had to know. Could he explain her dreams? But it wasn't only the dreams that plagued her. What she really wanted was to eyeball Mr. Songe. That was the only way she would know for certain if he had truly visited her last night or if it was indeed just a dream.

****

Garrett spent most of the afternoon finishing a trial brief defending his client's property lines. Not that he intended to rely on the finesse of the written word. But it was important to keep up appearances, and it gave him something to do while he waited for Barnes to return to the office. The minutes ticked by. What kind of hold did the Guild have over the senior partner? The prosperity of the firm certainly. In return, surely Barnes solicited favors for elite members from time to time. He'd hired Garrett as a favor, and that didn't seem so bad. Garrett had been an asset to this firm. But twenty-five years ago, Barnes had enacted something far more nefarious than blatant nepotism. He had broken the law to help a Guild member kidnap an innocent child, and Garrett needed to learn who that person was.

Minutes later Donna buzzed him that Barnes had returned. Garrett raced to the corner office nearly plowing into his quarry. He stopped and ran a flattened palm over his tie, allowing Barnes time enough to enter his domain.

"I hear you need to see me." Barnes loosened the knot at his neck and eyed Garrett with curiosity. It was not considered a good thing to find yourself in the office of the senior partner. The general consensus was the less you saw of upper management the better for your career. To intentionally call a meeting with him— well, that was an act of professional suicide. Unless you were a Guild member.

"Yes." Garrett clasped his hands behind his back and followed Barnes inside. "It's my understanding that you handled an adoption several years ago."

Barnes sat folding his hands underneath his chin scrutinizing Garrett. The old man didn't speak for some time. A trick he used in depositions to cause discomfort and make the poor bastard he was questioning blurt out anything to fill the silence. Usually to the detriment of the deponent. Barnes wouldn't be so lucky this time. Garrett accepted the silence waiting for his boss to respond.

"I've handled lots of adoptions. How long ago are we speaking about?"

"Twenty-five years." he said, watching him carefully.

Barnes shifted in his seat, eyes twitching. He rubbed them before he returned his gaze to Garrett. "That was a long time ago. Much too long to remember off the top of my head. Did you check the closed files?"

Garrett rocked back on his heels. "Oh, I believe you might remember this particular case. The adoption wasn't exactly above board. The child's name was Nikki Angelus. Ring a bell?"

Barnes traced the edge of his desk with his fingers. "What could possibly be your interest in a case that old?"

"So, you do remember." Garrett sat resting his elbows on the arms of the chair.

Barnes made no move to answer. Instead, he

continued to rub his fingers along the side of his desk. A stall tactic.

The silence expanded like a deep crevasse. The next move was up to the man currently ignoring his presence. Barnes' hands slid back and forth over and over before he finally made eye contact with Garrett.

"I don't remember the case."

Garrett flew from the chair, palms flat on the surface of Barnes' desk. He leaned in against the cool mahogany scrutinizing the lying bastard's face. "I don't believe you."

Barnes gave him a thin smile. "Such passion for dusty old records that have nothing to do with you."

Garrett growled. "On the contrary, that case stinks of Guild business. And that has everything to do with me."

Barnes frowned, a finger against his lips. His next words were uttered slowly. Thoughtfully. "You don't know what you are talking about. What could you know of the facts of any case that occurred when you were a child?"

"You'd be surprised."

Barnes' eyes widened, shock evident. He dropped a trembling hand to the arm of his chair and gripped it so tightly his knuckles showed white. He said nothing further. But Garrett had the distinct impression that his boss knew exactly what his words meant. A restless quiet descended upon them. Although he didn't deserve it, Garrett chose that moment to end Barnes' discomfort. "Let me make this simple for you. All I need is a name."

Barnes' head shot up, his mouth twisted with hatred. "Simple? Last time I checked I was *your* boss.

This matter is closed."

"As you aren't a member of the Guild and live off our largesse, in this matter I out rank you."

Barnes pilfered through the paperwork on his desk, obviously dismissing Garrett. Garrett didn't move. Until now, he hadn't realized how beaten down by the Guild Barnes had become. Instead of being grateful for his prosperity, he appeared to resent it. The price tag attached to the organization's assistance was too high. In trade for wealth, Barnes was required to follow the directives of the Guild without question. It was no secret Barnes hadn't wanted to hire Garrett nor had he wanted to be the Guild's lackey. But that was exactly the position the man had found himself in. Barnes didn't have anything the Guild didn't give him. What must that feel like?

But he already knew. Hadn't Garrett felt the same way every time his mother brought up his birthright to lead the Guild? Unlike Barnes, however, Garrett refused to let anyone control his destiny. His life was fully in his charge. Now he was acting just like those dried up husks bending people to his will. A fact that left a bitter taste in his mouth.

He would have let the matter drop if it wasn't so important.

"When the Guild is involved, I am in charge. Quit your posturing. Give me the name."

"Thank you for that little reminder." Barnes glowered opening a file, inviting Garrett to leave. "But you aren't in charge, are you?"

"What are you driving at?"

He pierced him with a look of pure venom. "In matters of the Guild," Barnes sneered. "I answer to

Adelaide not you."

Garrett stiffened, resisting the insinuation that he held no real power. Barnes was getting ahead of himself. Was he really that stupid? Garrett considered calling his bluff but that option had a serious downside. He couldn't complain to his mother every time someone bucked his authority. He had other ways of getting the information he sought. All he needed was a little patience and a small item from Barnes' office.

He grinned at Barnes. "We're not through with this conversation."

But Barnes ignored him, burying his nose in some inconsequential file. He palmed Barnes' stress ball and headed for the door.

"Don't bother visiting me tonight. You won't get anywhere there either."

Maybe not, but it was worth a try. Garrett seriously doubted anyone protected him. And if someone did? Well, that would be an interesting turn of events, because only a powerful caster could shield a mind.

"Until tonight, Barnes." Garrett chuckled. He slapped his hand against the door frame. In the meantime, he had another avenue to check out.

Chapter Nine

Garrett entered the courtroom and scanned the area for Nikki. Almost quitting time. He hoped to catch her before she left for the day. He should have known. She was at the bench, her hands gesturing emphatically with Judge Weatherly intently focused on her. With each movement, she drew all attention to her like a magnet.

She stood tall, ready for anything. And why shouldn't she? There wasn't an eye that wasn't watching her. Garrett couldn't help being drawn to her passionate pleas in her recommended placement of a child. Her reasoning lucid. There was no hostility directed toward her today. No one argued against her. She tossed her hair behind her back. Her confidence was breathtaking.

Once the hearing ended, she stepped away from the bench, and was stopped by another attorney. The familiar way he whispered in her ear set Garrett's teeth on edge. With a playful smile she pulled back, laughing and slapped him lightly on the shoulder. Garrett swallowed wishing she relaxed as easily with him.

But their case was not simple, routine, or easy which only increased her prickliness. Somehow, he would find a way to soften her attitude toward him. He followed her into the hallway of the courthouse complex. She leaned against a wall furiously scribbling on a notepad. In this domain, she was all business. But what occupied her time outside the office? Was there room in her life for play? For him?

"Nikki," he called, giving a friendly wave.

Her shoulders flinched almost imperceptibly. She raised her head, face devoid of emotion. Only her eyes hinted at the annoyance beneath the surface.

"Are you stalking me now?" The words were smooth. Nothing that indicated his intrusion bothered her in the least—until he approached. As he neared, she dug in her purse. He smiled. She was bothered all right.

"No, I was serious about my offer of dinner. I especially don't want any hard feelings after the way we left things this morning." He took the apologetic approach, hoping it would be enough to coax her into a casual meal. If he no longer offended her, he might be able to insinuate himself into her daily routine. Then maybe he could find a clue as to her unusual resistance to his persuasion. At the very least he could learn about her family ties.

"No need. The incident is already forgotten." She smiled brightly as she pulled out her keys and flung them around her wrist. Behind the action was a little too much force to convince him that she wasn't still annoyed. "As for dinner, I already have plans and I'm late."

Was she meeting a boyfriend? The idea of another man irritated him. He narrowed his gaze on her certain her refusal to have dinner was more than due to a scheduled date. She was evading him. After the debacle this morning, he couldn't say he was surprised but he wanted…no needed a chance to explain.

Still, there was no indication that she was lying to him about meeting someone else. Innocent green eyes studied him. An urge to know the exact nature of her dinner appointment irked him. "I'm sure your boyfriend won't mind if you're a little late." The words escaped his mouth before his brain kicked in.

"Not that it's any of your business, but I'm not meeting my boyfriend. I have cases other than yours, you know. But if you wish to discuss more reasonable terms regarding the Hanover child, I will be in my office all day tomorrow."

The tension in his shoulder blades eased. She wasn't meeting a boyfriend. Although he had no legitimate reason to care what engagements were on her social calendar, it appeared he did and it suited his needs just fine that she was going to a business dinner. Business dinners were much more flexible. "Good to know, but this is more pressing."

"Not from where I stand." She tapped her foot lightly, flicking her keys back and forth over her wrist. "There's nothing about the Hanover case that can't wait until tomorrow."

"I disagree."

She fixed him with an incredulous stare. "I guess that's your prerogative but I really have to go. Call me tomorrow and we can discuss your issues."

Garrett grabbed her arm. He pulled her in so close her subtle jasmine fragrance filled his nostrils. Her breath hitched. His fingers trailed the soft skin of her palm. The memory of that kiss they shared sent a rush of blood to his groin. He spoke softly into her ear. "Do I make you nervous?"

"No, you just irritate me." The slight quiver in her voice belied the words. She drew in a deep breath and shrugged from his grasp. She turned on her heel and headed to the door.

His long strides quickly overtook her small steps. He eased in front of her, again stopping her progress. "Look, I'm not your enemy here."

"Could have fooled me. Really, I don't understand you. Don't you have something better to do?"

He shot her a wicked grin. "Not at the moment."

"Well, I do." She maneuvered around him. "I don't have the time for this right now."

"Sure." He stepped aside. "Later then."

Later would be much sooner than she thought. He let her get ahead of him, then keeping a safe distance, he followed.

****

Nikki entered the Starlight Diner more than a little rattled by her brief meeting with Garrett. It was annoying how she let him get under her skin. For some reason, she couldn't stop thinking about him, even when he wasn't around. That wasn't like her. His broad shoulders and wicked grin captivated her. But there was something more disturbing about her preoccupation. He was growing on her almost as if she wanted him around. She gritted her teeth. Right now, she had more pressing matters than the puzzle of Garret's inexplicable hold on her.

Inhaling deeply, she scanned the tables for the most likely candidate resembling her recollection of Mr. Songe. Most of the occupants could be dismissed easily. A short squat man with a full beard slurped his soup while the frizzy haired blonde across from him nibbled on a salad. A young couple in another booth shared a piece of pie while they gaped at one another with adoration. Her gaze narrowed in on an older gentleman at the corner booth in the back. Yep, that was him. He stood out from the rest of the crowd like a clown at a funeral.

His expensive tweed suit wasn't the only thing that set him apart. His regal air was offset by a sharp angular chin accentuated by thin gaunt cheeks. Even white teeth appeared to be his own, not dentures or caps.

A cold tremor thundered through her at his familiar face. He *was* the man from her dream. She closed her eyes against the onslaught of this impossibility. They'd met briefly one time. How had his face become so definitely etched in her memory? Though curiosity played a partial role in her desire to meet him, she had the unsettling feeling that they'd met before that day in the courthouse. Long before he'd invaded her dreams.

His eyes fixed on her and he waved her over with a smile that reached his clear blue eyes. She slid into the booth opposite him. She wasted no time on semantics. She said, "I'm here, what do you need to tell me?"

"Wouldn't you care to order first?"

"I'm not hungry." She held back a groan at the petulance in her voice. But who could blame her? She'd had a rotten day. Garrett Nightshade had taken advantage of her. Not only did she fail to stop him, but she'd reveled in that sensual assault—responded to his touch.

The indignity of her weakness still burned. Now this smooth talking apparition from her dreams had details about the necklace. And he was taking his sweet time spitting it out. Nikki ignored the traitorous rumbling in her stomach. The knowledge that some supernatural power was restructuring her life, turned any appetite she had sour. She would stay long enough to get the information she craved. There was no point lingering over a meal.

"Well, I am." He pulled the menu from between two greasy salt and pepper shakers and perused it. With a sigh, she did the same. Maybe if she played along, he would be more cooperative. Even with the hunger pangs, she found nothing of interest. Burgers and fries were the diner's main offerings and she wasn't going to eat that.

A waitress shimmied to their table. "What can I get you?"

Mr. Songe answered first. "I would like a theta burger with fries."

Both turned to her expectantly. "Just coffee for me."

"You sure you don't want more? I'm buying."

"Positive." The man gave all the appearances of a doting grandfather. An uneasy curl wound through her. As odd as all this was, sitting across from him felt natural, like she had always met with him to discuss her day over a cup of hot chocolate.

The flash of a young child in a cherry blossom print sundress laughing over bubble gum ice cream flashed through her mind. She closed her eyes as the image took hold and squeezed her heart. *This can't be happening*. She took a deep soothing breath. Ignoring the sweat beading on her upper lip, she opened her eyes.

"You really should eat something, Nikki. You don't look so well."

"I'm fine."

"Very well, just coffee for me as well." The

waitress drew a sharp line across her pad and stalked off.

Nikki leaned into the back of her seat, his voice relaxing her taut muscles. She realized with alarm that she trusted him. No matter how hard she fought the inclination, just a glance from him or the cadence of his voice, eased her mind. What was it about this man that offered comfort? She rubbed her temples inspecting every groove and twitch on his face. "I've seen you before that day in the courthouse, haven't I?"

He nodded but offered no further details, apparently content to allow her to ferret out the facts. She regarded him with closer scrutiny. The answer shot through her—ricocheting like a boomerang. Suddenly she knew exactly why he was familiar to her, now and in her dream. "You were at my sister's funeral."

"Yes." He looked entirely too pleased. "But you knew me long before then."

"When?"

"I was there when you were born."

"Like I would remember that." She ceased massaging her temples as she considered his words. Tension pooled in her stomach like a lead ball. "How is it you know my mom and dad so well?"

"Why wouldn't I?" His lips curved in a mysterious smile. "I'm your grandfather."

"That can't be," she breathed. Her nerves tingled all the way to her fingertips leaving a trail of electricity in its wake. It was too hot. She pulled at her collar to ease the stifling atmosphere. What kind of alternate reality had she entered? "I know my grandparents on both sides of my gene pool and you're definitely not in it."

He leaned forward. The madness of conspiracy glinted in his eyes. "You're not looking at the right gene pool."

She swallowed. Hard. "I-I don't understand?"

"I'm saying there is the Angeluses gene pool and then there's…yours." Incredibly, he winked. Where was the waitress when she needed one? She needed a stiff drink. Something she was pretty sure the diner didn't serve. She stared at the man across from her, warring emotions battling for power. Did she trust him? Yes. Was he crazy? He must be. Mr. Songe was just plain nuts and she had agreed to meet him like a half-wit.

The glint of neon and chrome propelled her mounting terror over the edge. He was lying. Had to be lying. Incredibly some part of her, the insane part of her, believed him. Unable to take any more, she grabbed her purse. "You must have me confused with someone else. If you had even met my father, you would know that he would take great pleasure in not being related to me. If what you say is true, he would have told me."

He laughed, a low rumble from the depths of dementia. "I see the Angeluses kept their word. And why wouldn't they, knowing what we can do."

She froze. His reaction was not what she expected but then nothing today was. He was way too confident about what he was saying and way too calm about her agitation. It was definitely time to leave. Nikki forced herself out of the booth. The plastic crinkled as she slid to the end. "I have things to do. Have a good day."

He grabbed her wrist. "You don't want to leave yet, my dear. This is too important an occasion."

And just like that, she sat back down as if compelled.

"You were adopted by the Angelus couple when you were very young. I have your birth certificate, the real one, to prove what I say." Mr. Songe placed a file on the table and opened it. He riffled through the papers and pulled out two documents and shoved them across the table. One read Certificate of Live Birth and the other Decree of Adoption. With shaking fingers, she picked them up. The name on the certificate read Nikki Summer. The Decree showed both Jorge and Eva Angelus's names. Nikki Summer listed just below with the typical language that her birth certificate amended to Angelus. Dots swam before her eyes. She put a hand to her mouth. What the....?

"My mom and dad aren't really my mom and dad?" It was all she could muster through the fog of cold shock. "They never told me."

"They were under strict orders not to."

She looked up from the documents into the serene blue eyes of her "grandfather." A few days ago her dead beat dad was the only family she had left. Today, her family had doubled. "Where are my biological parents?"

****

Outside the city diner, Garrett sat in his parked car. Nikki had been in the restaurant twenty minutes now. That was enough time for her to get comfortable with the individual she was supposedly meeting. She could be having dinner with a colleague, but his instincts warned him that her frazzled state had more to do with who she was having dinner with than irritation with him. Was she meeting with her protector?

He got out of the car and walked to the door. Through a glass smeared with grease he spotted Nikki and her companion.

Luckily, Nikki faced the opposite direction. Her dinner companion faced him but was immersed in presenting documents to her. Disappointment flooded him. By all appearances, Nikki was on official business. To be on the safe side, he would take the picture anyway.

Just how did one go about nonchalantly snapping the picture of a guy at a diner? Garrett decided it was best not to hide his infraction. Why bother? Nikki's back was to him and he doubted the guy would notice. The man's head rose and his eyes greeted the camera just as Garrett snapped the picture. He even smiled. The bastard actually smiled. It was thin and tight with a hint of mockery. It was as if the man was saying 'I see you and I don't care. Take all the pictures you want. I'm not afraid of you.'

Well if you're going to play it that way... Garrett raised an eyebrow and returned the grin. He shoved the diner door hard enough that the bell heralded his entry like a cannon fire. He sauntered over to Nikki, taking his time, making sure her companion was aware of his every move. Nikki's back stiffened. Her head turned, and she scowled at his approach. Her companion's expression never wavered from his thin-lipped smile. Garrett's grin broadened.

"Nikki." Garrett placed his hands behind his back. "What a pleasant surprise."

"Surprise my ass." She shoved the papers she was holding back in a folder and slammed it shut. "You're really following me, aren't you?"

"Such accusations," he tsked. His attempt to sound weary was falling short. He glimpsed at the writing on the tab of the file but the typeset was too small to make out.

Icy silence was her response. The old man's gaze traveled from Garrett's ring to his face. After a brief moment he stood and offered a hand. "You must be Nikki's young man. How are you? I'm William Songe."

"Actually, no. Nikki and I are opposing counsel on a case." Garrett shook his hand assessing the man. Songe's lines were delivered with a sincerity a pathological liar couldn't match. Garrett didn't buy for a second the old man believed Nikki was dating Garrett. He was being measured beat for beat as to how much a threat he was. A shiver passed through Garrett. Songe narrowed his eyes. Garrett wasn't adding up in the man's scrupulous estimation. It didn't matter. He didn't particularly care what he thought about him. If he was foolish enough to think Garrett a wuss, all the better to use that bad impression to his advantage.

"I see." Songe regarded Garrett with an air of amusement. The way he looked at Garrett reminded him of a cat with a play thing. "Well, young man, I'm at a slight disadvantage here. I've given you my name but I have yet to learn yours."

"How impolite of me." He cleared his throat in his best 'I'm an idiot' act. "My name is Garrett Nightshade."

A dark shadow passed across Songe's face. His eyes no longer held a glint of amusement. Hostility replaced the 'devil may care' look. It was clear Songe recognized his name, and the association was not a pleasant one. Just as quickly, Songe's face went blank.

He coughed. "No, it's me who is being rude. Would you like to join us?"

Nikki gasped. Songe turned his penetrating gaze to her. "Come now, Nikki, no need to be rude to Barrett—"

"Garrett." They said in unison.

"My mistake. Let's not be rude to *Garrett*?"

Nikki pulled her hair out of her face so that it laid in a smooth slick plait down her back. "I'm sure Garrett has better things to do."

"Actually, no. Slide over, Nikki."

Nikki made no move to accommodate him. Garrett stared her down, daring her to make room. Songe decided the victor of the standoff. "Nikki, please allow Mr. Nightshade a space beside you."

Nikki rolled her eyes but acquiesced. Garrett was disappointed in how easily the man issued the order and got his way. As spirited as Nikki was, Garrett expected her stubbornness to last at least five minutes longer. Instead, she moved over. A sure sign Songe was her protector. So why didn't he wear the Guild ring?

Garrett slid into the booth close to Nikki. It was almost comical how she pressed herself against the far wall, putting as much distance between them as the space allowed. Which wasn't much. Just to piss her off, he crowded her leg with his. For a second he considered placing his hand on her knee but given their interaction earlier that day, he thought better of it.

The waitress approached the table, showing her full set of teeth. "What can I get you?"

"Coffee is fine."

The waitress looked from Nikki to him and huffed. Her irritation at the lack of a large order didn't stop her from swiveling her hips suggestively as she strode off to the kitchen.

"So," Garrett began. "How do you and Nikki know each other?"

"My, my, you are direct." Songe laughed. "Let's just say Nikki's association with me is confidential."

Nikki shifted uncomfortably beside him. He wasn't sure which one of them set her nerves out of control. Whomever it was, she clenched her jaw and kept her eyes focused on her folded hands.

Unlike Nikki, Songe's hands were evenly spaced palms down on the table looking as at ease as a man sipping iced tea by the ocean. Garrett drummed his fingers on the hard surface and scrutinized the man. Quite aware Songe did the same. Neither gave ground. Garrett wondered how much it would take to push Songe over the edge.

"Did I interrupt a business meeting?" Garrett raised his eyebrows.

"In a manner of speaking." Songe pressed his lips together but gave nothing away. His eyes traveled to Garrett's hand. "Nice ring."

"You're the second person to comment on it this week." Garrett turned his gaze back to Nikki who sat impassive, refusing to acknowledge him. He placed one hand over the other concealing the object of their interest and shifted his attention back to Songe. "As long as I've worn this ring, no one else has noticed it."

"How could you miss such a gaudy ornament?" Nikki finally said, tilting her head in his direction.

"Indeed." Songe chuckled. "Where did you get it?"

"Oh, I think you know." Garrett shook his head at Songe as if scolding a young boy.

Nikki slammed her fist on the tabletop, jarring their water glasses. "What is it with all this cryptic verbiage over that ring? I mean, what's the big secret?"

"That is the question, isn't it Mr. Nightshade?" Songe grinned. "Why don't you enlighten her to the secret of the ring?"

Garrett crossed his arms over his chest. "I'm more interested in why you don't wear yours."

Songe studied him. "What makes you think I have one?" Smugness oozed off him like thick goo forming a puddle. He didn't fool Garrett. His feigned ignorance wouldn't fool a deaf-blind mute.

"Because you aren't just mildly interested in my ring. You know what it is and what it's for. Which indicates you have one."

Songe shifted. It was a subtle movement, but his expression altered. Had he caught on he'd underestimated Garrett? Instead of confessing, he merely shrugged. "I have no notion of what you're talking about. Perhaps you'd care to enlighten us?"

The situation was ridiculous. Songe insisted on engaging in his feeble fishing expedition. That made no sense. If he was a Guild member, as Garrett suspected, the man wouldn't be this cagy dancing around the subject. If he was an ex-member, Songe would wear the guilt tattooed on his forehead. Songe was hiding something and Garrett was determined to discover his secret.

From the corner of his eye, Nikki assessed him with the same scrutiny Garrett gave Songe. She was that much closer to learning the truth about the ring. The waiting must be killing her. Garrett smirked, allowing a long pause.

"Look, this is stupid." Nikki pushed a stray hair behind her ear. "You wear the ring in full view so what's the big secret?"

"Tell her what the ring means, Mr. Nightshade." Songe smiled clearly enjoying his discomfort.

Garrett's initial instinct was to dig in his heels and stay silent. But what good would that actually do? There was little benefit in remaining quiet. "The ring is the seal of the Guild of the Celestial Night. All men wear the ring. All women wear the amulet."

"And you couldn't tell me this earlier?" Nikki looked frustrated and fascinated.

"I wasn't under the impression you were all that interested. The information isn't exactly available to the general public. To them it's a piece of clunky jewelry. To us," Garrett placed his hand on his chest. Nikki's gaze followed the movement like an entranced captive. "It's how we recognize each other as members."

"So the fact that I am not wearing a ring," Songe chimed in, "would indicate that I am *not* a member."

"But you are. I don't understand your reasons for hiding the fact, but I'm going to find out."

A snicker. "Bring it on, Mr. Nightshade. I've dealt with more powerful men than you."

"Maybe, but I'll bet I have more resources than they do. So you aren't doing yourself any favors by not telling me."

Songe shrugged. Garrett held his gaze, challenging him to buckle. One minute ticked by. Two...the man failed to yield. Three...four... Songe raised an eyebrow, lips curving into an unrepentant smile. Five.

Garrett clenched his jaw.

"Fine, I'll do this the hard way." Garrett pushed

from the booth before he gave into the urge to thrust his fist into the man's condescending face.

On his way to the car, Garrett snapped open his phone and quickly dialed his private investigator's number. Mark picked up on the second ring.

"I need you to track someone down for me," Garrett barked, sliding into the car.

"What's the name?"

"William Songe." He adjusted the rearview mirror and turned the key.

"Got a birth date?"

"Unfortunately, no." Garrett pulled out into the traffic. "But he seems to be in his early sixties."

"When do you need the info?"

"ASAP."

"I'll do what I can."

"Thanks." Garrett hung up. The sun had gone down. He flipped on the headlights and headed for the office. Barnes usually left around six-thirty. Nothing like the perfect opportunity to nose around a bit to dig up more information regarding Nikki's adoption. It was a long shot, but he had a hunch, and he needed to know if he was on the right track.

Chapter Ten

Nikki slid to the middle of the booth. A warmth occupied the area Garrett vacated. Still she was cold. She shivered filled with an intense longing for him to return. She could no longer deny her mounting attraction. Even at his most obnoxious, her body craved his. Distracting herself from him had been useless. She inhaled his cinnamon and clove scent. Her toes tingled in response.

Surely the electric charge that passed between them was strong enough to generate power for a month. She bit her lip and pressed into the booth. If only he would return and fill the empty chasm his absence had left. No. She wouldn't run after a man who only cared for himself and his needs. She wasn't that kind of fool. That was not what she had planned for her future.

Songe covered her hands with his, startling her back to the present. His earnest gaze, ripped through her. She pulled her hands from his and picked up her coffee. The warmth erased the chill from Garrett's departure. "Nikki, you must promise to stay away from him."

Yeah, he knew what she was thinking.

"A little difficult, wouldn't you say?" she said wryly. "I have an ongoing case with him." That was the most plausible explanation. It certainly made more sense than wanting Garrett in her life.

Truth was, she could pass it on to someone else. But she wouldn't. She shared an odd connection with Lori Hanover, one she couldn't explain. She couldn't walk away. Somehow, Nikki sensed the case required *her* not just any Guardian *Ad Litem*. Changing her actions based on the request of a newly surfaced grandfather was moot. At least not until she understood her place in his world.

"Right."

"You never answered my question. Where are my parents?"

His gaze shuttered. "That's best left in the past."

"Why? You were all a twitter to let me know you and I are related. It's not like my question is unexpected."

He exhaled. "I told you that to prove I was telling the truth. It's important that you trust me completely."

"Well, I don't." She hunched down in her seat. "I don't even know you."

Songe clasped his hands together as if keeping them in place would set order to his world. "There are more important things we need to discuss."

"More important than my parents?"

"If you are ever to meet them there are tasks you need to perform first."

Nikki tightened her fingers around her cup and glared at him. "If I'm ever to meet them?" The effort to restrain tossing water in his face was difficult. But she would. If...indeed. Nikki scowled. She had a right to know her parents and Songe's gatekeeping tactics were not only not appreciated, but now impossible for him to control.

Songe bowed his head and let out a long breath.

"The truth is, unless you fix things, you will never be able to see your father. He's dead."

His cold matter-of-fact words stung. There was no sadness or grief reflected in Songe's voice. He relayed the information as if he'd just read an obituary from the newspaper. What a cold-hearted prick. And he wanted her to fix things? How dare he. And how the hell was she supposed "fix things"? She couldn't bring someone back from the dead. An ache pulsed in her heart over the death of a stranger. A man who would never be her father. "And my mother?" she demanded stiffly.

"She is in a very fragile state. After your father's death, she fell apart." He studied his coffee before piercing her with a penetrating stare. "You can help fix this. That's why I arranged for the Angeluses to adopt you. It was critical for you to grow up outside of the Guild. With no restrictions." He paused, seeming to weigh his next words. "The Angeluses couldn't have children, you know."

Really? He was actually playing that card? "Are you forgetting my sister?"

"Ah, your sister," he said. His face took on a sage expression. "She came later. Sometimes when you accept that you can have no children, biology takes over." A small smile touched his lips, marking him as somewhat human. An aperture clicked in her chest. "She was unplanned and unexpected." His eyes turned to a calculating glint.

Unexpected for whom? Apparently, Cassie took everyone by surprise leaving Nikki caught between two worlds. "Again, I ask. Where is my mother?"

"I can't tell you." He sat so calmly, denying her access to her family tree, it infuriated her.

"Doesn't she want to see me?"

"She thinks you are gone." Sadness replaced the calculating glint. "As I said, she is fragile. Her mind couldn't handle the loss of Dale. She has been heavily medicated for decades."

"What do you mean gone?" For a man she was supposed to trust, Songe was very adept at skirting around a subject. He circled every question like a vulture hovering over road kill dropping bits and pieces, never giving enough detail to reason it all out. There were tidbits, however. Her father was dead and his name was Dale. Her mother, alive but unwell.

"I need to see her." Maybe then the surreal dizziness she felt would subside. If she could recognize the resemblance in her mother's face maybe she could make sense of the shaky ground that had become the foundation of her life.

"That wouldn't be wise. I told you, she doesn't know you exist. We felt it best that she think you died the same day as your father."

"Why the hell would you do that?"

"We had to keep you safe. We didn't want you raised by a society member of the Guild so I arranged for you to be adopted outside the Guild."

Now the facts were coming much too fast for her to comprehend. Nikki took a calming breath. It wasn't the information she desired but he was talking about the Guild. Hadn't she wanted to talk about this when she first walked into the diner? Yes. But she hadn't been expecting the impromptu history lesson. Her heart rammed against her chest. A deep seeded longing for a life lost nestled in her gut. Each word Songe uttered was foreign, yet changed her life. Was it possible to be thrust into something so fantastic, so unthinkable? Surprisingly she was beginning to understand, believe it was devastatingly true. She took another deep breath.

But first things first. She had no alternative but to enter into attorney mode. "Start with the accident. Tell me what happened."

He shot her a disgusted look. "We are wasting too much time on this subject."

"Humor me," she said calmly. "They were my parents after all." Nikki's insides burned with irritation. It was taking too long to discover the truth. Couldn't the man just spit it out? The unpleasant grease odor of the restaurant nauseated her. The stench suffocating. Her stomach rebelled. Nikki covered her mouth before the contents of her stomach emptied onto the floor. But she had a right to the information she sought.

"There was a fire. We don't know how it started but the authorities were sure it was arson. Your father died inside. The official cause of death was smoke inhalation. Your mother was visiting me at the time. I was to take her to the doctor the next day." He recited facts with no emotion, very little vibrato. So cold while sharing details of his son-in-law's last moments. But then he'd had more than twenty years to rectify himself to it.

"How did I survive?"

"You weren't there."

That couldn't be the full extent of the answer.

"Where was I?" She held his feet to the fire in relentless attorney fashion.

"I found you huddled in the bushes in the back yard."

"But if my mother was with you she should have

known I was alive."

He arched one eyebrow and cocked his head in a knowing fashion. "You underestimate my casting skills. Trust me, she doesn't know."

Sharp talons of panic pierced her composure. He had the warmth of a reptile to take advantage of a tragedy. Hiding her from her mother. "Skills? What the hell are you talking about?"

A feral smile lit his lips. "Now we're on topic. Your family is descended from a long line of dream casters. Specifically, the Guild of the Celestial Night. A society formed to give structure to people with these skills. Our people."

Nikki pressed her fingertips on her closed eyelids. As if this day wasn't strange enough, she'd now learned she was the lost daughter of some ancient family line. She couldn't have made this up if she were Dean Koontz. "Are you implying I have some kind of power?" The idea was incredulous.

"Come now, Nikki, are you saying you don't? You've already drifted about in other people's consciousness." Songe thrust his thumb at his chest. "I taught you how. And if I have done my job correctly, you will be my greatest accomplishment."

She shuddered. Those crazy dreams were events that actually happened. But what did that mean? "How come I didn't know about this so-called power until now?"

"Because I wiped out any memory you had regarding your past. It was essential for you to grow up outside of the Guild."

"What's the Guild got to do with me?" More importantly, how much was this Guild mixed up in her current situation? Hadn't her dad mentioned them? *Stay away from them, Nikki.* From the fog of her childhood, she remembered her dad didn't care for Mr. Songe. Yet they had the same agenda. At least on the surface.

"Long ago, the dream casters evolved to great potential. Our people thought some had too much power. It only took one bad incident to really scare them. A government of sorts was designed to keep the casters in line. Rules were created to follow, and the children carefully trained. Obliterating their true talents."

So the Guild policed 'her' people. That didn't sound so bad. Everyone needed rules and someone had to be in charge. "Why was that wrong?"

"We were reduced to nothing," he spat. "I tried to convince the Guild that we needed to let our powers develop into what they should have been in the first place. But they felt it was too dangerous to allow dream casting to go unbridled."

"What does that have to do with me?"

"You are what they fear. A dream caster without their rules and restrictions." He chuckled, sending a wave of terror up her spine. "They will be unable to stop you from changing everything they know to be true. I expect you'll do our family proud."

So, she was kept out of sight of the Guild to develop—but into what?

"How can they be scared of me when I don't *know* anything?" Frustration filled her.

Mr. Songe sat up straight. He beamed as if he'd discovered the cure for cancer. His intentions for her were far more serious than a simple family reunion. He expected her to do miraculous things. She wasn't

anything special. Her father, or should she say—
adoptive father, made that clear enough. All she had
ever been was a disappointment, but this man thought
she was the answer to obliterating all evil in this world.

"That's the best part. I have shielded and trained
you outside the knowledge and strictures of the Guild.
You have the tools to rewrite history. All you have to do
is let it surface. Unfortunately, I am not as strong as I
once was and can no longer protect you. But I have
faith in you. It's time you learned to protect yourself."

He was so earnest, his face so kind, that for a
moment she believed she was loved and truly wanted.
But how was that possible? The man kidnapped and hid
her from her own mother. He had another agenda.
Hadn't that been written all over him when she walked
into this dive? Instinct kicked in, warned her. She was a
piece on a chessboard. She bristled. A pawn in a game
she didn't create. "I don't even know what I've got."

He chuckled. "It's not a disease. What you are is
someone who can go into minds and alter their psyche.
Something we haven't been able to do for a long time."
Somehow his hands managed to stay gripped around his
cup, when his face showed he wanted to clap in glee.
"We've had to be satisfied with being neutered to the
point where we can only change small things. Maybe
sway a decision or lessen the pain of a critical event.
The Guild thinks that is all that we should ever be. I
know different. We are more. *You* are more."

"What does that even mean?" she whispered. The
minute the words left her mouth it dawned on her she
had already seen those talents in action. During her
meeting with Garrett and Sam yesterday morning, Sam
had been out of sorts. Talking nonsense about finances

and his client's health. Garrett must have been in his mind. Had he been in hers? It all started to make some kind of insane sense. Garrett wore a ring that matched her amulet. He had been so sure she would agree to his demands and when she hadn't he wanted to know who was protecting her. The events gelled, shifted into clear focus.

Songe was protecting her and, if he was to be believed, that time was limited.

Now more than ever, keeping Garrett at bay seemed paramount. Nikki blew out a pursed breath. She didn't want him rattling around in the attic of her subconscious. He couldn't know all the intimate details of her life. He could manipulate her. After all, he'd grown up in the Guild. No matter what Songe said, Garrett was far more skilled than she at this point. She did need to protect herself. She pulled herself up, squared her shoulders, and looked her grandfather in the eye. "Tell me what I need to do."

"Lock your mind, then start small."

****

Garrett parked his car in the office complex lot. Only a few vehicles remained. He scanned the scattered automobiles for Barnes' silver Lexus. Gone. His boss had left for the night.

One of the perks of Barnes' association with the Guild was that he didn't have to work late hours. Why would he when all he needed was someone to tweak a memory or influence a decision. Although the Guild could be very strict on the parameters, Barnes had reaped a healthy living off of their talents. Now it was Garrett's turn to take advantage of Barnes' absence.

He crept through the entrance, the automated lights

activating as he walked through the reception area. Judging by the time on the clock that hung on the far wall, he'd missed the security guard's first walkthrough. Good. That gave him some privacy for the moment. The guard shouldn't question Garrett's presence but why alert Barnes to his intentions? Especially if he was caught rifling around in his boss's office.

With a steady confident pace, he made his way down the hallway. Barnes' office held three filing cabinets reserved for the more delicate cases that contained information too sensitive to be sent to central filing. It was a long shot hoping the Angelus case resided here after sixteen years but it was a place to start.

Garrett grasped the handle and tugged. The drawer didn't budge. Locked. *Shit*. Now where would that pain-in-the-ass hide the key? Garrett approached Barnes' desk and eased open the middle drawer. He rummaged around. Only paperclips, an odd assortment of business cards, pens, and a small sewing kit. Sewing? A quick grin escaped. The remaining drawers yielded no key amongst the contents.

He pulled apart a fake floral arrangement on the credenza, looked under a CD rack, emptied the pencil holders but still no sign of a key, let alone something to even pry the thing apart with.

"Is there something I can assist you with, Mr. Nightshade?" Frank Gorman's nasal voice caught him off guard. He glanced over his shoulder. The young weasel poked his wiry red head in. He radiated curiosity. Always searching for that golden tidbit to use to his advantage.

Frank's antics around the office meddling in everyone's affairs was well known. The slimy bastard thought it would elevate his position in the firm. Truth was he was a toad. Not that it mattered at this moment because said toad caught Garrett, red-handed, rifling where he most definitely shouldn't. Trouble was he had no legitimate reason for being here. A fact the social climbing junior associate already suspected. Otherwise, the dweeb wouldn't have bothered him.

"Frank," Garrett acknowledged. Thinking fast, Garrett said the first thing that popped in his head. Some plausible excuse before Frank thought to place a call to Barnes. This one time, he might just rise in the boss's esteem. "Uh, I don't think so. I'm trying to find a pleading for Barnes, but it appears he forgot to leave me the key to his filing cabinets." Garrett held his breath.

"Boss man doesn't generally like anyone in those cabinets. That's why they're locked." Frank's eyes narrowed on Garrett. The jerk didn't believe him. And why should he? It was no secret Barnes steered clear of Garrett. Probably terrified his casting could be done while awake. In general, Garrett didn't mind the displaced notion. It kept Barnes from prying into his own business. Right now, however, he wished he had the power to influence Frank. Unfortunately, he had to be crafty so Frank wouldn't call Barnes. Later, he could easily slip into his mind and erase the incident completely.

"Usually, that's true." Garrett shrugged. "However, he forgot necessary paperwork for a trial tomorrow."

"So he'll get it in the morning."

"That's the thing." Garrett adopted his most

disdainful tone. "He's going straight to court. He knew I was coming by tonight and asked me to get it for him."

"If he wanted you in there," Frank pointed his finger at the cabinets. "He would have made sure you had a key."

Busted. Might as well call the man's bluff. What did he have to lose at this point? "If you don't believe me, call Barnes." Garrett glanced at his watch. "You should be able to catch him. It's just about the time he'd be sitting down to dinner with his family. Sooner's will be on at eight. So, he might have a moment to spare for you."

Frank rubbed his chin. "I don't know…"

The little turd was clearly weighing how much wrath would descend upon him if he did make the call. His eyes glassed over at the strain of his contemplation. Garrett growled. "Look, I don't have the time to wait around for you to decide. If you'll excuse me, I need to get back to locating the file."

"It just seems odd," Frank said. Definitely wavering.

Garrett pressed his advantage. "While I appreciate the irregularity, might I remind you that I still outrank you."

Frank smirked. Garrett knew he wasn't buying into his posturing. Frank looked down his narrow nose at him. "I don't know where the key is. Couldn't find it if I wanted to. Might check his secretary's desk though."

Of course. Shit. June would have access to all Barnes' files. With one last look of contempt, Frank sauntered down the hall. Garrett shot into action. No telling how long it would take Frank to figure out

Garrett's bluff. The clock was ticking.

Garrett darted to June's cubicle. He foraged through a monotony of staples, pens, and white-out. Then, nestled between rubber bands and a letter opener he found a set of keys. Hopefully one of them opened the filing cabinets.

Rushing back to the file cabinets, he inserted one key into the lock. It didn't turn. He chose another. Tried again. Failed. With each key, his gut dropped another notch, until—pay dirt! The sixth key.

He perused the names on the folders. An adoption would be in Nikki's original surname. There was no Songe among them. Good thing not all the files were adoptions. Garrett pulled every one with an FA adoption identification. There were three in all. Anticipation tingled his fingertips.

The second file held the adoption decree signed by the Angeluses. He quickly scanned the case style: In re the adoption of baby girl Summer. *Her last name was Summer.*

He searched through the file for Songe's name, but found nothing. Damn, he was certain there was a familial connection. If there was, this file couldn't corroborate his hunch. Hmm. Another interesting tidbit—no consent to the adoption. The order allowing an adoption without consent had been sanitized to the point where no identification of the biological family could be made. Only a member of the Guild could have encouraged such negligence from the judge.

Garrett took out his phone and snapped a picture, then sent the picture of Songe and the name Summer to his mother. Between her and Mark, they'd be able to locate the connection between Songe and Nikki.

Chapter Eleven

The next morning, Nikki pulled her car into the Juvenile Center parking lot, events of last evening still rattling around in her head. She wasn't sure what to think of everything she had heard. It was all too surreal. Discovering she was a descendant from an ancient line of dream casters? Talk about a weird family history.

Every family had some strange story buried beneath the depths of a normal façade. But every fact about her own life she thought she could rely on had now vanished, along with the knowledge that she was part of preternatural happenings. Insane. She pulled in a deep breath. There was no denying her abnormal abilities. She'd been given a taste of them, and inexplicably, a part of her was itching to try them.

She grabbed her purse from the passenger seat and removed the amulet. Should she keep it hidden? Everything changed the moment she acknowledged receipt of this strange object. Part of her wanted to shove it deep into a dark crevasse and forget she'd ever seen it. Maybe then life would right itself and let her go on as before.

No. No matter how much she wished for it, life would never be the same. If she was honest, life wasn't so great before gaining possession of the amulet. What good would hiding the damn thing do now? Besides, hiding wasn't in the repertoire of her natural behavior.

She'd always faced things head on.

She lifted the lid of the small box. The jewel sparkled in the sunlight, a little harbinger of her life in transition. *Stay away from them Nikki.*

"I can't, Dad," she whispered aloud. Her opposing counsel was one of them. Like it or not, she was part of Guild society.

Nikki removed the necklace from the box and clasped it around her neck. The weight was new, but comfortable, as if it belonged there. She clutched the amulet, drawing confidence from it. Maybe it did hold power. Its impression seemed to fill an empty space she hadn't realized existed until now.

Now I am truly one of you. The thought came unbidden.

A minute later she marched into the Juvenile Center filled with a new sense of purpose.

Marilyn slid open the glass window. "Boy, you're here a lot lately."

"You would be too if you were part of the 'case that will never go away'." She leaned against the counter anxious to speak to her ward.

"What can I help you with?"

"I need to see Lori Hanover."

"I'll have her brought to the room." Marilyn swiveled to her phone and dialed. A few beats later, she said, "Yes, Nikki is here to see Lori. Right." She hung up the phone. "You're in luck, Lori has no scheduled activities for the moment. She will be in room five shortly. I believe you know the way."

"You bet I do. Thank you." Nikki turned down the hallway but was stopped by the receptionist's next comment.

"Hey, is that necklace new?"

"Kind of." She fingered the amulet. "It's an old family heirloom."

Marilyn leaned closer, like she was examining a rare exhibit in a museum. The sense that she was on display didn't sit well. Naked in public.

"Sweet. Are those real?"

"I have no idea." More to the point, she didn't care. The amulet was pretty in its own way. Marilyn was a jewelry junkie judging from the huge gold hoops in her ears and mass of bracelets around her wrist.

"Well, it looks nice on you."

"Thanks." Nikki continued down the hall to the kids' room.

The interior was brighter than the last time she was there. The sun shone through somewhat grimy windows in spite of dust wind-tossed across the panes. The view outside revealed a barren lawn, bordering a black top with a solitary basketball hoop. The netting long since disintegrated, but a few kids were tossing around a ball, dunking it through the steel rim. It never ceased to amaze her how resilient children were. All smiles and good-natured jabbing, in the most desolate place on Earth.

The door opened, and Lori walked in.

"Hi, Lori."

Wide eyes signaled surprise, marred with a little trepidation as she made her way to the table. "Is something wrong?" She sat slowly, stopping short of actually taking her seat when her gaze spotted the amulet. "Nice necklace."

A common enough statement, but the intensity in the girl's eyes indicated much more beneath the surface. Although Nikki had doubts, Lori's reaction indicated a recognition of what necklace represented. It was in the way she slowly descended into her chair, sat, back straight, addressing Nikki head on. Waiting. Expectant.

Nikki decided to play the simple statement angle. "Thanks."

"How come you weren't wearing it the last couple of times I saw you?" Accusation threaded her question. A 'why didn't you let me in on the secret?' insinuation. Or at the very lease not hold back critical information. Heat rose from neck to cheek. Yes, Lori knew.

"I only just received it." Nikki covered the pendant with her hand, unable to meet Lori's eyes.

What the hell? Nikki felt chastised by this skinny eight-year-old. It wasn't as if she'd known about the Guild when she'd first met Lori. Surely, Lori's odd behavior at their initial interview could be attributed to a child's fishing expedition. Had Lori been asking if Nikki was one of them? Even if that were the case, Nikki hadn't known enough then to answer in the affirmative. But she did now.

Lori's expression morphed into something shrewd beyond her years. "How old are you?"

Taken aback by the question, Nikki pretended to write on her notepad considering her answer. This girl's forward manner made Nikki ill at ease. She bit back a small grin. Wanting to help Lori warred with the instinct to teach her some manners. She held back, however. There was no need to snap at a young girl just because she hadn't been taught the natural boundaries surrounding polite conversation. After all, Lori had only asked about her necklace. Something the receptionist had done. And asking Nikki's age was impertinent, yes, but not out of the ordinary for a young child. The problem was Lori had an uncanny knack of digging around in her emotional well and picking the one thing that would set her on edge. Nikki just had to assume that Lori wasn't doing it on purpose.

Nikki rubbed her neck allowing the tension to ease around her shoulder muscles. "I'm twenty-eight." What was the harm if Lori knew her age? It was one step closer to getting on a personal level with Lori. An area Nikki had successfully avoided to date with the other children she represented. Allowing a child to form an attachment, or act like a friend when all she was going to do in the end was walk out of her life was out of the question. Nikki refused to be responsible for another loss.

"You should have gotten the amulet way before now," Lori told her matter-of-factly. "How come it took so long?"

Nikki stifled the urge to drop her head on the table in frustration. From Lori's perspective she hadn't asked a personal question. She was just trying to figure out why Nikki hadn't been given her necklace like everyone else. That was fair.

Now it was time to turn the tables on this small girl. She was the one who should be asking the questions not an eight-year-old. At least her interest in this small piece of jewelry, gave her a place to start. "What do you know about this necklace?"

Lori leaned in close as if she was disclosing national secrets. "I know it means you're one of us. You're supposed to wear it all the time so that everyone knows you're a member. *And* you're supposed to get it at sixteen."

"How do you know all this?" Nikki strived for casual, but she was sure Lori could hear the loud drumming beating inside her chest.

"Duh." Lori rolled her eyes, head following the motion. "My family belongs to the Guild."

Nikki tapped her pen against her notepad, digesting this information. If she had her facts straight, everyone involved in the Hanover case was a member. But not everyone was marked with the Guild's signature. "How come your grandparents don't wear one?"

"They're not active members. They're on like super-secret probation or something."

"How come?"

She put her shoulder up in a half shrug. "Mommy knows more—" She choked off as tears formed in her eyes. Her head dropped.

"What about your dad?"

Her head shot up. The eye contact was fast, fierce, and angry. "*He's* not part of us. He was ex…com…" A sigh. "Shunned."

"Why?"

Her gaze didn't waver. Lori wanted this topic covered. "Mommy says that Grandma and Grandpa did this to him."

"Did what?"

"Made him an iso…" she frowned. "He can't do anything anymore."

"An isolate?'

Lori nodded.

"I don't understand."

"They were scared." Lori shrunk down, but her eyes remained wide and earnest. How did a parent become frightened of their own child? Nikki had seen parents file charges of assault and battery against their recalcitrant teenager. It never mattered that the child was defending himself from a lifetime of abusive behavior. Each and every time the parent claimed they were threatened by their adolescent. An adolescent of their own making. A sign the parent hadn't gotten their bluff in early enough. Not so unusual. Maybe that's what happened to the Hanovers.

"What's so scary about your dad?"

A shrug. "They say he did bad things. But Daddy says he was robbed—they shouldn't have done that to him."

Nikki studied her small charge. Lori was speaking in riddles. It was impossible to discern exactly what had been done to Mr. Hanover, but whatever it was, he was pissed off. "What do you think?"

Lori regarded her with what could only be termed wonderment. The expression of a child who'd never been asked their opinion. Nikki shuddered at how often she had witnessed this expression. Parents just didn't seem to get they were raising a little person instead of a lump of clay.

"I dunno. He's scary, I guess. He needs help."

"What makes you think that?"

She sank down further in her chair and rolled a red crayon back and forth with her palm on the tabletop. "That's what mommy says."

"I see." There was way too much talking about adult matters in front of this child. Another thing Nikki saw too much of. This situation felt different though. She had the strong impression that Lori was talking about Guild business and not just what happened to the

Hanover family. "What help does she think he needs?"

"He needs to be cleansed."

It occurred to Nikki she had a lifetime of learning to accumulate in a short amount of time. "What?"

"It's something the Guild does to make someone better."

Somehow, she doubted anyone would feel better after a cleansing. It had the connotation of purging and sanitizing. Like brain washing. "What was it your grandparents did?"

"Not that."

Perhaps this matter would be better taken up with an adult. But that would be an exercise in futility. Their members were tight lipped as it was, and Nikki was new to the organization. An outsider, and if her grandfather had his way, she would remain one. At this point she wasn't sure how she felt about either faction of the dispute. Before she could form another question, Lori reached for her arm.

"Did the Guild train you?"

"I'm kind of self-taught."

A broad grin spread across Lori's face. "Me, too! My mom and dad used to fight about it but Daddy always won. 'Cept he couldn't get into my mind, and Mommy kept Daddy's family away, too."

Apparently, just like Nikki, Lori wasn't completely a part of the Guild's exclusive membership. Lori, however, understood more about the society and had more contact with them. What must it be like for Lori to simultaneously belong and not belong? At least Nikki hadn't grown up outside looking into this small community. Nikki shuddered. She should be thankful. The room suddenly felt cold.

"Would you like to be formally trained by the Guild?" Even to Nikki's ears, it sounded like a stupid question. She hadn't intended on taking this conversation so off topic but she wanted to know what childhood was like for Lori from all sides. At least that's what she told herself.

"No." Lori tilted her head. "I like being trained by Mommy."

Nikki nodded her understanding, but Lori's eyes glazed over, and sadness tinged her expression. If only they could talk about her situation without bringing her mother up. Nikki promised herself she would steer as clear of Lori's mom as possible. Lori examined the ends of her hair like she was trying to count how many strands she had.

"You have to make my dad stop." Her eyes stayed on her hair, a pleading tone in her voice.

Nikki flinched. She didn't have to ask Lori what she wanted her dad to stop doing.

"You're safe, you know. He's in jail." Nikki hoped the words were reassuring. "He can't hurt you."

"What if he gets out?" Tears trailed down her cheek. "You have to make him stop."

"I'm not sure how I can do that."

"It's easy." In spite of her tears, she looked up at Nikki then. "All you need is something of his to get into his mind. Then you go in and change it."

Nikki didn't take the time to consider the ethical complications of what Lori suggested. After all, it wasn't as if anyone would ever find out. Even if Garrett shouted to the roof tops, who would believe him? The Guild was private about their business.

Most likely, things of that nature were handled

internally. A small fact that caused Nikki concern. Maybe what they did to Lori's father was how they punished people who stepped over the line.

She tapped her pen against the tabletop, thinking. She had to do something and her last instructions were to start small. Was this small enough? "What do I do?"

"Do you have anything of his?"

"No."

Lori looked left and then right. "I do," she whispered. She tugged a key attached to a dirty piece of plastic off her neck. "This opens the back door to my house. Daddy gave me his old teddy bear. It's blond and has round legs and arms. He has big blue eyes, but no tongue because it fell off."

Nikki squelched an urge to laugh. There was so much of Lori's world that belonged to a normal child, it broke Nikki's heart. And so much that was on a much larger scale. And those two parts mixed significantly.

Nikki caved into temptation, nodding sharply. "I'll give it a try."

Lori sat straighter, her wide grin returning. "See? You are my guardian."

****

Garrett answered his phone on the third ring. "Did you get the photo?"

"Yes. And I'm not pleased with the outcome." His mother's icy tone reached through the phone.

"Do you know him?"

"I'm not certain, he looks vaguely familiar, but I can't place him." She paused. His mother rarely handled well anyone messing with Guild business. "Are you sure he is the one protecting her?"

"Pretty sure." Why else would Nikki bend so easily

to Songe's suggestions? "If he has a connection to the Guild, someone should recognize him."

"I'll look into it." Another pause. As bossy and chatty as his mother could be, she was being very tight-lipped about the whole matter. "This might be a delicate situation."

"You mean not for my ears." Garrett hadn't ever been keen on heavy involvement in Guild business. Maybe that had been a mistake. The elders poured over antiquated documents outlining the ancestry of its family members. It hadn't occurred to Garrett they were anything but a family laminate. Frankly, he thought it was kind of sick the way they felt about their bloodlines resembling canine pedigrees. Perhaps the information contained in the sealed archives transcended more than a mere family tree.

"Some information is the domain of the head elders and, as you have so blithely put it, you aren't interested." His mother huffed but didn't even have the decency to hide the snide lilt in her tone. She was one up on him for now. "Let's just say there was a split in the membership years ago. Some wanted more leeway in raising their clan. We didn't allow it. If he is one of *them*, well…"

Guild business was beginning to sound more like the legal practice rather than some dry old men pursuing arid documents. "What happened?"

"Those who opposed us were ostracized but never stripped. The Guild kept close tabs on those families, and to our knowledge no one stepped out of line."

"Maybe someone did. Was there some kind of check in place?"

"Yes, but we detected nothing. With no activity,

we thought everyone involved in the dissent had died."

"Well, I can assure you this man was alive enough when I left him visiting with Nikki Angelus. Maybe you should check again." This was beyond belief. As careful as his mother was when it came to Guild business a lot of things seemed to be slipping by of late. An isolate with a gifted daughter? An old man back from the grave? For the first time Garrett wondered if he should take his rightful place with the elders. The notion sickened him. It had all but destroyed his father. All the obsessing and needling had driven him away. He didn't want that for himself.

"Interesting. What was his business with her I wonder?" Clicking on the other end signaled his mother typing. "William Songe's name does not appear on the list of known dissidents. This is as far as I can get here. I need to go to the archives for the rest."

"Why?"

"We've kept track of our people since we landed in America." Her voice was filled with irritation. "Only current information was transferred to the computer data base."

Garrett didn't like where this conversation was headed. Although Songe never admitted he was a Guild member, Garrett would lay odds that he was. The man never flinched or acted confused regarding Guild history. That meant he was familiar with its practices and, more to the point, part of it. If Songe was an ostracized Guild member, what was his interest in Nikki? Was Nikki a lost part of his family line? That might mean Nikki was the Shadow Dancer. Garrett groaned. His train of thought would not lead to positive resolution. The council would never allow Nikki to thrive. They would want Nikki eliminated. He couldn't convince himself isolating her mind was the right thing to do. "I think I should be allowed access to the archives." Urgency sounded in his voice. Desperation surged through his veins that if he was not an inside man on this matter, he couldn't protect Nikki from the council's wrath. A sentiment he didn't want his mother to detect. Her small laugh signaled he failed to conceal one or both.

"So now you're interested in the inner workings of our people. Very good. But you better tread lightly. There are elders who question your loyalty to the Guild. Some are concerned that you haven't cleared this matter already. That you are becoming too attached to the Angelus woman. Unless you clean up this mess, I'm not sure how much more help I can be. I've already told you too much because you are my son. But make no mistake, everyone involved in this matter must be erased. If the Angelus woman is part of this, she must be destroyed."

"Just so were clear. What exactly do you mean by destroy?"

"You are to do whatever is necessary to contain this situation. If that means the Angelus woman should die, you will not hesitate"

"Are you telling me the Guild has resorted to killing?" A chill crept down his spine. Surely his mother couldn't be serious.

"It is an unusual request. But an active Shadow Dancer developed without our knowledge. Our usual methods have not been successful at preventing this development. More severe actions may be necessary. Is that understood?"

"Yes, Mother." The cold edge of inevitability sliced away a piece of his freedom. But he'd hold on to whatever freedom he had left to extricate Nikki from this mess.

"Good. If you don't take care of this, the council will send someone else. I don't have to remind you what that could mean for you."

"Nope." After disconnecting with his mother, he dialed Nikki's office. It was past time finding out exactly what she knew. The need for subtlety was over. The sooner he discovered Nikki's part in this fiasco, the sooner he could resolve the matter of Nikki and her unusual associates for good. As long as this ended with Nikki still having a pulse, he would walk away with a clear conscience.

Chapter Twelve

Garrett headed to the Juvenile detention center thanks to Nikki's trusty assistant. His fingers twitched as he veered into the parking lot, scanning the vehicles. Spotting Nikki's sedan, he pulled into a vacant spot, waiting her to exit the building. He sank down in the seat low enough to escape her notice.

No doubt her visit was with Lori Hanover. He itched to hear the conversation. If only the Judge had granted the grandparents custody. It irked admitting they weren't the warm and fuzzy type, but that didn't mean they weren't capable of attending to the needs of a small child. Even the most cold and callous grandparent could turn to putty in the presence of their only grandchild.

If the Judge had bought Garrett's arguments *he* would have access to the child. More importantly, access to her mind. If she were the Shadow Dancer, he could quickly take care of any interference. If she wasn't, well…

Then there was the problem of the child's resistance to living with the Hanovers. He had to admit, Lori might have good reasons for wanting to remain away from them. He didn't have a lot of experience with children, but people in general rarely held beliefs without reason. He needed to know why she preferred remaining in the Juvenile center.

Maybe she was afraid they could take her powers away like they had her father's. If that were the case, he could reassure her they would do no such thing as long as he was their lawyer. But it didn't seem to him that they were inclined to strip her of her family legacy. They said she was talented. That meant they wanted to train her. It was like they were trying to gain an advantage over something or someone.

Then there was Nikki and her adoption. Suspicions churned deep inside. Just how much did she know? And how dangerous did that knowledge make her? Overwhelming qualms on her association with Songe burned huge grooves of reservations. Not to mention her role in the Hanover events.

Since the moment he'd kissed her, he'd had the unnerving sense of being a puppet in someone else's drama. Compelled to react to designed prompts and cues. Nothing could erase the realization of how neatly Nikki was wrapped up in this mess. He didn't like the reeling out of control any better than not knowing who was in charge. Nikki had answers and she was damned well going to answer them.

His phone rang. "What do you have for me?"

"Wow, you must be desperate." Mark chuckled. "Not even a how do you do."

"I don't pay you for chit chat. I don't have time for bull shit right now," he growled, eyes on the building exit.

"I ran the name William Songe through all my filters. Not a very common name so not much popped up."

"Anything of interest?"

"Actually, yeah. I found a wedding announcement,

two birth announcements and an obituary."

"Was the obituary for William Songe?" That was not good. If the man known as Songe had a previous identity there was no easy way to find out who he was. Unless he could pilfer an item. If Songe was as much of a threat as Garrett thought he was, getting something he owned could prove difficult.

"No, he's listed as next of kin."

"All right." The tension eased from Garrett's body. "Then who died?"

"That's the interesting part."

"Dammit, Mark, spit it out." Garrett opened his car window, allowing cool air to circulate.

"Is that petty sarcasm I hear?"

"Out with it," Garrett growled.

"Says here, William Songe had a daughter. Melanie. She married a man named Dale Summers in 1980. In '82, they had a son. Six years later, a daughter."

"Do you think that daughter could be Nikki?" Garrett thumped the steering wheel heavily. A loud pulsing thundered through his ear canal. He was close to the truth. He just knew it.

"Unlikely."

Garrett's hopes plummeted. He couldn't believe Songe was a dead end. "Why?"

"That's where it gets interesting. The baby's name was Nikki, but she died in a house fire along with her brother and father."

"They're all dead?" Garrett's vision blurred. How was that possible? He was so sure Songe was behind the adoption scam. Had his supposition been too simple? What he thought he knew was engaged in a tug of war with what he was now being told. He didn't want to let go of the idea that Nikki was Songe's relative.

"Yes."

Garrett's certainty depleted the same instant Nikki emerged from the detention center. She climbed into her car. "Scan the columns and email them to me."

"Right away, boss."

Garrett disconnected and started the engine. He followed Nikki out of the lot. If he had to dog her all day, he would. Whatever it took to find out what she was up to.

****

Nikki stood at the backdoor of the Hanover residence. Just a small rectangular box. The type of homes sold after World War II. A basic three bedroom, one bath, with no more than 1500 square feet. Her father would have called it a starter home.

Tired evergreen bushes framed the house in brown thick clumps. The grass barely held its green color. No flowers or other adornments alleviated the barren lawn. She doubted the Hanovers could have afforded much more beyond this house. Most people of their wage-earning potential were lucky to own a home at all. Notes from the file indicated the house had been inherited by Amy Hanover. Which was one of the reasons she was awarded possession of the home in the temporary order. All that changed when Amy dismissed her case. Amy's fatal error landed her in the hospital and sent Lori into the care of Child Protection Services. Nikki hoped she had the ability to alter Lori's tragedy. Then Lori could have a fresh start.

No crime scene tape crossed the premises. Luck

was with her. The local police had completed their collection of evidence several days ago. Otherwise she would have been stuck with no access to the residence. Now there was nothing to stop her from poking around. Nikki took out the key and slid it in the lock. She entered through a small kitchen laden with appliances dating back to the late 1950's. The most modern thing in the room was a microwave oven, and even that was old shown by its dial temperature timer. The strong stench of bleach hung over the kitchen. Clean dishes were stacked carefully in the drying rack. Nothing else appeared disturbed since the inhabitants' departure. But then this wasn't where the crime had occurred.

Nikki pushed through a swinging door that opened into the living area. Ah, the crime scene. The room was a disaster. Glass covered the carpet. Blood spatters stained the wall. A chair was knocked over, and what pictures remained on the wall were slanted askew just like in the dream when Parker drove the butt of a gun into Amy's skull.

Suddenly cold, she shivered before forcing herself to enter a tiny hallway. Family photos littered the floor as if tossed aside in anger. She tried imagining what it was like for an eight-year-old held hostage in the center of this sort of chaos. Scary, certainly. Each step on broken glass sent warning shocks up her spine.

As Nikki made her way through, she peered around open doorways. The first was a large room with a queen-sized bed. Books and papers were strewn from wall to wall over the floor in such haphazardness, it occurred to her the fight began here. A bloody fingerprint stained the door frame. She closed her eyes briefly, breathing through a wave of nausea. She swayed but stopped herself from drifting into the sullied area.

The urge to flee was overpowering. But she'd made a promise to Lori. Teddy bear, where the hell was the teddy bear? She gathered her bearings and forced herself to move on to the next room. Just an old stained couch and a TV. Completely untouched. No glass or other indication the fight invaded here. The next, a bathroom.

Then, finally, the room she wanted.

Busted hinges and splintered wood had the door hanging by a thread. A feeble remnant of the last barrier blocking Mr. Hanover from his prized possession, a small quaking child. Nikki turned on the light surprised by how ordinary the room looked. A white dresser and desk rested against the far wall. It was painted pink with sweet pea stencils over an arching window. A large white posted canopy bed occupied the center. The canopy and comforter had tiny rose buds threaded within green vines. With the exception of the broken door and a dust ruffle flipped up over the side of the bed, there was no indication a domestic disturbance had even occurred. She was looking at a perfect little girl's paradise, right down to the small tea set resting on a tiny table in the far corner of the room. Sometimes the sweetest places held the darkest secrets. It broke her heart.

A pet net hung from the ceiling on one side of the desk. It was too high to reach without assistance, so she dragged the desk chair underneath and stepped onto it. Nikki rummaged through the stuffed animals, sneezing a time or two as dust sailed into the air at the disturbance.

Clearly no one had touched these toys for a long time. They were there merely for decoration. She pulled out a red dog, a green bunny, and a blue poodle before finding the teddy bear she sought. It was just as Lori described, minus a patch of fur here and there. Cuddling the bear to her chest, Nikki jumped to the floor.

"What are you doing here?" A smooth silky voice spoke from the other end of the room.

She froze. Caught like a criminal in the act of breaking and entering. Bullshit. She was here by invitation. So what if it was that of an eight-year-old. Lori may not have the authority to grant access, but *he* didn't know that. He stood in the doorway, confident and sure of himself as always. "I have a key. Can you say the same?"

"I was asked to check the house to make sure it was secure." He rubbed a finger against the broken door frame. Maybe he'd get a splinter for scaring the crap out of her. "Imagine my surprise seeing the back door open and you inside."

Although she was certain that every word that dripped from his lips was a lie, at this point she was in no position to argue. It seemed every time she saw him they were at opposite ends of the pole. Arguing at every turn. She sighed. Right now, she just didn't have the energy. Too bad she didn't think to lock the door behind her. Ugh! She hated explaining herself. "Not that I have to answer to you, but Lori asked for her favorite toy."

"From way up there?"

A lame excuse, but that's all that came to mind. If he wanted to contradict her, he could prove it. Right now, all she wanted was to get out of this house and away from him. "Yes." She tried edging passed him but his shoulders filled the doorframe. "Step aside and let me leave please."

"I see you're not as innocent as you pretend." He reached and fingered the amulet on her neck. His touch was warm and vaguely comforting. It had the effect of transporting her back to her most recent dream—about him. *And* that kiss. She resisted the urge to move closer and breathe in his masculine scent. To rest her head on that broad shoulder. He was the enemy. Her mission was to stay alert and armed. Nikki stepped back. The amulet slipped from his hold, dropped onto her breastbone. His eyes held her mesmerized with an unpleasant gleam.

A slow smile spread across her lips. Her eyes traveled to his ring, letting him know there was no point in pretending.

He got the message.

"You don't know who I am do you?" He stepped closer, leaned in. His breath grazed her neck, and despite the efforts of avoiding him, a whiff of cinnamon and cloves assaulted her. She moved away allowing reason to filter its way in. But he followed again, closing the distance between them. "Answer my question."

"I don't care," she blurted, then clamped her lips shut. She hugged the bear close. Using it to shield her from Garrett's overpowering presence. It wasn't working.

"Did Songe give you this amulet?"

"Who gave you yours?" she retorted. He would not get the best of her. Two could play this game. She drew closer and lifted his hand, inspected his ring. His hand trembled, surprising her. "Is this an heirloom, too?"

"Quit the cat and mouse games." He eased his fingers from her. "You need to answer my question, right now."

"Why?"

"Because I'm an Enforcer."

"So? I don't even know what that is." How was she supposed to know or understand the inner workings of the Guild? She hadn't thought to ask a single question about the politics. She'd been too caught up in what her abilities were for it to occur to her that the Guild had a social structure. Songe hadn't exactly been forthcoming on the inner workings. In typical cryptic fashion, Garrett tossed out a position title that had absolutely no meaning to her.

"Well, you should." He was so close their noses almost touched. The gleam in his eyes mocked her.

She pulled back, taking in cool fresh air, mastering a calm she didn't feel. "I don't understand."

"An Enforcer makes sure the rules are followed." He placed a hand on her shoulder like he was her mentor. She tried another step back but his hand tightened, held her in place. There was no wriggling out of his grasp. His voice lowered, turned husky. "So tell me, Nikki, are you following the rules?"

"As far as you're concerned, yes." She bluffed once more pulling the teddy bear into her chest.

"I'll just bet you are." He clucked his tongue and shook his head. "Be careful because if you break the rules I will have to come after you, you won't like that. I would prefer sitting down and discussing things like civilized human beings."

She pushed him away relieved when there was air between them. "There is nothing civilized about you, Garrett Nightshade. You skulk around trying to intimidate me. When that doesn't work you resort to outright threats." She poked him in the chest with her finger. "Don't tell me you want civility. That's the last thing you want. We aren't on the same side. This is war."

His jaw twitched. "It doesn't have to be."

"You could have fooled me. I know what you did the other day. You may have succeeded in changing Sam's mind, but it won't work on me." She laughed. A brittle sound. "It must irk you to know that I'm not that pliable."

"Irk, no, but it does concern me." He leaned in. "Do you know how many people can do that Nikki?"

"No."

"None." He formed his hand into a semblance of a zero. "A big goose egg. Tell me, is Songe protecting you?"

"I don't know what you're talking about." Courage deserted her and she didn't feel that certain about her stance anymore. She stepped past him into the hallway. To her surprise, he let her pass, but his eyes trailed her every movement. "Even if I did, you are the last person I would cooperate with."

"I suggest you reconsider that one." His voice followed her out the door, but she stepped into the fresh air alone. For the moment.

Chapter Thirteen

That night, Garrett prepared to enter Nikki's mind for the second time. He wouldn't attempt to alter her motivation in order to win his case, he vowed silently. Nikki's surface memories were of no use to him in unraveling the mystery of her true parentage. He would have to probe deeper into events she'd forgotten long ago. He relaxed his muscles, assured he was armed with enough information to pilfer the truth from her subconscious. Soon he would have his answers. Even the person protecting her would have trouble interfering now.

Once he was successful, she would know what it meant to defy an Enforcer of the Guild. He would take special pleasure in teaching her respect. If she wanted war, he was in. All the way. *Be careful what you ask for, darling, I'm about to deliver it in abundance.* Her ignorance was his fortune. He grinned. Wouldn't she be shocked at what he could do, now that he knew she was one of them?

Using the same card still in his possession, Garrett crossed the barriers and slipped in. The same twelve doors greeted him but he wasn't stymied regarding which one to choose. The answers he sought wouldn't lay behind the door with the scales of justice. Those memories were nothing more than Nikki's legal education and career. Not the kind of information that would answer his lingering questions about her childhood.

Neither would the memories behind the doors with the cat, dog, and peace sign. Although, they undoubtedly held memories from her childhood with the Angelus family, they were too close to the forefront of her consciousness. Much too recent to be of any use.

He tested the theory by trying the knobs. As expected, the doors easily opened. His information was located further in a place even Nikki didn't venture. He surpassed the corvette, crystal, and brass knobs. Those had to be current memories of adolescent and young adult years.

Finally, he stopped before the door with the ivory knob. He tried it. Just like he had the first time. Still locked. A surge of anticipation rushed through him. This was where her deepest secrets lay.

He ran his fingers around the edges and over the top of the frame hoping Nikki could access her hidden knowledge with a hidden key. It couldn't be that easy. All he sensed was the rough texture of raw wood. The lacquered door was smooth to the touch revealing no clue on how to enter. There was no weakness in the surface or any hidden panel that would give way with pressure. He placed his hand over the key hole. A shallow breeze filtered through as if nothing but emptiness lurked behind.

He'd bet the door wasn't locked to just him but to Nikki as well. An event she couldn't yet face. A memory so powerful, it remained hidden until her psyche was strong enough to digest the details that lay behind it. Garrett took a moment to focus his thoughts. Maybe all he had to do was give her a little push in that direction. He took out Nikki's card and mentally formed it into an old-fashioned key.

His heart hammered in his chest as he bent down and inserted the key. It fit but didn't budge. Frustrated, he rattled the key around trying to get it to catch.

Nothing.

He cast the key aside and cleared his mind. Then traced his fingers around the shape of the key hole, focusing every ounce of his energy on the card. A new key appeared, cold and solid in his grasp. That was more like it. He inserted it and turned it. *A soft click.*

He grabbed the knob and turned. The door creaked open. A small shaft of light filtered through. He only saw a glimmer before it slammed shut shrouding him back into darkness. The hairs on his neck prickled. Another presence.

"What the hell do you think you are doing?" The voice familiar, the words softly spoken. Strength engulfed them.

Garrett stiffened. He turned and met the steel blue eyes accosting him. "Ah, Songe, how did I know it would be you?"

"Aren't you the clever one?" Songe's short, clipped words sent a shudder down Garrett's spine. "No matter how skilled you think you are, dear boy, you will never be good enough to get to the secrets of my granddaughter's mind."

"We'll see about that." Garret growled. He'd been right all along. Nikki was related to Songe. And the bastard had gone through a lot of trouble hiding the fact his granddaughter lived. Until now. Songe must have a reason for divulging his relationship to Nikki at this moment. Garrett needed to keep the man talking to find out what Songe's motives were. "I was almost there until you slammed the door."

Songe shook his head, favoring him with a condescending gaze, a smirk curling his thin lips. "That wasn't me."

Garrett's eyes narrowed. "Her?" He couldn't bring himself to say her name. To utter it would mean admitting her true nature waiting outside the edge of his periphery. He wasn't ready for that. Not yet.

"Yes." Songe's lips spread into the maniacal twist of a man who could eat his own children if it served the higher purpose. Maybe he'd done exactly that.

"Then why are you here?"

Songe shrugged. "Think of me as Nikki's alarm system."

"If she can deny me access to memories I suspect she doesn't even know, why would she need an alarm system?" Garrett crossed his arms and leaned against the door he'd so nearly walked through. Wishing he could simply melt under the door, he schooled his face into a mask of patience and waited for Songe to make a mistake. From the looks of the older man's placid expression, that could be awhile.

"I'm here because you were prying into matters that don't concern you."

"Really?" Garrett steeled his jaw. How far could he push the situation until it shifted to his advantage? Songe acted like a man who planned things to the nth degree. How much of his bravado was for show? "Maybe I don't need to open the door when the man who can answer my questions is right here."

"Your point?"

"You know all her secrets don't you?" Garrett

pushed himself from the door and sauntered toward Songe. Close enough to detect a slight twitch in the man's right eye. Other than that, the man was cold as a cucumber. "Care to enlighten me?"

The twitch ceased and the bastard actually grinned. "Also, not your concern."

"I disagree. Especially when my law firm was used to affect a dirty adoption."

A sudden chill invaded the air. With the twitch's return was an ugly twisted grimace. "You may think you know a lot, sonny, but I can promise you, you know nothing."

Garrett raised a brow. "Don't I?"

A short maniacal laugh burst from him. "No, allow me to demonstrate." With the authority of a true mentor, his arms raised. His voice boomed across the hollow expanse, eyes closed tightly. "Nikki, you're ready. Come defend your mind."

With that Songe disappeared in a golden mist. Time was about up. Garrett picked up the fallen business card and stooped in front of the door. He fumbled with the newly fashioned key. Just one more attempt. The ground quaked beneath Garrett's feet. Startled, he gripped the door frame. Trouble appeared in the form of Nikki Angelus. Garrett squared his shoulders. If she wanted confrontation—bring it on. Now he would find out exactly what she was capable of.

****

Nikki huddled deep in the arms of unconsciousness. The place where daylight memories met fantasy. A freight train blew through the center of her mind leaving a large chasm of chaos in its wake.

Pain filled the void with an elasticity of a bull whip smacking against the side of her brain. The pounding shook her in a rhythmic motion every second she slept. She had to get up, take some aspirin and hydrate, but no matter how hard she tried, her eyes refused to open. Her breath quickened as she fought to rouse from her comatose state but some barrier stood between her and the conscious world.

Slowly it dawned on her that it wasn't pain she felt but an alarm warning her of danger. The pounding mirrored her heartbeat as it prepared to battle an unwanted presence. Someone was rummaging around in her head and not being polite about it. She couldn't wake up until the intruder was annihilated.

Stop!

Her mind screamed the word. She shot through her slipstream until she stood before the prowler. A figure knelt beside a door. Every jolt and rattle of each impact sent tiny tremors through her. It didn't matter that his head was hidden behind his arm as he worked the lock or that his body was crouched in an unnatural stoop, she would recognize that muscular shape anywhere. "Garrett. What are you doing digging around in my head?"

He jerked his head around and gazed at her, his jaw firm and obstinate.

She crossed her arms over her chest. "What? Surprised that I would know someone was attempting to tamper with my mind?"

An object dropped to the ground before the door. Her business card. She huffed. Sometimes you miss the simplest things. "Not bad. Taking possessions from unsuspecting people and then penetrating them. Do you have no shame?"

He didn't respond. Made no movement at all. Didn't even appear to be breathing. "What's the matter? You shouldn't expect tampering with my mind would go unnoticed."

He rose to his feet, features schooled into his usual unruffled appearance. Did anything unnerve him?

"No, I was expecting you." His dark eyes bored into her. "I was just hoping you wouldn't show up so soon."

"You must think I'm an idiot." She tapped her foot in rapid staccato clicks. The motion only agitated her further when she realized how childish it made her look. And to make matters worse, she *felt* childish. She drew in a sharp breath, attempting to regroup her thoughts. "Do you know how painful it is to have someone rummaging around in your head?"

She searched his face for some indication of remorse. His neutral expression didn't change. His actions remained academic rather than personal. A cold burn of anger swept through her. What did he think he could accomplish here? This was her domain. A place to champion her cause. He didn't belong here.

"Actually, no." His expression stayed placid with no hint of apology. Totally at ease with invading her thoughts, stealing whatever facts he pleased.

She relaxed. A few easy breaths and her true power emerged with electric precision. The burn became a buzz vibrating through her entire being. The bastard expected admission. Felt *entitled* to her private thoughts. Irritation seared a trail of fury at such arrogance. "Get...out...of...my...head."

The ground trembled beneath them, but still Garrett

didn't budge. One shoulder rested against the door he'd been caught attempting to enter. His lips curved into a lazy, self-satisfied smile. "Not until I find out what lays behind this locked door."

She didn't know what was worse, that he persisted in delving into matters that didn't concern him or his total lack of distress. Fury consumed her. *How dare he*?

He should be scared. She wanted him scared. Instead, he acted as if her presence didn't matter in the least. "What's there belongs to me. You aren't entitled to any of it."

He raised one eyebrow and pushed himself from the door frame. He sauntered toward her. No signs of distress. A man in complete control. Her confidence wavered. He'd invaded *her* mind, and she was totally ineffective in protecting it. It didn't help that she was a novice while he was experienced. He'd roamed the heads of others many times before. Surely, there was a way to eradicate his presence.

"You might be surprised to learn that this is the first bolted door I have ever encountered." He pointed at the locked door. He treated her like a child who needed information spoon fed. The sheer condescension corroded her last bit of tolerance.

She sneered. *He* was the intruder, not her. She took several deep breaths, letting the oxygen clear her muddled thoughts. Whatever he was trying to convey eluded her.

If only she knew more about dream casting. But Songe assured her she did. He said he'd given her all the tools she needed to handle any situation. The biggest problem with this scenario was that all her skills were hidden deep within her psyche. If Songe hadn't told her about them, she wouldn't have been aware she had any special skill set. How did one gain access to something one had no clue about?

"That surprises me, Garrett. You act like you've seen everything." Stalling. She was always stalling when dealing with Garrett. He always seemed better prepared than her, leaving her to play catch up. The worst part was that he knew it, and like any good attorney, was using her weakness to his advantage.

She pulled her head back and lifted her chin. She needed to gain control of this situation fast. Not easy when he was standing so close. An electric heat hummed between them.

"Come on, Nikki, unlock the door," he coaxed, touching her cheek. A strange sense of wellbeing consumed her. His nearness fit. She was paralyzed, caught within the thrall. His gaze held hers far too long.

"No."

"Or maybe you can't." A simple statement. No taunt in his tone or even a dare.

"Why wouldn't I be able to unlock the doors to my own mind?" She pulled away and circled him like a cat observing her prey. That question worked both ways. She didn't know if she could open it or not, but she was certain she wasn't going to attempt it with him witnessing. "Or could it be that I am the only one who can lock my doors?"

"We, as a rule, don't lock our minds to others." For the first time in this insane confrontation, he looked away. Interesting. Maybe he wasn't as confident as he let on.

"Why is that?"

"Because." He turned his head. His eyes bore right

through her. The intensity of his gaze sent shivers of doubt trembling up her spine. "We don't hide our true natures from our people. That leads to other kinds of dangerous deceptions."

"I'm a private person." She allowed the disdain in her voice to amplify. "By nature, I don't share my personal life with many. Most especially those who creep around in secret. I suggest you leave."

"Or what?"

"Or this." She faced all her doors and whispered, "Lock."

"What are you doing?"

"Making sure my private life remains just that. Private."

Garrett raced around rattling doorknobs. He pounded on wood. Slipped his fingers underneath and pulled. They didn't budge. He rested against the last one, his breath ragged. "You can't do that."

"I just did."

"It isn't allowed."

"Isn't it?" she said a bit too smugly. "If I am forbidden, how is it I'm able to?"

Garrett's face went slack. He didn't have an answer.

Good. If she were going to retain the upper hand, keeping him off balance was crucial.

Garrett snatched up the card that had fallen to the ground and focused his attention on it. The card shifted and curled into the shape of a key. He inserted it into one of the doors. She turned her efforts on his actions. Pulled down into the farthest places of her mind. She sent out a force so strong it ripped through her skin, pulsing toward the keyhole. *Stay locked to everyone but me*. The key crumpled into bits of paper that drifted to the ground.

"You won't get away with this." A strange glint simmered in the depth of his gaze. He didn't appear sure of his words, but concern lingered beneath hooded lids. Concern she would succeed or concern for her? She wasn't sure.

It didn't matter. She found the source of her power and it was intoxicating. A slow smile of triumph crossed her face as a curious notion occurred to her. "Wait a second, does that mean that you can't lock your doors to me?"

"Don't be a fool. You don't know what you're playing with." He stood, arms crossed, his feet shoulder length apart. He was bluffing. Nothing he did or said could erase the fact he hadn't answered her question, but it hung there—between them. He couldn't keep her out of his mind.

"I'll take that as a yes."

"Don't make me hurt you." His voice softened. Torment raged within his chocolate brown eyes. In two short strides, he was within inches of her. He gripped her shoulders and pulled her to him. "I know you don't know what you're doing. I really don't want to hurt you."

"Then don't hurt me." Heat radiated off him, urging her closer. Without thinking, she ran her fingers up his firm arm. His breath hitched. She smiled as a pleasant warmth spread, punctuating an aching need she didn't even know existed until now. She should move away. Hadn't he all but threated her a moment ago? But his eyes were no longer tinged with anger. A new intensity burned beneath. A soul scorching gleam.

Dangerous, yes, but not life threatening. Her traitorous heart quickened. She leaned in.

He pulled away. "What are you doing?"

"Distracting you." A low throaty tone crept into her voice, surprising even her. Confident. Secure. She put her hand on the back of his head...pulled him to her...brushed her lips against his.

He stiffened. Hesitated. But then in a bruising crush, his arms circled her waist and his mouth pressed against hers, his tongue stroking her own, ravaging her. A fire blazed a wicked trajectory inside her. Awakening her through to her inner core. A giddy sort of dizziness entrapped her in a soft cocoon. Her arms tightened around his neck, and she held on reveling in his solid frame. Stroke after stroke of his tongue threatened the stability of her knees. She trembled, never wanting this moment to end. It had been such a long time since she'd wanted anyone this much.

He broke away, breathing harshly, cupping her chin. "Are you sure you want this? Astral sex has complications. Another thing you know nothing about." His voice was raspy. Nothing like the day-to-day indifference and hostility she was so accustomed to.

"You're in my mind, remember?" She swayed against him. "I-I'm in charge."

"Don't say I didn't warn you."

"I've been warned enough. Thank you very much—"

His mouth covered hers, cutting off her sarcasm, softer this time, igniting a slow simmer in her veins. She shuddered wanting him to go further. He didn't disappoint. His hand trailed down her back, rousing a surge of longing that left her breathless. They shouldn't fit this perfectly together. They weren't supposed to even like each other. But none of that mattered now. All that mattered was her endless aching need. He lifted her off the ground, and she wrapped her legs around his waist, pressing against him, reveling in his arousal. He slipped his hand under her shirt, brushing against her breast. She moaned as her nipple hardened in response.

"Yes," she breathed against his lips. The familiar smell of cinnamon and cloves sent her into a frenzy. She arched her back. Now. She wanted him. Now. She ripped his shirt from his shoulders, buttons flinging against wood. She slid her hands across the solid plane of his chest.

He groaned and tumbled them onto the ground, his weight holding her down. She tugged his shirt over his head. His lips moved down her throat, soft but insistent. Telegraphing his need.

He unbuttoned her shirt one button at a time leaving a trail of damp sizzling kisses along the path of her sensitive flesh. She wrenched her fingers through his hair wanting him to move faster, at the same time needing him to slow down. His mouth moved to her breast. He flicked his tongue over her pebbled nipple. Her body tightened. She couldn't take any more of this torment. Their garments constricted their ability to explore each other, driving her further insane. She shifted her leg and flesh met flesh. She gasped.

"Couldn't wait to get my clothes off, huh?" Garrett chuckled.

"What just happened?"

"The mind knows what it wants. And it gets it." Garrett thrust his rock-hard penis into her, his body building an incredible pressure. She shuddered, raking her fingers down his back. Gasping for breath. He pulled out, and with a groan plunged deep inside her. Blinding spasms erupted. She cried out.

Garrett's neck stiffened beneath her fingers. He gripped her hips hard against him…spilled himself into her…his own cries bounding against the walls in her head. His head fell into the crook of her neck, his ragged breaths searing her skin. Her body shook from the aftermath, a pleasant, relaxing sensation she wanted to savor forever.

After a long moment, Garrett rolled off her. She stared upward, suddenly feeling exposed and unprotected. "We-we shouldn't have done that."

Garrett laughed. A low guttural sound. "It's a bit late to reconsider. Don't you think?"

She lifted onto one elbow and scrutinized him. "We're enemies, Garrett. We won't ever be on the same side."

He brought his face close to hers. "I'm not your enemy, and it's not that simple."

She fell back down and ran her fingers through her hair. "It is that simple." Even as she said the words, a cold emptiness filled her. She couldn't undo what had happened. But no way would she allow Garrett to muddle her thoughts any longer. She needed to stay focused, free of distractions. "This can't happen again."

"You still don't understand—"

Nikki put her hand over his mouth ignoring the soft tingle of his breath against her skin. "I may not, but whatever this is, is over." She waved her hand. "Now, get out of my head."

With those words, he vanished. She had no idea what she was doing, but it was like…magic. Magic that now left a yawning ache deep in her soul.

Fighting off tears, she sank into the ground and back into her body.

Chapter Fourteen

Nikki woke with a start, unsure of where she was. As her eyes adjusted to the dark, the familiar shapes of her rag doll collection emerged. Over on the nightstand, Lori's doll slumped over her clock. Three in the morning. Too early to be up. Her nerves prickled alerting her she'd left something undone. Memories of Garrett and their reckless abandon came back in a flood. In effort to distract him, she'd allowed herself to be blindsided. She'd gotten swept up in her own desire and need. Now she just felt stupid and empty. But she still had time. Garrett had only stalled her progress. He hadn't stifled it. She thought of Parker Hanover. If she truly could alter the course of events in his life, perhaps she *could* change the outcome. How good it would feel make the bastard really feel remorse. Bring him to his knees. A heady sense of the good she could do surged through her.

She yanked the teddy bear off the comforter. A sense of time and space crackled from her finger tips to her toes. The pressure built. Strong. Certain. She was ready. She reached. A suction pulled her into the slip stream. Excitement bubbled in her stomach. Nikki soared through the portal and landed on solid ground. Confidence seized her.

She turned her head right and left. Alone. She bit back the acid taste of disappointment. Whatever she'd done to cast Garrett from her mind must have been very potent. There wasn't even a twinge of his presence. Really for the best since she didn't need his interference if she was to complete her task. Taking a deep cleansing breath, Nikki let the tension wane from her aching muscles and turned her attention to the layout of Parker's mind.

Like her mind, there were doors. But they were haphazardly placed. Unorganized. An indication Parker adhered to no structure or impulse control. That would explain the capacity to beat his wife senseless with no plan to escape the authorities. Each door was adorned with a primary color, red, blue, and yellow. But nothing solid. It was more like blotches of color as if the surface was hastily painted with no thought for uniformity or tidiness. No other ornamentation or design decorated the surface or knob.

Nikki examined them but wasn't sure that it mattered which door she entered first. Other than the colors they all looked the same. So the tint on each panel must be the clue. She considered each one, attempting to discern the entrance to the most volatile aspect of his personality. If he were like most parents of the children she represented, he had a great deal of hostility and paranoia thriving inside. Blamed everyone, other than himself, for his predicaments. He was caught in the cycle of pointing his finger with no understanding that the only behavior that needed adjustment was his. She grimaced. The crazy person was always the last to know. Nikki gravitated to the red door, the color of anger, and peered inside.

The memory before he'd been arrested.

The moment Parker beat Amy wouldn't help. By

her calculations, that was too late. She needed to locate the motivation for his actions. She pushed further.

There. He sat as an adult on a child's full twin bed. A comforter covered in footballs and sports logos was draped over his hunched shoulders. Posters of sports stars, faded and worn around the edges, adorned the walls. The furniture was small and toy-like next to Parker's hulking presence. At his age, his room should have reflected a more mature decor but maybe she was a little too harsh. Until recently, Parker hadn't even lived there. And true, some parents kept their children's rooms as a shrine.

She wondered how the room would change now that Parker was living in his parent's house again. Would he replace the juvenile twin in favor of a queen-sized bed, or tear down the posters and hang the artwork that resided in his marital home? She swallowed, realizing he wouldn't be able to do any of those things if she failed to keep him from beating Amy senseless.

Chin resting on his fist, brooding, he appeared more like a rebellious teen than a full grown man. She drew nearer, forced her mind closer. She needed to hear his thoughts, and he hers. She paused and just listened.

Filthy bitch thinks she can keep my Lori from me. Better think again.

The thoughts were intense and focused on Amy and her desire that he seek counseling before he returned home. Amy dismissed her case but wasn't ready to let him live with the family. Rage radiated from him—all over his lack of control over his situation. Yeah, tough break. Nikki imagined that sort of injury went deep and festered. But was that enough to compel him to clobber his wife with the butt of a gun? Surely there was more to it.

The door to his room opened, and Carolyn Hanover stuck her head in. "Parker, honey, you need to eat something. Keep up your strength."

"Not hungry." The edge in his voice curdled the acid in Nikki's stomach.

"Now, Parker, don't be that way." Carolyn's placating tone grated on Nikki. Cloying and meddlesome. Her syrupy sweet words disguised the controlling aspect of the woman. But Nikki saw it as clear as the sun in the Caribbean. The woman expected Parker to heed her word.

"Go away." He threw a basketball at the door. "This is all your fault. If you hadn't taken my powers away, I wouldn't have lost my family, *my Lori*," he hissed.

Instead of retreating, Carolyn stepped inside. She made her way to the bed and sat next to him. "Parker." She patted his hand. "That's not true. We did what was necessary. Darling, we aren't responsible for what happened to you. Amy can't keep Lori from you forever. She just wants you to get some anger management classes before you go back home."

He pulled his head from his hands, eyes filled with tears. His menacing gleam shook Nikki to her core. Carolyn flinched at his expression. The mixture of sadness and hatred was startling. "No one will help me."

"That's n-n-not true."

Parker jumped to his feet, arms waving with vigor. "You don't understand, Mama, Amy might be a liar but Lori isn't."

"What?" Carolyn's gasp sounded sincerely surprised.

Parker's eyes widened to the look of a caged animal. Caught in a trap of his own making.

Until this moment, Carolyn hadn't considered that Parker had harmed his child. "I thought it was an accident. How can you hurt your own child?"

"Don't you judge me," he said harshly. "How else was I to reach her? *I have no power.*"

Carolyn stared at him. Shocked at the monster before her. Nikki wasn't surprised. Most parents had no inkling the part they played in their child's evil behavior. How could they? If they looked close enough, they would be horrified to see their own reflection. It was always easier to blame others for one's failings.

Carolyn stood, her face contorting into a mask of disgust. "You've made your bed, boy. Your father and I can't help you anymore. You're on your own." She marched from the room leaving Parker to stew.

He sank onto the bed. Large gulping sobs erupted. Then stilled. From the depths of his despair, anger sprung forward to take root.

There was no court order keeping him from his daughter. He would go over there and demand to see her. Amy would be quaking in her boots. She didn't have her jackass attorney standing between him and her tonight.

His intent came through loud and clear. Nikki's hands trembled.

The right to see Lori overrode any rational thought. That she would be glad to see him. The slow smile that erupted on his face made him appear menacing.

Alarm coursed through Nikki. *This was it, the*

turning point. The moment things wrenched out of control. What he wanted was to see his daughter. Memories of the beating she'd seen from Amy's mind came back in vivid detail, she knew Amy fought valiantly to protect her daughter. With the hair trigger on his emotions, Parker must have snapped as evidenced by the gun he'd retrieved.

That one act changed the course of their lives. Nikki compressed her lips. She could switch it back.

No Parker. Think of what you are doing. You are too angry to confront Amy tonight. If you go see Amy, it will only lead to disaster. Calm down. Wait a couple of days.

To Nikki's profound relief, Parker's thoughts began to shift. He was too exhausted to think. He needed rest. Maybe things would look different in the morning. Things would be all right.

Things will be better, Parker. You'll see, she assured him. Inhaling deeply, Nikki slipped away.

****

Parker shot up. His heart rammed against his chest. Terror? Or excitement? Every nerve ending trembled and twitched. Something had changed. He rubbed the last vestiges of sleep from his eyes, allowing time to adjust to the dark. For a moment he couldn't recall where he was. Shapes began to form. A small dresser. A chair. The stupid poster he'd hung on the wall at seventeen when he thought he could do almost anything. Even get his powers back. But this room ceased to hold the promise of new awakenings a long time ago. His parents had seen to that.

Last thing he remembered he'd been locked in jail. But the solid cinderblock walls faded and a different image began to form. He sat up messaging his neck recalling the most recent events in the Amy/Parker drama. It'd been a bad fight. Why couldn't he control the rage that burned through him every time Amy defied him? All she had to do was look at him with that blank innocent look in her eyes. The 'I haven't done anything wrong' pout. When it was completely evident she'd messed up big time.

All he wanted was to come home to a welcoming family and not trip over Lori's damned toys. That wasn't too much to ask. But Amy wasn't the kind of woman to feed that desire. She had to willfully defy his one simple request. His fingers curled as he recalled her response.

"But Parker, I haven't had time."

But there was no excuse for the utter chaos that reigned supreme in his absence. Toys all over the house. A laundry basket filled to overflowing. There was no reason she couldn't keep the house clean. All she needed was a little organization. But she was so scattered, order was impossible without his guidance. Lori stepped in the middle of their fight. Her eye smacked into his elbow. And now Amy wouldn't even let him move home. She sent him to his childhood room as if he was in time out. But he wasn't a child. She should know that by now.

He was charged up enough to teach her that lesson. Then it occurred to him to give it a rest. To step back and take a break. Which was odd because he hadn't ever done that before. That meant only one thing. Someone had been in his mind. Altered him enough to make him think holding back was the right thing to do. So, he'd come back to his childhood room to think it over. Believing if he just gave it a little more time, they could work it out. He would convince her to be more organized. Once he was back in control of everything, they could be happy again. They would be the family he deserved.

He laughed. Must be the work of that nosy woman sent to protect Lori. He knew she'd be handy eventually. The stupid twit had no idea what she was doing. That kind of ignorance could be very useful to him. On a whim, he expanded his mind but the familiar barriers clamped down on his efforts. Well, he was out of jail. That was nothing to discount. Ms. Angelus had figured out how to turn things around this much in a measly three days. It didn't even matter that Amy had marched right back to court the next day after he'd blackened Lori's eye and refiled for divorce. He'd overcome supervised visitation before. Maybe it was time to encourage the mighty protector of children a bit more. With a little nudge, Nikki Angelus would come through. Then everyone would know not to mess with him. He lay back down and went to sleep certain of his upcoming triumph.

Chapter Fifteen

Garrett woke to a sledge hammer hacking at his brain. Each dig sent an explosion of pain, followed by a blinding light behind his eyeballs. It took a second to remember. He held his head to quell the aftershocks of Nikki distracting him with mind blowing sex then slamming him back into consciousness.

Damn her. He rubbed the back of his neck massaging the stiff muscles. The tension didn't ease. Shit! There wasn't enough aspirin to cease the pain. The last time his head felt like a disaster after a train wreck was after an especially rigorous training session as a teenager. Had to give her credit, the woman dealt a hell of a whollup. No novice could inflict this kind of agony.

What was he going to do about her? On one hand, she cared about the children she represented, truly wanting to help them achieve a healthy adulthood. That much was obvious when he'd gained access to her mind. Those actions demonstrated compassion. Her intention to do the right thing was admirable. He wished more than anything he was in a position to help her. Unfortunately, while she'd been trained in the arts of casting, she hadn't been taught to respect the laws of the Guild. That meant she was dangerous.

Garrett took a slow deep breath. The steady throb in his head increased. He squeezed his eyes shut. An inkling there was something up with Parker Hanover bobbed to the surface of his thoughts. What was it exactly? His wife had filed for divorce. Garrett was hired to represent him. The child had a bruise. The realization clocked him sending another surge of pain hammering through his consciousness. Parker had been in jail three days ago. Today he wasn't.

There was no longer any doubt Nikki was the Shadow Dancer. That meant she could forage farther back than any other caster he'd come across. Beyond the forty-eight-hour window. As a child, he'd heard tales of others with the same ability, but that was hundreds of years ago—before the Guild slammed on the breaks and curbed those abilities for the good of mankind.

Now here she was, a rogue caster with the capacity to change more than allowed. He rolled his head from side to side. It only succeeded in increasing the surge of echoing pain. His insides churned. Nikki was trouble. If she wasn't stopped she could bring down the whole culture in one fell swoop. Changing history despite her good intentions. That wasn't going to play well with the elders and it certainly placed him in a tenuous position with the council. He groaned. She didn't trust him and she certainly wouldn't listen to him.

He sat up, curling his toes along the cool wooden floor. He had to stop her. But without access to her mind he couldn't do it in the traditional fashion. And that was just fine with him because he didn't want to cripple her mind. He would have to find some other way for her to see reason.

Unlike Nikki, he wasn't able to lock his mind. That was the first thing the Guild prevented. A mechanism to curb the power hungry. Now the very measures designed to protect him left him vulnerable to her attack. He could forgive Nikki's transgressions. None of this was her doing. It was her grandfather who disregarded the Guild's checks and balances. Garrett dropped his head in his hands. His fingers twisted and pulled their way through his hair. What exactly was the old man up to? He couldn't fathom any one of his kind wanting a dream caster to go unchecked let alone one as powerful as the Shadow Dancer.

The ceiling spun. A wave of nausea descended. He rolled over on his side and curled into the fetal position. He held onto the edge of the bed, waiting for the room to return to normal. He was in no state to figure out William Songe's motivation. When the room stilled, he looked at the clock. Five a.m. Another early morning with no hope of sleep returning. Letting out a long tortured breath, he stood on unsteady legs and fixed himself strong coffee.

He sipped the bitter liquid then rummaged around in the cabinet for aspirin. Grabbing the bottle, he yanked off the lid that sent little pellets skittering across the kitchen counter. He scooped up three tablets and popped them into his mouth relishing the acid taste while he contemplated the turn of events. Maybe it wasn't as bad as it seemed. If he couldn't get through the front door, he would go through the back. That path led him directly to William Songe. It was time to pay him a visit. All he had to do was find him.

Garrett pulled out his cell and dialed Mark. Thankfully, he picked up on the first ring. "It's early. This better be good," Mark barked.

"It is. Have you found an address on Songe?"

"Sorry, not yet. I was putting out another fire yesterday."

"I need you to find him now."

"On it. I'll see what I can dig up right away."

Garret slipped the phone into his pocket, feeling better already. It was always interesting to shake the trees to see what kind of nuts fell lose. While he was waiting for Mark's answers, he might as well pay a visit to Nikki

****

Nikki opened the door to her office and stopped short. Garrett sat perched on the edge of her desk, tossing her bean bag dog up in the air with the flair of a juggler, his face fixed on her expectant and waiting.

"You shouldn't be here." An overwhelming urge to fling herself into his arms consumed her. She swallowed holding the door knob firmly before she behaved like a love-sick puppy. Oh *hell*. After last night, she shouldn't be surprised to find him here muddling her thinking with his smoldering gaze. She touched her tingling lips. Memories flooded back. His strong arms encircling her waist crushing her against him. The sizzle between her thighs as their lips touched. Pulling him nearer. Needing him inside her.

"You can't get rid of me that easily." He was so calm. Not a lock of hair out of place. Unruffled by their night tangled up in each other. As if things like that happened to him all the time.

She sucked in a breath putting a halt to her rambling thoughts. She tugged at her suit jacket gathering her composure. "Let me guess, you visited my receptionist in the night so that you can barge into my office at will."

"I had to find some way to get to you since you've blocked the usual route." He studied her. "You've made some changes since I left you last night."

"Changes?" She slipped past him. He turned and planted a palm smack in the middle of her desk. Her heart thudded in her chest. Had she made a difference? She bit her lip. Garrett had the upper hand on her. He knew what she'd done. From his downturned lips, he wasn't happy about it either. "How bad is it?"

"Could be worse."

"Stop being so cryptic." She searched her memories for any differences in the events of the past few days. But her vision was cloudy. Other than their recent tryst, not one salient fact emerged from her jumbled mind. "I'm a little disadvantaged here. Tell me exactly what's changed."

"Can't remember, can you?"

She shook her head.

"That's the thing about meddling in matters you shouldn't. The meddler never sees the consequences of their actions."

"Care to enlighten me?"

"At this point, the damage is minimal. Parker is back at his parents and the divorce has been refiled. Nothing the Guild can't handle." He grimaced as if what he had to say next was very distasteful. "You would be wise not to make another attempt to change Parker Hanover."

Letting out a sigh of exasperation she faced him. "From what you are telling me, things have moved in a positive direction. My I remind you, you are not my keeper."

"If you don't heed my words, you have no idea

how bad this can get." He didn't smile in his usual cocky way. His eyes pleaded for her to listen.

She softened. As irritating as it was to have him dogging her everywhere she went, it was hard to see him looking so worn down. She refused to examine why it should matter one way or another. Last night was simply a moment of carnal lust. She wasn't supposed to care about him. She wouldn't let herself care. But she did care. "Oh shit!" She fingered her necklace looking at anything but him.

"Pardon me?"

"Sorry, I just remembered something." Not the real reason. But she wasn't about to let him in on her personal train of thought. He would probably laugh. And that would hurt. She chewed on her bottom lip. Who cared if he didn't believe her? It was enough of an excuse to get away from him. "I have to go."

She turned to leave. He caught her arm when she was half way through the door sending a strong tingle through her like they had just completed an electrical circuit. Buzzing filled her head, fogging all sense of reason.

"Nice try. You're not getting rid of me that easy." His grip was strong. Clearly his confidence had returned.

She whirled, yanking her arm from his grasp. "You sure are spoiled. *Always* believing you can get your way."

"Is that what you think?"

She leaned against the door frame. "In a word, yes." What was wrong with her? She wanted to get rid of him not bait him into another argument. But another emotion consumed her with superiority. As if she was in control of everything. She wasn't certain she liked the feeling but she couldn't help the surge of glee at her apparent domination. Her cheeks burned in shame. She wasn't power hungry. But Garrett was under her thumb and he knew it.

"This isn't a joke, Nikki. You don't know what you're playing with."

That was true. She had no idea what she was doing. "As I see it, I'm doing pretty well."

He pulled her so close she could lean in and kiss him. His masculine scent made her dizzy. The memory of them laying together exposed and naked flooded back. She licked her lips knowing if she gave in she would lose what semblance of control she had. But if it would stop him from chastising her… She dismissed the notion. Allowing physical contact would only complicate matters further. It was already bad enough she succumbed to her desires last night while she slept. To do so while she was awake was only asking for trouble. Her musings were interrupted by her receptionist.

"Do I need to call the deputy, Ms. Angelus?"

Nikki glanced over at the wide-eyed woman. She had been so caught up in wrestling with her warring desires she had forgotten anyone else was there. Now she realized what a spectacle she was making. She was acting like a teenager in heat. In plain view of the entire office complex. The idea sapped her strength.

"No, that won't be necessary." She walked behind her desk. "You have fifteen minutes."

He was still much nearer than she would have liked. A hint of cinnamon compelled her to lean in closer. She fought the urge. A wave of guilt washed over her. What was she doing? He was an attorney on one of her cases. In any other circumstance, it wouldn't be strange to let him into her office to discuss the case. But the events of the past few days weren't normal circumstances. Her initial surge of dominance faded. His presence crowded the room. That was dangerous enough. Even more appalling was how much she was willing to do just as he wished. She grasped anger to control her desire. Remaining rational with the man was impossible. The sooner this case was over, the sooner he would be out of her life. A thought that didn't bring much solace anymore.

"Fifteen minutes," she said again. "But make it quick. I don't have all day." She held her breath, stilling the butterflies in her stomach. Surviving the next few minutes would be a godsend.

****

Nikki sat behind her desk. "I don't want to talk about what we did last night."

Garrett tried to suppress an amused grin. Her lame attempt in side-stepping the real issue was laughable. Maybe not so lame. The fire that burned in the depths of her green eyes rekindled the need to feel her smooth skin against his as she responded to his touch. He wanted her again and again until the spark of their passion went out. If last night were any indication, that would take a long time. He didn't want to talk about dream casting any more than she did. Still, the matter had to be discussed. "As pleasurable as that would be, that's not why I'm here."

"Then we have nothing to discuss." She picked up as stack of papers and straightened them, avoiding any eye contact.

"On the contrary, you and I have a lot to go over." Garrett sat back in his chair and steepled his fingers in front of his nose.

"I'm not discussing my abilities with you."

She put a huge amount of effort into restacking the already voluminous documents from one pile onto another. He wondered briefly if the stacks had any real order. But that was irrelevant. It wasn't the papers he was interested in.

"You're heading into dangerous ground."

She slammed the stack of papers onto a smaller heap. Good, he had her attention. "I don't think you're the one to guide me in this matter."

She put up a good front but he could tell that she wasn't as confident as she would have him believe. And she appeared…guilty.

He leaned forward. "It doesn't bother you that I'm an Enforcer?"

Now it was her turn to sit back. "Not one bit."

"It should." Garrett began slowly.

She wasn't a neophyte. Instead she was a very powerful caster who knew just enough to be dangerous. He didn't pretend he was doing anything but wasting his time trying to warn her. But it just didn't seem to be good sport to catch her unaware. Everyone should know the rules before they engaged in war. She was an innocent bumbling around in an unfamiliar world. She wasn't informed of the stakes. If only she could see reason before it was too late.

He had to admit she'd caught him unaware last night and that didn't sit so well. She was so soft. So willing. So exciting. Blood pounded in his ears at the memory of her in his arms. The fullness of her lips pressed against his. He had to get her to see reason. She'd already gotten a taste of what she could do and was a larger liability than his mother already suspected. After last night, he knew he couldn't hurt her. There would be no greater shame than destroying a mind as captivating as hers. If the elders caught on to his reluctance, somebody else would step in. Garrett wasn't sure he could protect Nikki if that were to happen.

"Oh yeah." She brushed a lock of hair behind her ears. "Why's that?"

"Well," He paused for effect.

Nikki squirmed.

Good. Maybe, she would listen. "I'm the guy that comes after the people who don't adhere to the laws of the Guild."

"I'm not a member of the Guild."

"No. You're one of those people who think the rules don't apply to them."

She leaned over her desk as far as the mountain of paper work allowed. "What if I am?"

He was struck by her courage. But then she really didn't know how dangerous *the Guild* could be. Maybe she thought that the mere locking of her mind to them would keep them at bay. She didn't need to know it had stalled them. And quite a bit, but they weren't done yet. They would find a way around her obstruction. "That would not bode well for you."

She let out an exasperated sigh. "To set your mind at ease, I believe that everyone should follow reasonable rules. However, I *do* question authority. In case you hadn't noticed, that *is* my job."

"As is mine." Garrett let loose a slow smile of appreciation. She was very good at wordplay. A necessary skill for an attorney. As a caster, not so much. "But you need to be aware that the Guild will not allow even the slightest infraction. You have already gotten away with far more than they usually tolerate."

"I've seen how the Guild deals with small infractions. It seems a bit draconic to me."

Garrett loosened his tie and swallowed. Had he not said the same thing to the elders numerous times? But there was no way Nikki knew that. "What experience could you possibly have with Guild?"

"Oh, I haven't met them—just seen the trail of their destruction." She smoothed a hair running her fingers through dark locks. Her voice silky, evasive and cagy.

"Jesus." He hadn't missed something important, had he? Garrett was certain he knew all the changes she'd made last night. But he'd never dealt with a Shadow Dancer before. It was possible she could alter things without his knowledge. "You haven't gone too far for me to correct your mistakes, have you?"

"Well, Mr. High and Mighty, I did my job. Rest assured, there's nothing to correct."

"Last time I checked it wasn't your job to meddle in people's affairs. At least not when they're asleep."

She slammed her hand on the desk, sending one of the stacks fluttering to the floor. "Listen, you arrogant prick. It's my job to help families mend allowing ample opportunity to raise healthy adult children." She bent down and gathered the strewn mess. "Now, as it turns out, I can help in a permanent way."

Garrett's pulse shot up. He squeezed his hand into a fist until his knuckles whitened. He remained anchored to his chair willing the throbbing in his ears to cease. If he rose, he wasn't sure where his hands would go. Around her neck? "You are in dangerous territory altering people's minds. You don't know what you're messing with."

"Says the guy who tried to change my mind about the Hanovers and compelled my receptionist to let you in my office at your whim. I get it. It's only okay when *you* do it."

"I'm trained."

"So am I."

"Look, I can't go beyond the forty-eight hour window. I have never used my powers to help anyone who doesn't deserve it. But I don't have to justify my actions to you. I am working for the good of the Guild."

She gifted him with a benign smile. "Are you sure about that?" She stood. He was surprised at how much she towered over him. He didn't budge. He refused to let her get to him, forcing himself to remain calm.

"Absolutely, just as sure as I am that you aren't working for the good of the Guild."

"I don't care about your stupid Guild." She moved back behind the desk. "I care about the families I represent."

"Fine, then why don't you sit down and tell me how you think you've helped." To his surprise she did sit. But she remained tight lipped about the events of last night. "Look, if I don't know how far you've gone, I can't guide you."

"I don't need your guidance."

"Yeah, you do."

****

Garrett was everything Nikki despised in a man. Good looking, dressed to the nines, and bossy. So sure that his solution was the only one, that he alone had all the answers. She'd spent years avoiding his type. How had destiny dropped this one in her lap whose every move sent another wave of desire coursing through her? The worst part was she was actually beginning to...like him. She squelched the notion before it got the better of her. "I have my own source for guidance, thank you," she quipped.

"Your grandfather isn't going to help you with matters of the Guild."

"Oh yeah? How would you know? It appears he has functioned just fine without the Guild." She wasn't sure she should have confirmed Garrett's suspicions but she was a little out of sorts that he knew about her grandfather. Just how much more did he know?

"I also have my sources." The cocky bastard was as slippery as she wished she was when doling out information.

"As I said, I am not a member of the Guild."

"Ah. But he was *and* he was excommunicated."

She narrowed her eyes. "You're lying."

He shook his head slowly, looking like a man at the top of his game, certain of his assertions. Nikki's understanding of the situation was changing so fast she was sure to get whiplash. Just what part did the Guild play in her life?

Dealing with Garrett was bad enough. But the idea of a whole group of people dictating her actions—

She bit the inside of her cheek and considered the ramifications of what it meant to be a caster. Things had gotten, well, complicated and she wasn't sure how to handle it. "I'm sure he had his reasons for leaving your precious Guild."

"We all have our reasons but some of them aren't that good. Do you happen to know his?"

She was pretty sure she shouldn't say anything but couldn't stop herself. The urge to wipe the arrogant expression off his face took hold. "They took his family."

To her surprise his expression softened. "Why would he say that?"

"There was a house fire. He blames the Guild."

"The Guild had nothing to do with that Nikki. I swear."

He sounded sincere but how was she supposed to believe him? "According to the records, it was arson."

"And Songe holds the Guild responsible?"

"Yes."

"The Guild doesn't kill people. They protect them."

"So, *you* would be my protector?" Nikki let out a derisive snort. "Do you really think you've built a case by prancing around threatening me on behalf of the Guild all the time?"

He rubbed his forehead with his index finger and thumb. "Okay, so I haven't been great at this. You—the extent of your abilities has thrown me. I'm trying to warn you that the mind is very complex. Not everyone is capable of change. Some people are just monsters."

"Like me?"

He leaned in, ran his thumb over her lower lip, stirring the butterflies in her stomach. "That's not what I meant at all, and you know it," he said softly. "You would be wise to listen. I'm not the most dangerous thing out there." He pulled back and pointed to the window as if evil would manifest itself.

She jerked her head from his touch. "Could have fooled me." She glanced at the clock and stood. "Your time is up. Since your client is no longer in jail, I expect to see him in my office soon."

"I suspect you've done enough damage. There's no way I'm going to allow you further access to my client." Garrett was out the door before she had time to think of a pithy response.

****

Long after Garrett left, Nikki considered his words. What had he meant he wasn't the most dangerous thing out there? She got the distinct impression he was saying monsters were born rather than created. But that would mean some people couldn't be redeemed. Everyone deserved a second chance as far as she was concerned. She picked up the phone and dialed the newest number in her cell. It rang only once.

"How'd you sleep last night?" her grandfather asked.

"Fine. I did as you asked."

"Who'd you start with?"

"The father." She waited like a child hoping to bask in the approval of a parent.

"Interesting choice. How'd it go?"

She sighed. "It's hard to say. That's not the crazy part. Guess who met me there."

"Who?"

"Garrett Nightshade. He was in my mind but I was able to lock all access before he could do any damage." She left out the rest. Some things weren't anybody's business but her own.

"Good for you." His raspy voice turned cold. "What did he say?"

She hesitated unsure how much to reveal. If Garrett was telling the truth, Songe couldn't be trusted. Both men had reason to manipulate her. She was the lucky one stuck in the middle. "Not much at that time. But he came to my office and once again informed me he was an Enforcer. He warned me to back off."

"You need to be wary of him. If he is an Enforcer, he has more than one way to get to you."

"What can I do?"

"Just be on guard when you go casting. If he can get into *your* mind, he can get into any. The Nightshades are very strong and they have the ear of the Guild."

"What, exactly, can the Guild do to me?" She had been raised apart from an entity that now seemed to have her life in a vice. There was no justifiable reason a group she knew nothing about should have such a huge impact on her choices. But from the moment she received the necklace the walls had closed in with no sign of relenting.

"For one, they can stunt your abilities. We can't have that now that we are so close to our goal."

Alarm shot through her. She had just been introduced to her talents and now there was an agenda? One that she was being brought into piecemeal. If Songe let her in on the whole plan, would it stop her from doing as he wished? A shiver shimmied down her spine. Maybe Garrett had good reason to fear her. She was casting without all the facts. It just felt so good to assist floundering parents. All she wanted was to create healthy families. Had she been wrong to try? She didn't want to be part of a larger plan she knew nothing about. "What goal is that?"

"Bringing your father back."

What? "How the hell am I supposed to do that?" Seriously, her grandfather had forgotten she was a mere novice and knew next to nothing.

"Just keep doing what you are doing, Nikki. All of these events are intertwined. Once we find out which Guild member set the fire, we'll settle things. It's important to get to the information before Nightshade."

A chill of regret engulfed her. Maybe she shouldn't have been so candid with Garrett. What if she'd delivered information right into the enemy's hands "What makes you think they're looking?"

"Now that our family is back on the grid, they'll be looking. I can promise you that," he said harshly.

She drew her brows together and sighed. God, her life had become complicated. Last night she had started a chain of events that would end in disappointment for someone or worse. But she couldn't back track now. There was no alternative but to move forward. "What do you need me to do?"

"You have access to Garrett, and therefore Guild business. Be on the lookout for things that appear off kilter. For now, see what you can do for the Hanovers. You need to practice your skills before you go back that far."

"How far?"

"Farther than any caster has gone in a long time. Back to where it all began."

She hung up the phone. Everyone was speaking in riddles. If she read her grandfather accurately, he wanted her to reach back in time and change events that happened when she was a child. How the hell was she supposed to do that?

Chapter Sixteen

For someone who had been hiding for sixteen
years, Mr. Songe was a little too easy to find. The
minute Garrett left Nikki's office, Mark called with the
address. William Songe seemed to be thumbing his
nose at him. Garrett quelled the uneasiness brewing in
his gut. Just what was Songe up to? The series of
coincidences were stacking up at an alarming rate.
Nikki's assignment to the Hanover case just as her
powers surfaced had *fix* written all over it. That meant
there had to be a connection between the Hanover
family and Songe. There could be no other explanation.
He would explore this connection when he spoke with
Parker this afternoon. But first up was a visit to Songe.

Garrett pulled up in front of a two story, white
brick house with iron fenced wraparound porches on
both floors. Songe hadn't suffered much during his
exile. The house gleamed with mockery. The well-
manicured lawn and exquisite landscaping was lush—
every plant and bush expertly placed along deep green
healthy grass. The man who lived here didn't care about
watering bans or droughts. He was rich enough to pay
the fines, and arrogant enough to flaunt his financial
status. When you had power to influence people, money
wasn't hard to come by. It didn't matter what Songe
said he did for a living, the man could weasel his way
into any business from a purloined pen or business card.

Songe isn't much different from me. Acid roiled in the back of Garrett's throat. It had been a long time since he helped someone in any significant way. As misguided as she was, Nikki was at least trying to make things better, and he was the man hired to bring her down.

He rapped on the door, not expecting Songe to answer, but the door swung wide. The thin man with thick white hair and glasses delivered an unnerving grin. His eyes gleamed. Had he been expecting him? "How nice to see you so soon, Mr. Nightshade."

"I'm sure it is," Garrett retorted. Nikki must have tipped him off. "If you have a moment, I have a few questions."

"I always have time for my granddaughter's friends." His emphasis on 'friends' made it sound like a distasteful word. Nevertheless, Songe stepped back, allowing him to step inside.

The interior surfaces gleamed deep, rich, golden brown without a speck of dust despite a faint musty tinge tainting the air. The long plush carpet runner absorbed the impact of their footsteps so that no sound intruded during their solemn walk down the hall. Songe turned right into a large living area. A stark green Victorian couch stretched across the backside of the room facing a vast stone fire place. A large mahogany coffee table occupied the space between the couch and a wing back chair. Songe dropped into the chair and motioned for Garrett to take the couch. "What can I do for you?"

"I need to talk to you about Nikki."

His grin broadened. "Exquisite, isn't she?" Songe settled into his chair with a self-satisfied tinge as if he was contemplating a rare work of art.

Garrett's lips twisted. Nikki was nothing but a mere tool to Songe. Sure, she was a bleeding heart who wanted to rescue the world, but it was also charming the way her hair dropped in her face like she was a shy teenager rather than a competent attorney. Songe didn't appreciate her real value. He saw her as a means to an end. Garrett crossed his arms and glowered at his adversary. There was no way he was going to let Songe use Nikki. "You think you have created the Shadow Dancer."

A deep chuckle. "I *have* created her. Everything I have done was to bring her to this moment."

Songe's arrogance festered in Garrett's gut. An air of madness clung to the man like a shroud. "What moment might that be?"

"You'll find out soon enough, Mr. Nightshade." He offered him a toothy grin, picking crumbs from his pants. "I'm not quite ready to expose my plans just yet."

"I don't think you have a choice." Garrett kept his voice even. No matter how much this man goaded him, he refused to play that game. "You do know that I'm an Enforcer. It is my duty to look into these matters."

"Ah, yes. My plans would annoy your precious Guild. Not that it matters much. They won't succeed in stopping me. Nikki is strong. You won't be able to touch her."

"We'll see about that."

"Yes, we will." Songe leaned forward, elbows on his knees, smile never wavering. "The Guild is such a pious organization—so filled with their own virtue— they don't even know when to stay out of matters not their concern."

"This is a concern of the Guild."

"You think so, young man?" Songe leaned back, rubbing his fingers across his lips. "What would the hired help really know about Guild matters?"

Garrett bristled. Songe was clearly trying to egg him on, determined to send him in the wrong direction. Getting under his skin was apparently some family trait. If Garrett was to gain the upper hand, he had to skirt Songe's diversion and narrow his focus.

"Maybe." Garrett surveyed the opulent room with contempt. He trailed a finger over the stiff back of the couch. Stiff and immobile like Songe. There must be a way to get through to the man. "But you have allowed a Shadow Dancer to survive, and that is against the dictates."

His expression went grim. "She is my granddaughter, and no one will tell me how to deal with my family. Making her an isolate was out of the question. You have no idea what that will do to a person."

"And you do?"

"Oh yes." His eyes grew harsh. "I wasn't always an outcast. When Nikki was born, I pleaded with the Guild to allow her develop naturally. They forbade it of course. I was left to train her myself."

Garrett stood and crossed to the far wall taking in the oil paintings depicting scenes from more pastoral days. An old rickety farm house, golden fields of grain and fine English gardens. The room reeked of archaic traditions. The exact type, Songe mocked. No pictures of family lined the walls or the hearth. Just trinkets and nothing more.

Nikki was born exceptional. And the Guild knew. His mother had left out that choice detail. A potential Shadow Dancer had lived, yet they locked the information away insisting such a person couldn't exist. Garrett shuddered to think how many other secrets lay hidden within the Guild's sacred walls. "The Guild knew about Nikki?"

"Indeed they did, and then tried to destroy her. First, by attempting to curb her abilities. Thankfully, I was able to protect her from that. When they couldn't make her an isolate, they tried to kill her."

"*What*?"

"That shocks you?" Songe's eyes narrowed with a wicked gleam, his smile widening. "People will try to control what they fear, and when they can't—they kill them." He shrugged. "The Guild never understood we could be so much more."

Garrett wondered if Songe weren't a little nuts. Even if he didn't care to admit it, the years of exile had to have taken their toll. The loss of association with other casters was hard on all of them. They needed one another to survive. Songe's maniacal speech was evidence of what the Guild had done by sending him away. "The Guild doesn't kill. If they did you would be dead."

"You think so?" Songe stretched out his legs with a casualness that belied the seriousness of this situation and winked. "You underestimate my talents."

"Even you can't manage to evade the will of the entire council."

"I already have." He cocked his head to one side. "It took a lot more effort than I'd have liked but I was successful in hiding from the council for twenty-four years. You know about me now because *I* allowed it."

"Why?"

Songe bared his teeth his voice seething with venom. "Because when I bring down the Guild I want them to know exactly who did it."

"What would that accomplish?"

"I'd get my family back." Songe spit out the words with the certainty of a preacher's faith in a higher power. But surely Songe knew what he wanted was impossible to obtain. Didn't he or had insanity taken a firm hold?

"You can't change the progression of events." Garrett spoke in the soft tone one used to ease a troubled mind.

"True enough," Songe said. "But Nikki can. And she will."

****

"Come in, Mr. Nightshade." Lars Hanover opened the door to his house and led Garrett straight into a living area with a couch, love seat, and chair with a matching ottoman. Mrs. Hanover already occupied the large overstuffed chair. She switched off the TV, rested the remote on the arm, and waited for both men to have a seat.

Parker waltzed into the room. The lines on his face had eased since the last time he'd seen him. He walked with a bit more swagger. He still wasn't much to look at but the Hanover family resemblance was more apparent in the set of his nose and jaw.

Garrett took a place across from Carolyn Hanover. Parker leaned against the wall smirking and picking at his nails. For some odd reason, Garrett's agitation increased in Parker's presence. It didn't help he was already burning from his meeting with Nikki's grandfather. The bastard was bat shit crazy and he was going to drag Nikki down with him. But what puzzled Garrett most was the Guild had knowledge of a potential Shadow Dancer. His mother had conveniently left out that little detail. Maybe she truly thought Nikki had perished in the fire. But Garrett suspected a far more insidious reason. Could the Guild have been involved in Nikki's biological family's destruction? When Mark came back with the answers, he would be able gauge that for himself.

Garrett turned his attention to Parker.

"Took you long enough to get back with me." Parker dropped into his chair with a loud thump. "If you had waited any longer, my wife and I would have reconciled." Nothing in his tone indicated he was joking or being sarcastic. No eye tic or twitch of his lips. His expression remained placid, completely void of emotion. Had Nikki's intervention caused Parker's lack of concern?

"Now, Parker, that's no way to talk to your attorney. Show some respect." Although her words were meant to be a reprimand, her voice held no conviction. She didn't meet Parker's or Garrett's gaze. Both Lars and his wife stared at anything but the people in the room. Garrett knew things had not gone well the last time he'd met with the Hanovers, but they seemed more uneasy than someone who had just lost one round in court. Something else was going on and that something had to do with their son and his bizarre statements.

"There's no point in engaging in wishful thinking, Mr. Hanover." Garrett placed a legal pad on the table and picked up his pen. "I'd like to start preparing your divorce case."

Parker sniffed. "Not necessary."

"Pardon?" Garrett leaned forward from the edge of the couch clasping his hands in front of him. His palms grew sweaty. He wasn't certain what it was about this meeting that made him nervous. Every breath he took was harder than the next.

"You heard me." Parker's eyes measured him steadily. Was he considering dismissing Garrett as his attorney? For a fleeting moment, Garrett considered pushing the point. Just a little nudge and he could be free of this loser. His jaw tightened. It was better to see this thing through especially since there were aspects to the case that extended beyond his client.

"Mr. Nightshade, can we turn this situation around?" Carolyn Hanover's milky blue eyes poured sincerity as if she was asking how her son fared at camp. But hidden beneath the layers of her wrinkled skin lurked panic.

"I can't help him unless he cooperates," Garrett said mildly. He'd often met with Parker's kind of arrogance from a client who wasn't paying the bill. The last ditch effort of those who couldn't manage their own affairs to maintain some semblance of control. Not that his bristling made any difference. He didn't stand a chance of ever having more than supervised visitation if his attitude didn't improve.

"See," Parker leaned in conspiratorially. "I really don't need your help anymore. It's all been handled."

"Parker…" Anything else Carolyn Hanover might have said was stilled by Parker's acid glare. She closed her mouth and looked to Lars for help. But Lars wasn't paying attention. He was still staring off into space in his own separate world.

Garrett dropped his pen onto his legal pad eyes never wavering from his client. "Usually my clients don't come to terms with losing custody, their home, and having limited visitation this soon. What's your secret?"

Parker drummed his hands on the chair arm and fixed him with a saucy stare. Confidence oozed from him. It wasn't just false bravado, or even stupidity, there was substance behind his air of certainty.

"I don't have one. I'm reconciling with Amy soon." Parker traced a nonexistent design on the chair's faded material with his index finger.

"And how do you plan to manage that?"

A slow satisfied smile crept across his face. "It's already done."

"What're you playing at, Parker?" Garrett squeezed his pen so hard its cheap plastic flexed with the tension. He didn't know why he was letting this 'I've got my life under control' wannabe irritate him so much. Maybe it was the way Parker so easily said the words. Like they were fact. He was so sure of himself that Garrett almost believed him. That set him on edge.

Parker's expression melted into amusement. "You have no idea what I am do you?"

"Yeah, I do. You're the schmuck who gave his daughter a black eye. Now you have to be babysat just to see her."

Parker shook his head slowly from side to side. "Lori's eye was an accident. Besides, that's about to change."

"Fine." Garrett pushed himself from the table with

such force the table trembled. "I don't have time for your games. Since you have nothing more to offer, I'll come back another time."

Parker rose his unruffled grin never wavered. "I don't think that'll be necessary."

"Right." This guy was seriously out of touch with reality. A trait that had probably landed him in this situation in the first place. Providing zealous representation for Parker would not be easy.

"It's true." His velvet soft voice wound through Garrett, setting each nerve ending on edge. Nails across a chalkboard couldn't have been worse. Garrett winced. "So I don't have use for you after all."

Garrett allowed a slow smile. This spoiled weasel was about to be out of macho posturing. After attacking the ability of your attorney, there was really nowhere else to go. He folded his hands on top of the table. The jewels on his ring glinted under the light. "You about done?"

Parker's eyes traveled to the ring and then back to meet Garrett's gaze. Although the arrogance had not completely left Parker's face, he appeared more contrite. "I should have had one of those." Parker swept his hand around the room and laughed. "But I wasn't allowed to grow up in the usual way."

Despite the macabre tongue and cheek shtick Parker was laying on him, Garrett had no doubt that Parker blamed his parents and anyone else in the way of his finger for his situation. "I'm aware. But that doesn't explain leaving bruises on your daughter."

"What do you know about it?" Parker pushed off the chair and paced waving his arms emphatically. "They took everything. Everything. They should have listened to him."

"Now, Parker…" Carolyn Hanover began more edge to her voice than before. Garrett waved off her intrusion with his hand.

"What are you talking about?"

"The man who came to help."

"Parker, you can't…" Lars Hanover had finally decided to pay attention but Garrett wasn't about to allow him to silence his son. Not when Garrett was finally getting somewhere.

"Will you two quit interrupting?" He glared at Parker's parents. They flinched. Satisfied there would be no more intrusions, Garrett turned back to Parker. "A Guild member?"

"Yeah. He told them I was very powerful and would like to train me. But they wouldn't let him."

"Was his name Songe?" A tinge of dread pricked the back of his neck.

"That was the name."

Parker never stopped moving batting at the air as if an unseen force blocked his progress. Given the level his agitation had risen at the mention of his non-caster status, Garrett wondered if what his parents had done might be the crux of the problem. Even if he couldn't use the rationale, Parker had been excommunicated. Denied his birthright. He stood without a people. He was alone. Even worse, his wife and his daughter didn't share in his situation. Lesser emotions than envy compelled people to act violently. Garrett sighed. It wasn't enough. "I'm sorry you were neutralized but I need you to focus on the present. Maybe it shouldn't have happened but it did. You can't rewrite history."

Parker clasped his hands together cocking his head

in Garrett's direction. "That's where you're wrong." Parker snorted. The amused superior glint was back. "She already has."

Garrett straightened his tie and readjusted his seat. "Who has?"

Parker sat down in his seat a sly grin spread across his features. He drummed his fingers on the mahogany coffee table watching Garrett observe him. Parker was again in control of his feelings. A man who had all the answers addressing someone no more significant than an ant. "You haven't figured it out?"

"No." Garrett frowned as an uneasy feeling crept upon him. Parker said nothing. He was waiting him out. A technique Garrett had often used in deposition to get the deponent to divulge more than he should. He loosened his tie surprised at how effective this strategy was. Comprehension dawned. When he spoke it was in a whisper. "Nikki."

"That's right, you have no idea how useful she has been to me."

Garrett rubbed his forehead taking in the offered information. Just what exactly was he talking about? The only thing Nikki had done was keep Parker out of jail. A boon to his client, to be sure. But not enough to inspire this kind of gloating. Garrett was sure Nikki hadn't crossed that far over the line. Not what Parker desired above all, anyway. Unlocking a sanitized mind was next to impossible. Re-establishing Parker's power would require traveling back to when his mind had been stripped. No caster had that ability. The mocking words of Songe returned. *Nikki can.* Garrett was beginning to believe it.

"She didn't change that much." No matter what

Parker thought Nikki had accomplished, he was still facing divorce and child abuse charges. Parker just quirked a brow and stalked off.

"Well, I guess that's it." Garrett made a motion that ended up a half shrug. Carolyn Hanover flinched so slightly, he would've missed it had he not been looking. Determined to keep this interview calm until he could ferret out the information he truly sought, he decided to contain his focus on the child abuse charge. "I'm attempting to find a good defense tactic. Since Parker wasn't unable to give me any insight into his demise, is there any explanation you can give me?"

"No." Lars ground out. "He blames us but he's a bad seed if there ever was one."

Garrett turned to Lars. Apparently the man could find his voice outside of his son's presence. "He blames you because you made him an isolate."

"He never could handle consequences. Always was a pampered child." Carolyn Hanover wrung her hands not quite meeting Garrett's gaze. "That is our fault, but we had no choice. We had to make him an isolate."

"Yeah, that boy never conformed to the teachings of the Guild." Lars looked at the floor, shoulders slumped. "He was always breaking the rules, messing with his classmates' heads."

"Now, Lars, he didn't do anything other kids hadn't tried." Carolyn scolded her husband. Yet her hands never stopped moving. She didn't meet her husband's eyes either. "But," she turned to Garrett, tears collecting on her lashes. "We had to isolate him. He wouldn't conform."

"That's why we said we isolated him," Lars said. "No need to get into that, though."

Garrett's skin tingled with promise. More half-truths were forthcoming. It seemed everyone, including his mother, held back something crucial. What happened to the Guild's motto, 'revelation with truth and light.'? No one seemed to be following those words. Instead, his people had turned into sniveling sewage rats, skulking around, hiding important details. Behaving ashamed of who they were or, more aptly, who they had become.

"Yes, Lars, it's time." Carolyn fixed her husband with a stare that never wavered despite his intense glare. "He's our attorney. He needs to know."

Lars fidgeted, focusing his attention back to the floor. "Fine."

Garrett looked to Carolyn for the answers. "Why did you strip him if his abilities?"

"Because left alone, he would have destroyed us all."

"No need to be so dramatic." Lars held up his hands to stop her diatribe. "The truth is, we don't know if he would have hurt any of us." He looked up at Garrett. "He manifested an ability that concerned his mother and me."

"What ability?" Garrett wasn't sure what these people were driving at. Besides the Shadow Dancer, there couldn't be another legend of an ability larger than the one they all shared as a culture.

"He could push," Carolyn said.

"Push?"

"Yeah. Push. You know, when someone influences another with a push of his mind."

"How is that different from the rest of us?" Isn't that what they all did? Get into people's minds and influence their choices and decisions. They'd all done that at one time or another.

"Because," Mrs. Hanover said. "He could do it while he was awake."

****

Outside her grandfather's residence, Nikki rang the doorbell twice. She leaned against the pillar waiting impatiently. Too much had happened since learning she was the Shadow Dancer. Not that she truly knew what that meant. She hoped she was doing everything she possibly could to help the Hanover's. After her review of the case file, she wasn't certain she was making any difference at all. The divorce was back on file. An emergency order gave Parker supervised visitation because Lori had a black eye. At a loss of how to help this family, there was only one person to which she could turn. Her grandfather finally opened the door after the third ring.

"Hello, Nikki." He smiled his 'trust me' smile. "This seems to be my day for visitors."

"I have a question for you."

"Just one?" The amusement in his voice permeated the atmosphere, lightening her dark mood.

"How far back can I go to influence a person's choices and decisions?"

"You get right to the point, don't you?" He chuckled, throwing the door wide open. "You better come inside."

She followed him down a long corridor, dogging his heals like a blue healer. "I don't see the sense in wasting time."

"A good quality to have." After a deep breath, he situated himself in a lazy chair. "The short answer is,

I'm not sure."

"What's the long answer?" Nikki watched several emotions cross his face, ranging from skepticism to elation.

"It has been theorized for decades that our kind can do more than a simple tweaking of outcomes within our subject's mind." He placed his hands on the armrests and leaned back with a smug glint in his eyes. "But it has long since been abandoned as practical."

"Why?"

"Because, the Guild is afraid the consequences of having a person who can reach back into someone's mind and change events of the past."

He paused never taking his gaze from her.

Silence invaded the room, descending like an oppressive cloud. It dawned on her that grandfather thought he might be looking at that kind of person. Someone who was feared because of her abilities. What did it matter if she could solve her current problem? If she could change events of the past, then she could make the Hanovers behave differently and Lori wouldn't have to endure a flaky mom and an abusive dad. And if she could go back far enough, she could make both parents healthy. Allow Lori to grow up as all children deserved. "Well, what if the results of the change were a good thing?"

"I'm not sure they care."

Her brain flitted in a million different directions. "If it were possible, how would one go about accomplishing it?"

"I'm not going to say this is possible." Songe shook a paternal warning finger at her but didn't disguise the triumphant gleam in his eyes. His expression radiated the arrogant satisfaction of an adolescent who had just discovered his science project had won the Nobel Prize. He blurted out the next words. "But it would require going deeper into the mind than anyone has gone before. Such a person would have to be able, not only to access childhood memories, but change what the participants remember."

"Has anyone ever tried to do this?"

"No. No one to my knowledge has ever been able to accomplish that task." Disappointment shadowed his face. "We can view past events to garner understanding of a participant's development, but no one has been actually able to adjust their memory for a different outcome outside a forty-eight hour window."

Nikki was disheartened with these words. If she couldn't change what a person perceived how she could change their outlook on the world? She needed to be able to access and change those memories in order to alter events.

Wait. Hadn't she made Parker change his decision about beating his wife? Her shoulders slumped. But it didn't seem to make any difference. A divorce was still pending and Lori had been injured. Maybe she imagined the effect she had on Parker's mind. "I'm not sure but I think I might have already done that."

Songe leaned forward. "What do you mean?"

"Last night. I went into Parker's mind. To when he decided to beat his wife."

Songe narrowed his eyes. "And did it make a difference?"

"Not really. They're still getting a divorce and Parker hit his daughter."

Songe stroked his chin. She waited, surprised her

247

little foray interested him so much. She assumed all casters could do what she had. The possibility they couldn't filled her with tingles of excitement. If he took her activities this seriously, maybe she could make a difference.

"It appears you may not have gone far enough in time. We have to think of a better test."

"Like what?"

"Go back in, change a critical childhood event. We'll see the results the next day."

****

That night, Nikki prepared for bed, clutching Parker's teddy bear. Her senses tingled at the thought of seeing Garrett again. She gritted her teeth in a vain attempt to dampen the anticipation. Her heart and mind were divided. She pushed away the notion of resolving it for now, willing sleep. She scanned her mind checking the doors to her private psyche, making sure they remained locked to any intruders. A small assessment assured her. She could vacate it and go to work.

She relaxed and slipped through the constraints of her earthly body. Instinct thrust her into the slipstream, straight into Parker's psyche.

The moment she stood on the precipice of his mind, the more uncertain she was that she had entered the right one. The terrain spanning before her was not the one she had seen the night before. Although the doors were still disorganized, they were misshapen and bent. Some rippled and phased almost transparent. Barely there. Others leaned in a distorted back bend until they almost touched the ground. Some twisted, overlapping with others braided, interweaving into each other.

A slight tremor shifted the ground beneath her feet, the pounding insistent until the doors rattled and shook. An edge on one of the woven doors snapped off with a loud crack. Soon all the doors vibrated, their forms contorting until they splintered into a thousand pieces. The remains bounced and skittered across the surface, growing smaller until they dwindled into nothing.

Then darkness. Nikki crawled through the eerie black fog. Every nerve ending tingled on edge. It felt as though something slimy had crawled up her back and wouldn't leave. She shuddered as a gooey shroud took hold. She pulled her hair over her shoulder but her vision didn't improve.

This has to be dream. Parker's mind didn't look this way last night. What had changed? There was no place on earth as muggy and desecrated as this wasteland. Then, again, there was the problem of how his mind had changed in the first place. What was a gray blank slate yesterday was dank, dark, and blanketed with fury, hatred.

Nikki straightened her back and ignored the slippery eel like thing squirming along her torso. She squinted. A brown spark flashed in the distance. A small narrow opening in the fluttering ebony veil. A minute tear caught in the wind. She headed toward it. Pushing back the veil she spotted a golden light pulsating in the distance. It glittered with a million fingers flaring in all directions. Taunting her need to step through, she crossed over the threshold of yesterday. It wasn't much of an improvement. Murky clouds surrounded narrow brown crystalline threads that pulsed with intermittent light. She inched around them heading further into the web.

"Where are you going?"

A whisper wrapped around her heart, soft, kind and gentle.

Nikki looked up. She could see nothing but darkness behind her.

"To the light," she said to the air.

"You can't go there."

"I have to. There is no other way out." Nikki felt a tug within her. A warning. A gentle nudge compelling her to pay attention to the voice. But her feet kept moving toward the opening. She *had* to get there. She *had* to cross over. An internal compass guided her. She had no choice but to follow.

"Go back," the whisper persisted.

Nikki looked around her but saw only the formless empty void. There was no sign of any other presence, yet she knew he was there, stalking every footstep, monitoring every breath. "Okay that's enough. Show yourself."

Why was this intrusive voice interfering with her affairs? For that matter, why did she care so much? It wasn't like it mattered in the grand scheme of things. But it did. That was the problem. It mattered a lot. Ever since she entered this strange realm, a need gnawed at her to stop a monster.

Ahead of her another figure appeared dressed in a crisp white shirt and jeans his features concealed in shadows. The head turned in her direction. "You shouldn't go walking around in a mind this dangerous, Nikki."

Nikki froze. "Garrett?"

She frowned as she neared the form in front of her.

His voice sounded familiar but it was garbled and distant. The lack of clarity made it hard to pinpoint but there weren't that many people she had met in this strange new world. Her heart pounded in her ears the same time her expectations fell. He was here to stop her.

She rushed the intruding form. In a flash, she stood before him. She swiped out her hand and a spark of light illuminated his face. Shocked brown eyes stared back under strong bushy eyebrows and immaculately groomed hair. Garret's mouth appeared twisted in pain. It was almost comical.

"What are you doing here, fancy pants?"

"Protecting my client. You shouldn't be here."

"Whatever, Garrett." She threw her hands in the air and stalked away, stilling her racing heart. "This isn't the type of situation covered by our legal ethics. I don't know why you should have anything to say about it."

"You don't know what you are doing. Look at what one trip into Parker's mind has done. You've caused this destruction. You need to stop now. Let me fix this."

The edge in his voice stopped her. She had disappointed him, but much worse was the flood of shame rising to her cheeks. His fingers curled around the light extinguishing it, hiding his expression.

"How are you going to do that? Sanitize his mind like his parent's did. Admit it, you don't know what's going on any more than I do. At least I'm trying to make things better." Knowing she provoked his anger didn't stop the torrent of words. She was sick of his meddling superiority. A surge of power from the dark places in her mind took hold urging her onward. It was imperative she erase his presence so she could quell the sense of humiliation threatening her from the edge of reason. Pulling assurance from every instinct she shooed him with her hand. "If you aren't going to help you need to step out of my way."

Garrett vanished. *That was easy.* Still she couldn't shake the strange feeling something important had happened. The rush of power coursing through her body made her dizzy. She was sure no other caster could erase another from a mind. It was one of those pesky rules of the Guild's checks and balances. Rules that didn't apply to her.

Charged with the fuel of righteous power, she almost didn't notice as a foreign thought invaded her mind. It was full of arrogance, vengeance, and venom. It slithered through her brain leaving ice trails in its path.

Kill the Bitch. It screamed.

Full of new found purpose Nikki sought out the source of the thought. The need to squelch the slimy little toad that owned the thought overwhelmed her. She pushed her way through multifaceted interlocking sticks. Each intermittent spark of energy sent a twinge through her as she neared the well of consciousness. She stepped into a circle of pulsating awareness. She found the source of the thoughts.

Parker Hanover.

His mind was getting stranger and darker. She caught each thought as it slinked through the air. *Kill the Bitch. Punish her. How dare she do this to me? She isn't worthy. Trample her to the ground. Take her child.* There was no agony only retribution and hostility.

Nikki waved her hand over the source of the

outpouring. *Stumble*, she thought.

"Stop this!"

She looked over her shoulder. *Garrett*. No longer calm. No longer speaking in soft whispers of desperation. Brown eyes glittered fury at her in their brilliance. She glared back.

She faced him drawing up to her full height. Even at her highest elevation she only met his chin. She tilted her head further to meet his eyes. "This isn't your place…"

"This isn't your place either. You're dabbling with things you don't understand."

"What are you talking about?"

"I told you I couldn't allow you to ignore the dictates of the Guild."

"And I told you before, I am not a member of the Guild." She took off for the pulsating light in the distance prepared to escape behind it. Garrett stayed on her tail. His breath touched her neck even in the shadow realm. His feet thundered after her. She reached the light and shot through it.

"Nikki, you have to stop. You don't know what you're doing."

Was that terror in his voice? Maybe she was making better progress than she thought. *Parker, take me to where it began.* Instinct propelled her on. The ground beneath her feet quaked and hurtled her forward. Then she was flying toward a door she hadn't seen before. Garrett still trailed her, but she was creating a gap between them. She landed in front of the door. She stood and placed a hand on the knob.

Garrett had caught up. He tried to grab her.

"Don't follow me through this door," she snapped.

"What door?" His eyes froze wide.

"This one." She opened it and stepped through.

Chapter Seventeen

Garrett walked around the area Nikki had vacated. It pulsated with dispersed energy, but no solid object occupied the space. A subtle silver haze shimmered around an oval void. The faint odor of sulfur permeated the air. But there was no door. An uneasy edge cut along his insides. A snap of electrical energy lingered. Where was the mental conduit? He waved his arms through the emptiness but the only thing his limbs met was thin air. No sign of an opening. No portal. No Nikki.

She evaporated, leaving no residual trail to follow. He clenched his fingers into fists, his hearing muted by the thunder of pounding blood. He shook in frustration. "Where are you, damn it?"

But he already knew. The pieces of the puzzle assembled into an abrupt moment of clarity. She was still here, deeper inside the timeline of Parker's psyche. Right where she shouldn't be. Where she *couldn't* be.

Somehow she found a way to crash the time barrier. A trickle of fear pricked the back of his neck. *That* was crazy. No one could do that. He sucked in a deep breath. Garrett could no longer ignore the evidence. Nikki had done the impossible. She'd bridged the gap between the present past and the far distant past. The hair stood on the nape of his neck. Cold uncertainty snaked deep in his gullet.

A caster that could jump through endless threads of time could alter more than small changes within the individual mind. With the right tweaks and modifications their actions could be devastating. Whole families wiped out. A tyrant revived wielding destruction. Historical events from the last hundred years changed.

Impossible, he reasoned. No one had that much power. But hadn't he been warned? Was Nikki capable of such horror? He'd refused to see her for what she truly was—an unindoctrinated caster with the power to destroy them all.

Dear God. He clenched his jaw. He had to stop her before it was too late. Before another Enforcer was sent after her to wipe her mind or even worse kill her. If he couldn't trace her in Parker's mind, perhaps he could reach her through hers. He clutched Nikki's card so tightly it crumpled. With a quick jerk, he swept the card and crossed into her mind.

Twelve doors were still there. He grabbed the knob of the closest. Locked. Just to make sure no one was in residence, he went from door to door, rattling each one loudly. Waiting for her to appear. Demanding she stop. Only silence greeted his efforts.

Nikki was either too far away to notice or she was past caring. Why should she? He couldn't gain access to her mind. Couldn't *change* anything. He sank to the floor. Every door mocking his unsuccessful efforts.

"Nikki, you don't know what you're doing. You have to stop, darling," he said so softly, the words were barely audible. Nikki was what the Guild feared. They wanted her taken care of.

And he was the one elected to destroy her. It

couldn't end that way. Nikki was a good person. A little misguided by her bleeding heart and way too powerful. But her intentions were pure. That had to count for something. If Parker was any indication, eradicating a mind sent a person into a dark place. No one to trust. No one to count on for support.

Nikki deserved better than that. There had to be a way to reach her. If he couldn't invite her presence here, he'd locate her in Parker's mind. Dogging her wherever she went. And if she knocked him out. He'd go right back in. Because he had to stop her before it was too late.

****

Nikki waded through the thick dark muck of Parker's mind. Green black globs of goo dripped from overhead, oozing into distorted webbing. The stench of garbage in the hot afternoon sun permeated the atmosphere.

She covered her nose with the edge of her shirt, but even that failed to prevent the odor of decay. Parker's parents hadn't cleansed his mind. They had prevented any healthy growth. The consequences seemed to have turned it into a twisted malformed destruction. Why would any parent do that to their child? It was barbaric.

Filled with a need to help the man, she fought her way through the sludge, searching for the critical memory. Sorrowful moans greeted her followed by sharp snaps. She swung her head in the direction of the tortured anguish. An image of a young boy around twelve years old enveloped her. He sat at the dining room table bent over homework covering his eyes with his hands, weeping into his sleeve. Parker's mother, then a stocky woman hovered over him, slapping a plastic ruler against the table top. Each time it whistled by, the boy's ear, he flinched.

"Concentrate!" she snapped.

"I'm trying," he wailed.

"Try harder." She slammed down the ruler again. This time it nicked his ear. He rubbed the edge and sniffled. "Pay attention." She raised the ruler again.

What you've had to endure, Parker. No wonder Lori didn't want to live with her grandparents. No child should be exposed to this kind of terror. Nikki's stomach flipped with sympathy. Her hand flew to her mouth and she blinked back tears. She rushed past the sight assaulted with another image. This one a few years earlier.

This time a tall, rail thin man chased Parker down the hallway, unbuckling his belt. "Come back here!" The man was too scrawny to be terrifying. Unless you were a seven-year-old boy. "What were you doing in my office, boy?"

The small figure flew down the hall not stopping until he reached a large oak chest. He slipped inside, peeking through a sliver of space. With each step the man took, large thumps clamored throughout the room.

Nikki didn't think it was possible that a man of such slight build could create so much noise. Yet the sound of his thundering feet, ricocheted inside her, leaving tremors of aftershock. She sucked in her breath. Her hand flew to her throat. She gasped for air. *It's not real—not any longer.* She forced her breathing to ease. The suffocating terror of a young Parker as he waited for his father to give up was mesmerizing. The scene unfolded in excruciating detail. The man approached the chest, stood with feet shoulder length apart. "Come out of there and face your consequences like a man."

The boy didn't move. Sweat dripped down Nikki's neck.

Parker's father reached down and opened the lid so slowly Nikki counted fifty heart beats. Parker's wide-eyed terror tore through her watching him look up at his father, sliding further into the corner.

I have to stop this. Nikki raced into the man, obliterating the scene into mists of smoke. The horrible image dissipated. She wiped away a stray tear.

She was only able to take one gulp of soothing air before a pulsating wave crashed into her feet, thrusting her further into Parker's mind. Memories coursed around her. They flashed by too quickly for her to comprehend their contents but this man had been through a horrifying childhood. She focused on one of the memories. It emerged into living color.

Parker at five. He lay beneath the covers of a twin bed shaped like a racing car. The bedspread sported automobiles of all shapes and sizes. This was not the bedroom of an underprivileged child. Nikki could discern no indication he wasn't loved. Yet he wept under his blankets, howling sobs engulfing the room. His mother sat beside him patting his leg so tenderly it was hard to believe she was the same woman wielding the ruler.

"I'm sorry we have to do this but you aren't following the rules."

Punished? With a time out or something equally mild. Yet an aura of significance clung to the atmosphere.

"I'll do better," he cried, desperation evident. What could this little boy have done to cause such anger?

Break a window? Steal a cookie? His blond hair curled over an unappealing cowlick. His mother smoothed the cowlick only for it to spring back up.

"You know that's not true, Parker. We have given you more than enough time to adjust to your training but you just won't behave. Please understand, darling. We don't do this lightly."

Good grief, not the 'this hurts me more than it hurts you' scenario. *Let me see what you did.* Any images Nikki could conjure were vague and opaque, like a dark fog covered Parker's misdeeds.

Show me what happened next. A mist fell over her, then cleared for a new setting. The playground. Parker stood within a circle of other boys laughing and pointing at him. "Loser!" They jeered. "You can't do anything right."

Silent tears ran down Parker's face. Nikki felt the impact of each child's words. Each one chafed and churned inside of Parker igniting a rage he was too young to understand or handle. It seared inside even as his tears fell. Through choked sobs he spit out venomous words. "Someday you'll be sorry."

"Yeah right," the others said.

Parker shifted his weight. His empty words had no effect. It no longer mattered what he said. He had no power now that his parents had annihilated his ability to dream cast. No means to turn their opinions to his favor. Amongst his people, he was the lowest form of being.

Why had Parker's parents taken such action against their son? He didn't seem any more dangerous than other children, yet his parents must have felt they'd chosen the best course. She looked about, searching for the last piece of the puzzle. Maybe, just maybe she could help this lost boy.

Easy, Nikki thought. *Easy*.

Parker stared right at her, no longer crying. Could he sense her presence inside his own trace memory? His eyes pleaded with her, sending shock waves of pity into her depths. "Help me."

The gaggle of kids laughed, a cacophony of squawking noises.

"Who you talking to?" One voice rose above the rest. "Your imaginary playmate?"

The rest of the children roared with laughter but Parker kept his attention on her. Red-rimmed eyes and the tracks of tears were the only indication that he had wept. He wiped his nose. The aura of depression fled and another emotion took its place. Hope? Arrogance? Nikki wasn't sure.

"Please?" His soft voice wrapped around her heart and squeezed.

She couldn't ignore his plea for help. But she didn't know how to erase the past. And Parker in the present was no picnic. She remembered the odor of dirt and moss filtered up her nose. The searing pain when the butt of Parker's rifle rammed against her head. As an adult, Parker was a monster. Could she change the course of Parker's life by altering events that had long since happened? It probably wasn't possible but if she could gain some insight into Parker's pain, she might be able to redirect his future for the better. "Show me what you did."

A spark of triumph appeared in Parker's eyes. The expression was enough to send a jolt of uncertainty up Nikki's spine. But it was too late to pause the momentum. The images changed once more and she was tossed back into his early childhood. He wandered in another child's head scattering the seeds of a suggestion.

Can you hear the sound of a waterfall? Parker laughed. *The water is so warm. Go swimming.*

Soon the child wet his bed. Parker tossed his head back and crowed. He laughed so hard, he fell to the ground. He couldn't stop giggling. Every time he thought he had it under control it rumbled back up to tickle his nose. He snorted as another wave consumed him.

An adult male entered. "Stop, Parker. This is forbidden."

He froze. His laughter stuck in his throat. His father stood five feet away with arms folded over his chest, mouth in a severe twist. The hard glint in his expression always meant trouble.

"It's just a joke, Dad."

"No, you are punishing him." His father closed the distance between them, put a hand on his shoulder, and squeezed. "How many times have you been warned not to cast without proper supervision?"

Even in his dream form, pain coursed through Parker. Tears pricked his eyes. "But he beat me up. He should be in trouble not me."

"His parents have taken care of him. He won't bother you anymore."

"That's not enough." Parker ripped his shoulder from his father's grasp. "He's not sorry and he should be."

His father shook his head soberly. "Parents guide their children. Not their classmates. Now get out while I discuss an appropriate punishment with your mother."

Parker's mouth set in an obstinate thin line. "I didn't do anything wrong."

"Don't make this harder. Leave." His father pointed into the darkness like a compass and he stared his son down.

"Dad." Parker took a step back.

"Go back, now. Your mother and I will deal with this tomorrow."

Parker and his father vanished.

What was that about? Convincing a child to wet the bed was as innocuous as dipping a sleeping friend's hand in warm water at a slumber party. Nikki and her pals had played around with that on numerous occasions just to see if it would work. How often had she snickered over the results? But there'd been no real harm. It was a silly childhood prank.

Parker seemed to have acted out of revenge, not silly foolishness. Even that didn't justify the level of intensity his father projected. There was a more insidious meaning behind the boy's actions. Something important was missing.

Left to her own devices with only the light-filled threads of Parker's mind to keep her occupied, Nikki dug deeper. She stumbled upon Parker's dream web. Maybe she could follow those memories to their true origin.

She trailed one strand. It twisted into a tangled mass, each strand interwoven into another with no indication of where one began and another ended. She ran her hand along the length of the ball surprised by the smooth texture. No ridges or gaps broke the continuity of any strand. She took hold of one and worked on unraveling it until it fell from the rest of the knots, floating freely.

She walked around the cord. It bobbed and weaved, reminding her of seaweed in the ocean. Electrical impulses zipped up and down the shaft but she couldn't tell what memory the strand held. No matter how hard she tried she couldn't see or hear or detect any memory trace. It was as if she had been transported outside of the area that assimilated Parker's experiences, placed directly into the cerebral cortex. Why weren't there any doors to pass through?

Nikki tore at the threads, pulling each one apart, examining them in turn. Where was the memory she had just left? If she could get to the beginning of the sequence of events she might understand why Parker had been stripped of his ability for what appeared to be a harmless prank. There was so much she didn't know about this new society she had entered. It was so frustrating. From all appearances, Parker's parents were a bit overbearing. If she'd been Parker's Guardian *Ad Litem*, she could have saved him earlier. Now was her chance to change things. Hopefully, it wasn't too late.

Just as Nikki was about to cave, an errant strand curled around her wrist. Suddenly she was propelled back into the school yard. Parker lay in a bloody mass on the hot asphalt. Even through his sobs, she sensed his lust for revenge. She could feel his detailed plan to punish his tormentor. *Now is not the time. Go back.* She whispered to the child wanting to play his prank. His head shot up and he looked around.

Help me. Make them stop.

Nikki was startled by the voice. The adult Parker was aware of her presence. She backed away, searching for the quickest exit, disconcerted her mind extraction had been discovered. She stopped short by the sudden realization that Parker asked for help. He *wanted* her help.

I don't know how.

The ground quaked propelling her forward into a dark churning abyss. Her body whipped back and forth through the tides of his mind. A flash of light, and she was thrown onto solid ground. She stood and brushed the dust from her pants, surveying her new surroundings. She had no idea where she'd landed, but based on the color and formation of the doors, she was no longer in Parker's mind.

She was in someone else's.

****

Garrett stood behind a black gauzy barrier waiting for Nikki's next move. Following her psychic footprints hadn't been easy but he'd finally found her. But something about the path was unsettling. Nikki didn't want him to locate her but someone did. And that didn't feel right.

He ground his teeth. How had Nikki found the way into Parker's mind so easily? She hadn't been anywhere near Parker's personal possessions. Just as the question formed, he saw the teddy bear in her arms, covered with patches of missing fur on the arms and legs. It was the same stuffed animal she retrieved from the man's house a couple days ago.

Obviously, he had misread the entire scene. He'd let her prance out of there with Parker's teddy bear without question. Too distracted by her attractive ass. Chalk one up for Nikki. He had to tighten up his game. Now she was grilling his client, gaining access to all sorts of confidential information. Then Parker's words permeated like a sharp slap to the face.

Help me. Make them stop.

****

The ground shuddered, and Garrett found himself propelled alongside Nikki down the monstrous consciousness of an abuser. He remained hidden from her sight but the atmosphere shifted immeasurably. It was brighter, clearer, although still gray and dingy. Had Nikki adjusted things yet again? But then he heard a new thought.

What will become of my boy now?

Lars Hanover. How had they gotten into his mind? The teddy bear didn't look old enough to belong to Lars before it belonged to Parker. Even if it was, his signature would be too weak after having given it to Lori. A tingling sensation raced from his toes to his head, matching the rapid beat of his heart. Rock hard dread settled in the pit of his stomach. Parker brought them here as a deliberate act.

He was no longer an isolate. *Oh, Nikki, what have you done?*

****

Nikki stood on the precipice of a significant event. Electrified tension sizzled the air. All she needed was the identity of the mind Parker had sent her into. *Show me.*

In an instant, she landed at a park. The soft gust of springtime warmed her skin. Clovers dotted the green grass. Parker and his father were in the middle of a baseball diamond tossing a ball back and forth. Peace and calm descended over her as she watched the two of them.

"I can throw this really far." A young Parker—age four?—flung the ball back into Lars's gloved hand.

"That's a strong pitch, son," Lars chuckled as he tossed the ball back. A proud Papa dreaming about Parker being a pitcher on a major league team. Or a coach for a prominent college. All options were open for Parker at this young age. Even if he never obtained these goals, Lars would be gratified. His son was excited about everything new, unafraid of anything. Pride surged through him.

The image blurred. Inky fingers spread across the happy memory, fracturing it into a patchwork of doubt and despair. Nikki plummeted into a chasm below, unable to bear the weight of the hopelessness. Fear the pair would never find their way back into the sun. As Parker grew older Lars' pride migrated to fear. His son was strong but too obstinate to get his way. Lars' vision for his prodigy's future crumbled into dust as Parker veered from his early teachings.

His studies within the Guild were failing. He challenged everything. So sure he knew best. So certain he was right. The scene changed again. Parker, being led out of school by Lars, his tight grip on Parker's shoulder.

"Owwwww, Dad. Let go of me." Parker struggled against the pain. His ten-year-old scrawny body no match for Lars' solid build.

"I've told you before, you can't do that to your classmates," Lars growled through clenched teeth.

"Awe, it was only a joke." Parker waved off the rebuff cocking his head with a half-smile.

"No, it wasn't." Lars yanked his son the rest of the way to the car. Parker had been messing with his classmates for over a week using an ability others didn't have. Try as he might to hide it, Parker continually stuck his foot deep into trouble, honing those forbidden skills. He couldn't help it. Lars had to stop it. Nikki read the desperation in the older man's face.

"They wouldn't leave me alone," he whined.

Lars looked about helplessly. Where had he gone wrong? Had Carolyn coddled him too much? No. The boy had been born defective. That's why he was picked on at school. Why he couldn't conform to Guild instruction.

Lars hadn't had those childhood problems. Carolyn either, as far as he knew. There was no reason Parker should. Unless he was flawed in his own right. Surely, they'd done their best for him.

Now he had to repair the snake pit nipping at his heels before the Guild sanctioned them for Parker's impurities. The dreams Lars had of Parker being a popular athlete spread three sheets to the wind.

Parker wasn't interested in any of that anyhow. All he wanted was to make other kids obey him. When he wasn't exploring mind control, he was off talking to himself. Parker was a weird kid. The kind of weird that kids zone in on and tease mercilessly. What had happened to his sweet boy?

Nikki observed the scene, taking in Lars' poisonous thoughts. Parker was a boy not a conniving monster. Lars' faulty reasoning needed modification. So Parker hadn't lived up to his father's plans for him, what of it? Lars either refused or wasn't capable of seeing his son as an individual with wants and needs of his own. Too disappointed to see Parker wasn't interested in sports. He failed to grasp what Parker truly craved. His parent's approval.

If Nikki could give him that, perhaps Parker wouldn't be so interested in controlling his peers. She could fix that.

Embrace who Parker is. Encourage him.

She began the intricate work of weaving a new beginning for father and son. *He doesn't need to be number one. Let him discover who he is on his own.*

Be proud of him. Don't be afraid.

Nikki continued to work, her fingers moving fast, interweaving new memories. Happier ones. *Now* Parker's future had a chance.

****

Garrett tensed in the shadows, watching Nikki work Lars' mind. What the hell was she doing? Glimmering silver threads of memory, she weaved and reworked, into a different pattern. Sparks flew while her hands sifted deftly through each one as intricately as a weaving loom. The complex design was far superior to any he had ever witnessed. What would've taken him a decade to decipher she did in a matter of seconds.

He attempted to peer into the design, pick out the memories she altered, but to no avail. What she was doing was incomprehensible. A chill settled into the pit of his stomach. He had never seen anyone pull the threads of memory past the last forty-eight hours of their lives. And yet her weaving went deeper into the most inner sanctum of Lars' consciousness. How many years he couldn't tell.

Her fingers braided the tendrils so fast, he had trouble following her progress. He should intervene, but how, when what she did went beyond his skills? Dread curled from his gut, taking a strangle hold on his throat. He massaged his neck. What she changed could not be undone. Not by him. Not by anyone.

He *had* to stop her. The consequences would be devastating not only to the human race, but especially his kind. If she continued in this vein, history would be rewritten. Her less than subtle activities would lead to the Guild's discovery. The consequences would land them, like the dark days of the past, where they would be used and manipulated by humans. Or worse, those who feared their power would hunt them down, destroy them. Reminiscent of the Salem witch hunts.

The Guild had very good reasons for restraining the powers of their members. Just because one could venture into the past to change events didn't mean one should. Nikki needed warning before it was too late. Her best intentions were harmful and ill-advised. Unfortunately, getting her to listen was a whole different ballgame. He wasn't sure how long he could stall the Guild, but time was running out.

****

Parker woke with a start. His heart hammered in his chest like it was in a horse race. But it felt good. As if he was in charge again. Able to get anything he wanted. He was twelve again bending the weaklings to his will. Enamoring the strong to agree with him. Big man on campus.

But that was when he was able to manipulate minds. Mold them to his liking. A thing he hadn't been able to do since his parents stripped him of his abilities. But something was different. A crackle. A charge. Inhaling deeply, he expanded his mind. It was more of a stretch because he no longer expected to reach out. He did so out of habit. Hoping sheer willpower would restore his abilities. All efforts thus far had been stripped, failed.

Until now.

A small release of barriers clanked as he gained access to places he hadn't been since childhood. Swallowing a shout of triumph, Parker pushed further. The footprints in his mind, soft and light, his movements swift and smooth. Paralyzed by this unexpected gift of freedom, he was unsure of his next move. If the walls that blocked his abilities had crumbled, he should be able to use…it was too much to hope. He brought his trembling hand to his lips. What he needed was someone to experiment on. A way to find out how much had been unlocked. Right now, his mind felt like a vacuum that held infinite possibilities. But could he bend minds to his will like before? He blew a gust of breath through his fingers. Had he finally been released from the hell that had become his life?

Dark giddiness engulfed him. To walk amongst the dreams of others. Not just walk—trod and stamp them out. Just as his parents had squashed his ambitions. They would pay for the agony he'd endured as an isolate.

All he had to do was sleep to test the waters. Damn, he didn't have any of his parent's personal items in his room. There was no need before. No matter, he would forage around downstairs for exactly the right item. Then he'd show them. He'd show them all.

****

Nikki rushed to work the next morning, expecting to see Garrett perched on her desk a mercenary gleam in his eyes. He wasn't there. She frowned at the empty space. It was almost disappointing. No one to spar with or justify her actions to. Really, she had to pull herself together. Despite the fluttering in her stomach every time he was near, she had to get used to the notion he wouldn't be in her life forever. Pain squeezed her heart. She ignored it. There were more important things to worry about than the emptiness left by Garrett's absence.

She slid into her chair and focused her attention on her work. A manila envelope lay in the center of her desk, her name scrawled carelessly across the front. At first glance, it appeared from a parent in one of her other cases who neglected to include a return address. She tore through the crease with a letter opener.

A newspaper clipping slipped out. She snapped it up curious to discover which parent had been arrested or committed some other inane activity. Something that merited an article to solidify their stupidity in writing.

Fire Ransacks Home—Three Dead

She dropped heavily into her chair. She wanted to look away, but couldn't. The article had nothing to do with any of the people in her cases. It was regarding *her* family.

The few paragraphs didn't contain any information she was unaware of, but drew the embers of the past into the raging inferno of the present. Inside the tiny print was her own obituary.

Family of Three Perished In House Fire
No Survivors
The body of three-year-old Nikki Summers was never recovered, but presumed consumed by the blaze.

Remnants of Nikki's former life tickled the edge of her consciousness. Long ago forgotten. Now threadbare. Pain sprang from every frayed edge with each recollection. The smell of smoke: Thick. Suffocating. Bitter. Tall flames blazing out of control. Crackling. Spitting. Consuming. Her lungs tightened. She coughed.

This wasn't history. *This* happened—to her. Something concrete and real. She slammed her fist down on her desk, crumpling the paper. There were more important things to concentrate on than her tortured childhood.

Nikki riffled through the paperwork stacked on her desk, attempting to find something…*anything* to shake her mind of the obituary. But nothing worked. Words jumbled into senseless phrases. Guilt gnawed a hole in her gut. Her attention fixated on the envelope. Finally, unable to resist, she lifted the envelope and turned it over. There was no indication of the sender. Her grandfather? Unlikely. He had all too readily imparted the information when they'd met at the diner.

Garrett? Doubtful. He was much more prone to delivering his messages in person. Physically. No, this package came from someone who wished to remain subtle. A person connected to the Guild determined to let her know that he or she possessed information about her.

She massaged her temples. It was a threat, clear and simple. There was no other reason for such secrecy. Her phone buzzed, bringing her back to the present. She picked up the receiver.

"Nikki, Parker Hanover called and said he'd be a little late for his appointment this morning." It was Misty, her receptionist.

"Who?" she asked.

"Parker Hanover, your next appointment."

She froze, then said slowly. "Right, I haven't had my morning caffeine yet."

She checked her docket, heart thumping with excitement. A quick glance revealed Parker's name in the nine o'clock slot scrawled in her handwriting. Something significant changed. Patience, she schooled herself, until the intercom buzzed. "He's ready."

"Great."

Nikki walked quickly to the front slowing her steps when she reached the waiting area.

"Mr. Hanover, follow me please?"

Parker smiled as he set down a magazine and got to his feet.

"How are you doing today?" Nikki asked, leading the away to her office, fully aware that the man who beat his wife in another time frame lumbered behind her.

"I'm tired. Didn't sleep well last night."

"I'm sorry to hear that. Please come in and have a seat." She skirted the desk and sank into her cushioned chair. He took his place in the facing chair, eyes downcast. He chewed on his nails.

"Parker," she began gently. "Do you know what my role is in this case?"

"You're here for Lori."

"That's right. I'm here to protect her best interests. I know that most parents come in with an idea of what is best for their kids. I want to warn you that I might not always agree with you."

"You're here for Lori and that's good enough for me." He gazed out the window, rubbing his hand on his pants leg. He looked so normal sitting there nervously awaiting the outcome. Not at all like the monster from before. Things had changed so drastically, she wasn't exactly sure where the case sat at this point.

"Do you have an attorney?" How she kept her voice from shaking amazed her.

"Yes, Garrett Nightshade. I'm probably not supposed to speak to you without him present."

She let out a breath. So that hadn't changed. She shuffled quickly through the file. The paperwork indicated Parker represented himself at the temporary hearing and when the judge dismissed the case. Garrett was hired after Mrs. Hanover refiled for the divorce, just like she remembered. Still, Parker hadn't been so willing to speak with her before. Something Nikki did last night must have altered his behavior. She was deeply curious to find out what else had changed in the lives of the Hanovers.

"It's perfectly fine that your counsel is not here. As a Guardian *Ad Litem*, I have the authority to speak to you without your attorney. However, if you would be more comfortable having your attorney here, we can reschedule."

"No, I would prefer to get this over with if you know what I mean."

"Very well. How long have you and Mrs. Hanover been married?"

"Well," he looked to the ceiling for answers. "Lori is eight. So nine or ten years."

Like most fathers, he wasn't clear on the exact date of the marriage. She bit back a grin, relaxing slightly. But that wasn't the event of the biggest impact. "How...uh...long have you been separated?'

"Six weeks."

On the dot. Nikki hid her amusement schooling her features into an unreadable expression. "What happened that caused you to separate."

"I couldn't handle all her cheating."

Cheating? "How did you know she was cheating on you?"

"I saw her talking to this guy after work when I picked her up. She denied everything, but I could tell there was something going on. Then the Sunday before I left, he called."

So, Parker was still the jealous type and could be set off with very little data. Those two events, without more, wouldn't raise her suspicion but if one was looking for something then it was most likely to be found. That was the problem with these cases, everyone found meaning in the smallest circumstances and blew them up into a volcano. She blew out a breath. But right now, she would play along.

"What did she say about the call?"

He waved his arm in a dunking motion. "Some bullshit about him giving her a ride to work." He looked at her then, his expression chagrined. "Pardon my swearing, ma'am."

"Of course," she murmured. When one observed a person in their own habitat one learned who they were. The people who came to her office were generally on their best behavior, which made it difficult to gauge the exact issues. The more at ease Nikki could make them, the better the interview revealed the true individual. "So you discovered her cheating? Then what?"

"We got into a big fight about me spanking my kid. She threatened to keep me away from Lori. Guess she made good on that threat," he spat, "because she accused me of abusing her in court."

Parker was raising the oldest smoke screen there was. The accusation was made to keep the child away from him. At least it wasn't a black eye anymore. What Parker didn't know was she'd already seen his true nature. There had been changes but bruises from a spanking was just as serious. "So you deny hurting Lori."

Parker nodded soberly. He lifted three fingers in the scouts' honor sign. "Honest to God. I was just disciplining her. That's not abuse, it's letting her know I love her."

Why you slippery little devil. He looked so sincere, if she hadn't already been involved in this situation, she might have believed him. *Might* have, but she knew him for the liar he was. "Did anyone accompany you for me to talk to?" She had to ask though she'd known the reception area was vacant. Parents sometimes brought others to assist in validating their worthiness. Apparently, Parker didn't have that kind of support system. No neighbor, counselor or grandparent accompanied him.

"No."

"What do you suppose your mother would tell me regarding this situation?" It was a calculated question, and it didn't fail to hit its mark. Parker's face grew red and his eyes widened in panic.

"Uh, I, uh…what do you mean?"

"What will your mother tell me about the allegation of abuse?"

Parker's expression went blank, regaining composure quickly. "Amy is a liar."

That might be part of what she would say, but

Nikki would lay odds that wouldn't be everything. She held out no hope that Mrs. Hanover would reveal Parker's confession. The woman would protect her son no matter what. She wasn't so certain, however, his mother would completely side with him anymore.

"I need the name and phone number of your parents so I can speak with them."

"I would prefer they not be involved, ma'am." Parker met her eyes with deep concentration. A slight pressure wafted passed.

"I understand." For a moment he seemed relieved by her words. "But I need to talk with them regardless. Often times, grandparents have great insight into their grandchildren."

Red crept up his neck, but he dutifully wrote their name and number on the paper she indicated. He pressed on the paper, and the angry flourish ended in scribbles nearly tearing the paper.

He tossed it to her, sneering. He hadn't gotten his way, but his reaction was way over the top of frustration. Had he expected *her* to comply with *his* wishes? Curious.

His attitude portrayed that of someone with high status who demanded respect. A lofty expectation for an auto mechanic with less than two years of college. "It's not my intent to upset you, Mr. Hanover. It's in Lori's best interest for me to speak to as many family members as possible."

"I'm sorry, it's just that I'm her father. What's in her interests should be up to me...and her mother." He steepled his fingers against his chin.

His attention focused on her, but something in his expression seemed ...off. His pupils dilated, making his gaze too intense.

A chill hung in the air.

She rubbed her hands up and down her arms but refused to reach for her suit jacket. Alerting him to how his behavior unsettled her didn't seem wise.

She leaned back in her chair. "I understand how you feel. However, while this case is ongoing it's up the court to decide what's in your daughter's best interest. My investigation helps with that."

"Fine." His expression relaxed but his gaze never left her face. He said nothing further drawing out the silence staring at her. Waiting. Expectant. But for what? Since he'd calmed down it was probably best to continue as usual.

"One of the things that might help you, would be if you attended counseling. I would recommend Dr. Sanders. She is very familiar with situations such as yours."

"Oh, I don't know that there is any counselor familiar with *my* situation." His voice was slippery. "Nor yours."

Her back went rigid. "I'm sorry?"

"Don't play dumb with me." His eyes burned through her, evaporating any façade he'd mustered. Nikki clasped her hands together to stop them from shaking.

He measured her with his gaze. Never blinking. Never twitching.

"Why are you really here, Mr. Hanover?"

"I thought it was time we had a chat." He grinned.

"About?"

He scooted his chair closer to the desk.

She pressed into the back of her own chair. The

stacks of files failed to fend off his intruding presence. The intensity in his gaze returned. "I think you have done enough to assist *my* family. From now on, I suggest you keep out of our business."

Hackles raised, she bit out. "I'm sorry, Mr. Hanover, but it's my duty to look after Lori's best interests." Nikki riffled through her rolodex and pulled out a number. She copied it on a piece of paper, then stood and held it out to him. "Here is Dr. Sander's number. Allow me to walk you out."

"I'm not finished." A warm blanket of air blew past, freezing her in place. Parker rose, placing both hands on her desk. A slow sinister smile curved his lips. The air squeezed around her. She gasped, unable to get a complete breath. "You *will* leave us alone."

She squirmed under the pressure. All she managed were a few grunts.

He nodded. Apparently, pleased with the outcome of his visit, he turned his attention to the contents of her desk. Nikki fought against the constraints of the invisible barrier. She had to do something to keep him from reading her files.

He picked up a small piece of paper. The article.

She struggled to get free. Desperation seized her. He was holding personal information about her family.

"What is this?" His eyebrows lifted as he scanned the contents. He slipped the article into his pocket. "I think I'll keep this. You have a good day now."

Parker strolled from her office. Once he was out of sight, the pressure on Nikki's lungs eased. She inhaled a huge gulp of air then sprang into action. She raced down the hall. But Parker had disappeared, along with her private history. She leaned against the wall, its cold surface the only thing that kept her standing. What had she done?

Chapter Eighteen

Adelaide Nightshade couldn't curb the mounting anxiety pounding through her veins as she drove into the upscale neighborhood on the west side of town. These were houses filled with people who could afford professional landscaping, never believing their idyllic lives could topple over in a split second.

They decorated their lawns with red, purple, and yellow flowers, forming rings around trees placed equidistant from each other. The order of the foliage mocked her as she wound her way down the road. Everyone went about their business fearing nothing. She hated them all.

No one in this community, save one, knew of the benefits her society gave them. The pain the Guild eased and suffering erased. They were blissfully unaware of the delicate balance and order necessary to serve mankind. She compressed her lips tightly. And that structure had been breached.

Her tension level was at an all-time high since Garrett paid her a call earlier that morning. She pounded her fists against the steering wheel. How could the Guild have missed such an important development as the birth of the Shadow Dancer? Arrogant bastards! So sure no member could slip through the boundaries set for them in childhood. But one of them had. And there was only one person it could be. The outsider.

All children raised within the Guild had boundaries set for them from childhood. Even if their thoughts led them to alter more than they were allowed, they wouldn't have mastered the skills to do so. All signs they had more powers than the Guild allowed were expunged early on.

She could no longer deny someone had evolved to the point that they could change real events, not just feelings and opinions. If Garret was right, it was all William Songe's underhanded work.

Garrett refused to confirm how deeply involved Nikki Angelus was. Since her son had made the unfortunate acquaintance, he'd behaved as if the Guild was the enemy. As if someone *messed with his mind.* Fury surged through her veins. It was past time to pay Mr. Songe a personal visit. And *that* she lay at Garrett's unhelpful feet.

"Your destination is on the right," the annoying GPS voice-over said.

"So, I have arrived," Adelaide mimicked. She considered the grand structure with its meticulously manicured lawn. So this was where the traitor lived.

Adelaide stepped from the car and made her way up the long curving path, bordered by white periwinkles on either side. A welcoming scene. One she was certain would disappear once she met the monster residing inside. She lifted the door knocker and let it drop. The sound reverberated hollowly. The door slid open revealing a man around sixty dressed in an elegant navy blue pin-striped suit.

Her breath caught. He'd aged well. He should be shriveled, bent and tortured by his defection. Not the picture of health and fine living.

"May I help you?" His eyes landed on the Guild crest hanging around her neck. To his credit, no crack appeared in his composure. He smiled as if greeting a stranger. They'd never officially met but he knew what she represented. Yet he chose to play daft? She bristled under his show of ignorance.

"Don't play coy with me, Mr. Songe. You used to wear the Guild ring. I'm sure you know why I'm here."

His lips curled in amusement. "Do I? I'm sure I don't. You have me at a loss. You know my name but I don't know yours."

She squared her shoulders, pulled herself upright. "I'm Adelaide Nightshade."

He lifted his eyebrows although she was certain he wasn't surprised by her response. "Garrett Nightshade's mother I presume."

She gave a sharp nod.

He stepped back, swinging the door wide. "Why don't you come in?" He said with all the reception of a host greeting an honored guest.

"Thank you." She didn't mean to sound so stiff, but Mr. Songe's tranquility threw off any semblance she might have of a calm demeanor.

"As luck would have it—" He motioned her into a large living area, managing the temerity to execute a slight bow, "—we have the house to ourselves."

"Good." She smiled, hoping he didn't pick up on her uneasiness.

He poured himself a cup of tea, adding milk, then sugar. He stirred the brew in lazy circles before giving her his attention. Irritation burned behind her eyeballs. She wanted to shake his composure. "I suppose you don't want anyone to hear what you're up to."

"And what is that?" He lifted the cup to his lips.

He hadn't offered her any. His manners were positively barbaric. She wouldn't have accepted if he had, she decided, piqued. Her gazed scanned the large overly furnished room. She chose the couch across from him and sank onto the cushions. Her bones ached from the change in weather. The soft couch was a short respite until her journey back home. "Messing in Guild politics that don't concern you."

He handed her another of those ingratiating smiles. So condescending. "Oh, but they do concern me, my dear."

She observed the expensive furnishings. Dark mahogany end tables and a matching coffee table that framed the overstuffed couch and two chairs. Shelves stacked with books and a silver tea service sat atop the sidebar.

Songe lifted his dainty china cup and picked up its mate, a plate with a half-eaten scone.

"You scoff at the very rules that provided you with all this. You've done well for yourself."

"We've all done well," he said, setting down the teacup and scone. "And I'm certain you didn't come here to discuss my circumstances. Out with your suspicions, my dear."

She didn't hesitate. "Have you unleashed the Shadow Dancer?"

He considered her from beneath hooded lids, fingers steepled at his chin. "The fact that you are here tells me you already know the answer to that question. At the very least suspect."

"Garrett tells me that someone has skills far beyond what the Guild condones."

"Does he?" Songe leaned closer.

She resented his smug face. His attitude indicated a disrespectfulness of her title, her *authority*. He believed there was nothing she could do to stop him? *Think again, Mr.* "Yes, he does. What have you done?"

"I have merely accomplished what your precious Guild didn't have the guts to when I asked them to simply let us evolve." He shrugged, and picked up his blasted plate again.

Adelaide's heart thumped hard against her chest. She wasn't surprised by his answer she just hoped it wasn't true. "You won't get away with this," she hissed.

A chuckle. "I already have. My granddaughter is by far stronger than any of your brood. Stifled by your own constraints. They are no match for her."

"I wouldn't be so sure." Adelaide stood, knocking the table askew in the process. Tea spilled over the rim of the dainty cup sitting there.

"Why hasn't someone put a stop to her actions?"

Adelaide was brought up short by this question. He was right, no one had stopped her. Not even Garrett could get close enough to dent Nikki's progress, and he had tried. She narrowed her eyes. At least, he said he had. Was he committed though? She'd considered sending someone else, but no one was as strong as Garrett. Still, she didn't trust him any longer. She had no choice but to find someone else to deal with the aberration. "Don't be so sure of yourself."

"Oh, I'm quite sure of myself." His grin widened, and she felt a little like red riding hood peering into the toothy gullet of the wolf. "She *will* change things."

"What could you possibly hope to attain from this

treason?"

"You can't be that naïve, Adelaide. The Guild stole my family. I intend to get them back."

"At what price? The Guild will sanitize *you* just as they should have done years ago."

For the first time she'd entered the lion's den, his carefully structured composure cracked. "I don't care what the price is," he said harshly. "The Guild needs to learn whose bad side they end up on. They incurred my wrath the minute they set that fire."

Adelaide's hand went to the collar of her cotton dress. It felt as flimsy as she did at that moment. "The Guild had no involvement in that fire."

"Don't bother lying to me. You were just a cog in the machine when my family was stripped from me. I doubt the Guild is forthcoming with the truth to one so wet behind the ears. They did as surely as I live and breathe."

"I beg you to stop this craziness before your granddaughter gets hurt." She turned on her heel and stormed from the room.

"Warn Garrett. He is the one that needs to be careful. You wouldn't want something to happen to him."

She spun. His face was red and he grabbed his chest. Any calm he'd presented prior, completely obliterated. He crumpled to the floor shaking. His frail hand reached in his pocket. He drew out a small bottle. Nitrogen. The plastic bottle dropped from his hand and rolled away. He crawled after it, clawing inch by inch to reach it.

In two quick strides she was upon it. She raised her leg to kick the bottle away then though better of it.

Songe lay gasping like a fish out of water. His helpless desperation touched a nerve she'd thought had long been obliterated. He believed the Guild responsible for his family's destruction. Guilt filled her because it was possible someone out there had done as he said. She snatched up the bottle and placed it in his hands. As he struggled with the top, she dialed 911. If he ended up dying, at least her conscience would be clear.

****

Parker pulled up in front of his small brown ranch house hoping to catch Amy before she left for work. It had all the basics—a kitchen, living room, dining room, three bedrooms, and one bath. Not as large as he preferred but it was home. At least until that stupid judge handed it over to his whiney wife. The bastard didn't care that it was *his* family's money poured into the mortgage and the fireplace she held so dear.

Things were going to change. This house belonged to him. No one was going to tell him to stay away. Parker gave the door a swift hard knock.

Amy opened the door. Terror filled her widened eyes. "What are you doing here? I have a restraining order."

"This is my house, too," he said, maintaining eye contact. Would it work? It hadn't on the Angelus woman but it was worth a try. His wife's mind was more pliable. He held her gaze.

Amy held the door wider, tilting her head in a slight bow. He stepped into the entryway brushing his arm against her. She didn't flinch. Encouraging.

She followed him into the living room then sat in her graceful way, smoothing her pants legs as she did. The very quality admired at one time was a sick reminder she thought she was too good for him.

Parker leaned against the stone fireplace careful not to disturb the glass figurines. Now that he had her attention he couldn't spoil it by irritating her. He took a few minutes to digest what had just occurred. Merely by telling her they didn't have to listen to the judge's order, she had complied with his wishes.

"What do you want?" She sat across from him, fidgeting. Dark circles under red eyes indicated she had been crying. About their separation? Warmth spread through him. He thought she had wanted the divorce, but maybe just maybe, she wasn't as sure as he'd first thought.

"I want another chance." He maintained eye contact willing her to submit.

She broke it and focused on her feet shuffling against the wood floor. He dragged a finger around the edge of his collar. Maybe he didn't have enough discipline to manage her yet. Fighting to regain composure, his eyes swept the room. She had removed the stained throw carpet revealing dark gleaming wood grain. The faint odor of lemon hung in the air. He couldn't detect a speck of dust. His stack of Motorcycle Madness Magazines were gone, and a brand new remote control caddy hung off the arm of the couch. She'd been cleaning to work out a problem. Maybe getting the house in order for his return. That was promising.

She pulled at a string from the hem of her sweater. "I don't know. It hasn't been right between us for a long time."

"Look at me, Amy," he said softly.

Her head snapped up at the command. Limpid

pools took on the edge of a cornered rabbit. So innocent, sweet and scared. Who knew such a raging bitch hid behind those placid eyes? "We need to try again—for Lori's sake."

"I am doing this for Lori." But the conviction in her voice days ago was absent. She didn't sound half as sure of herself.

Parker smiled his best 'I'm a good guy' smile. He went and knelt by her side, took her hand in his. Suspicion clouded her expression but she didn't pull away.

"Lori needs both of us now," he said, gently. And for good measure he played his final card. "Aren't you tired of strangers looking into our business, Amy?" He thought of the Angelus woman, all her nosy questions. He knew Amy was thinking about that too. All he had done, after all, was punish Lori. So it left a few bruises. It wasn't illegal to spank his kid.

"Yes." It was a weak answer but at least she wasn't fighting him any longer.

"It was just a spanking. I never meant to hurt her. It could happen to anyone." That was true. How many of his friend's kids had welts on their rear end because of a spanking with a belt or a wooden spoon? Lots he'd wager. He'd done less than that and was getting brutalized for applying simple discipline to his own child.

Rage spiraled inside his entrails. He stifled it. This wasn't the time to let loose his anger. This was his one chance with Amy.

"Maybe," she said, looking at the floor again. "We could try one more time but I'm not dismissing my case until I'm sure."

"I can live with that." And just like that he was back in the game. In a few hours he would have this matter settled for good. He had his powers back. He could push his way into anyone's mind *while they were awake*. It felt good. Real good.

Parker grabbed his keys and tossed them in the air. "I'll move back in tonight."

****

White walls gleamed an icy welcome when Nikki crept into the hospital room. The usual sterile antiseptic smell assailed her nostrils. She rubbed her nose at the unpleasant acidic after bite. The same odor clung to the air when her sister and mother died. Her eyes watered. She bit back the tears. This was not the time to recall these emotions. Not when she was here to see a man she barely knew. She could hardly even call him family. She shook off the remnants of grief and approached the only bed occupying the room.

Her grandfather sprawled across the length covered by a thin blanket. The hospital gown engulfed his thin torso dwarfing him. IV tubes sprung from his pencil thin arms then arched upward toward several bags holding saline, penicillin, and other medicines. He looked fragile. Breakable.

She was angry with her blustering, manipulative grandfather. Not this fragile old man whose shallow breathing and unsteady blips on the heart monitor marked his mortality.

His eyes opened and a weak smile formed on his lips. A gratifying glow flooded through her. She wrapped her fingers around the cold steel guardrail. One moment she was furious with him, the next filled with this tender emotion. The knot of anxiety in her

291

stomach eased.

Was she relieved because he was her only link to the new life she had entered? Or because he was her grandfather? Her only tie to a life she didn't remember. She couldn't lose him now. He was the only true family member she had left.

"What happened?" she asked.

"Heart attack." His once robust voice held a reedy quality like he spoke in a vacuum. He coughed. "I hear you've been busy stirring up a mighty hornet's nest."

"I'm sorry." She patted his arm awkwardly. He might look too weak to lift a spoon but the man had a narrow focus on his agenda. Not that she was clear on his objective. But he seemed pleased with her progress. "I don't think I'm doing the right thing. It's all gotten so out of whack."

"You're making their lives miserable. That's a very good start." A small laugh wheezed from him, setting up another fit of hacking. Despite his weakness, an amused twinkle danced in his eyes. "Keep them on their toes. You're on the brink of success."

She tossed him a fierce frown. "Is that all you can think about!" she demanded. Then, "How exactly do I do that?"

He searched around the bed for the remote. She snatched it up and handed it to him. He pressed a button that raised his bed. He pushed aside the sheets and edged into a seated position using the bars on each side of the bed. His loose-fitting gown fell off one shoulder. A wire trailed his skin to the sensor attached to his chest. The rhythm on the monitor spiked. Angry beeps matched the jagged lines running together like the scribbles of an angry child. She leaned over to assist him but he grunted and waved her off. Once settled, he said, "Change the minds of the weak, that's how."

"I'm only trying to help the Hanover family." Every time she spoke to him confusion muddled her mind like a thick fog. He wanted more from her. But she couldn't figure out what. She needed to do her job not cater to the whims of a mad man set on vengeance.

"As you should be." He waggled a finger at her, some of the rich quality returning to his voice. Yet it wasn't the sound of a healthy man. He would sacrifice his life if it suited his cause.

She paused. "Parker threatened me."

"Of course he did, dear." His tired lid winked. Or was that a twitch? "All snakes show their fangs before they strike."

"If I continue will it hurt you?"

"Don't worry about me. This is what you were meant to do. Don't stop simply because I landed here."

"I don't like the sound of that." She took a deep breath. Someone had to act responsibly when it came to her talents. Difficult under the circumstances. She barely understood the realm of her capabilities. There were rules she didn't follow. Rules she didn't understand or know, blundering through a diseased mind of an atrocious parent.

Garrett was getting angrier by the second. *And she cared.* She'd rather face her grandfather's disappointment.

"I didn't take the risk training you so you could chicken out at the last second. You're making the Guild nervous. That's good."

"But I don't know what I'm doing." And she was making powerful enemies in the process. Garrett had warned there were horrific ways to stop her. He hadn't used them so far. Out of reluctance or inability, she didn't know. That was a puzzle she had yet to work out. The more time she spent with Garrett, the harder it was when he was away. She trembled with the need to be near him. She couldn't track when the change happened, but the desire to see his face churned full throttle. And if she didn't get a handle on who she was and where her loyalties belonged, this situation with Garrett would not end well.

"You know what you're doing. I've trained you well. Continue working with the Hanover family. The little girl is the key."

Nikki's mouth fell open. "How?" How did Lori have anything to do with her grandfather's goals? Having been brought through the veil of this society recently, she still didn't comprehend how close knit the Guild community was. Everyone knew the business of all members. Even hers. A small village she had become a citizen of without relocating her homestead.

He leaned in conspiratorially, voice low. His eyes darted around. "Parker Hanover was stripped of his power when he was a child. He didn't do well with the dictates of the Guild. Although it was never said, I think the boy had other abilities the Guild feared. Now he has a daughter and I hear she is very talented."

Frustration with all the innuendos had Nikki tempted to pull her hair out by the roots. "What does that mean exactly?"

"I think we are evolving." His heart rate went up on the monitor. He leaned back.

"Calm down. You don't need another episode."

He waved her off. "Don't worry, I'll be fine." His

heart beat settled. "The Guild is trying to prevent us from evolving. Protect that girl at all costs."

Nikki's life could not get any more bizarre. A couple days ago, she protected children from the *non*-paranormal. She defended against bruises, lack of food, and parents who confused a child's needs with their own. A serious enough job without adding the extra element of mind control. Now, it appeared, anything could happen. "I'm not sure I can."

"Trust your instincts. They'll lead you."

"Yes, but where?" she muttered under her breath. Pressure folded in on her. The enormity of the situation dragged her downward into uncertainty. What if her instincts steered her wrong?

Chapter Nineteen

Nikki sipped her tea with some misguided notion the liquid was elixir to ease her tension. It wasn't working. She leaned into the soft pillow willing her muscles to relax. She ignored the Hanover file sprawled across her bedspread. She wasn't able to concentrate enough to absorb the details anyway. Just one moment of peace wasn't too much to ask. Her cell phone rang. So much for peace. She jerked it off the night stand. "Hello."

"Did you miss me?" Garrett's silky tones emanated dripping with sarcasm on the other end. Her heartbeat quickened. Irritation surged through her system. He was the last person she needed to speak to right now.

"For pity's sake, it's late, what do you want?" She massaged her temples unable to stem the iciness. Why did her professionalism desert her when it came to him? One minute she wanted to throttle him. The next jump his bones. It's like she'd all of a sudden become bipolar. Weariness seeped into her bones. As long as the Hanover case was ongoing, she would have to deal with him. She ignored the warmth that spread along the length of her thighs at the thought. He was the enemy. He should be contained, not toyed with.

"This can't wait. There's been a new development in our case." He sounded a bit too superior. Like a man who had discovered the fountain of youth rather than some mundane fact in a legal battle. As important as the information could be to this case, it was unlikely to have the far-reaching effect of immortality. "One I bet you're not aware of."

Resentment at his taunt twisted her insides. "What would that be?"

"The Hanovers want to reconcile."

"*What*?" The inane question slipped passed her lips. She pulled the covers up to her torso as a protective shield. "Ridiculous. Parker Hanover is accused of abusing Lori."

"Mrs. Hanover had a change of heart. She now thinks she…*overreacted* to the situation."

"But there are bruises. I'm sitting here with the pictures." Her heart hammered against her rib cage. If they reconciled, the case was over. She wouldn't have any authority at all. And without current information, she'd no longer be useful as a caster. "Is she dismissing her case?"

"Not yet." He didn't sound so smug this time. "But it does put the case on hold."

Nikki waited for her heart rate to adjust from panic mode to mere concern. If she was to prevent the Hanover matter from being swept into a dark corner, she had to act fast. "Thanks for letting me know."

"I trust this development will keep you from head hopping tonight."

"What do you think?" She pulled the phone from her ear to disconnect but his guttural growl kept her on line.

"I know I've said it before, Nikki, but you have no idea of the chaos you are causing with your meddling. You've caused enough damage. Please leave the

Hanovers alone before you do something I can't fix."

"I'll take that under advisement. I have to go." She ended the call and tossed the phone on the bed. She fixed her attention once again on the file spread across her mauve comforter, searching for some clue as to how Parker had managed to weasel his way into Amy's house. She examined each component of her case. Petition for Divorce. Check. Allegations of abuse. Check. Temporary order for supervised visitation. Check. Nothing had changed enough to merit reconciliation. But not all developments were contained in the file.

She'd changed his psyche last night but not for the better. What she'd actually unleashed remained unclear. His past memories indicated Parker had a power other casters didn't. A more insidious development than she'd intended. She'd experienced Parker trying to bend her to his will this morning. But whatever he'd been attempting hadn't taken. Had he been able to use his powers on his wife? She was certain he lacked the necessary object to control Amy's mind. Maybe he didn't need one. A chill shivered up her spine. She shook it off. Parker and his powers weren't the only explanation. Abusers were slippery, their victims often compliant. It wouldn't be the first time Amy had caved. She hadn't spoken with Amy recently. Hadn't gauged whether she would buckle at the first sign of pressure or not.

Now that Amy wasn't in intensive care, perhaps it was time to visit her mind. Nikki shoved the papers back into the folder and placed it on the floor. All she needed was a personal item. She'd retrieve one when she visited Lori tomorrow.

****

Nikki walked up the small sidewalk to the Hanover residence. The tip of her foot caught on an uneven portion of the concrete. She tipped forward and stumbled a few steps before, regaining her balance.

She'd only drunk two cups of coffee before heading out this morning. Nothing cleared the fog in her head created by Garrett's announcement the Hanovers were reconciling. The cracks and tuffs of grass were much more challenging than they should have been. She rolled her head back and forth. Her muscles eased with the motion but her nerve endings remained on edge.

She smoothed her skirt though it was recently pressed and knocked on the Hanovers' door. One final tug on her suit jacket and she was ready when Amy opened the door.

"Ms. Angelus." Amy's eyes widened, and her voice rose. There was no reason Amy should be surprised. The appointment had been arranged days ago. Unless...just how much *did* she change the other night?

"Hi, Amy. How are you all doing?" She spoke slowly uncertain where things stood in the investigation. Altering events had distinct disadvantages. Nikki stayed calm. No use revealing too much information.

"We're fine. What are you doing here?"

"We scheduled a home visit, remember?"

"Not really." Amy shook her head, then smiled. "That's all right. Come on in."

Nikki stepped over the threshold into the small living room. It was neat and tidy. The figurines were all in their place. Nothing smashed or broken. She felt a wave of pride at her accomplishment.

"Is Lori here? I would like to begin with her."

"She's in her room."

Nikki followed Amy through the hallway where picture frames that previously littered the floor, now hung on the wall. One picture in particular caught her attention. Parker and Amy stood next to each other beaming in their wedding finery. Next to that, another photo depicted the happy couple gazing in adoration at their small newborn wrapped in a pink receiving blanket. A happy family.

But pictures sometimes lied. A snapshot of one moment didn't tell the tale of what lay beneath the surface. In this household secrets slithered beneath doorways, hid in the darkest corners.

Amy tapped once on the third door on the right, jolting her back to the present. It was time to focus on those elusive pieces of the puzzle, pull them in the open where they could no longer harm this family.

Nikki found Lori laying on her stomach at the foot of her bed, feet flailing in the air.

"Now Rags, that's not how we play this game," Lori chided her doll.

A wave of pleasure pressed against Nikki's heart seeing Rags back home where she belonged. Apparently, the changes also altered things Lori was able to keep. Nikki tucked that nugget to the back of her mind. Lori glanced up and grinned.

"Nikki!" She scrambled off the bed and threw her arms around Nikki's waist. She stiffened, startled by the show of joy before quickly returning the hug. Feeling awkward, Nikki extricated the child to arm's length.

Allowing the children she represented to become attached to her was inexcusable. If she performed her job correctly, her involvement with families was for a short time. A requirement of a Guardian *Ad Litem's* position, so the children didn't suffer another loss once the case was completed. "How are things going?"

"All right." Lori's soft reply didn't sound convincing. There was a pinch in her face that alerted Nikki that there was more to be done.

Nikki cast Amy a glance, indicating for her to leave them. She needed Lori's perspective.

"Well," Amy said, "I'll just be in the other room."

Nikki nodded and led the child further into the room. The bedroom looked similar to the last time Nikki was there. It was the one room that had remained untouched by her father's rampage through the house. She wondered briefly if Lori remembered those events. Lori looked worried. Maybe some remnants of the past still seeped into the present.

Nikki sat on the edge of the canopied bed. "How has it been since your daddy moved back in?"

Lori moved beside her. It was very much like an aunt talking to a niece sharing secrets, but far more serious.

"It's been okay." Lori picked up Rags and toyed with her red hair.

"Anything you'd like me to change?"

Lori looked up, hope on her face. Nikki still wasn't sure how powerful her abilities were. How much she could address. She made progress with the Hanover's condition but she suspected Lori was about to poke a hole in her soaring mood. That her changes weren't good enough.

"He isn't spanking me anymore but…"

"What?" Nikki bit her lip holding back the edge of dread threatening to surface.

"He's just weird." She thrust Rags onto the bed. Her doll's arms fell over its face, one leg curled around the other.

"Weird how?"

"I don't know. He doesn't get that red face anymore but he still seems…mad somehow." Lori's soft brown eyes implored Nikki to help her.

"What do you mean?"

"His face does this weird twitching thing." Her hands fluttered in an attempt to mimic the motion.

"What do you think that means?"

"I think he's hiding that he's mad. And my mom's not right either."

Nikki's heart pounded out the rhythm of distress. She'd definitely made matters worse but couldn't grasp hold of what she'd actually done.

It sounded like Parker was a powder keg with the fuse lit and about to blow. Nikki wanted to sooth him into a loving father, not mask his darkness. "How so?"

"She does everything he says no matter how stupid it is. Last night I caught Mommy scrubbing the floor—with a tooth brush."

"Really?"

"Yes."

"What did she say about that?"

"She said it was the only way to get the floor really clean. But she's never done that before."

"I bet she hasn't."

"He won't stop looking at me with that bizzaro way."

"Like how?" Lori's face went placid and her eyes widened staring at Nikki with extreme concentration. Nikki'd seen that look before when waves of warm air brushed over her. The day Parker came to her office and tried to exert his will. "Oh no."

"Look," Lori peered at the doorway before continuing. "I'm not strong enough to fix my mom. She's an adult. Even if I could, I'd never go into Daddy's mind. But you're strong enough."

Whatever Parker was capable of, his abilities appeared to have returned. Amy was being manipulated. That was not good. And he was trying to use his powers on Lori. If she could report her mother's odd behavior, it was a sure sign he wasn't controlling her. Yet.

Chapter Twenty

Nikki gazed at her reflection while preparing for bed, wondering when her life had gotten so complicated. Dark circles shaded the area beneath her eyes. Frown lines crossed her forehead in deep grooves. If she didn't get control of the situation, she would look older than some of the mentally ill parents she dealt with.

She shook her head and squeezed the lotion bottle. A large glob pooled in her palm. With long broad strokes, she smoothed out the frown lines. She relaxed, realizing the wrinkles weren't as deep as they first appeared. The exaggeration was no doubt a symptom of the toll her casting was taking on her. She swiped the remainder off with a towel.

She couldn't quit casting until she rectified the situation.

Nikki leaned against the sink contemplating her next move. No matter how hard she tried, she couldn't characterize what the Hanover family needed.

She stopped Parker from beating his wife, but something still remained...off. Especially since he was using his powers again. She spread toothpaste onto her toothbrush and scrubbed her teeth so hard her gums bled. Not once during the time she was mucking around in Parker's head did she stop to consider his parents might have been right to strip him of his gifts. She'd focused on Parker's pain, not on the reasons for his parents' actions. She spat into the sink. She had to make this right. But where to begin?

Parker would have his guard up. Resistance would make her task more difficult if not impossible. In truth, she wasn't quite sure how to go about mending such egregious errors. Perhaps focusing her efforts in strengthening Amy's defenses against Parker's wishes would net better results. She wrapped Amy's velvet scrunchy around her wrist, the one Lori had given her.

Nikki glanced up in the mirror again, pressing her lips together. She wouldn't be deterred from her mission until she fixed this situation. She stalked to the bed, crawled in, and pulled the covers to her neck. She closed her eyes and drifted into oblivion. She raised an arm toward the slip stream. Before she was caught up in its electrical surge, steel fingers wrapped around her arm and yanked her around. She looked into Garrett's hard gaze.

"You've done enough damage. I won't let you cause anymore."

"And how are you going to stop me? I've evaded you before." She was getting weary of his pestering. Didn't he understand she was trying to fix her mistakes?

"Like this." He moved closer. The heat of his breath trailed her skin, tickling the back of her neck. He kissed her, sending shockwaves of need charging to her most private places. The smell of cinnamon and cloves drove her to a frenzy. Fire coursed through her veins. The charge sizzled on her lips. She fell into him, kissed him back. Her traitorous arms circled his neck. His hands locked against her spine, sending warm shivers through her.

She dragged her lips from his, gasping for air. Her heart ached but she willed herself to stay put. This was all a game to him. A desperate ploy. "I know what you're trying to do. It won't work." Her mind reeled.

He smirked. "If you knew what I was trying to do, we wouldn't be in your head. You'd be in my bed."

"I told you this would not happen again." She balled her fists, refusing to give credence to the pleasure of his words. Oh, to fade into oblivion, here, with him. So easy to give in. But the bastard was only trying to distract her like she had him. Did he think her that stupid?

"Come on, Nikki. We had so much fun the last time."

Rage replaced the need. She shoved at his broad chest. "Get away from me." The words were weak and hollow, her ragged gulps sounded like cannon fire. Her lips burned from his touch. She planted her feet firmly in place. Ready for his next move.

He didn't budge. His eyes raked her over, searing every inch with the promise of an expertise she had never encountered before she met him. Her body hungered for his skilled fingers to graze her skin. The kindled blaze of intimacy. For…No she refused to succumb to the aching throb of desire. *Rain now*!

Cold water poured down, jolting her senses to reason. Wind howled. Sodden hair clung to her face and neck. Her clothes drenched. But her mind was clear.

"In need of a cold shower?' Garrett laughed.

"Look." Nikki gulped down embarrassment. "I'm trying to help this family."

"You know, sometimes things are best left alone."

Water dripped from his hair, down his nose. His flattened hair plastered to his head like a helmet. Wind blew his shirt, stretched by the pelting drops, against a chest accentuating well-defined muscles.

Rather than the water cooling her ardor, however, she found herself wanting to lick away the moisture. His eyes held the embers of their kiss. Her heart lurched. Heat scorched a trail down her limbs. Damn him. Even drenched with ice water she craved him.

"I'm making progress," she insisted. "They've asked for a counselor. They want to work on their problems."

Garrett shook his head, never taking his eyes from her. "Don't be so sure. A leopard's spots don't change, you know."

"A leopard is born with spots. People aren't born bad." She edged around him, looking for the slip stream. The blue glow shimmered above. She jumped, ready to sail through to Amy's mind.

"Oh, no you don't." Garrett leapt and grabbed hold of her leg. The sheer weight of his body dragged her to the ground. They landed with a thud inches from one another. His shirt had come unbuttoned, revealing evenly tanned skin. Her fingers itched to trail across his chest. "A woman doesn't kiss like that without wanting more. Why not give into what you want?" He tugged her into his body, his words a seductive stream of its own.

Her gaze fixated on his biceps. Strong. Powerful. She longed for them to enfold her. To lay her head against his broad chest. It would be intoxicating. A few minutes. Just a little time. Forget what was truly important. She pulled away before she succumbed to the temptation.

"Quit messing with my head."

A slow smile curved his lips. "You should take your own advice. Messing in the heads of others is dangerous when you don't know what you are doing, and you don't, Nikki." His finger trailed her jawline, sending more delicious shivers into those forgotten parts of her body. He leaned in. "You remember how nice astral sex can be. I promise you'll enjoy yourself."

"Stop." She jumped again. This time success. Unfortunately, not quick enough to keep him from following. He soared through the air beside her.

"Think about what you're doing."

"I have," she shouted.

They tumbled into Amy's mind. Wind lashed at her face. A mass of dark clouds hung overhead. Flashes of light skittered across the surface though not enough to illuminate the area. She couldn't see two inches in front of her, let alone any doors. "What happened?" she whispered.

"You happened."

A dull ache settled in the pit of her stomach, tears pricked the backs of her lids. She shook her head and looked around. She hadn't been there before but she could guess who had. Garrett was right, this was her doing. She winced. "I can fix this."

"Haven't you done enough?" He prodded gently. "Without expert training, there is nothing else you can do."

A hot volcanic heat rushed through her. She clenched her fists. "You're right, I haven't been traditionally trained. But at least I'm *trying* to make a difference. What has all your training done for you?

You're paralyzed."

"No, I'm cautious."

She cringed at the venom in his voice. "Caution has no place when people are in crisis."

"Because of you."

She faced him, limbs trembling, but she stood firm. "Fine. You're right, this *is* my fault. Now watch me fix it."

She focused her attention inward. *Light*. Amy's mind cleared. *Happy*. Brightness surrounded them. *Good choices*. A sigh resounded. Nikki poised, prepared to jump back into the slip stream.

Garrett pushed up his sleeves and crouched ready to follow. "Be careful, I'm not the most dangerous thing out here."

"Like I haven't heard that before." They plunged back into Nikki's head. Unable to resist any longer, she jumped into his arms and all but dared him to knock her socks off.

Chapter Twenty-One

Nikki paced the width of her grandfather's overly ornate living room. The mahogany and oriental carpets she'd stood in awe of mere days ago now stifled her movement. Every glint off the gold edged, fine china mocked how far her adoptive family had fallen. The Angeluses would have lived in a house such as this if it hadn't been for her grandfather's interference. She swallowed the burning regret. If it hadn't been for her.

"Those rugs are antiques, dear. I'd appreciate it if you didn't wear a groove in them." Her grandfather sat in his favorite chair sipping tea. But there the routine stopped. Instead of a costly suit and polished shoes, he wore striped pajamas and slippers. As he lifted the cup to his mouth, his gnarled hand shook. His thin neck didn't appear capable of holding his head that had become too large for the rest of his slight body. Even in this frail state, arrogance oozed off him like lava flow.

She paused. "The Hanovers are a mess. No matter what I try things get worse. This is all my fault." Her legs shook. If her knees locked, she would fall. He still believed she could save them all. Her insides trembled and rocked like an angry sea. Her limitations gnawed and nipped at her heels. If he couldn't help her she would be adrift. Alone, without recourse.

He watched her with a sharp, piercing gaze. "Don't be so hard on yourself. Look at all you've accomplished in this short time. I'm very proud." His voice sounded his actual age. Like a very weary grandfather.

She cringed. "I've made a bigger mess. The Hanovers are reconciling, but their marriage doesn't seem to have improved. I've tried to fortify Amy's mind, but it doesn't seem to have done much. No matter how hard I've tried, nothing is making them better parents."

"Ha!" He leaned forward, tea cup leading the way. Dark liquid trembled over the side as the cup barely made it to the saucer on the table. He leaned too far for a second before inching his way back in his chair. Nikki raised her hand to assist him, but he waved her off. He huffed, grasping the armrests. His chest rose and fell quickly.

"Are you sure you should be out of the hospital?"

"There's nothing they can do for me that I can't get right here." His index finger tapped the armrest. The touch was so light, it didn't make much sound. Guilt challenged her constitution.

"Maybe I should come back later."

He crooked an eyebrow. "I'm fine. We're fine. Tell me what you need."

"I have to fix this. Parker has powers I haven't seen before."

A hard edge glittered beneath the surface of his expression returning a bit of his command. Her words hadn't surprised him. They were expected. He must have realized Parker would regain his abilities and what that entailed.

Hope bubbled up from the well of her mistakes. For a moment, she could believe her grandfather hadn't suffered a heart attack. That he would always be there for her. That he would always be able to assist her.

"He's not as strong as you think." He smiled slyly. "And he doesn't know what you can do. Keep working on it. You'll see."

With that statement, hope fled. His teeth bared like a dog marking his territory over a juicy bone. He wasn't going to help. He was tossing her into the abyss with no safety net.

"But I don't know what I'm doing." She hated the edge in her voice knowing she was repeating the very words Garrett uttered frequently. She was so out of her depth. No matter how hard she tried things just kept getting worse. Things had gotten too out of control and her grandfather was abandoning her. *Again.* She couldn't do this alone.

"Don't be ridiculous." His soft tone belied the intensity of his raw-boned face, frozen in that sardonic grin. The strain of his belief reddened his features. He grasped the arms of his chair, knuckles turning white.

Just what did he want from her? What did he believe about her abilities?

"The more he comes at you, the more you will learn and adapt. You're more powerful than them all. That's why they seek to destroy you. But you won't let them will you?"

"You're using me," she accused. How could he? His granddaughter. His own flesh and blood. Nikki's toes curled and a sinking weight pulled at her insides—tugging and tearing her apart. Ready to hurl her into a dark pit. There was no one on her side. Except maybe Garrett. And that didn't sit so well. She wasn't sure he had her best interests at heart. Her grandfather didn't contradict her. No amount of familial affection encouraged him to deny her accusation.

"Hate me all you want but it's too late to walk away now. Parker is out there and you're the only one who can stop him." His index finger punched the chair arm. This time louder and harder. Where was he finding the strength? "And when you do, it will be as I predicted. You may not want to now, but rest assured you *will* give me what I want." A shrewd gleam lit his eyes, a tinge of madness colored his voice. Did he even think of her as his granddaughter or was she merely a pawn in his crazy game?

Nikki's mouth went dry. She couldn't swallow. All she could do was stand there like a piece of artwork, peppering the living room of his already overpopulated mausoleum. That's all she was to him. A thing used for his own purposes. But he was right, damn it, someone had to stop Parker.

He pulled his Guild ring out of the drawer of his end table and held it out. "You'll need this to complete your task." The tremors were back. An insidious worm of guilt curled in her gut. He might be obsessed with his own need but he was her grandfather and she needed him. She snatched the ring from his trembling fingers and rushed out.

****

Nikki slipped beneath the bed covers, no longer feeling the sense of comfort and security, when she sank into the cocoon and the soft cushion of her pillow. Those days were long gone. She was on alert all the time now. Her dreams didn't integrate the day's events. They were stuffed with nightmares where anyone could toy with the inner workings of the mind. Lost in a world to which she now belonged, she was part of it—like it or not.

She closed her eyes and entered Parker Hanover's head. Wind swept across a barren foundation. No doors. Nothing. Just an inky fog hurled with wrath at her intrusion. Tendrils struck her arms and legs, leaving black burns across her skin.

Stop this. Her voice rose above the cacophony. The wind roared and the tendrils snapped back before striking her again, shoving her backward. Blood oozed from the slash marks. She chewed the inside of her cheek knowing she had created the monster.

Forging on, she surveyed the area for an access point.

Again, nothing. Parker seemed to have shielded his mind from the poor saps who entered—locked in some sort of solitude or anger.

The attacks grew more aggressive, but Nikki accepted her due. Bloody gash after bloody gash appeared, the burns searing pain. *You can't want this. I can heal you. Make you whole.*

Leave me be or I will destroy you.

I can't do that.

Then suffer the consequences. A large flash of light darted from the clouds, landing just inches from her feet. She dodged the bolt. The ground blazed orange on the surface beneath her feet. Hot spikes pricked her soles. She screamed, jumping back. The relief was an instant cooling.

Reasoning with him wouldn't to work. Parker's sanity was too far gone. She looked around. There must be a way through.

Another flare flew in her direction. A flaming ball racing through a sky of nothingness. She hit the ground just as it whizzed by her ear. A crackle of singed hair and it was gone. Nikki stumbled from the onslaught as more fire balls were launched.

She ran. Sweat dripped from her forehead into her eyes. The salt stung but she did not stop. Flames crashed on either side of her. Licked her heels. Her heart thundered in her ears. She dodged flames left and right.

The temptation to wake was overwhelming. But that wasn't a permanent solution. She was committed. Parker *would* hurt others. From a sadistic kid, his dark mind found pleasure in picking on those weaker than himself.

He laughed, a maniacal chuckle. An image flashed in her head so fast she wasn't sure she understood. A young Parker on the playground, goading and beating another kid. No matter how hard the child wailed his pitiful sobs, and they were heart-wrenching, Parker punched and laughed.

Nikki choked back a scream with such force she almost wretched. This child's anguish was her fault. If only she could step into his place. Could she?

She'd found her way in. Holding on to the scene, she pushed further in. Parker stared, shocked—punch frozen in midair. "What… What…"

Nikki grabbed his fist and bent it back. She held her position until he screamed. A high-pitch shrill. More soulful than the boy he'd used as a punching bag. *You're a pathetic loser.*

"The problem with you bad guys is you always want witnesses. I won't let you hurt anyone ever again," she said. She didn't even recognize her own voice, it was so deadly calm, cold.

"How are you going to stop me?" His eyes narrowed sending the same pressure he'd used in her office.

It wrapped around her, squeezing the air from her lungs, clouding her vision. Her hold loosened. He thrust her backward. The tension eased and air rushed into her lungs. Panting, she slid to the ground.

Nikki glared at him, expecting his taunt. But what met her was a surprise. Somehow more chilling than gloating, his mouth twisted. Bewilderment mixed with a hard need to crush her will to his. "Why doesn't it work on you?"

"What?"

"You should be mine. Do my bidding. Especially here."

Confused, Nikki forced herself to think quickly. Parker's power far exceeded her own—didn't it? Yet, he acted as if he'd failed. Frantically, searching her memory, she thought back to the other day. What had he been trying to do that hadn't worked? He issued a command followed by paralyzing pressure. Was that not his expected outcome?

"Stay away from me." He backed away. She followed. He turned and fled. She stayed close. Visions of his past flooded her. Parker was flanked by his entourage. Safe amongst his friends, Parker knocked a Cubs baseball cap off a skinny red head. "Haven't you heard, your team sucks?" Laughter and chortles exploded from Parker's buddies. Their smiles easy. Clapping him on the back. Playful body slamming as they sauntered away. A bully. King of the school. Parker was cruel. The most popular guy in school.

A short kid rushed past them, his eyes on the floor.

"Hey." Parker said. The boy looked up. And Parker fixed the kid with the same stare he had used on Nikki. "Pull down your pants."

Without a word, the child unzipped his fly. His pants pooled around his ankles. The other boys roared with laughter. Parker smirked. "That's better."

Oh no. What she had done was far worse than she imagined. Parker wasn't contained in the dream world. He could influence a person merely by looking into their eyes. His life was better than ever. His dominion over others gave him a rush of power.

His laugh was crazy. Insane. No one noticed. They were too besotted with their chum to discern the evil. His parents did his bidding. They were no longer afraid, but looked upon him with pride and encouragement. Parker may no longer be an outcast but he wasn't a productive citizen either. He abused his powers, seeking revenge upon anyone who hurt him in the past.

No. Nikki's thoughts resonated in his mind. *This is wrong. Go back to the beginning. Be responsible*. She wasn't sure if he heard her words.

His child form vanished and she was left in darkness. She could find no real indication he was present or that he comprehended. The murkiness of his mind held no spark. A cold tremor of realization shocked her core. If the possibility of making amends existed, she needed to try elsewhere.

Nikki fled into Amy's mind. Her mind was different too. Instead of someone aware of what she was doing, Amy operated as an automaton. She wore a short skirt, a pearl necklace, and high heels. She stood at the sink washing the dishes by hand, though a perfectly sound dishwasher was built in just next to her.

Nikki watched her prepare sandwiches for twenty people with growing horror. Parker hovered in the background barking orders. "Cut the crusts off and toast the goddamned bread first."

Amy nodded. With meticulous movements removed the crusts.

"That's right. You know how I like it."

Amy put two tablespoons of pimento and cheese mixture on the sandwiches and cut them into triangles. She placed each wedge on a platter, repeating the process over and over, expression placid. Her dull eyes focused on her task and nothing else. She moved the platter from the counter and carried it to the dining room. Parker flipped the tray before she reached the table.

"You clumsy fool." He back-handed her across the cheek. "Make them again."

"Okay." Amy rubbed her hands on her apron and bent to gather the sandwiches strewn across the floor. After depositing them in the trash, she washed her hands and began again.

"Dear God." Nikki breathed.

She pushed further into Amy's mind. Like Parker's, no spark of life remained. Nothing but brown goo and skeletal tendrils greeted her. She swiped them away as far as she could. Until she located the real Amy trapped behind a barrier. Amy beat her hands against the wall, her mouth open and screaming. But no sound emerged. Nikki tore at the barrier and Amy tumbled out. Nikki grabbed her arms. *Stop listening to him. Be your own person.*

Amy nodded her face no longer devoid of emotion. Her lips trembled. Tears streamed down her cheeks.

Shakily, she got to her feet with Nikki's assistance. "Will you be all right?"

"Yes."

One last task. Nikki entered Lori's mind. Thank God. Lori's mind was solid. Nikki let out a huge breath and rolled her head, willing her muscles to relax. Parker hadn't gotten to his daughter yet.

Upon further investigation, Nikki realized, it wasn't from lack of effort. Parker had tried, but Lori had resisted his influence. He'd tried many times. Each and every time Parker's eyes bored into Lori's, Lori shrugged and turned away. Again and again he attempted, but was somehow always thwarted by his little girl.

Nikki studied Parker's movements. His technique. She was rewarded by a glimmer of hope. She could do the same. She was sure of it. And she would use her powers for good.

****

Nikki shook her head on her way to the Hanover house, grimacing. Not a good idea. Hot knives sliced through her brain, raking a trail of pain. She shouldn't have tried going into three minds in one night. But she had to be certain everything was all right.

She stopped in front the house. The fresh mowed lawn was green. Purple and red flowers bordered the house flanked by two blossoming Crepe Myrtles. The walkway was clear and clean. Her pulse raced. Had she finally done something right? She crossed her fingers in her pocket, and with a light step made her way up the walk. She knocked on the door.

Amy answered. Nikki detected no recognition in her eyes. "Yes," Amy said tentatively.

"Mrs. Hanover, I'm here to see Lori."

"Who?"

Nikki stepped back from Amy's vacant expression. If there was one thing Nikki was certain of, it was Amy's devotion to Lori. Nikki searched Amy's face for some kind of sign she was making a joke. She found none. Amy frowned at her scrutiny. "I'm sorry. If you're selling something, I'm not interested."

A chill trickled down Nikki's spine. Amy began to close the door. Nikki stopped her. "I'm here to see your daughter, Mrs. Hanover."

Amy's hand flew to her chest, the other one wrapped tight around the screen door. "I don't have a daughter. I-I'm not ready for children. You must have me confused with someone else."

"Who's there?" Parker came to the door. Unlike Amy, recognition did dawn in his eyes. His cheeks burned with a rage so deep Nikki's throat closed. She swallowed, grasping to regain her equilibrium.

"What do you want?" Parker growled. He stepped forward, forcing Nikki so far back she almost stumbled off the stoop.

"I want to see Lori," she whispered.

Parker's eyes narrowed. "No one by that name lives here."

"I don't understand." Nikki blinked rapidly. Her stomach churned. She'd gone too far. Changed too much. Lori was gone. "I was s-s-sure she lived here."

"Parker and I don't have children." Amy's voice took on a sympathetic tone as if speaking to the mentally imbalanced. At this point, Nikki wasn't sure she wasn't. Remorse flooded her with a weight threatening to drag her through the ground. It was less than she deserved. She stood there with Amy's confused stare and Parker's malevolent one. *What had she done?*

"Please leave. You're upsetting my wife." Parker leered at her in a way that alerted Nikki he knew exactly what she was talking about. A flicker of discontent colored his rage. His eyes bored into her head. Familiar pressure reeled against her. He was trying to influence her.

She adjusted her stance in equal measure with his and pushed back. Parker stepped behind his wife, his eyes wide and mouth agape.

Bet you didn't know I could to that.

"What happened?" She addressed Parker, carefully gauging his reaction. "I can fix this."

"You've done enough. Get out." Parker drew Amy into the house.

Amy turned to him, a gentle hand on his arm. "Parker you don't have to—"

Parker slammed the door in Nikki's face cutting off Amy's words. Message clear. He knew his daughter had been erased and he held her responsible.

Nikki cringed, sure phantom hands would appear and drag her to hell. She deserved no less. In her attempt to help, she'd gone too far. Now the child she was trying to save was gone. Just gone. And it was all her fault.

****

Back at the office, Nikki trailed down the hall on wobbly legs. If she didn't get to her chair soon, her legs would buckle. Her high heels weren't cooperating. She should have worn more sensible shoes but how was she to know her acts had erased Lori? A torrent of guilt sucked the wind out of her. She should have known. It was her responsibility to consider all the consequences. She'd acted without thought. Tears pricked her eyes. Yeah, she should have known. Garrett was right. She was a fool.

Finally, she reached her office. The light filtered through the doorway, a beacon of safety. How did you fix a mistake of this magnitude? She needed to think, sink down in her soft chair and work it out. Alone.

She bit her lip. As a caster with no real training, she must be kidding herself. There was no way out of such a mess.

After what she'd done, Garrett would wipe her mind for sure. And her grandfather had his own agenda. Correcting this situation meant she was on her own.

Nikki rounded the corner seeing the last man she wanted to see sitting in her office. At least he wasn't perched on her desk. Despite that, he sat there like a cobra ready to strike.

"Garrett, this isn't a good time." She waved him off but he made no move to leave, he sat firmly planted. What had she expected?

"Oh, I think it is." His voice brooked no argument. He rose. And lord help her, she was going to back down. She skirted the desk and sank into her chair. Weariness crept through her bones. Her mind spun. And Garrett was breathing down her neck. Judging from his intense glare he'd already learned of her misdeeds.

She sighed, grateful for once for the stacks of files that partially obliterated him from view. She heaved in a breath and waited for him to start the worst conversation of her life. But she was too tired to fight with him anymore. He was the only one who could understand her predicament. The only one with answers of any kind. "I've made a huge mistake."

"I know." His voice was filled with a tenderness she didn't deserve. Her mouth went dry. Tears filled her eyes. There were no words to explain. Lori didn't exist anymore. He was here and knew she was responsible.

"I don't know what to do." The words were weak and sad. How do you slap down the enemy when *you* are the enemy? The tears that she held at bay blurred her vision. Self-disgust at showing such emotion in front of a man she didn't trust consumed her. The man was hell-bent on annihilating her, given half the chance. Even worse, she deserved that fate.

"I suppose you've come to make arrangements to eradicate my mind." She shuffled a file.

Garrett came around and cupped her chin in his hand. A gentle tender touch, that sent the tears spilling down her cheeks. "No, I'm going to help clean up your mess."

She blinked and looked up at him. His lips were twisted in chagrin. His jaw twitched but the strain was apparent around his eyes. Compassion lurked behind that stern expression.

"I don't deserve it." She hiccupped.

"I know." He leaned in and touched his lips to hers, then perched on the desk. "This has never happened before. In one fell swoop you have destroyed everything the Guild has taken centuries to build. If I don't miss my guess, Parker will be coming after you if we don't go on the offensive. The Guild might be satisfied with letting him destroy you but then he will be out there. An evil man with powers far beyond what the Guild would allow. At least your intensions are pure."

"Really?" She pulled open the center desk drawer, searching for a napkin or tissue, to blow her nose. A reprieve was a gift. Gladly accepted, for now. "I'm going to fix this. I promise."

"No. *We* will fix this."

"We?"

Her question hung in the air. He shifted uneasily, she was sorry to note. He moved back to the chair across from her, rubbing the back of his neck not meeting her gaze. "Yes, but don't think there won't be consequences for you, Nikki. Playing God is wrong. The Guild has laws and consequences for this very reason. No one should be capable of doing what you have done."

"I understand." She pulled in a deep breath, resolved. "Okay. How do we fix it?" She moved in front of the desk and sat on the edge one foot over the side. He looked at her. Defeated. Sullen. Stubble framed his chin. Dark shadows underneath his eyes. "You look like hell."

He arched an eyebrow.

"You could have warned me this could happen."

"As I recall, I tried."

"No, you threatened. Threatening doesn't teach anyone anything."

He leaned back and crossed one leg over his knee. "I'll give you that." Garrett rose and kneaded her shoulders. Nikki froze, so tempted to settle against the hard plane of his chest. He leaned in and whispered against her ear. "I think it's time you met my mother."

Chapter Twenty-Two

The house Garrett grew up in held no surprise for Nikki. A massive stately mansion constructed of stone, complete with a turret and wrap around porch. Perfect landscaping of bushes and red, orange, and purple flowers lined the pathway of a vast lawn. She'd bet no one in the Guild lived in squalor. The structure rose with sharp edges. Ghastly shadows loomed over her. She inhaled deeply feeling doomed like the women of the Salem witch trials must have felt on their way to judgement. And Nikki was set to be judged just like those unfortunate souls who burned alive.

Adelaide Nightshade opened the door without a word. She wore a simple blue sheath dress. No doubt the creation of some famous designer. Diamond studs glittered at her lobes. The coldness of the stone matched the ice in her eyes.

Nikki wasn't welcome but she stepped into the entryway with flair, refusing to let anyone sense her discomfort. She followed Garrett and his mother along the bare wood floors. A creak with every step. No carpeting to warm the drafty interior. It smelled musty and barren.

In the living room, Nikki slid onto the couch. Adelaide stood behind a wing backed chair, resting both arms over the top, drumming her fingers as she surveyed Nikki.

Nikki resisted the impulse to fidget. Adelaide's irritation was as clear as the absence of dust on her expertly arranged furniture. Nothing out of place. Everything where it belonged. No inviting warmth. Just order. The aggravation in Adelaide's brown eyes was made more severe by the tight bun at her nape. Nikki longed to jump up and shout her presence was at Garrett's insistence.

"Well, my girl, you've caused quite a stir." Adelaide fingered the amulet at her neck. The same kind that hung from Nikki's.

"Yes, ma'am." Insulting her host would serve no one's purpose.

Adelaide glanced at Garrett as if she were sizing him up too before returning her attention to Nikki. "My son tells me that you are in need of Guild assistance."

"Yes."

Adelaide walked around the chair. The lack of distance unnerved Nikki. Garrett's mother was a scary, birdlike creature, and Nikki had the sense that any moment the woman would grow wings and pluck out Nikki's eyes with a newly formed beak. Shuddering, she longed to be anywhere but here facing the retribution of her crimes against the Guild.

"Well, I'm not so certain you *can* solve this problem," Adelaide snipped. "To do so means you will have to go back even farther than you have in the minds of others."

"I will do what I must." She swallowed meeting Adelaide's gaze.

Garrett lowered himself next to Nikki. She'd never admit it, but she relished his presence. He lifted his hand and pressed it over hers. "Mother, I think there is a way."

Nikki shifted a startled glance on him.

He met her eyes, and spoke gently. "How far back have you gone into Parkers mind?"

She blinked back sudden tears. She didn't deserve his kindness. "As far as five years old."

He arched an eyebrow. "And you could alter them?"

The question confused her. "Of course, isn't that what being the Shadow Dancer is all about? I understand no one else can do that."

"No, we can observe, but we can't alter more than the last forty-eight hours. The Guild is very strict on limiting the amount of change one can make."

Nikki understood the necessity now but realized her grandfather didn't agree with this philosophy. How could he have allowed her to run amuck in the minds of others without censure? At the very least, guidance? She knew he had an agenda but how nefarious was that agenda? She had been created for a purpose, and that purpose had not yet been tapped. She knew that too.

"How far back can you go?" Adelaide asked.

Nikki was surprised by her lack of animosity. A new sense of respect filled her. "I don't know."

"I'm guessing as far as she wants to go but she'll need a gateway," Garrett said.

"Yes, and she must travel through someone she hasn't touched. Someone who was there at the beginning."

A gateway? Wasn't that what the doors were for? Nikki's gaze shifted between mother and son as the solid weight of destiny settled over her. She needed a mind without a shield. Someone who wanted her to travel that far without restriction. Excitement flooded her. Songe. He had given her his ring for this reason. She just knew it. She patted her pants pocket assuring herself the ring was still there. Its solid shape gave her hope. "How about my grandfather?"

"I don't trust him," Adelaide said.

Nikki straightened her spine and looked Adelaide in the eye. "You don't trust me either, but to fix this situation, our families must work together."

Adelaide pursed her lips. Nikki's statement riled the woman, but then she caught the slightest twitch at one end of her mouth. Adelaide didn't like her choices any more than Nikki and her cold glare reminded Nikki she was nowhere near out of the dog house. Hell, she most likely never would be.

She had to change this nightmare, and pray she could still the dark tremors that pursued her afterward.

"Fine," Adelaide finally said. "Your grandfather will be the portal. Do you have a handler?"

"No." *What the hell was a handler?* She held her tongue.

"Garrett will be your handler."

Nikki glanced at the man next to her. From his startled stare, Adelaide had taken him by surprise. "I'm not a handler," he said.

Given that Garrett had explained in excruciating detail that his job was to hunt her down and eradicate her powers, he didn't seem the best candidate. She'd prefer a handler who wanted her safe. But Garrett had brought her here to help solve her problem. That, at least, was a vote in his favor. Later, there would be consequences. Right now, they were on the same team. Her heart ached at the thought. It would be nice if they were always on the same team. Maybe, after this was over... No, she couldn't think about the future. Not when Lori's existence loomed in front of her. Lori was the most important consideration. No matter what it cost Nikki.

"Nevertheless, that's what you'll be." Adelaide was saying. "She needs a handler while she travels that deeply into the mind of others. You may have to pull her back."

****

Nikki prayed she had everything deep casting required. She placed the day's newspaper on her night stand. Armed with her grandfather's ring shoved snuggly onto her thumb, she looked to Garrett for further instructions. All her nerve endings were on edge. Tingling static, staccato rhythm. She itched to begin. Anxious about the outcome. She whispered a silent prayer her instincts would serve her well.

"Are you okay?" Garrett watched her with a troubled grimace. His brow furrowed, forming deep lines at the center of his forehead. His jaw set so tightly, his muscles twitched. He was nervous.

Nikki looked into Garrett's concerned eyes. "Yes."

"Are you ready?" he asked softly.

How amazing things had turned from him wanting to eradicate her mind to wishing her a safe journey. She wasn't used to people having such an amorphous quality. They were usually just what she initially believed, but Garrett no longer resembled the spoiled, oily man from her first impression. Had that only been mere days ago? Now he was the hero. Someone she could rely on. *Someone she could love.* She pushed away the intrusive thoughts and concentrated on his words.

"Don't do anything rash," he coached.

"Really?" A rough laugh burst through. "I thought that was exactly what I was supposed to do."

"Nothing is worth your death."

"Look at you being so protective." She nudged his forearm playfully. "That's so unlike you." She spoke seriously. "I beg to differ with you. Lori Hanover is worth that and more. And I will do *anything* to get her back." Nikki lay down taking confidence from her grandfather's solid silver ring. It was just old enough to tap the ancient parts of his mind. To take her back to where it all began.

Garrett drew his hand through his hair less confident than she had ever known him to be. "What if I won't remember you?"

"I'll find you," she said with more surety than she felt. She caressed his face. Not remembering the last few days was much more daunting than her task at hand. If she forgot, what would happen then? She'd gained so much. If it wasn't for Lori, she'd grab her future in a vice grip and never let go. But Lori was gone. Nothing should be more important than that.

"You'd better find me," he said gruffly. He bent down and kissed her full on the lips. His touch tingled, sealing her resolution to make things right. "Now. Let's get to work."

Jocularity with a tinge of sadness filled every word. He thought she was going to leave his life. Sadly, she couldn't guarantee she wouldn't. From what Adelaide said, no one had ever ventured as deep in the mind as she was about to go. No one knew for certain what would happen. Or if she would be successful. There was every possibility that her mind would not be strong enough to do this task. She could die. Nikki swallowed as the burden of her task squeezed her chest.

But the thought of Lori erased through time propelled her onward. She closed her eyes and drifted into the familiar dream world. She found her grandfather's slip stream and flew through it.

She wasn't alone. Another presence skulked around the edges of the stream. Someone was following her. It wasn't Garrett. As her handler, he stayed behind, awake.

Nikki glanced around but didn't see signs of another entity but she felt his presence. A sinister nuance of the danger ahead.

Suddenly, her grandfather appeared and the atmosphere melted into a state of calm.

"Hello." He grinned. Satisfaction marred his features. "Are you ready?"

"As ready as I'll ever be." And she was. Nikki's essence hummed with an unknown need to get on with it. She wanted to go back as far as possible regardless of the consequences. It was time.

"Step through here." He motioned to a mahogany door.

She opened it and they both stepped through. "I can only go so far but I might be able to guide you to the access point," Songe said.

She followed her grandfather, fascinated with the images of his past.

Her grandfather slipping a package to Nikki at the courthouse. Their first meeting in the diner. His voice warning her to get out of Amy's consciousness before the gun butt came down on her head.

Then, the images of her grandfather dream casting in her mind. Wiping out all traces of her memory to the past. Willing her to believe the Angeluses were her biological mother and father. Warning them to never reveal the truth. Her grandfather had been near her the whole time turning her life into a web of lies all so she could one day do this. Nikki closed her eyes. These pictures could only hinder her efforts. She must succeed. It could not be for nothing.

Songe pulled up. "Here." He pointed to an access point. "Start here."

Nikki stepped where he indicated. The feeling of someone tethering himself to her refused to dissipate. But her grandfather seemed unaware of the presence. Surely, he was skilled enough to sense an unwanted intruder. She shook off the paranoia and rolled her head to dispel some of the tension. Having to perform such a task, knowing every step forward could lead to her death was trying.

"I can do this. I will do this." She hugged her grandfather then pushed further into her grandfather's mind leaving him behind in the mist of his past. She ventured deeper and saw his decision to create and protect the Shadow Dancer. He'd been very aware of her talents from the time she was in her mother's womb. He accessed her mind while she was developing to ensure her position as the most powerful dream caster born.

Which begged the question, if she was the most powerful, how was Parker so powerful?

Something made him dominant. Where the link? She had to find a way to neutralize him yet again. Pain threatened to overwhelm her. She shoved it away and forged on.

Nikki accessed the Hanovers' early mind through the portal her grandfather showed her. The mess she made materialized before her.

Yet, the angle was different. A mass of interwoven chords. Twisted. Tangled. *Ugly.* She began the long process of unravelling it.

She worked on unweaving the knots of time until she happened upon her first scene. *Parker crying. I'm sorry son.* Just as she started to leave, a psychic wind whipped around her stinging her cheeks and ears.

No.

Parker. She shouldn't have doubted her instincts. He followed her to the very depths of his history. Right where he could gain control.

"What do you hope to accomplish, Parker?" she demanded.

He emerged before her. "I won't let you take my powers away," he hissed.

His eyes blazed so hot they glowed. *Never mind me. Go find yourself.* Familiar pressure tightened around Nikki's chest. She shoved against it but her strength ebbed.

Parker's will burst into her, shifting and splitting her objectives.

"No." She pressed her palms against her head. "You shouldn't be able to push me."

"They didn't tell you, did they? Going this far weakens you."

"Then you should be weaker, too."

He tossed his head back and laughed. "I didn't expend any energy. You did."

Now go.

She plummeted backward flailing down a large hole. Darkness swallowed her. She grappled for something to grab on to. There was nothing but the wind whistling in her ears. A free fall through space. She tumbled on the ground. Slowly she crawled to her feet.

She found herself in a church where a funeral party was receiving mourners. Nikki's fist went to her mouth. Her twelve-year-old self stood next to her mother hugging a rag doll to her chest. Nikki's throat closed, choking back tears. *I remember.* Letting go of the present, she succumbed to the memory of her younger self at her sister's funeral.

Twelve-year-old Nikki pressed a hand against her throat, trying to hold back the sourness churning her stomach. Sunlight filtered through stained glass windows, casting multi-colored shadows on ebony pews. Her nausea grew. The greens, blues, and reds that she and Cassie used to skip through on church days were no longer fun. Now, they twinkled like evil demons threatening to devour anyone brave enough to step close to her sister's small coffin adorned with a spray of colorful flowers on top of the bottom half.

"No one should lose a child." A woman hugged her mother, who was frozen with grief. "At the young age of nine." She shook her head in sympathy. "It was God's will."

Nikki edged closer to her mother and grabbed her hand, watching the long line of people move past. Her mother nodded to their words of comfort, but nothing in her face indicated her belief in those words. Nikki didn't believe them either. What kind of God would snap his fingers and make her baby sister die? How could he kill someone as sweet as Cassie?

Another stranger approached and swept her mother up in a bear hug before turning to Nikki's father. "I'm so sorry. God must have wanted an angel in heaven."

That made everything better. Nikki forced herself to remain still, but everything inside ached to scream. God didn't need another angel in heaven. Her sister was destroyed by something evil, and God hadn't stopped it. He hadn't protected Cassie.

Nikki wanted everyone to quit saying stupid things. They didn't help. She wanted them to leave what was left of her family alone. Her body quivered with stifled anger. There was no fair explanation for what happened to Cassie. She was fine one minute and rushed to the hospital the next. No one gave Nikki a good reason why she died.

Nikki clung to her mother's hand and clutched Cassie's favorite cloth doll in the other. Her mom squeezed back, but her focus was on each person who walked by, nodding after each silly statement. Nikki avoided eye contact with her father. He stood on the other side of her mother. Since Cassie's death, he had been looking at her funny. She would catch him staring in a way that made her insides curdle. It was an accusing glare, as if she had caused the condition that took Cassie away. But how could that be? Cassie died of an infection in the brain. Whatever that meant.

Nikki stayed clear of her father's line of sight. She didn't want to do anything to make him angry. She didn't want him to notice her. She just watched in silence as everyone went by telling her parents how sorry they were. Lies, all lies.

A tall thin man with short brown hair, speckled

with gray streaks, worked his way up the line. All the screeching that warred within her body stilled. She had seen those long strides before. But where? His dark blue suit looked familiar and she couldn't shake the feeling he didn't belong there with her relatives. He was as out of place as the amused glint in his blue eyes. He turned his gaze on her.

She looked away.

"I'm so sorry." Another person lied to her parents. "She's in a better place."

How was a big hole in the ground a better place?

A shadow loomed over Nikki's younger self. She glanced up at the man. He squatted before Nikki.

"You don't remember me, do you?" His gentle voice was different from the others. Honest. Direct.

She shook her head, but she kind of did. Where had she seen him before?

"That's okay." He placed his hands, one on each shoulder. "It was a long time ago. I want you to know everything will be all right. I promise."

His blue eyes were kind. Trust filled her. She believed him. Though she couldn't say why. He stood and greeted her mom.

"Thank you for coming, Mr. Songe." Her mom held out her free hand to him. "It's comforting to see so many…friends here today."

"Just wished to pay my respects. I'm sorry for your loss, Mrs. Angelus." He turned to her father. "Mr. Angelus."

Her father grunted a harsh guttural sound. Dad didn't trust him. Nikki edged behind her mother, her hold tightening on her mother's hand.

"I know it's difficult to lose a child. But grace will

come when you need it." Mr. Songe didn't even acknowledge her Dad's rudeness. Nikki stilled the twitch on her lips. Smiling would be inappropriate. She withdrew her hand from her mom's. She didn't want to embarrass her by laughing. The almost laughter died in her throat as she glanced over at the small open coffin. Nikki was drawn to it. The last remnant of a life no more.

Slipping away from the crowd, Nikki walked up the aisle to the front of the church where her sister lay. She slowed her steps as she neared, wanting to shut her eyes, but unable to make them close. It wasn't right. Cassie should be at home playing with the doll Nikki clutched tightly to her chest. Not here, where people spoke softly and cried.

But she was there, still and quiet. Soft brown curls gently framed Cassie's face, her eyes closed as if she were resting. Her mother called it the "forever sleep", but Cassie wasn't breathing. She was still. So still Nikki couldn't believe her sister had ever drawn a breath. Appearing, instead, like a doll in a cradle.

"I'm sorry," she whispered. "I wish I could wake you up."

Tears streamed down her face. In her mind, she saw Cassie lowered into the ground—a dark hole that would forever separate the living from the dead. She swallowed the burn at the back of her throat. This was the last time she would see her sister. Life was so unfair.

A strong hand gripped her shoulder. She turned. It was Mr. Songe. He gazed at her so intently it creeped her out. A moment ago, he'd felt like a friend. Now she just wanted to escape his grip.

"There's no need to be afraid of me, Nikki."

She shook his hand from her shoulder. He made no move to touch her again. "This is part of your journey. To become what you were meant to be. If you do what you must, someday, you may be able to right this wrong."

"That's impossible. No one fixes the dead." Fresh tears welled, and she turned back to her sister's casket.

He gave a low chuckle. "Not all is as it appears, Nikki. Not everything they tell you is the truth."

Nikki frowned after him. Soon, Cassie would be in darkness and would never be able to return to the light.

"I can't leave you alone in a box without something to keep you safe." Nikki put her hand on the edge of the cold wooden surface and placed the doll next to Cassie's face. "Your doll will stop the monsters. Goodbye, Sissy Boo."

Nikki jerked herself from the memory, sobs wracking her chest. As a child, she hadn't understood her sister had died of Pneumococcal Meningitis. She did now and another certainty came with her comprehension. Her mother was so frazzled because Songe used her mind as a training ground for Nikki. It'd sapped her mother's ability to reason. She'd missed how sick her youngest was until it was too late.

Another death Nikki was responsible for. Maybe not directly. But it was because she existed. Nikki dropped to her knees filled with remorse. Tears streamed down her cheeks. The weight of her missteps pulled her deeper into the well of sorrow. If she hadn't been there, Cassie might still be alive today.

A jolt of realization shot up her spine. Parker was using these memories to paralyze her. That she couldn't allow. She stood screaming at the emptiness. "Fuck you, Parker. When I find you, I will squash you like the worm you are."

Nikki sent out feelers in all directions. She sensed his presence again and took off after him. She found him standing over his mother. His hands around her neck. "You won't hurt me again. I can kill you here."

Nikki thrust out her hand and yanked him off the weeping woman. Parker's mother cowered in his shadow, arms raised to fend off another strike. Nikki had never touched Parker before, but the force of her will dragged him to the ground. She lifted her foot to stomp on his head but he was too fast and grabbed it, knocking her backward. Then he was on her, crushing her windpipe with his arm. She clawed at his arm, gasping for air.

"I told you not to mess with my family."

She closed her eyes shielding herself from his influence. He might kill her, but she wasn't going back to the time of Cassie's death.

"Look at me." He bit out.

She squeezed her eyes tighter, shoving at his arm trying to pry herself loose. She kicked her feet but they met dead air. Stars exploded behind her eyelids.

"Look. At. Me." A sharp slap stung her cheek. Pain seared down her neckline. Her eyes shot open and she found herself staring into the gaze of a madman. *Go back further*.

Pressure leaned against her body before she could muster the strength to fight back. Parker disappeared.

She materialized on cold linoleum, staring up at a dim light fixture, gasping for air. A mewling sounded to her right. She rose on her elbows. A small child of three pushed against a door. The child was too small to reach the door knob. Her lips trembled as tears fell.

"It's all right. I'll get the door." Nikki rose. After a few steps someone entered the kitchen.

"Nikki. I'm here." Her adoptive mother held out her hands to the child. The baby turned her head and toddled into her mother's arms. A welcoming embrace enfolded the small body and kissed the top of her head. *Little Nikki* snuggled into her mother's bosom.

"Daddy doesn't want me."

Her mother chuckled. "Of course he does sweetheart. He just left for work. He'll be back."

Little Nikki leaned away and looked into her mother's trusting face. "R-r-really?"

"Yes, sweetie, we'll always be here for you." Her mother stood and brushed the dust from her pants then held out her hand. "How about some breakfast?"

"Oatmeal, please."

Her mother set her at the kitchen table. Swept away her tears then went about assembling breakfast.

I remember you, Mom. How many times had she dried her tears? Helped her with homework or picking out clothes? Nikki watched her mother and her younger self, laughing and joking with an aching heart. This was her home. Her safe place. When had things gone wrong?

"I love you, Mom." But the woman didn't look up from the stovetop where she stirred the oatmeal with a wooden spoon. She glanced back at her tiny charge, eyes brimming with pride and adoration. Little Nikki had made them a family long before Cassie.

Nikki breathed deeply. Her mother smelled of fresh linen and lavender soap. A deep calm settled over her.

This moment was right. A time when things were simple. A place where love occupied every corner. Darkness didn't linger here. Her mother brought two steaming bowls to the table. She set one before Little Nikki and then sat down to eat. The scene broke Nikki's heart. As much as she wanted to, she couldn't stay here and bask in the warmth her mother provided. That would be cowardly. A way to avoid the dangerous things she had to do. That wasn't behavior worthy of a mother who kept her safe from harm. Now she would have to break the Angelus family to make them whole.

Nikki walked over to mom and child who ate in silence. A sense of contentment hovered around them. If she defeated Parker, she would never be a part of this happy home again. She must sever the connection. Her heart ached. But it had to be done. She placed a hand on her mother's arm and knelt to see her face. The woman never flinched or acknowledged Nikki's actual presence. "I can't explain this but I have to leave. If I'm successful, you won't ever even have known me. I'm so sorry. But I can't stay here. That's what Parker wants and I won't be distracted. When I go through that door I won't ever be back."

Nikki started for the door. Before she opened it, she took one final glance at the blissful domestic scene. "Goodbye, Mom. I love you."

She stepped through and closed it shut, the click loud and decisive.

****

Garrett stood next to Nikki's bed. A gust of wind caught him, and he grabbed on to one of the posts to prevent himself from slipping to the floor. Another gust hit him, shoving him back. His fingers slipped from its

341

firm grasp on the pole. The surroundings of Nikki's bedroom began to change.

A vanity replaced a desk. Two end tables became one. Stacks of magazines piled up, then down. Garrett threw himself onto the bed. As he did, the four poster bed turned into a sleigh bed. The comforter switched from mauve to green.

He snatched up the paper they had laid out before she went under. The date remained the same but the print was changing. Not the major events but smaller ones, altering faster than he could read them. He grabbed Nikki's hand, wondering how he would change. What he would lose. He couldn't lose Nikki. *He loved her.* He tightened his hold on her hand.

Another gust slammed against his chest pushing him into the air. A dark hole formed on the wall behind him. Churning and whipping the air around. Icy tendrils wrapped around his ankles pulling his feet toward the chasm. He tightened his hold on Nikki's hand. Perspiration burned between them loosening his grip. His fingers slipped an inch and he lurched further away pulling Nikki with him. If he held on Nikki would be pulled with him into the void. Then they'd both be lost. Garrett brought her hand up, pressed his lips against it, then let go. "Don't change me, Nikki. Take care to save the important parts."

Nikki shifted in her sleep. A shaky sigh slipped from her lips. He held fast to the possibility she heard him as he tumbled through the endless void.

****

Heat shot over Nikki. A tall house, white and stark, against the night sky burst into flames. Orange and yellows crackled as the blaze devoured the structure against a lush lawn. A halo of light chewed at the insides. Two people rushed outside. A small girl and an older boy.

"Go to the safe place," The boy yelled at her.

"No, Sean—I want to stay with you." She threw her arms around his neck. He lifted her up and tore her away from the burning embers.

"No, Nikki, stay out here. Grandfather will be here soon. I have to find Dad."

Terror tolled through her at the mention of her name. She looked closely at the little girl wearing a flannel nightgown, clutching a teddy bear. The scene sparked recognition as flames consumed the house. A long ago buried place she had forgotten or perhaps been willed to forget. She had an older brother. Sean. He was born eight years ahead of her? A brother she'd adored and looked up to.

Memories of Sean flashed by. Reading her a book. Teaching her to tie her shoes. Sneaking her favorite box of cookies down, index finger pressed to his lips.

Love, known and lost, washed over Nikki, watching her eleven-year-old brother hug her for the last time as he raced into the house. She ran to the far corner of the yard, as promised, squishing herself behind the large rose of Sharon bush.

She held tea parties there with Sean. It was their secret spot. The place they whispered about the odd things that occurred in their home.

Where was her mother? Memories pounded through her. Mom was at Nikki's grandfather's to go to a doctor appointment. She left Dad and Sean to watch over Nikki until she returned.

Nikki let out a psychic scream. One her mother

would hear. Her grandfather had to come and save them. She screamed and screamed. Sean was still in the house getting dad. Who would save them?

Nikki cowered in the corner of the yard, heat covering icy skin. Her brother rushed outside, tears streaming down his face. When he reached her, he pulled her close. "I couldn't get to him. He made me leave."

Tears rushed down her face as she remembered the terror that had frozen her three-year-old self. The intensity of the fire. Ashes floated and fell as the house crumbled in on itself.

"Daddy!" she screamed. "We have to get him out."

"I'm going back in," Sean whispered. "I won't let him die in there. I'll be back soon. Grandfather will be here soon."

Sean rushed back into the house his form getting smaller and smaller against the light of the blazing inferno. She waited in the fading light of the fire watching for her daddy and brother. Waiting for her grandfather. "It's going to be okay. It's going to be okay," she murmured over and over.

Little Nikki rocked back and forth, speaking meaningless words as she sobbed into the sleeve of her nightgown. Waiting for her family that would never return.

Nikki stepped away from her younger self. How could she have forgotten her older brother? Songe hadn't even mentioned she had one. Rage burned through her similar to the white hot fallen embers of her childhood home. He would pay for leaving out important details.

Just as quickly, her shoulders slumped. Thinking

like that made her no better than Parker Hanover. There must be a better way to handle such fury.

She glanced about. Parker had thrust her here, but it was time to find her way out. Now that she knew the truth, she controlled the rewind button. She whirled away from the scene. "I'm coming, Parker. There are no more secrets to tell. You can't stop me."

****

A sizzle of energy slashed through Nikki, dropping her to the ground. Parker rounded on her. "Stay away or I'll send you back."

He marched to the cords of his memory. He pulled, wove, and reshaped them.

"There's nowhere else to send me," she said. Her voice remained controlled and steady. "Your time is up."

Parker ignored her, weaving through his intricate ritual. Nikki lunged to stop him. He whacked her with one hand, staving her off. The taste of blood touched her mouth. Bitter. Acidic. Rejuvenating. She wiped it away. This time she would win. She lunged again. "You will stop. *You* can't change the past."

"You did." He pushed her away.

Nikki toppled to the ground. Rearranging history devastated nature's equilibrium.

She spat out the blood and rubbed her bulging lip. "If you do this you won't ever see Lori again."

At those words, he paused. A slow smile crept upon his lips. "It isn't a choice between my powers and Lori. I can have both."

Parker turned back to his weaving. Somehow the man had piggybacked onto her essence and now sought to destroy all of her work. A surge of energy erupted

345

from her. It shot from her fingers. Electric tendrils sliced at Parker. He screamed swiping them away.

Nikki didn't have time to consider what she was doing or how she was able to do it. She allowed static to build, rage fueling her charge. It swelled and pulsed, filling the emptiness. All the lost souls. She would undo everything to set the world right. With the strength of a woman possessed, she sent the electric current after him—through him, until Parker shifted farther and farther from the tapestry.

"How did you?" His voice came out in a harsh whisper.

"I'm sorry, Parker, but I can't save you. You're unfixable." Nikki neared him, eyes fixed on his. "You will stay out of your parents' minds."

His eyes glazed over in terror. "Stay away."

"All evil you have done will now be aimed at you. Any anger you feel you will turn on yourself." Instinct sent the command spewing forth.

"Myself," he repeated.

"You're done." Nikki waited, breath held. Seconds later, Parker dematerialized.

She dropped to the ground, all energy sapped. She took a breath and dragged herself up. With painstaking surety, Nikki approached the tapestry. The threads dark and leathery. Dry and unwieldy. With a sigh, she pulled at one cord and began weaving. The color lightened from dark brown to tan. Dry husks softened into pliable fibers rich with recharged life. She stepped back and inspected her work. She nodded. Parker's mind was as it should be.

But she wasn't done. There was one more thing she had to do before she could return home.

****

Parker Hanover woke his heart slamming against his chest. His arm burned, itched, on fire. He clenched his teeth against the seething pain. He rubbed his arm, sending jagged pricks like a million pieces of glass. He bolted from the bed and switched on the light. His arm was covered with small circular welts and red sores oozing blood. Black skin crusted the edges. *What the hell*? He jumped back.

Amy turned on the bed and sighed. Her eyes closed. She'd always been a deep sleeper but couldn't she notice he was in pain? "Wake up, bitch."

Amy's head shot up. "Parker?"

"Look at this." He shoved his arm at her. "What happened?"

She focused on the burn marks with wide eyes. "I d-d-don't kn-kn-know."

"You did this."

She hugged the sheets to her neck. "No."

"They sure as hell didn't get there on their own." He stalked toward her. Her eyes bulged in a mockery of the little porcelain doll he'd met years ago. She trembled, whimpering like a mewling kitten caught in a thunderstorm. Every flash of light and quake of thunder broadcasting a consequence she couldn't escape. *That's right, little kitten. This is your fault.*

"Please don't. Things have been so good," she whimpered. A sickening weak sound. She didn't deserve this house, their daughter, or the diamonds glittering in her lobes. He'd gone into debt to provide her with such luxuries. And this was how she repaid him? Acting demur, innocent, and pitiful? She was a demon. She'd burned him while he slept. He reached for the studs in her ears.

A blunt force struck him in the face. Pain exploded behind his eyeballs, white specks blinding his vision.

Suddenly, Amy was at his side. "Parker? What's wrong?" She caressed his face. But acid sizzled his cheek. He reared back, crawling from her. Poison. She was poison.

"Get away," he screeched.

"What happened to your face?"

"You hurt me."

"No, I would never..." She drew near.

A heavy weight slammed into his gut, robbing him of air. He curled into a ball and glared but she was two feet away. She couldn't have possibly body slammed him. He forced out ragged breaths.

"This is no good." Tears of frustration formed. He was no blubbering fool but excruciating pain intensified each time Amy drew close. A new stab of pain sliced his thigh like a knife through yielding skin. "Stay away...from me." His words huffed out in ragged pants.

"What?"

She was poison. Toxic sludge. He edged his way to the living room. Still she followed. "No. Stay where you are."

She froze. Confusion muddled her angelic face. But it was a veneer. She wouldn't fool him again. "Amy," he stated as calmly as possible, "this isn't going to work. I want the divorce."

"No, it's been so perfect." She ran toward him. "We can't give up now."

She grabbed his arm sending another onslaught of pain to every nerve ending. He writhed like he'd landed in a bed of fire ants. He yanked his arms away, gritting his teeth against the burning scrape of her nails as he wrenched free. He crawled on all fours. The effort mustered every ounce of his withered energy. He trapped Amy's gaze and sent the force of his will into her. "You will divorce me and never come near me again."

"Parker, I don't understand." Her voice grated on his eardrums. "Let me help you. I'll do whatever we need to make this work."

Parker observed his wife through slit lids. He was sure he'd held eye contact. Why was she fighting him? He gathered his frayed power for one more go. "I said stay away from me." He gritted out the words.

"After all we've been through." She moved toward him and waves of agony ripped up his abdomen, knocking his head against the floor.

"No." He held up his hand but the bitch kept coming toward him. Pressure built against his neck choking off air. He clawed at his shirt, gasping. His vision dimmed.

Then blessedly Amy stepped back, her hands up in a placating gesture. Air flooded his lungs.

Her hand flew to her mouth. "I'm sorry. I'm sorry. Tell me what to do."

"Just stay back." He worked his way to the door. "Just let me go." With the last of his strength, he wrenched open the door and fled, impervious to her pleas. Deaf to her anguished screams. Every step closer to the street brought another wave of relief. Balm to his skin. Once outside, he glanced down at his arm. *The burns, gone*, the swelling under his eye down.

He was free!

Parker raced to his car, sucking in deep breaths of soul-soothing oxygen. Each precious inch down the crooked sidewalk taking him farther away from the nightmare that occupied his house. He thumped against the car, sending a throbbing sting up his arm. But that was nothing compared to the bone searing agony inflicted by his wife. He yanked the door open and settled into the velour interior. Safe. Thank God. He was safe.

He'd have to go back to his parents' house but that was only temporary. He reached for his keys and froze. The familiar bulge wasn't there. Shit! He'd left his keys in the house. His eyes fixed on the twin rectangle windows flanking each side of the front door. There was no movement. Could Amy have gone back to bed? Dare he risk it? His parents lived over ninety miles away. He couldn't walk. Maybe they would come get him. He moved his hand to his back pocket. His phone wasn't there either.

Fuck! He couldn't do anything right. He slammed his fists against the steering wheel. He couldn't do it. He couldn't go back in. Not with *her* there. His stomach clenched.

He surveyed the surrounding houses. Occupant's peacefully sleeping while he was forced to live through this hell. Wasn't a chance any of them would help him. Not after all the lies Amy had spread. He gripped the wheel as if the force of his will could power the car. *Turn your anger on yourself.*

He shook his head. But a foggy remnant of a memory intruded his mind. The front door flew open and Amy charged toward him. The devil incarnate. Destroyer of his world.

No.

She would not put him through that hell a second time. He opened the glove compartment and grabbed his hand gun. He lifted his hand, pointed the glock to the space between her eyes and squeezed. But sharp pains raced up his shins. Burning, festering. Moisture clouded his vision. *Turn your anger*. The words teased him, challenged him. *Go on, you can do it. Turn your hand. Look down the barrel.*

Being this close to Amy caused too much agony. *Yes. It's no good shooting Amy.* He shook his head. "No!" His voice cracked in the quiet car. *Shooting her would rip a hole through your heart.*

His head throbbed. A pulsating twinge that grew stronger the closer Amy drew near. It was too much. He was powerless to stop it. He had nothing left. His hand moved without thought. He took the barrel into his mouth.

Pulled the trigger.

****

Nikki made her way to the access point of her adoptive mother's place in her grandfather's memory. She entered through the portal Grandfather opened long ago when he coldly handed Nikki over to the Angeluses.

She searched back, looking for Eva's reaction in receiving the news of having a baby. Most especially when they learned they couldn't conceive on their own. Then the bliss when she became pregnant with Cassie.

Things grew complicated as Nikki aged. Strange things began to occur. Events almost wiped out with only the smallest remnants to trigger their memory. Or Nikki would remember things that hadn't happened.

The niggling doubt. The strange looks. Events her parents couldn't remember.

They were so distracted by the mystery of Nikki that they failed to recognize Cassie's illness. That it wasn't just a cold as they'd believed. Then she'd died. Aching guilt sent shockwaves through Nikki.

I can fix this.

She located the stream and slipped in.

Take her to the doctor no matter what you are dealing with when she is nine. You will know when. Take her even if you're unsure.

The guilt stilled. Nikki faded back to her own unborn mind. So innocent and unformed. She had to warn her infant self so no one could misuse her powers again. *Let no one in. Remember.*

****

Someone shook her. Disturbing her despite the gentleness of the touch. "Nikki." Weariness saturated her body muddling her mind. She pushed the irritating intrusion away. But the shaking didn't stop. Masculine hands gripped tighter and shook her harder. More insistent. Demanding. "Nikki, you have to wake up. I'm not going to let your penchant for being late allow you to miss your own engagement party."

She rolled over pulling the blanket over her head. "Go away."

"Nikki." That was a command. Rich, warm and sexy, but an order nonetheless. Only one person spoke to her that way. She tore the blanket away and her eyes shot open. Garrett stood with his arms crossed, irritation clouding his deep chocolate eyes.

"Did you say engagement party?"

Garrett let out an exasperated groan. "What is it

about family gatherings that puts you off so much?"

"I don't mind family gatherings."

"Really? There's a party less than an hour away where you're the guest of honor." Garrett pointed at her. "And here you are napping."

Nikki rubbed her eyes. "I was dream casting."

"Why?" Garrett sank down next to her. Strong arms pulled her against a chest that smelled of cinnamon and cloves. She breathed deeply. He smelled like home. "What could you possibly be trying to fix now?"

"You don't remember?" she murmured.

He set her away and searched deep into her eyes. "Am I missing something?"

She squirmed under the scrutiny. There was nothing on his face that hinted at her success—or failure. He didn't seem to remember anything. She peered around her room. It was kind of the same but there were changes. She glanced at the brass bed covered by a floral print bed spread and grimaced. Floral patterns, though popular, were not her thing. But the blending of green, mauve and lavender weren't unpleasant and the comforter did match the curtains.

Her gaze lit on the nightstand. It was cherry wood instead of mahogany. Over the window stood a desk where her hope chest used to be. No papers or files littered the surface. Only a pen holder and small clock occupied its broad expanse. Her skin tingled and despite the down comforter she was cold. "Where are my dolls?"

"I don't know what you're talking about."

"My dolls they were right there on the…" She was about to say hope chest. But there was no hope chest anymore. How much had she changed?

"As long as I've known you, you've owned no dolls."

"How long have I known you?"

He caressed her cheek. An action so welcoming. So intimate. "Are you all right?"

A memory stirred. But it was difficult to determine which Garrett she was remembering. The Garrett before she casted or the one sitting next to her now. She scrutinized him. Despite the concern etched in his face, she crushed her mouth over his in a harsh surge of emotion. Her head spun by the time she broke away. The coldness in the space between them sparked a glimmer of recognition. The recollection of Garrett on bended knee holding up a two-karat princess diamond lined with emeralds. How fitting.

"I'm fine," she smiled. "I was just worried about Lori."

One arm, firmly around her. "Well, that's one thing you don't have to concern yourself about anymore."

"What?"

"Lar's called me this afternoon. Parker shot himself last night."

"I made a man kill himself," she said, shaking.

Garrett frowned. "This isn't your fault, darling. The man has always been a bit off. He did this to himself." Every word Garrett spoke shook the very foundation of what she knew to be true. When she'd embarked on this journey, Garrett was with her. Cognizant of her actions. Now, it was as if that life had never happened. A new existence had sprung in its place. The details unclear. Nikki wasn't so sure how she felt about that.

"So Lori's safe?" She grasped his shirt with trembling fingers.

"Yes. Not the way our firm likes to lose a client but Parker was a mess. Wasn't sure Gorman was going to be able to do much for the man. I'm just glad you conflicted me out of that case."

But Lori was back. She and her mother, safe. Those changes were positive. Parker's death filled her with guilt. She knew she played a part in his demise. It was a burden she dare not share with Garrett, and that saddened her. Why didn't he remember their life before?

"Now get ready." He kissed her on the top of her head. "I hear Sean is bringing a date to this shin dig."

"Sean?" She swallowed. Her brother had returned. She'd altered the fabric of time for more than a small child. Had her family returned?

"Don't look so surprised. I told you our confirmed bachelor might finally get serious about someone."

"I'll be ready in a flash." She leapt off the bed. Her arm slid through Garrett's hand. He tightened his grip and pulled her back. His lips met hers, kindling the burn between her thighs. She pulled away. "Do you want me to get ready or not?"

"Touché." He smiled. "I'll be right outside."

Nikki hurried to the bathroom and closed the door. Both hands pressed against the cool counter top, she studied her reflection in the mirror. The dark circles under her eyes were gone. Her tank top and loose fitting pajama bottoms were the same as when she'd closed her eyes to cast. They were a little wrinkled but nothing to indicate what major changes had been implemented. Mussed hair. Rumpled clothes. Just as if she'd woken from a regular, restful night's sleep. But she'd reformed reality, which meant she had changed too. She shook her head trying to extricate the differences between the old Nikki and the new one. The details were hazy in her muddled brain. It wasn't even clear if she still retained powers.

Her powers! That's where her problems began and that's where her problems should end. She glanced in the mirror, holding her eyes steady. Her pupils dilated and a jolt of energy shot down her back. "Remember the changes you made."

Warm wind whipped past her sending her stumbling into the wall. A wave of dizziness overwhelmed her. Her stomach rebelled as the room twisted in motion. She held onto the doorframe, biting back rising acid. Images of long past events flashed before her. Sean helping her with an algebra problem. Her father teaching her to make a campfire. Helping her mother bake a cake, licking the spoon with chocolate batter dripping down her arms. They were alive. She inhaled deeply, willed herself steady enough to stand.

That answered one question. She still had her powers. As near as she could surmise, she hadn't misused her casting abilities. But the events of her other life warned against power as great as hers. She'd kept everyone but herself out of her head. It was up to her to choose how strong a caster she would be. She'd almost destroyed the life of an innocent young girl because of her inherent meddling. A mistake she didn't care to repeat.

Nikki leaned toward the mirror, making eye contact once more. "You will never use your powers for an unjust cause, and you will take no action until you are certain of the right course." The warm wind whipped past her as she clung to the counter.

Once the queasiness subsided, Nikki washed her face then hurried to her closet to pick through her clothes. All familiar soft silk shirts. Gabardine and woolen suits. Ha! Some things never changed. She edged to the back and sifted through her cotton dresses. Black? Classic but too morbid. Teal? No, the brightness gave her a headache. Green? The color of her new family tree. Perfect.

She slipped the dress over her head and smoothed out the skirt determined to face life anew.

****

The reception hall glittered with a million twinkling lights, casting an ephemeral glow to the festivities. Nikki walked, her arm intertwined Garrett's, through the crowd of well-wishers.

"Well, Mother's outdone herself." Garrett glanced dubiously around the room. The subject of his comment moved toward them, sleek in her mauve colored dress, hair pulled into a tight bun. Diamond studs gleamed from her lobes. The perfect hostess.

"Darling," she said to Garrett, kissing him lightly on both cheeks. "Glad you finally made it."

"Nikki had some primping to do." He smiled down at his mother. "You can't rush perfection."

"Indeed." Adelaide turned to Nikki taking both hands. Nikki squirmed under the woman's scrutiny but her eyes weren't unkind. "You look adorable. Now, I won't keep you from the rest of your guests. Enjoy the party." She waltzed off to greet another couple who'd just entered the hall.

"Don't look so pensive." Garrett said. "This party

is in our honor."

"Sorry." Nikki was unsure what to make of her future mother-in-law's thawing attitude. "This whole thing is just so odd."

"Come on," He wrapped his arm around her waist. "This is supposed to be fun. Want a drink?"

"Definitely."

As they made their way to the bar a tall blond man stepped forward raising his glass. "Congratulations, you two."

"Thank you," Nikki extended her hand to…Mark? Ah, yes, Garrett's private investigator. Her lips curved. The images were coming faster, making it easier to navigate the new terrain. "I'm so glad you could join us."

Garrett clapped his colleague on the back and grinned. "Don't drink all the beer."

"I'll just drink all the best ones." He winked.

"Smart ass."

Garrett and Nikki drifted to the bar. Her grandfather sat on a stool sipping a whiskey. His face lit up when he saw her. Years fell from his face. He looked good. His cheeks were plump. His blue eyes sparkled with energy compared to when she'd last seen him. "Hey, baby girl." He pulled her into a bear hug.

"Hi, old man." Nikki hugged him back, surrendering to the sudden giddiness at seeing him again. Images of walks in the park, swimming in his pool, Sunday afternoon barbecues rose into clarity. No longer a puppet master. Only a loving grandfather. "You're looking well."

He pulled away. "Well, I should. You're finally getting settled, and the whole family's here. What more can a man my age ask for?"

"Nothing, that's for sure."

Garrett returned with a glass of chardonnay and a pilsner of beer. He handed her the wine as he took a long pull from his glass.

"I'm guessing Mark didn't raid the entire selection." She laughed enjoying how easy the adjustment was.

Garrett shrugged. "Not yet."

"Don't worry, he still has plenty of time."

Songe tapped her arm. A gesture filled with familial connection that hadn't been there mere days before. "If you two are done sparring, I think your Mom and Dad are trying to get your attention."

Nikki's gaze followed the direction her grandfather indicated and gasped. A woman with long brown hair waved her over. The tall man next to her smiled with pride. Nikki's mouth went dry. Mom and Dad. *Her* parents. Like spectral images from the past, memories flooded her mind. Filled with a need to touch them, reassure herself they were truly there, Nikki rushed forward.

Her mother beamed, folding Nikki in her arms. Their first hug ever, yet one of many since childhood. Nikki couldn't let go. If she did, her mother might disappear. Her mother grunted. "My goodness, child, what has gotten into you?"

Nikki pulled back, staring into green eyes so like her own. "Nothing. Nothing, Mom," she choked out. Blinking quickly, Nikki wiped her eyes. "I'm just so happy to see you."

Her father laughed, pulling Nikki into another hug. Tears threatened to spill over. She swallowed them back. "Congratulations, sweetheart."

"Thanks, Dad." Nikki stepped back as her dad shook Garrett's hand.

"How's the new power couple?" Her mom leaned in to kiss Garrett's cheek.

"Still getting our sea legs," Garrett said.

Nikki froze in stunned silence. She'd done it. She'd brought her family back. Oh, my God. A warm rush of adrenaline shot straight to her head making her light headed. Every mistake she and her grandfather had made was undone. The improbable made possible. An achievement she would never take for granted.

Someone tapped her shoulder. "Hey, sis, congratulations."

Nikki turned, seeing Sean for the first time since her memory of the fire. That recollection melted away. There was no fire. Her brother had grown up with her after all. Teasing. Goading. Protecting. She threw herself into his arms. "Sean, I'm so glad you're here."

Sean hugged her then held her out at arm's length. "What is it about these occasions that turns normal people into emotional wrecks? You're a council member for crying out loud. Try a bit of decorum."

"I'm not sure." Nikki took a few beats to digest this new information. "It's just so good to have the whole family together."

"Where's your date?" Garrett slipped his hand into hers and squeezed. She squeezed back.

"Funny story," Sean tugged at his neck tie. "We had a fight last night. I'm single again."

"Typical Sean." Nikki was surprised at how easily those words spilled from her lips. Like she'd known her brother all her life. But two realities warred within her mind. Despite her random confusion, she'd been able to keep them straight so far.

"Excuse me." A soft feminine voice intruded. All eyes turned in her direction. A diminutive woman with auburn curls that spilled past her shoulders and soft brown eyes studied Nikki. "I'm Cassie Angelus from the Hazelwood monitor. I'm covering this party for the society page. Might I have a moment of your time?"

"You've got my attention." Sean's interest was evident in every word. Cassie smiled, amusement lighting her eyes.

"All in good time." Nikki edged in. "I believe she wants to speak to Garrett and me first."

Cassie offered her hand to Nikki. "I'm so glad to finally meet you. My mom is a very big fan of your work."

"Really?"

"Yes, she volunteers at the shelter and really admires the work you do for children. She's always prattling on to my dad and me about you."

Well that was a huge change. If Cassie only knew the truth. Oh, God. The implications. Again, tears welled. Her sister lived, but now things were different. Memories of another life swept through her. Life with her biological mother, father, and brother. There was no adoption. Cassie couldn't know her as anything other than a feature for her society page. Nikki let out a breath. Resolve seeped through her. Good enough. "I'm very pleased to meet you, too."

"Could you tell me how you two met?" Cassie pulled out a pen and notebook.

"Why don't you tell that one Garrett?" She glanced up at Garrett, her smile so wide her cheeks ached. "I'm so happy right now, I'm not sure I could give the story justice."

"Where to begin? You should know my life wasn't complete until I met her." He leaned in, his breath whispering her skin. "I love you so much." He lowered his mouth to hers.

She cherished the moment, heat travelling through her body. "I love you, too," she murmured against his lips. *We did it*. Together they'd changed the past and created a brighter future. With him by her side, nothing was impossible.

A word about the author...

Krysta Scott has always been a daydreamer, imagining worlds far away with happy endings. When she was in fifth grade, she was so caught up in fantasy she earned the dubious distinction of being named the girl who daydreams the most. The award for this questionable honor was a colorful transparent plastic poster made to look like stained glass. It was very cool.

Given her flights of fancy, it came as no surprise to her family when she announced she was going to be an actress. Unfortunately, her pursuit into theater didn't last long, because she was too withdrawn and shy to exhibit any talent in this area.

Left with no other choice but to pursue a more practical avocation, she decided to major in psychology and then go to law school. Not able to let go of the worlds she created in her head, she returned to writing and was very excited when the Wild Rose Press contracted her first book.